Praise for

THE CURSE *of* PEN

South Florida Sun Sentinel—on
of the Year
B&N—one of the Most Memorable Mystery Debuts of the Year
Goodreads—one of the Best Books of December
Amazon—one of the Editors' Picks for Best Mystery, Thriller &
Suspense of the Month
LibraryReads—one of the Top 10 Reads of the Month

"Armstrong's lively prose will make cynics believe in curses and witches. Ruby's intelligence, insight, fearless nature, and complicated background will make readers eager for a sequel."
—*Shelf Awareness*

"A solid start with its evocative gothic atmosphere, a rich sense of post–WWI England and an intriguing, strong heroine who is tasked with delivering rare books to a folk healer in a tiny Cornwall village." —*South Florida Sun Sentinel*

"The author's prose and imagery are powerful like a seasoned cinematographer's eye for details. You will find yourself immersed in the eerie silence of the woods and whispers of Penryth Hall. . . . The notion of crime and curse, reality and foul play keeps moving from one page to the other till the end."
—*Deccan Chronicle*

"Armstrong keeps the tension cranked high. . . . Characters are rounded and distinct, the setting remarkably realized, and the blend of gothic gloom with rustic charm and war-hardened pragmatism makes a highly palatable formula. The prose style is rhythmic and assured. . . . Fans of gothic mystery as well as more realistic detective fiction will enjoy this confident debut." —*Historical Novel Society*

ALSO BY JESS ARMSTRONG

THE RUBY VAUGHN MYSTERIES

The Secret of the Three Fates

THE
CURSE
of
PENRYTH
HALL

~

A RUBY VAUGHN MYSTERY

JESS ARMSTRONG

MINOTAUR
BOOKS
NEW YORK

Published in the United States by Minotaur Books, an imprint of St. Martin's Publishing Group

THE CURSE OF PENRYTH HALL. Copyright © 2023 by Jess Armstrong. All rights reserved. Printed in the United States of America. For information, address St. Martin's Publishing Group, 120 Broadway, New York, NY 10271.

www.minotaurbooks.com

The Library of Congress has cataloged the hardcover edition as follows:

Names: Armstrong, Jess, author.
Title: The curse of Penryth Hall / Jess Armstrong.
Description: First edition. | New York : Minotaur Books, 2023.
Identifiers: LCCN 2023018003 | ISBN 9781250886019 (hardcover) |
    ISBN 9781250886026 (ebook)
Subjects: LCGFT: Gothic fiction. | Detective and mystery fiction. | Novels.
Classification: LCC PS3601.R5753 C87 2023 | DDC 813/.6—dc23/eng/20230531
LC record available at https://lccn.loc.gov/2023018003

ISBN 978-1-250-88603-3 (trade paperback)

Our books may be purchased in bulk for promotional, educational, or business use. Please contact your local bookseller or the Macmillan Corporate and Premium Sales Department at 1-800-221-7945, extension 5442, or by email at MacmillanSpecialMarkets@macmillan.com.

First Minotaur Books Trade Paperback Edition: 2024

10 9 8 7 6 5 4 3 2 1

For my dad

CHAPTER ONE

An Unwanted Journey

EXETER
AUGUST 1922

THERE were three things a girl wanted after the night I'd had. One: a proper breakfast. Two: a scarcity of sunlight. And three—possibly most important—coffee. Dark, bitter, and at least two pots. But I had none of the aforementioned. What I *did* have, however, was a splitting headache, a sunburn, and my octogenarian employer sitting alongside me in a deck chair with the *Pall Mall Gazette and Globe* in his hands.

I blinked in the bright morning sun, then shut my eyes back tight. I braved a glance down at myself, still dressed in the same ocher silk evening gown from the night before. Details of which returned in the vaguest of flickers, none particularly illuminating. The nearby bells of Exeter Cathedral rang out loud and clear, rattling around in my gin-muddled head.

"Is there coffee?"

"Is that all you have to say for yourself?" Mr. Owen flicked another page in his paper, his dark-brown eyes fixed upon the newsprint. "When you didn't come down for breakfast I thought you'd finally gone and drowned yourself in this death pit you've dug in my rose garden. But it seems you've nearly done the job in gin."

I waved a hand at him, ignoring the twinge of truth in the last barb. "It's a bathing pool, Mr. Owen. They're going to be all the rage one day. Besides, your roses were dead when I moved here. I daresay I improved matters."

He chuckled beneath his breath. At least he wasn't terribly cross. He seldom was, no matter how deep my provocation. I sat up in the wooden chair, pulling my knees against my chest, wincing at the light. The blackcap in the tree nearby was particularly effusive in his morning song. The fellow was a bit more cheerful than I.

He slid a wire-framed pair of sunglasses across the table between us, and I breathed out a sigh of relief, taking them at once. God bless him. A rapidly cooling cup of tea sat on the table beside me, and I couldn't help but smile. This was our habit, he and I, had been since I'd answered his advertisement for a room to let. Though I'd gotten quite a bit more in the bargain. We'd lived together in this strange little world here in the eastern part of Devon, and it suited us both fine. In name, he owned it all: the bookshop, the derelict mansion along with everything in it—with the exception of my little automobile and my clothing. Oh, and my jewelry. Not that I had much of that anymore as I'd taken a rather bare-bones approach to life since the end of the war. Fewer ties, fewer things to lose.

With the sun no longer assaulting my head, I opened my eyes to the jade and gilt tiles of the pool, which sparkled back at me like a jewel box in the midmorning sun. And while *he* might detest the thing, it was my greatest joy as we weren't along the seaside. "Has Mrs. Adams arrived yet?"

"After last night, lass?" Mr. Owen raised an incredulous bushy white eyebrow.

I bit my lip—well, if I could only recall last night it might clue me in a bit as to my current state of being as well as the location of our housekeeper. My parties did have a knack for getting out of hand. Last night, from all evidence, was no exception. And it started off so lovely too, with dinner and a bit of port—which I believe was the 1907. We still had half a case in the cellar that I'd brought up specifically for the occasion. Followed by literature and poetry. A smattering of philosophy until things took a more libertine bend. *And they always took a libertine bend.* Mr. Owen would join in the revelry for the first few hours, eager to debate Marx, Nietzsche, or Freud, his favorite—I despised the fellow, but no one was perfect. Not even dear Mr. Owen.

"How bad was it?" I wrinkled my nose.

He snorted again and took a sip of tea, glancing at me over a gilt-rimmed teacup. "It wasn't nearly as bad as the one in February with the . . ." He gestured with a furrowed brow. "You recall, the one with the goat dressed for the opera."

I snorted back a laugh. "She wasn't dressed *for* the opera, she was Brünnhilde *from* Wagner's *Götterdämmerung.* Come now, we even saw that one together in Hammersmith last winter. Remember?"

"I do not recall any sopranic goats when we were in Hammersmith."

"That's not a word—"

He shrugged with a quirk of his white mustache. "It is if I say it is."

I glanced around the eerily quiet garden. It was too quiet. Ordinarily by this time of day Mrs. Adams would be bustling about, casting me annoyed glances as she went about her duties. Likely gathering bits of information to carry back to the ladies' auxiliary or whatever they call that sort of thing in Devon. "Mr. Owen . . . where is Mrs. Adams? She hasn't taken ill, has she?"

The old Scot's dark-brown eyes were warm and amused. Not that he'd ever admit to either sentiment. "Gone. Within ten minutes of setting foot over the threshold. Something about a den of sin and vice. What's that make now? The third housekeeper that's scarpered this month?"

"Second." But really, who was counting at this point? Honestly, my parties weren't *that* scandalous. Even if I couldn't recall the exact details of the affair.

"It's for the best, as I wanted to speak with you about something, lass. And if that old hen were here she'd never leave us in peace."

Something secret—now, that *was* interesting. My morning was looking better already.

"You see, girl, I've been thinking."

Oh, dear. Mr. Owen's *thinking* never boded well. Usually, it was followed by my being flung hither or yon on some mad escapade of his. I wondered briefly what he'd been like as a younger man, traveling the world until he ran out of funds, and returning back home with an unconventional wife to set up the bookshop here in Exeter. Of course, she passed away before the war, and all three of their sons during it. Leaving him a father in need of a child, and I a child in need of a father. He never spoke much about his life before I came into it. Nor did I for that matter. The past was no good to anyone, and digging about in it only brought about unpleasantness. It was best to leave it where it was. Past.

I took a sip of the tea, letting it wend its way, dark and strong, down my throat. "Where am I off to this time?"

"Am I that easy to read?"

"Dreadfully so."

He folded his paper with a harrumph and set it down between us on the little metal table. "It shouldn't be too troublesome for you this time. I need you to carry a box of books to a little town outside Tintagel. I've an old friend, you see." He lifted his cup to his lips. "He's a bit of a folk healer."

I arched an eyebrow. "A *bit* of a folk healer?"

Mr. Owen ignored me and carried on. "Lothlel Green, I believe the village is called. Tiny little spot. Nothing but cows and cliffs and sweeping vistas dotted by creatures of the ovine persuasion. I daresay you might even find the place charming."

Lothlel Green. My stomach knotted at the name. A place I hadn't thought of in quite some time. *He's a baronet, Ruby. Don't you see what this means? I think, perhaps, I could be happy there.* Her voice echoed in my mind. In truth, I made it a point to *not* think on it. Or her. Or Cornwall for that matter. I'd expressly vowed to never set foot in the godforsaken county ever again.

"It isn't much of a town, mind. It's a handful of miles from Bodmin Moor, on the way to Tintagel. You've been there, haven't you? On one of your little sojourns. I could have sworn you'd gone off for a wedding some years back for a friend of yours. Just after you moved in here."

Yes, well. The old man seemed to have a very keen memory. Any trace of my good humor evaporated as I stared into my teacup, wishing for something a bit stronger than oolong in its depths. Oh, I'd been there. And I'd watched my best friend— the only person I'd ever truly loved—marry another. And not out of love—that I could understand—but out of . . . I wasn't even sure out of what. Inertia, perhaps? "I'm afraid I'm not feeling quite up to—"

"Nonsense, child, you were more than able to entertain your human menagerie last night. And if you could carry on in such a manner then, you can do this for me now. Tell me you took the handsome one to bed at least?"

Bed? I'd just spent the evening in a deck chair. What feats of acrobatics did he expect of me? Besides, I hadn't taken a lover in a scandalously long time, as sexual congress had lost a bit of its charm. I must be as dissipated as the neighboring ladies' association whispered behind gloved hands. No, it was worse than that—I was suffering the worst case of ennui since the dawn of the nineteenth century.

"What was his name?"

I sniffed and took another sip of tea. "I haven't a clue to whom you are referring. And I don't believe it's any of your business what cavorting I do, or do not do."

He laughed again and shook his head. "It's not the bed sport I take issue with, my darling girl, it's that you're wasting yourself on these young jackanapes." He pointed at me with his forefinger. "A girl like you, Ruby Vaughn, has more potential than the lot of those gents who come here every Saturday eve in hopes of getting in your good graces. Half of them couldn't decipher their arse from their elbows if given a Michelin guide."

I nearly snorted the tea out my nose. My eyes watered. He wasn't wrong. I was searching for something. Needed it. Only I hadn't quite determined what exactly I sought.

Fiachna, Mr. Owen's house cat, on the other hand, knew precisely what he was after. The great feline hopped up into my lap, purring loudly. I stroked his ebony ears. His claws caught the silk of my gown as he settled in for a good rub.

"I mean it, girl."

"Why don't *you* go if it's that important?" I shot back, changing the subject.

"You know my gout has gotten to the point I can hardly walk."

There was no arguing with him when he was in this mood.

He stretched, rising from his own deck chair, and steadied himself on a simple rowan walking stick. "Come along. I have something to show you."

Very well then. I scooped Fiachna into my arms and set off inside, following Mr. Owen through the terrace doors into his personal library. He tugged on the heavy velvet drapes, allowing the morning sun in through the ancient leaded windows. Illuminated dust danced in the air. The room was lined floor-to-ceiling in books. Dark. Hidebound spines facing outward.

All the mundane titles he kept in the bookshop, but *this room*—this room housed all the exceptionally rare and valuable tomes, along with those particular titles that the government took issue with.

He lumbered across the room and thwacked an enormous case with his walking stick. "These are them."

A box of books?! A trunk more like, and an old tatty one too. "What's in there? The butcher? Are you certain Mrs. Adams left, or did you do her in and stuff her in the trunk so I can dispose of what's left of her?" I wrinkled my nose, reaching down for the clasp and shifting Fiachna's snoring form to one side. The black cat let out a mewling sound of protest at the inconvenience and I set him down.

Mr. Owen's cane came down on the top of the trunk with a loud crack about three inches from my fingers. "You're not to open it. You understand me, girl?"

He'd never spoken to me that way before and I didn't care much for his tone. I opened my mouth to tell him the same when it struck me—in the nearly four years I'd lived with him, he'd never forbidden me to touch anything. Never forbidden me to look at a book, even handle one. I'd gone through some of his most delicate volumes. Pages as thin as butterfly wings and twice as fragile without him voicing a single protest. What in this box could be so different?

"These are ancient things, my girl . . . dangerous ones."

"Honestly, Mr. Owen, they're books. How dangerous can they be?" I was beginning to wonder if perhaps he was the one who had too much to drink last night.

He set his jaw firm beneath his thick white beard.

I glanced back down at the trunk. "They are books, aren't they? I was only teasing about Mrs. Adams . . ."

"Of course they are books, lass. But books themselves are seldom the danger, it's what's within them that carries the risk."

"Oh, good God, they're not illegal, are they? After the last time I thought you'd had your fill of banned books."

"Me?" He gave me an innocent look.

"Fine. After the last time, I had my fill. I thought I made it perfectly clear I wasn't moving any more illegal books for you after you got me locked up in Holloway Prison for four days!"

"It did wonders for your temper too, if I recall." He chuckled low and shook his head, waving me off. "Don't look at me like that. You're far too pretty to glare like my great-aunt Petunia. Besides, there's nothing in there to get you arrested this time."

"You don't have a great-aunt Petunia. And why can't you send me somewhere interesting? You know how much I'd like to go to Egypt with your friend Mr. Carter. He invited me to join him last time we spoke. Said he could use someone with my translation abilities."

Mr. Owen grumbled beneath his breath. "I haven't a clue why Lord Carnarvon is so patient with him. Mark my words, the man will find nothing in the Valley of the Kings. I don't even know why he keeps throwing good money after bad. Though I've heard Carnarvon's going to pull funding soon."

"I thought you liked him."

"Carter?" Mr. Owen drew his brows up. "I do. But even I know a bad bet when I see one," Mr. Owen snapped, putting an end to that conversation. Again. Lucky Mr. Carter goes to Egypt. I . . . I go to Cornwall.

"There's nothing illegal in the trunk. Stop glaring at the box."

"Oh, that's a fine assurance." But I was done arguing. I'd already made up my mind to go. His box of forbidden books piqued my curiosity more than I cared to admit, as I was quite certain he knew. I was a predictable thing. Dangle the faintest hint of mystery before me and I would be captured like a fox in a snare.

Mr. Owen sensed the change in my mood. His wide mouth curved up into a smile and he laid a hand on my shoulder. "Maybe this trip is precisely what you need, my darling. You'll come back with your head clear. I knew a chap once, William Bottrell, long dead now but he traveled all over the West Country collecting their stories. It's an ancient place— Cornwall—full of secrets and legends. I think you'd enjoy it if you gave it a chance."

"Did Mr. Bottrell die in pursuit of said stories?"

Mr. Owen laughed merrily, shaking his head. "The old Cornish folkways predate even the Romans. There are things that occur there no one can explain, no one dares question. After all, Tintagel is the birthplace of Arthur, they say. The seat of kings. Perhaps you'd find it interesting. Maybe it would help you to . . ." He gestured for a moment, a look of pain crossing his face before he shook his head. "Never mind me, lass. You go on. I'll write down Mr. Kivell's direction."

Folk healers, superstition, and likely no electricity.

Lovely. Just lovely.

Chapter Two

The Growing Storm

THE sixty-odd miles between Exeter and Lothlel Green passed in a series of craggy moors and sweeping vistas marked intermittently by granite tors. Sharp curves wending around fields separated by dry-stone fences. A more bleak and beautiful place I don't think I've seen in all my life. Mr. Owen was correct on that score: There was no shortage of cows or cliffs. I skirted along the edge of Dartmoor, heading farther west. No matter how long I lived here, it never ceased to amaze me how different ten miles in Britain could be. I'd left the lush woodlands of Devon and found myself in another world. And were I not headed toward the one place I'd sworn never to return to, I might have even enjoyed myself. Pulled off to the verge and enjoyed my lunch hamper overlooking a charming shadowed valley. But I did not stop, as I had no appetite, and the increasingly rugged landscape kept pace with my ever-souring mood.

Every mile that ticked by was one mile closer to *her*. It was an irrational thing to bear a grudge like this. I couldn't even bring myself to think her name—let alone speak it aloud—without growing irritable all over again about the whole affair. I'd seen in the papers a while ago that she'd had a child. The lovely Lady Tamsyn Chenowyth and her dashing war-hero husband. There. I'd thought it at least. I scarcely even recalled their wedding, having spent the evening half drowned in gin, as Mr. Owen so keenly describes it.

Tamsyn.

I gripped the wooden wheel of the Crow Elkhart roadster that Father bought me and paid a small fortune to have brought over after I'd been exiled from home before the war. Not precisely exiled; rather, sent away for my own good. But no need to think on that today. Memories had a way of begetting more of the dratted things, and I was full up on the stuff.

Tamsyn had written me in February of last year. It was the last I'd heard from her. Not that I'd responded then. Instead I'd kept her missive tucked away in my jewelry box beneath the strand of my mother's pearls the solicitor gave me after the estate was settled. And yet here I was driving myself to Lothlel Green, with that very envelope tucked into my luggage. Her words an enigma, as they'd always been. *We must speak, Ruby. I've made a terrible mistake coming to this cursed place and have no one to trust but you. I'm so afraid and alone. Ruby, I need you.*

Perhaps I should have answered. But what does one say after all that came between us? She often tended toward the melodramatic, always had. She was a writer after all, perpetually scribbling down ideas and notions. Speaking in hyperbole and parable, so I cravenly brushed away any concerns I may have had for her. I clutched the wheel tighter, flexing my fingers. I suppose I was answering now—in a fashion—as I couldn't very well *not* see her when I was in the village. Perhaps that was all part of Mr. Owen's nefarious scheme.

A sound came from the basket beside me. I turned to it, but there was nothing there. It must have shifted with the rutted road. I slowed the car to a stop alongside a tall hedge and pulled out the map. If I hadn't taken a wrong turn, I should be nearly there. I'd passed carts and wagons, a few lorries, but every village I passed through, every farmstead, people would stop to stare.

I ought to be used to it. People always *looked* at me. It wasn't that I was particularly interesting looking—if anything I was rather an oddity. With dark-brown hair cropped into a bob, which I thought rather avant-garde. However, Mr. Owen said it gave me the appearance of his great-aunt Prudence after she came down with the flux and they'd shorn her like a summer ewe. Not that he had a great-aunt Prudence either.

A sensible soul would have delivered the books directly and headed back to Exeter without rehashing old wounds. But no one had accused me of being sensible. I folded up my map and turned the car at the crossroads, away from this Mr. Kivell's home, and headed directly to Penryth Hall. To *her*. Best to get it over with. I'd never been a coward, and it was a poor time to start now.

PENRYTH HALL LOOMED at the peak of the hill. A great foreboding neoclassical fortress set against the windswept countryside. Designed centuries ago to vulgarly proclaim the owner's wealth and power over those who worked the surrounding land—now it only managed an anemic whisper of its own past. The money that once filled the Chenowyth coffers had long ago dried up, leaving the vaunted family's future to be saved by an upstart's fortune. Tamsyn's.

I'd been here only a few years before, though looking up at the house, it seemed a lifetime divided now from then. If I remembered clearly, from the top floors you could see the sea rising up beyond the cliffs. I'd stood there once, buffeted by the wind, taking in the vista and wondering if such a bargain could ever make me happy. The answer was always the same. No.

My parents had thought sending me here and saddling me with an impoverished peer would save me from myself. But instead it reinforced the sad fact that I wanted none of it. Never had, and I feared never would.

I continued the drive up the narrow tree-lined road ever higher, until it gave way to large lawns on either side. Once tended by dozens of gardeners with neat hedges and beds, now nature outgrew its bounds, turning the land on either side to luscious meadow. High grasses promiscuously tangled with weeds and gorse. Lovely white, pink, and yellow flowers danced in the golden midmorning light.

And it was in that moment I saw her. There in the distance surrounded by sun and air and flowers. My breath caught in my chest. She didn't see me. She was in the field to the left of the road by a great copse of trees bent down in the wildflowers. I drew the car to a halt and watched her. Engine idling. Half wondering whether I should go out to meet her, or continue on to the house and pretend I had not seen her at all.

Her hair fell loose around her shoulders, shining copper in the sun, as it often did when we were girls and away from the city. We'd summered in the neighboring village, in the years before the war. She always loved the country, whereas I despaired of it. A great basket was looped over her arm full of cut wildflowers. A child was with her. Her son. He must be over a year now, toddling along beside her, stopping every now and then to pick his own flowers. Chubby hands full of crushed blooms.

Turning at the sound of the car engine, she raised her hand to the sun and paused for a handful of seconds. She scooped up the child onto her hip and darted across the open field, wind whipping the loose layers of her skirt. Her broad-brimmed hat fell from her head, tumbling into the high grass behind. She didn't even slow at its loss. Tamsyn reached the side of my car in seconds, struggling to catch her breath. The boy giggled, his arms wrapped around his mother's neck. "Ruby?" Her cheeks were pink. "Oh, Ruby, it is you! I thought when I saw your motorcar, but I . . . I couldn't believe my eyes! What brings you to Penryth?" Her eyes sparkled brightly and my own spirits rose with her smile. She shifted the boy to the other side, his dark curls a stark contrast with his mother's fair hair.

"I had an errand to run and thought I might drop in to say hello."

"In Lothlel Green? What on earth could bring you all the way out here?" Her face suddenly fell, and she caught her lower lip between her teeth. "I suppose you didn't receive my letter?"

Guilt washed over me. "Letter? No, I hadn't received any." The lie tripped smoothly from my tongue. Better than the truth in any event.

"Well, never mind it. I'm so terribly glad you've come. There are things I must tell you. I only wish we had more time." She cast a glance back to the house, and that was when I spotted it. A faint smudge of yellowish brown on her cheekbone. "There never seems to be enough time in this dratted old place."

I lifted a hand toward the fading bruise, but she pushed it away. "Don't, Ruby. I should have put on powder this morning but I wasn't expecting guests. It's nothing. I woke up one morning with it . . . I . . . I must have done it in my sleep."

It didn't look like nothing, nor like something one could accidentally do, but I kept silent. Tamsyn glanced again back to the house, brows drawn tight in worry, before she turned back and grabbed both my hands tight in her own. "Come to dinner. Perhaps at seven? I need to speak with Edward first of course. Wouldn't that be lovely, Jori? Company all the way out here?" She jostled the boy on her hip, smiling fondly at him and brushing a kiss to his brow. Her expression shifted briefly, fine lines creasing her forehead. "Edward hasn't been himself lately. But I can have your room made up. It will be just like old times. Do say you'll join us. It would mean the world to me."

"Of course, goose. I'd love nothing more." I struggled to sound cheerful. Her guarded words, the old bruises. I didn't like what I'd found here one bit. I should have come when she'd first written, but I'd never imagined Sir Edward to be a violent man. Disagreeable, yes. But never the sort to harm his wife. Then again, I learned long ago that things are never as they seem.

Chapter Three

The Pellar

MY mind grew ever more troubled with worries for Tamsyn as I drove away from Penryth Hall. She was a grown woman who'd made her own choices, and yet I couldn't get the haunted look in her eyes from my mind. I'd not expected it. Not at all. As I reached the crossroads again, with its stone marker, I checked my pin watch. I had a few hours. And while I ought to have gone straight to Mr. Kivell's home to deliver the trunk of books, I also needed to clear my head. Mercifully we were only a dozen miles from the sea.

Surely with a couple of hours in the salt air, this sense of foreboding would pass. Yes. That was precisely what I needed.

I followed the weathered stone road markers toward Tintagel before turning off and parking my car at the top of a hill. It would never have made it down the path, let alone back up, and I needed the exercise. I made my way down the steep slope that led to the ruins and the sea beyond. The ancient castle walls rose up before me, stark against the brilliant afternoon sun. From the cove, if I looked up I could spot a handful of more adventurous souls gamboling about upon the clifftops, entirely disinterested in me. But here along the rocky shores I'd found my haven.

I quickly shucked off my pale-yellow frock, then, dressed in only my muslin shift and a pair of drawers, I walked into the sea. The water was angry, thrashing upon the rocks. I was angry too.

It was bracing and cold, even for August, causing my skin to prick and teeth to chatter. I swam farther out from the shore. Stroke by stroke as the waves pulled me back toward the rocks. The current here was far stronger than I'd expected—but I was stronger. Always had been.

A rock outcropping rose up from the blue-green water some handful of yards away. I reached it in a few easy strokes and pulled myself up and stretched out atop it in the warm sun. Finally, I'd outrun my thoughts. Only the violent crash of waves against the stone kept me company, ridding me at last of the growing sense of dread that had followed me all the way from Exeter. And somewhere between the sea mist and the sound of the greedy gulls crying out overhead, I fell fast asleep.

"Madam?" A voice startled me awake. "Madam, are you quite well?"

Where was I? I bolted upright, neck aching from the awkward angle I'd fallen asleep. A man stood there before me up to his knees in the water. Right. I was at Tintagel. I glanced past him at the shore, now much farther away than I'd remembered. The tide must have gone out. His hair was a riot of black curls shot through with silver strands. The wind had whipped it free, and it blew wildly around his shoulders. His sleeves and trousers were both rolled up with an old, stained British Expeditionary Force haversack slung across his shoulder.

"Are you quite all right, miss? Did you . . ." He paused,

running a hand over his jaw and glancing around the cove. "How the devil *did* you get out here?"

"I swam," I grumbled, rubbing my sun-flushed cheeks in an echo of his own movement before I tucked my knees up beneath me. "And yes, I'm quite well. I just need a moment to gather myself. I must have fallen asleep." I glanced up at the sky, where the sun hung decidedly lower than it had been, and swore. "I'm afraid I'm going to be terribly late." *Again.*

He snorted for a moment in amusement, a faint smile crossed his lips. It was then I noticed his eyes. He had the most extraordinary ones I'd ever seen—pale green mostly, except the left one bore a second color within it, like a gray cloudbank drifting across the sea. I'd never seen such a thing, and yet there was something about his face that tugged at me. It was achingly familiar. As if I knew him. Though I would have certainly remembered having met a fellow like that.

He turned his back to me then stooped down and scooped up something from the tidal pool. A small shell of some sort. He gingerly tucked it into his haversack.

"You'd best get back to shore before the tide returns. It's really remarkable you made it to this point. Many a foolish man has drowned in these waters trying to reach the far caves."

"I'm not afraid of the sea."

He gave me the strangest look. "Regardless, you should have . . ." He checked his pocket watch then tucked it back into his brown waistcoat pocket. "Another few hours at least before the tide cuts off the cove."

"What time do you have?" I inclined my chin to his pocket where the watch resided.

"Six. Why?"

Damn and blast. "I have to get back. I'm later than I thought." Scrambling to my feet, I slipped on the wet stone and began to fall. The man's hand shot up, grabbing hold of my hip and steadying me above him. I accepted his aid as demurely as one could when in one's unmentionables—which had mercifully dried in the sun—and slithered down the rock to join him in the tidal pool. The water was vastly colder than I recalled a few hours earlier, as it lapped around my bare skin.

He chuckled beneath his breath, shaking his head as he watched me with interest. It was as if he'd stumbled across some strange creature and couldn't quite decide what to make of it. "Will your husband be in a terrible temper if you're not back in time?"

I arched a brow and started back to the shore. "I haven't one. Nor am I in want of one if that's what you're insinuating. I am blissfully unattached and intend to remain so." Aside, of course, from a meddlesome octogenarian bookseller. But we were family now, of a sort.

"I didn't mean . . ." He raked a hand through his hair, matching me step for step as we splashed through the water back to dry land. My strides defiantly long, partly from the cold, partly from annoyance at his assumptions.

The wind picked up, spitting mocking mist at me, robbing me of those last few delectable moments of warmth on the rock. Another mark against Cornwall—its dreadful weather.

"It's just rather amusing is all."

I glanced over my shoulder, spine straight, and placed my hands on my hips. "What is amusing?"

He reached out, plucked a strand of seaweed from my hair, and tucked it carefully into his bag. "You see, there's an ancient story around these parts about an old man who stumbled across a mermaid in these very same waters."

My temper soothed. Just a bit, as the peculiar man went on.

"He thought at first she was a mortal woman in distress and went to save her from certain drowning. You see, she'd climbed upon a rock to sun herself, and the tide abandoned her, leaving her unable to return home. The poor maid was frantic, concerned her husband would be angry with her for being gone so long and eat her children."

I wrinkled my nose. "Lovely story."

But he was not deterred and continued on as we walked back to where I'd left my clothes. My own pace slowing in time with his. "You see, the old man slowly earned her trust and before long, he carried her back to the water. In return the maid offered him anything he desired. A gift for saving her."

I shivered, rubbing my arms for warmth, and stepped unconsciously into his shade. "What sort of gift?"

"Well, you see, the seafolk could have given the old chap any manner of prize. Gold. Pearls. Power. Riches beyond his imaginings. Anything at all his heart desired." His voice was deep and carried with it an unusual cadence that warmed me through and through despite the weather.

"And I suppose he became a fabulously wealthy man, then?"

The stranger shook his head. "No. You see, he didn't want any of those earthly trappings. Nothing like that. Instead he asked for three things." He held up his thumb and his first two fingers to underscore the point.

"It's always three, isn't it? In fairy stories, I mean."

The edge of his mouth quirked for a moment before he continued on. "The man asked her to bestow upon him the power to help his fellow men. To heal the sick, to break the spells of witches, and to find stolen goods."

"And what did they call such a fool, to give up the wealth of the world to find missing trinkets?" Secretly, I thought I might have made the same choice if given the option. After all, I had all the wealth I could want, and gave more of it away than I kept. I glanced up at the stranger, impossibly charmed by the story he'd woven. Enough to forget Tamsyn's troubles—if for the moment—and to forget the fact I was half frozen, or that I was standing in my underthings with a man I didn't know.

"Pellars. They call them Pellars, Miss . . . ?

"Vaughn. Ruby Vaughn."

"Pleased to meet you, Miss Vaughn." He ducked his head politely, before he brushed his hair back from his brow with a rough hand. "I'm Ruan Kivell."

My breath caught in my chest at his name. Now, that was a surprise. Surely he couldn't be the same fellow Mr. Owen had sent me after? But the name was unusual. There couldn't be two in this area.

I raked my gaze over him, trying to make sense of him. I'd imagined someone suitably aged and perhaps with a stoop. Not . . . *A man like this.* "You . . . are Ruan Kivell?" Perhaps that was why he seemed so familiar? Had I met him before back in Exeter at one of Mr. Owen's book meetings? No. No. Impossible. He was not the sort of man one forgot.

He nodded uncertainly, as if my shock was catching.

Mr. Kivell stood a good head and shoulders above me—which was quite a feat, as I was not an insubstantial woman. Handsome in a fashion, I supposed, with a square stern face with faint lines between his brows from worrying too much. Though he possessed an odd ageless quality that made it hard to guess his years.

"From Lothlel Green?" I asked slowly.

It was his turn to be surprised. "How did you know?"

I gave him a crooked grin. "Because Mr. Owen sent me here to bring you some books."

If he'd startled me on the rock when I'd woken, I'd doubly shocked him now. His expression so comical, there was nothing to do but laugh.

CHAPTER FOUR

A Dreadful Dinner

AS it turned out, Mr. Kivell had been brought to the shore by a local farmer and the fool man had every intention of walking the several miles home—which boggled the mind considering he had collected half the seashore in that haversack of his—so for the sake of time I delivered both him and the box of books to his cottage. He was amiable enough, and it made for a pleasurable trip back to Lothlel Green, pushing Tamsyn that much further from my thoughts. It wasn't until I parked in the lane outside his cottage that I recalled my reason for going to the shore in the first place.

Tamsyn. The bruises.

A coldness set in my belly, doubly worse than before. We said our farewells, and I watched him lug the great trunk through the gate and into his house. It was a charming, if small, white structure situated high up on the cliffside—likely only two rooms down and one up, if that—with an obscene preponderance of greenery surrounding it, all seemingly held together by a dry-stone fence. Leafy vines climbed up hazel trellises filling the air with scents I couldn't even begin to categorize. Herbs and flowers. Bees buzzed everywhere. Cattle and sheep appeared like figures from a child's wooden play set grazing in the lowlands below.

I sat watching his closed door long after Mr. Kivell disappeared inside. I don't know why I waited, nor why I watched him so intently. Perhaps it was just dread of what I'd discover at Penryth. My little excursion to the seaside had been a pleasant diversion, but now I had to face the truth. Something wasn't quite right at Penryth Hall.

I checked my pin watch and snapped it shut. A habit that irritated Tamsyn when we were younger. She was always convinced I'd break the thing if I wasn't careful. I was late for supper already, but there was nothing for it. Just as I resolved to leave, and set the car into gear, something meowed. Yes. It was definitely a meow. I looked around, glancing over at the basket in the seat beside me just as it shifted and I heard the sound again.

Cautiously, I lifted the lid and out popped Fiachna, stretching as he extricated himself from his makeshift bed, one paw at a time. Crumbs from bits of my lunch stuck to his crooked whiskers as he rubbed against me. There was no end of surprises for me today. I scratched his ears. Well, I certainly hoped Tamsyn's housekeeper was fond of errant felines.

SOME TWENTY MINUTES later, I stood on the great stone portico of Penryth Hall. The wind howled across the hills, catching the still-damp hem of my skirt and plastering it to my legs. A deep fog gathered, rising up from the fields below, casting the world behind me in muted shades. Just as I lifted my hand to the great bronze knocker, the door opened, revealing an elderly woman some forty years my senior with silvery hair bound up into a tight bun at the back of her head. She wore a drawn expression, her weary eyes tracing over me top to bottom, before settling upon the mewling basket in my arms. She looked vaguely familiar, though she ought to, as I'd been here three years before. But my memories of the wedding were murky at best.

"You're late, maid." The woman frowned.

Other women of my station would have likely taken umbrage at her familiarity, but she was most certainly correct. Tardiness was one habit I couldn't shake. "I was . . ." I racked my brain, struggling for an excuse other than the truth. "Detained."

"The master hates tardiness," she muttered beneath her breath. Something flashed across her face, a half thought that disappeared into the gathering mist. "But he'll have to wait. You can't very well show up for supper dressed as you are. I'll show you to your room to freshen up. They've waited half an hour, I daresay they can wait another."

I followed the anxious housekeeper through the halls of Penryth, cavernous and dark. She muttered to herself the names of the ordinary rooms as we passed, almost a litany rather than a tour. Library. Morning room. Dining hall. The dark umber curtains were pulled tight against the outside world, shutting out any prayer of light. We passed each door at a brisk clip, going up the stairs to the farthest corner of the third floor. Out of sight, out of mind.

· "You'll be comfortable enough in here, my lover." She smiled at me faintly. A memory tugged at me. One I couldn't quite place.

"You don't remember, do you?" she asked, brushing my hair back from my brow. The sensation altogether too familiar. I'd been here before. In this room. With this woman. I knew her voice. "Probably for the best. Some memories are best forgotten." She cleared her throat and straightened, snipping the tie to the past and knotting the thread tight. "The mistress often uses this room. She prefers the view of the orchard to her own. It's her favorite place on the estate." The old housekeeper's voice softened at mention of Tamsyn. At least Tamsyn had one ally in this great monstrosity of a house. The housekeeper crossed the room, her dark-gray skirts rustling as she pulled the curtains wide, filling the room with golden evening light.

It was a grim yet serviceable space. Everything in this godforsaken place was grim. I'd forgotten quite how dreadful it was. With dark wood paneling and a bed that looked large enough for Henry VIII and at least three of his wives to occupy concurrently. I set my small valise down in the corner, along with Fiachna's basket. Faint snoring emanated from inside. Dreadful little stowaway.

"Do you need anything?" she asked with a pause, her hand on the doorframe, lines etched deep in her face.

I smiled halfheartedly and shook my head. There was nothing at all she could give me now.

"Ah, Miss Vaughn, you've arrived at long last. We feared you'd changed your mind about joining us." Sir Edward didn't bother standing to acknowledge my presence, as any proper gentleman would do when a member of the opposite sex entered. Instead he gestured to a seat on the far side of the table without ever meeting my gaze.

"Sir Edward." His name dripped like acid from my tongue. "It's lovely to see you too." I crossed the room to take the proffered chair.

"I was just observing how Americans seem to lack the ability to tell time. Wasn't I, my love?" His gaze went from me to Tamsyn, who sat across from him pale and shrunken. Her once vibrant green eyes now fixed on the plate before her. She didn't respond.

He stabbed at a lone parsnip with a silver-tined fork. The bone handle clenched in his tanned fingers. "So what have you been about in all these years? I seem to recall last time you were at Penryth you caused quite the stir. I hope we aren't to expect a repeat performance?" he asked, biting into it with an audible snap.

His words struck a guilty chord, just as he'd intended. I didn't recall what had happened here, but between his barb and the housekeeper's concern it must have been quite the scene indeed.

On the whole, I supposed Sir Edward Chenowyth wasn't an unattractive man. Unappealing, yes, but even considering the fact he was a good twenty years our senior, he kept in good form and had his hair and all his own teeth as far as I could tell. An active, vigorous fellow that one might even like if he had anything resembling a tolerable personality. For it was his temperament that made him insufferable. That inborn belief that he was superior to all around him by the sheer happenstance of blood.

"Well?" His word was clipped.

"I'm renting a house in Exeter now, working at a bookstore."

"A bookstore? How terribly common. Then again, wasn't your father in trade?" He knew good and well it was Tamsyn's father who made his fortune in commerce. I didn't dare look to see how she fared, for fear I'd lose my temper, which was already on an increasingly taut tether.

"Nothing so industrious as all that. I'm afraid he made his fortune in speculation."

Sir Edward grimaced and shook his head before turning back to his plate with another irritated stab at his food. Excellent.

"A gambler, I'm afraid. Surely you know the sort."

He made an almost choking sound but swallowed it down, his face pinker than it had been a few moments before. A thin sheen of sweat appeared at his brow. Good. The bastard deserved a bit of what he doled out.

I chanced a glance at Tamsyn. A mistake. Sitting there at the table with her hands folded meekly in her lap, she was nothing more than the delicate shell of the girl I'd known so well. And in all my life, all my journeys, and all the people I'd encountered, I'd never wanted to kill a man more. To drive the meat fork sitting in the roast joint straight into his skull for what he'd done to her. Tamsyn had never been outspoken, instead allowing others to lead, but she'd always had a vivacity that I'd admired. No. That I'd loved. And he'd all but snuffed it out like a candle at the end of a too-late dinner party. With only a wisp of smoke as evidence it'd ever burned at all.

Edward made a rather unpleasant sound. That slight beading of sweat had now turned to full perspiration. He dabbed at his brow with a crisp white handkerchief and cleared his throat. Clumsily he slid his chair back from the table. Banging into it, making the crystal clatter. "I think I shall take some air before retiring for the evening. I'm not feeling quite well."

Good riddance.

Tamsyn murmured something to him that might have passed for concern. He pressed a kiss to her brow and departed. As the door snicked shut, she quickly straightened and reached out for the roast joint, slicing off a chunk and setting it onto an empty plate. I eyed it, rather thinking twice of eating.

"Parsnips?"

I patted the chair beside me with a shake of my head. "I'm not hungry. Come sit. Talk to me."

She sighed heavily and set the knife on the table before grabbing the half decanter of wine and her glass. "Please don't say anything about him. I don't want your judgment, Ruby. Not tonight."

The beaded hem of her skirt brushed my own. It wasn't so

long ago that we'd spent every dinner like this at her parents' town house in London, sharing our secret world between the soup and fish courses. The rest of our companions none the wiser. It all seemed so long ago. "Why would I judge you?"

She gave me a puzzled look and glanced toward the closed door. Her hands knotted in her napkin. "I chose my path. I know. It's only that sometimes . . . sometimes I wish . . ."

My stomach clenched and I shook my head. "We won't speak of it then. Not tonight."

She squeezed my hand and for the briefest instant the past was close enough I could grab it if only I reached out. Except when I turned to her, her eyes were those of a stranger. "Well then, what do you want to talk about?"

"Not the past. That's for certain."

She laughed lightly, a strange hollowness in her voice. "You always did hate the past. And I've always been wed to it. I think that's the difference in us. Even before . . ." She lowered her lashes. Before my parents died, she meant. "You were always racing to the future. To the next thing and I . . . I think I was always falling behind."

"That's because *you* weren't caught at the Vanderbilts' Christmas ball with your skirts rucked up and a married man beneath them for all the world to see." Not that I'd known that final point at the time. He'd been a promising young alderman whom my father had taken as his protégé. No one in our set knew he already had a wife in the country. Not until he'd ruined any prospect I had for a decent society marriage. I'd fancied myself in love with him and see where that useless sentiment had gotten me?

Tamsyn gasped at the casualness of my words. "Ruby!" But she knew the story, as did her family. It was the condition my father set when he sent me off to England, that his old business associate knew precisely what he was getting: a naive and utterly ruined sixteen-year-old girl.

I shrugged. "It's in the past. We cannot change it. I do still find it strange that Mrs. Vanderbilt's son was on the same ship as my parents, though. What are the odds of that?"

She furrowed her brow. "So he was. I had nearly forgotten. Do you keep up with the Vanderbilts still?"

I shook my head with a small smile. "Of course not. I think they were happy to see the back of me." I snorted at my unintentional pun. "Besides, it's the past. Remember?"

She laughed at that, her eyes brightening for just a moment, and I could have clutched on to those precious seconds for an eternity. The old Tamsyn wasn't dead. At least not fully. She existed still, somewhere, beneath it all.

"Well then, since we're on the subject, tell me everything that's happened since you left France. Don't leave out anything." The strain was still all over her face along with the faint bruise that neither of us would speak of. But she was trying, and so would I.

"Not even the racy bits?" I teased. Not that there were many of those as I'd become dreadfully boring lately.

"Especially not those."

I played my part, weaving her a tale more cheerful than the sad song of ancient books, expensive gin, and a troublesome house cat that made up the backbone of my existence. Instead I told a story of sparkling parties, interesting bedfellows, and starry nights. With music and art and beauty all around.

A convincing charade, but a charade, nonetheless.

Perhaps it was the wine on an empty stomach, but somehow my hand found hers again. I squeezed her fingers in my own and continued talking. Words spilling out in a desperate ploy to keep that familiar flicker of light in her eyes. Too afraid that if I stopped nattering on, even for a second, she would disappear entirely. And I couldn't bear that thought. Not now that I'd seen what Edward had wrought.

And I drank in her hollow laughter. Because perhaps even this shell of her was enough to ease my guilt at not coming sooner.

CHAPTER FIVE

Bad Dreams

RETURNING to Penryth was a mistake. It was one thing to allow Tamsyn to transform into this fantastical monster of my imaginings. It was an entirely separate one to see her fate with my own eyes. To pity her. How was I to go back to Exeter in clear conscience after seeing what had become of the girl who had once been my dearest friend—my closest companion? The one person who had seen me at my very lowest point. And the only person to willingly walk away. My eyes pricked at the memories, tears coming hard and fast of their own volition.

I pulled a bottle of gin from my suitcase and uncorked it before unpacking the barest of essentials for the evening. I took a swig straight from the bottle, letting it slide smoothly down my throat, then laid out tomorrow's clothes upon the dressing table and began combing out my knotted hair. The changes in Tamsyn since I'd last seen her were so marked and terrible I hardly recognized her.

Hell. Looking into the mirror, I hardly recognized myself. I touched my face for a moment, running my fingers down my cheek. I hadn't spoken of the scandal that caused my exile from America in years. I'd been such a foolish little girl then. But no more. Between leaving America, war, and the death of my parents, I'd become a different creature. An almost feral fatalistic thing, living from chance to chance, existing only because death didn't want anything to do with me. At least not yet.

I took another long drink of the gin and stripped out of my clothes, replacing them with a thin cotton nightdress. The evening air thick and damp. I washed my face in the basin, scrubbing away layer after layer of day. The room was dark as evening set in, with thick paneled walls and heavy velvet drapes that reminded me of those in a mortuary chapel. A great silver candelabrum provided the only light, casting large shadows that leapt and danced upon the walls.

Fiachna had surfaced from wherever he'd been hiding and rubbed himself against my ankles before making himself at home on the blood-red coverlet, curling up into a little ball at the foot of the bed.

"I agree, old man. I agree." I blew out the candles, sinuous smoke crawling up from the damped wicks, and I slid into the bed with him much as I did every night in Exeter.

Something creaked in the hall. A maid perhaps, though I hadn't seen anyone but the housekeeper since arriving. Despite the recent infusion of the Turner fortune from Sir Edward's marriage to Tamsyn, the entire estate remained threadbare, only a few steps away from dereliction. I'd recalled hazily from my last visit several Greek marbles, along with a collection of Gainsborough landscapes that I thought quite fine, but none of that remained. At least not that I saw. All likely sold for taxes, or improvements, making a dour house even more so. One would have thought Tamsyn's money would have brought some modernization, but it seemed the house simply swallowed the funds, greedy for more. I waited with my face turned toward the door for the inevitable knock—but nothing else followed. The house was evidently falling into slumber.

Old houses had a tendency to make noises. Stretching and creaking in the night. Some more fanciful people believed them to be haunted. But I didn't believe in ghosts. Nor anything else I couldn't explain. I was a student of reason. Logic. Things that I could touch, taste, feel. And there was no room for ghosts in that sort of a world.

When I succumbed to sleep at long last, it wasn't of specters that I dreamed, but of *her*. Drawn and broken as she'd been at supper, standing there in her nightclothes. A great snake curled around her body, slithering up, round and round her until it reached her throat. Winding tighter and tighter. Noose-like, choking the life from her. My own chest constricted in response. I couldn't breathe as I watched the color slowly drain from Tamsyn's face.

I moved closer, but my steps were weighted. I couldn't reach her. Struggling against the darkness. Heart racing. I reached her at last. But just as I laid a hand on the serpent at her throat, she melted away to someone else entirely.

Edward.

His smile curled up into a sinister sneer as he stumbled toward me in the darkness.

One step. Then another, reaching for me. A great blade in his hand.

He caught me by the collar of my gown. Tugging me closer. Closer.

I fought him. Struggled. Heart now slamming into my ribs, fit to burst from the bone cage that housed it.

Damp.

Sweat.

Heat.

I couldn't get away.

He was too strong. His hands around my throat squeezing harder and harder.

I opened my mouth to scream but silence followed.

My fingers grew numb as I clawed at him, reaching for something. Anything.

Then my hand found it. The handle of the blade. Fingers curled around the warmth, I drove it deep into flesh. A loud howling sound reverberated in my ears and I dragged it upward. In and up.

He still wouldn't let me go.

I bucked against his weight. Fingers still gripped around the knife in his belly.

My pulse grew slow.

Thud.

Thud.

The hands at my throat grew tighter as the last of my strength began to fade. Fingers numb, slowly slipping from the knife. Then suddenly my captor slackened his grip. Another scream came. Feral and sharp, cutting through my dreams and the distance. In an instant the bonds were gone.

I jerked upright, gasping for the thick night air. Body drenched in sweat. My nightdress stuck to me. My hands went to my own sore throat. I'd had my share of night terrors but never before had they *hurt*.

Fiachna sat at the foot of the bed, hissing at the tall bureau, a shadow cast against the wall. His back arched, tail fluffed out three times the size of normal. My throat dry and tight, unwilling to let the air come.

Only I would have a cat who shared my nightmares. He must have been smothering me in my sleep. I ran a hand over my face, trying to shed the last remnants of the dream. My limbs still clumsy. Numb and weak like those of a newborn kitten. I flexed my fingers, pushing the eerie sensation away.

It was just a dream, Ruby. Just a dream.

Slowly my breath returned to normal, and Fiachna, having

given up tilting at windmills, settled himself against my thigh. His wide yellow eyes flashed a spectral green from the moonlight coming in through the open window.

I hadn't recalled leaving it open. In fact, I was most certain it had not been open at all when I went to sleep. The curtains billowed inward as the sky outside lit with heat lightning. One. Two. Three. I counted on, waiting for the rumble that never came.

The moon was low and full overhead, with a strange ghostly halo around it. Pinprick stars flanking it in the pitch of night. Odd for lightning on such a clear evening. A hint of movement caught my attention and I turned toward the wood. A figure dressed all in white disappeared into the copse, robes trailing behind as it hurried into the dark. I blinked sleepily, rubbing my face as I stared after the spot where the specter disappeared, but it never returned. Perhaps I should rethink my opinion of ghosts after all. But whatever it was or was not, the creature was in the orchard and I was here, safe and sound within the drearily thick walls of Penryth. I pulled the window firmly shut, fastening the old metal latch hard for good measure, and went back to sleep—that is, until I heard the bells.

CHAPTER SIX

The Bells of Penryth Hall

A baleful clanging rang out through the foggy morning silence, jolting me from my sleep. My body was accustomed to springing to action from the years I'd spent along the Western Front. But this time there were no explosions. No shouts. No wounded men needing to be loaded onto lorries and carried from the casualty clearing station farther from the front. Confused and cloudy, I tugged on my riding boots one at a time, hopping down the hall as I struggled with the laces.

All the while the bells tolled. I stumbled down the stairs seeking out the source of the commotion. Dressed in my wholly inadequate nightdress, I followed the infernal sound out the back door and toward the wood. But as far as I could ascertain, no one else was running. No one came. Something was dreadfully wrong.

A stillness passed through the thick air. The fog dampened every sound, every sensation, aside from the clang of the fire bell. Wet high grass, thick with dew, clung to the hem of my gown as I ran after the sound. A few late poppies dotted the grass in bloodlike splotches, unfurling the blossoms to the early-morning sun.

Faster and faster through the fields I ran, my lungs grateful for the clean air, until at last I found the source of the commotion. The fire bell was on the far side of the decaying stable block. The wooden siding had rotted clear through and the structure had a drunken lean to the south, making it appear that a stiff gale might send the whole thing toppling over in defeat. But still no smoke. No fire. Nothing except Mrs. Penrose, the housekeeper, stretching up on the tips of her toes to tug down on the old frayed rope, wholly unaware of my arrival. Her graying hair had come free of its confines and whipped around her face, giving her the selfsame windswept appearance of the fields beyond. A shotgun was propped up against the stone wall, alongside a tipped-over basket of blackberries spilling onto the grass.

She stopped and glanced past my shoulder to the house warily. Her eyes were haunted. "Where's the mistress?"

"Asleep, I suspect. No one was stirring when I left. What's happened?"

"It's for the best, the poor dove." Worried, she continued to watch the house. "Did you see anyone on your way out here? Anyone at all?"

I shook my head again, hugging myself to ward off the damp air, which cut through the thin fabric of my nightdress.

She paused, hands on her hips drawing my attention to her blue-gray skirt, which was smeared in myriad shades of reddish brown and green.

"I suppose you'll have to do." She clicked her tongue, turned, and grabbed the shotgun. She thrust the butt of it into my hands, along with a heavy waxcloth bag of cartridges. "If half the things she's said of you are true, I'll trust you know what to do with this."

Hesitantly, I glanced from her to the weapon in my hands. I *did*, but why I needed it escaped me. "Mrs. Penrose . . . Please tell me what's happened."

"The master's been killed."

My blood froze in my veins. The dream. It'd been so vivid. So real . . . I swallowed hard, shaking away the sensation that it had happened again. My dreams . . .

Mrs. Penrose's voice broke through my troubled thoughts. "I don't know what, beast or man, has done the deed. But the ravens have already been at him. I won't have him any more disturbed than he already is. We need to keep them away until the constable comes or the Pellar."

The Pellar? That was the second time I'd heard that word—but I was still focused upon the fact that Edward Chenowyth was—

"Dead," I whispered.

"Dead. Aye, maid. That he is." Her mouth took on the shape one does after biting into an unripe persimmon. A mirror to my own thoughts. "Come along then." Mrs. Penrose turned on her heels, marching off toward the orchard as if finding a dead man happened every day.

And perhaps it did in Cornwall.

The grass along the center of the path was beaten down shorter than that along either side. It was only yesterday I saw Tamsyn out here picking wildflowers with her child, but that image seemed miles away now. My hands grew damp around the shotgun's solid reassurance. It had been a dream. Just a dream.

With each step, the way remained stubbornly familiar to my mind. Something in the angle of the trees, the path, the gentle curving arc of the land tugged at the periphery of my memories. A wholly unsettling feeling considering my dream last night. Finally, as we reached the edge of the copse, the sensation grew too great to bear. I paused and turned back to the house.

And there on the third floor on the farthest corner was my

room. My window. My pulse sped as the memory of the night before came back in full force. The figure.

This was the spot. The very one in which I'd seen the ghost, or whatever it had been. My fingers rose to my aching neck hidden behind the high collar of my nightdress.

"What is it, maid?" Mrs. Penrose paused, huffing out her breath in annoyance, brushing the hair back from her damp brow.

What is it? What a preposterous question for the woman to ask after she'd thrust a shotgun in my arms and told me there's a dead man in the woods that I may or may not have killed.

What isn't the matter? I shook my head and turned back toward the path. "Nothing. Nothing."

"It's not a pretty sight. I'd warn you to keep your eyes away from him if you can."

"Have you sent for a physician? The constable?"

"No physician's going to help him now. One of the house-maids heard the bells straightaway and set off for the Pellar. He'll know what to do." She wrung her hands into her stained apron. Twisting then untwisting, my gaze locked on them. "Aye. He'll know what's to be done."

I gave an unsteady nod, not liking the sound of her words.

Mrs. Penrose drew in a shaky breath before continuing. "The bells of Penryth Hall haven't rung in thirty long years." Her hands fell to her sides in defeat. "I'd hoped not to hear them again."

Thirty years? I followed after her into the woods, panting to keep up. "What happened then?" I managed to ask between gasps.

But she just shook her head and continued down the path. Not the most auspicious response. Another five minutes or more, we continued through the orchard, trudging through ancient tangled undergrowth that had flourished where dappled bits of light broke through the thick canopy overhead. Unripe apples dripped from the branches with promise of a harvest yet to unfold. It was bucolic—peaceful even—or would be, if not for the heavy stillness of the shotgun on my shoulder, and the ever-growing dampness of my palms. The birds sang, chittering out their summer songs oblivious of what had occurred here.

SIR EDWARD CHENOWYTH was laid out in the middle of the orchard beneath a verdant canopy, with lace-like bits of sunlight breaking through the leaves casting a pattern on the ground below. At first blush one might assume the fellow had fallen asleep watching the wind play in the leaves above, were not his body contorted in a peculiar serpentine position. Or were his face not ripped beyond recognition. Bits of white bone peeked out through the gnawed flesh. His mocking mouth, largely unscathed, was twisted into a snarling and cynical smirk— even in death. My pulse quickened. Breath grew short as the dream from the night before thundered back to the forefront of my memories. I'd seen that smile. That sinister line of his mouth as he came for me.

But he hadn't been dead in the dream.

Instead he'd had a knife.

One I'd taken from him.

I stumbled backward from the body, reeling. It had to have been a dream.

Had to.

A knot of bile lodged in my throat as I tried to swallow it back down, my gaze fixed upon his rent-open belly. The same one I'd driven the knife into . . . No. No . . . It was a dream. A dream. I couldn't have killed a man. I *couldn't*. My thoughts came so violently and fast I nearly doubled over with the force of them.

Misunderstanding altogether, Mrs. Penrose laid a warm hand on my shoulder and I jumped. She shushed me like a mother cat. "I warned you, maid. 'Twasn't a pretty sight."

I swallowed hard, trying to gather my wits. To let my old companion—rationality—win again. One did not commit murder in one's sleep. I sucked in a breath, then another, before my pulse began to slow. There was a logical explanation. Surely.

A pair of crows flapped down from the branches overhead, pecking at his face, and the bile returned. Gathering what remained of my addled thoughts, I fumbled in the waxcloth bag at my hip, loaded two shells into the shotgun, and braced it against my shoulder. I set my feet and fired a round up into the air to scare off the blasted creatures. White-hot pain ricocheted through my shoulder. But it was worth it, as the nuisances fluttered off in a wave of indignant squawking and flapping. I broke the shotgun open and plucked out the empty shell before dropping it into the sack. Once the birds settled into their new position in the branches above, the woods grew silent again, except for the cacophony in my head.

I drew nearer Edward's supine form. The stench of his rent bowels was overpowering. Surely, if I'd had a hand in his demise, I'd recollect the scent if nothing else. I brushed a sweaty lock of hair back from my brow and peered down. Edward's stomach had been opened much like one would a fish, entrails ripped and spread across the grass giving the appearance that whatever had gotten into him had been startled away. An animal then. Yes. That made a great deal of sense. I hugged the shotgun to my chest and stepped even closer. A great moving sea of black with flecks of green undulated upon his abdomen, making his chest appear to rise in breath.

Flies.

Hundreds of fat ones feasting upon him. And at long last I lost my nerve, the bile returned for the third time, and I turned away.

Coward. I wet my lips and took a step back from the body, careful to remain upwind of the ill-fated Sir Edward. "What do you suppose did it?"

Mrs. Penrose didn't answer.

"You don't happen to have wildcats about?" I gnawed my lower lip while pacing about, feeling slightly reassured that I probably hadn't gutted a man in his sleep.

A vee formed between the older woman's brows and she gave her head a shake. "Not in many a year. Perhaps a boar could have done it. Aye. That would make sense, maid. A boar . . ."

A rustling came from the bushes nearby and I spun around, closing the shotgun with a click. Satisfied—for the moment— that my dream was just that, my imagination ran amok with all sorts of *other* creatures lurking in the wood with a new-found taste for human flesh.

A few seconds later, a slight man came through the under-brush, his head bent beneath a low branch. Neatly dressed in an ill-fitting suit. His hair a medium brown beneath his similarly hued low-slung cap. As he stretched upright, I discovered he was also in possession of a rather spotty set of whiskers grown to cover up the inexpert surgical repair of his lower jaw.

"Ah, Constable. Thank the Lord you've come! I wondered if she'd found you." Mrs. Penrose's shoulders immediately slack-ened with his arrival.

The man eyed me curiously as I realized I still had the shot-gun aimed at his chest. I hastily dropped the barrel and broke it back open, cradling it against my body.

"What's happened here, Mrs. Penrose?" he asked as he ap-proached the body cautiously. The constable wasn't a large man. No taller than me, but he exuded an air of competency and calm, which in this moment was worth more to me than all the works of David Hume—Locke as well for that matter—sitting in Mr. Owen's private library.

"I'm not certain what befell the poor soul. I came out to pick some blackberries to make a tart and came across him . . . I haven't seen anything like it since . . ."

The constable grimaced as he stooped down to inspect the body. Since what? But Mrs. Penrose did not continue.

"Who is she?" he asked gruffly, not bothering to look in my direction.

"A guest from up at the house. She came to help me keep an eye on him after I chased away a fox who was having his supper."

The constable withdrew a handkerchief from his pocket, covered his nose and mouth, and gently began probing the body. He tilted Edward's head from side to side cataloging the wounds, as the flies grew annoyed at the intrusion.

Mrs. Penrose averted her gaze.

Another rustle came from the path, and I turned to the sound to see the very last person I ever expected to see in these woods.

Ruan Kivell.

Except this wasn't the charming man I'd seen only yesterday at the seashore. No. He had thunder on his face, and there was something different about him. Something untamed, uncivilized, and entirely terrifying.

And worse, he was staring directly at me.

CHAPTER SEVEN

The Pellar Returns

"MISS Vaughn?" Mr. Kivell slowly took inventory of me, stem to stern. A sensation I didn't much enjoy. "What are you doing here?"

"Me? What are you doing here?" I shot back.

He grumbled a response, his steady gaze giving me the uncanny impression he was looking straight through me. Into me. Which was impossible. I set my jaw and stared back at him and into those unusual eyes, which shone brighter in the shade of the copse than I recalled from the day before.

He certainly hadn't been so fierce looking yesterday with his trousers rolled to his knees and smelling of salt and sun and water. Then again, yesterday I wasn't standing with a shotgun over a dead body. I worried my lower lip to the point it began to bleed.

The constable cleared his throat, breaking the moment—such that it was. Mr. Kivell turned his back to me and moved silently across the copse to join the constable by the body. He slipped his old British Expeditionary Force haversack from his shoulder and set it on the grass before dropping himself down on the ground beside the body. The two men whispered together, shoulder to shoulder, and I got a sense this wasn't the first time they'd been thus. An image of two war-weary soldiers flitted to my mind. A gesture here. A point there.

I leaned closer, curious despite the frisson of fear that snaked its way up my spine. Would they be so intent if it had been an animal that killed him? I picked at something dark brown beneath my thumbnail.

Mrs. Penrose took me by the arm, tugging me back to her. "Let them work, maid. It does no good to hover."

"What . . . what is he doing?"

"Pellar business. He's to tell us if it's the curse or no." She made a strange gesture with her hand, then shook her head.

"The curse?" The word settled rather uncomfortably on my thoughts. I didn't believe in curses. Nor Pellars. But I *had* dreamed of Sir Edward last night. Drove a knife into his belly, and then here he was . . . carved up like a Christmas goose. I swallowed hard. No. *Something* did this. Of that I was certain.

Mr. Kivell glanced up from where he worked, his brows drawn up, and gave me the queerest look before returning to his work. He shucked off his neat rust-colored field jacket and rolled up the sleeves of his shirt. He then rummaged around in his bag and pulled out a small brown cloth-bound parcel. Unwrapping some cuts of meat, he threw them one by one into the underbrush, where they landed with a swish of foliage. The crows above immediately set off after them, abandoning their predatory vigil. Mr. Kivell folded the cloth back, tucked it into his pocket, and pulled out a small bottle, pouring it over his hands, then rinsing and drying them.

The story he'd told me at the seashore came back to me in a rush. I'd thought at the time it was little more than a folk-tale, but apparently it was something more. *He* was something more. Mr. Kivell dropped down on the ground beside the body and laid his hands along Sir Edward's still form. All three of us stared at him transfixed. My breath tight in my chest.

It's just a dead body, Ruby. You've seen them before. Yet I was unsettled all the same. Any remaining thoughts of Tamsyn's betrayal and my tangle of emotions had long since fled, and my mind was fixed upon one thing and one thing only—the curious shape of Mr. Kivell and what he was *doing* to Sir Edward's body.

The cursed man was now kneeling over him. Not examining as the constable had. Not at all. Instead he was . . . I took a step closer, as if drawn on an invisible tie, pulling myself free of Mrs. Penrose's outreached grasp.

Another step closer.

The air in the copse suddenly took on the strange, almost electric smell that occurred after a lightning strike as Mr. Kivell placed his hands gently on top of Sir Edward's rent-open chest.

"How are you?"

The constable spoke from just behind my elbow. He'd moved across the grass, quiet as a hare, and I'd not even noticed his approach.

"I didn't mean to startle you, Miss . . . ?"

"Vaughn. Ruby Vaughn," I managed to whisper, my attention fixed upon Mr. Kivell's back.

"Miss Vaughn." His voice held a hint of a smile, and at last whatever spell had been cast over me broke. I turned to him at last and ran a hand over my jaw.

"I suppose it's rather par for the course today, don't you think? Startling things."

The constable looked over my shoulder to where Mr. Kivell worked and sighed. "I'm afraid it is. I'm Fredrick Enys. You're a friend of Lady Chenowyth, I come to understand. Mrs. Penrose said you'd been here a few years ago for the wedding."

I wet my lips and nodded, glancing back to where Mr. Kivell continued his . . . *ministrations* . . . for lack of a better word. "What is he?"

Constable Enys huffed out a breath, resting his hands on his narrow hips. "I suppose some might say he's a sort of a healer."

"So he's a doctor?"

The constable let out a dry laugh. "Ruan Kivell? Certainly not. But he knows his way around a sickroom. Let's say that."

"It's a bit late for that sort, isn't it?"

Enys cocked his head to one side. "You don't have Pellars in America, Miss Vaughn?"

"I scarcely know what a Pellar *is*, Mr. Enys."

That earned me a smile from the rather dour constable. "He's a witch." He paused before adding, "More or less."

"A what?" I would have choked had I been drinking. Surely he couldn't expect me to believe in witches.

Enys rubbed his scarred jaw with the back of his hand as we both watched Mr. Kivell work. "Aye. A sort of conjurer. Surely they have wisefolk where you're from?"

"Witches, in New York City?"

The damaged side of his mouth quirked in amusement. "Perhaps it's best if he explains it to you."

But before I could think any more on the subject, Mr. Kivell rocked back onto his heels and gave his head a low long shake.

"Bloody hell!" the constable swore, the easygoing expression he'd worn seconds before faded to one of fear. His whole body tightened on a spring, unable to make out what to do with the silent information that Mr. Kivell had imparted. "Pardon my language, ladies."

"What is it? What's he found?"

The constable and Mrs. Penrose stared blankly at Mr. Kivell as the man procured that same small glass bottle from his bag and washed his hands.

"It's what he didn't find is the trouble, Miss Vaughn." His jaw settled into a deep frown.

"It's the curse, isn't it, Ruan? Tell me true." Mrs. Penrose's voice rose with each word. Her eyes wide, frantic for the first time since she'd rung that damnable bell.

Curse? I mouthed the word, half to myself.

The elderly housekeeper's breath trembled in her chest as she clutched at her breast. "Thirty years ago, the beast came. It killed them all." As her words spilled out, the copse grew even more silent. My own heart beating in my ears.

"You can't possibly . . ."

She looked up at me with such a forlorn expression my heart cracked in response. "The Curse of Penryth Hall, maid. It's the Curse of Penryth Hall."

"YOU CAN'T POSSIBLY be contemplating that Sir Edward was killed by a curse?" I spluttered out once Mrs. Penrose and Constable Enys were out of earshot. The younger man had taken her by the arm, like one would their favorite aunt, leading her back to the house presumably to wheedle more information out of her.

Mr. Kivell, *the Pellar*, slung his haversack over his shoulder with a groan. He raked a hand through his dark hair and shook his head. "Have you any likelier ideas as to the cause, Miss Vaughn?" He gave me a knowing look.

The shotgun cradled to my chest provided cold comfort. I glanced down at Edward's splayed form and cleared my throat. "I'm an antiquarian, not an inspector. But there are no such things as curses, Mr. Kivell." Because if that was a possibility, even a remote one, then perhaps my dreams were more than just coincidences. And that thought couldn't be borne.

He narrowed his gaze at me, penetrating through the thin layers of my nightdress. Not in a lecherous way. No. It was worse than that. It was as if he was adding up my bits and parts and gauging the sum.

I turned away from him and stalked across the copse. Distance was precisely what I needed from this man. "What is a Pellar?"

"Didn't I tell you the story yesterday?" he grumbled as he stooped down again next to Edward's body, still puzzling over his death.

"I'm afraid I'm a poor student."

"Who," he gritted out while he ran his fingers over Edward's pallid cheek, probing gently into the garish wound with a tenderness one would reserve for a thing of beauty, not this . . . horror that lay out before us.

"Pardon?"

"Who is the Pellar?"

I was quickly losing interest in our little verbal spar. "Evidently you. But I still don't understand what you are supposed to do about him—" I pointed to Edward's body. "He's *dead*, in case you've not noticed, and while I understand from the constable that you're some kind of healer, unless you have the ability to walk on water I don't think he's coming back anytime in the next century."

"I can't."

I snorted.

"At least not as last I checked." The edge of his mouth curved up in amusement before he grew grave again.

My jaw dropped. How could this man be irreverent over a corpse? Then again, how could I? We were arguing about something inconsequential when there was a much larger problem here. Tamsyn's husband was dead. I suppose not an altogether unfortunate event. However, someone in this village had gutted Edward Chenowyth like a fish, and I was only *fairly* certain it wasn't me.

He startled then shook his head hard as if he'd been struck by a wayward thought or been stung by a bee. What a very peculiar man. My fingers drummed impatiently on my forearms. "Pellar or no, you surely can't believe it's a curse that killed him. Could it have been an animal? A beast of some sort?"

"Why can't I?"

I couldn't tell if he was having me on or if he was serious. My pulse thundered in my ears and I shifted the shotgun. "Forgive me, Mr. Kivell, but I'm not feeling very clever right now. I do wish you would tell me what is going on. I come here to deliver books, see an old friend, and I wake up to . . ." *All of this.* I gestured broadly at him, unwilling to even say the word. "*And you.* And a whole lot of nonsense about curses and *Pellars.* I didn't sign up to be in the middle of some sort of—"

"Some sort of what, Miss Vaughn?" He drew closer.

"Story, Mr. Kivell. I didn't sign up to be in someone's fairy tale."

"It's not a fairy tale." The wind rustled through the leaves overhead as shadows descended in the woods. "Least of all for him."

Something about this man set my teeth on edge. The way he seemed to see me. To know me. And yet I couldn't help but push back. "There's no such thing as magic, Mr. Kivell. No curses. No monsters in the night. None of it. There's a perfectly rational explanation for what happened to Sir Edward and I intend to get to the bottom of it."

He took another step nearer. Close enough I could catch his scent, earthy and dark. "It's not a folktale for them. No matter what actually happened here last night. To the people of Lothlel Green the curse is as real as you or I."

"You can't possibly believe in this nonsense. It's the twentieth century, Mr. Kivell. We have science. Logic. Mathematics! There's no room in the modern world for magic or curses." Even as I said the words, I saw how pathetic my reasoning was. The simple fact was I refused to believe. Couldn't even conceive of it. Because if such a thing *were* real, it opened up a box of questions about my own past that I wasn't ready to answer.

Something in his expression softened at that. As if he sensed my distress, and for half a second the charming man from yesterday stood before me. "I'm not sure what I believe. But until I prove for certain it's mortal hands that've done this work, there's not another soul in all of Cornwall that's going to want to be within ten miles of Lothlel Green. The old ways are strong here."

"But you're an educated man—"

"—I'm a Cornishman first, Miss Vaughn. My blood runs through the very rock and sea and soil here. And while you may not have respect for these people—my people—I do."

Chastened, I hugged my arms to my belly.

"You're in Cornwall now, Miss Vaughn. It's best for you and I both that you remember that."

So much for our warm repartee of yesterday. It seemed that Ruan Kivell and I were at odds. Likely always to be. And if that was the case, I would have to bring sense to Penryth Hall all on my own. "Well, I for one intend to prove that it's a man at the root of all this, not a monster."

For a moment—just that—I thought I'd had the best of Ruan Kivell. He turned, slinging his haversack over his shoulder and making for the western edge of the copse before he turned back to me, destroying my bravado with five simple words.

"Or a woman, Miss Vaughn."

Or a woman, indeed.

CHAPTER EIGHT

Rumors Abound

I left the *Pellar* and all his unwelcome observations hovering over Sir Edward and headed back to the house more unsettled than when I'd first joined Mrs. Penrose in the orchard a handful of hours before. I needed to get to Tamsyn, to be the one to tell her about her husband's fate—minus the crows. And flies. I'd spare her those little indignities of death. It was irrational the pull she still had over me—that had to be the reason for my staying. A reasonable woman would have walked away—said that Tamsyn had made her own bed and would need to deal with it herself—and yet I couldn't do it. For some inexplicable reason I needed to protect her—*had* to protect her.

Besides. I knew all too well how quickly idle rumors spark to conflagration. While Tamsyn was the mistress of Penryth Hall, she was still a woman living alone with a child and a husband dead under very bizarre circumstances. Oh, could the man not have choked on a fish bone? The very last thing she needed was whispers of a curse just when she'd freed herself of that dreadful man.

Freed herself. An odd turn of thought as Tamsyn was the

less likely of the two of us to do the deed. Which brought me back to the rather unpleasant recollecting of my dream. I'd had ones like it before and yet this was different somehow. More visceral. More real. Which terrified me to no end. And when conflated with the ghostly figure I'd seen entering the copse, I began to wonder if I wasn't going half mad myself.

I'd rounded the edge of the garden, pondering the merits of a hot bath and a strong drink to set my thoughts in order, when I heard voices nearby. A pair of them. I slowed my steps to silence my approach.

Two maids—a miracle that the place even had them, as I'd been entirely unaware of their existence up until this very moment. Though it should be no surprise, as Mrs. Penrose was certainly in no condition to keep the house as tidy as it was. A hint of tobacco smoke hit my nose.

"You heard what Mrs. Penrose said—it's the curse!"

"—you know we aren't supposed to be talking about this. She forbade us to say a word inside the house. Said the mistress is beside herself with worry."

"Well, we ain't in the house now, are we?"

The other girl laughed huskily.

"Besides, if I was the mistress, I'd be glad he's gone. She may as well kick up her heels now. He never was a right husband to her. And the way they'd row."

The whiskey-voiced one laughed again.

Row? Tamsyn scarcely spoke in his presence, I couldn't imagine her summoning the passion required to argue.

That was worrisome.

I closed my eyes to memorize the sounds and cadences of their voices, in hopes that I could place these to the girls when I saw them inside. I edged closer to the rectangular yew bush, to better catch what was said.

"That bird isn't heartsick in the least. You saw how she was. She's glad he's gone as she ought to be. He was a beast, and I say he got as good as he deserved."

She'd get no argument from me on that score.

"Hush now," the one nearer to me started. She shuffled in the gravel. "You shouldn't say such things."

"And why not? The man was a terror."

Touché, bloodthirsty maid.

"Do you suppose it's that poor Smythe girl? Remember how she carried on in the street about it only a fortnight past."

"Rose, don't be a dolt, you know they wouldn't call *him* for that. The Pellar only gets brought out for serious business. Speaking of . . . what took you so long to come back with him?"

I heard Rose make a sound low in her throat, and the playful smack of the other maid against her arm.

"You're redder than an apple, love. You have to tell me now." Another giggle.

"It was nothing. He wasn't in his cottage is all. I had to go look for him."

"And where was he?"

A loaded silence sat between the two maids.

"He wasn't doing that! I just found him down at the lake . . ." She hesitated before finishing. "Bathing."

"Did you at least get a good look at him then while he was there?" Whiskey asked.

"You shouldn't talk that way. He's the Pellar!"

"And he's still a man, ain't he? With all the bits and parts? Or did you not get a good look to tell if he had 'em?" Another hushed pause before the more brazen maid continued on. "All's a pity. But it's probably for the best. You know as good as I he's not for the likes of us."

More laughter from the other side of the hedge.

"Well, he might not be for marrying, but no one said I can't look at him. There's not a one in the village half as good-looking."

"Not since poor George Martin passed, that's for certain. Now, he was a right handsome one."

A yellow-and-black hoverfly buzzed around my nose, and I shooed it away, growing increasingly bored of village gossip and the debatable charms of the irritating Pellar. I was of half a mind to continue on to the house when the whiskey-voiced maid continued.

"Speaking of George Martin. I still can't get over what happened to his poor Miss Smythe."

"She wasn't *his* anymore, he broke things off with her before he even came home from the war."

The other maid huffed out her breath in a way that made me think she didn't care too much for whatever this George's reasons were for jilting poor Miss Smythe. But as George was no more, perhaps it was for the best for the girl. Whoever she was. Good God, I needed a drink to listen to much more of this, although it was more diverting than staring at a dead baronet.

"But for his lordship to put her out on the street without so much as a reference after all this time? You'd think he could have done the decent thing and given her a little blunt after putting a babe in her belly."

"Sir Edward hadn't a decent bone in his body," the first grumbled.

A mistress and baby then. With a dead lover to boot. Well, that would certainly give me a new avenue to pursue. Not that a *dead* lover would mean much, but a jilted mistress would have plenty of reason to wish ill on Sir Edward. Only I had no idea who the Smythe girl was. Or how I was to find her.

I listened while they finished their cigarettes then disappeared back into the house. Once I made certain they were well and truly gone, I followed them inside determined to wash the stench of death from my skin and put on a decent frock before seeing Tamsyn. After all, it was the very least I could do.

CHAPTER NINE

Promises Made

TAMSYN was sprawled out across the bed when I found her, in the room just beneath my own, staring at me with dry vacant eyes. The sight of her so hopeless and resigned broke something deep inside me.

She sniffed and patted the lush jacquard coverlet, pulling herself up to sitting. She'd grown thinner over the years. Bones too close to the surface, and sitting here with her reedy arms wrapped around her legs, she looked more like a china doll than a woman grown.

Wordlessly I joined her, the mattress giving beneath my added weight. "Did Mrs. Penrose speak with you about . . . about . . ."

"Edward?" she asked before shaking her head. "No. There was no need. I already knew. Everyone knew." She lifted her hand, pointing out the open window. "The bells ring when the curse has returned. I suppose I should have expected it after all. Edward had become obsessed with the thing. Going on and on about it."

"Mrs. Penrose mentioned it too."

Tamsyn nodded. "She would. She was here before, back

when—" Something stopped her and she turned away from me, looking out toward the copse where the clouds had begun to build in earnest. "I suppose I should have listened to him. Should have believed. He was right after all, wasn't he?"

"You don't seem terribly upset." I hesitated.

She shook her head. "Why should I be? There's no changing what's happened. Nor is there any changing what will happen next." Tamsyn drew her lower lip between her teeth, biting hard, her eyes still not meeting mine. "It's coming for me."

Her words were so calm, so emotionless, that at first I didn't register what she'd said. "Tamsyn, that's . . ."

"It's the truth. It took his uncle and his wife. It's only a matter of time." She cleared her throat, folding her delicate hands in her lap. She'd always had the finest hands with long elegant fingers a pianist would envy. I brushed a tangled lock of hair from her face and tucked it behind her ear.

Touching her had an uncanny ability to bridge the space between then and now. The house was silent aside from the rapid thundering of my heart in my chest. This was a mistake. Always a mistake to be this close to her, yet I couldn't leave her. Not now. "Nothing will come for you. I won't let it."

A weak smile crossed her face and died away. Stubbornly she refused to meet my gaze. "You were always too brave by half. I never had your courage, though I wish I did. I could use a dose of it now."

"Do you remember that night we spent near Soissons?" I brushed her cheek softly. Her skin cool. Damp.

"How could I forget? I thought I'd die that night when the Germans started strafing. It was just you and I and a handful of half-dead men. I swore to myself if I survived that night I'd never join you on another run to the clearing stations." She closed her eyes tight against the memory. "I don't know how you bore it. The responsibility of their lives in your hands. Knowing that most of them wouldn't even make the journey."

How many nights had I spent driving that battered ambulance from the clearing station closest to the fighting back to the main hospital in Amiens? Hundreds of miles. Thousands of miles over three interminable years. Looking back on some of the risks I'd taken and the orders I'd blindly followed, it was a marvel I'd survived the ordeal at all. But the devil rarely takes those determined to meet him. I'd already lost my parents and younger sister, the only thing keeping me tethered to the world back then was Tamsyn—then I lost her too.

I cleared my throat, the past uncomfortably close. "You were brave that night. The two of us kept every one of those men alive because there was no other choice, Tamsyn. I need you to be brave now. Because we don't have a choice. Not anymore."

She blinked at me uncertainly. "You can't stop a curse, Ruby. No one can."

I took her hands in my lap, squeezing them tight. "There's no such thing as curses. You never believed in them before, why should you now?"

"Perhaps I should have done. Everyone knew what happened to Edward's uncle. I should have listened to the stories. Heeded the warnings and perhaps Edward wouldn't be dead."

I opened my mouth to ask what had come before, no one had spoken of it—but she laid her fingers on my lips, silencing me before I could pry.

"I need you to promise me something."

"Anything."

"Protect him. Keep him safe. No matter what comes. No matter what happens to me." Her eyes at long last took on a shade of viridescent emotion.

"Protect who?"

"My son."

I stared at her, not comprehending.

"The curse will come for me. I don't know how long. Perhaps days? Weeks? And then Jori will be next. I'm certain of it. It's what happened before. It'll happen again, and when it does—I need to know he will be safe. There's no one in this world I trust more than you to make sure of that."

Perhaps the maids were right and Tamsyn had lost her mind. Never before had she believed in the old stories—she knew them, of course she did, having been weaned on them at the knee of her nurse. And later on, she'd whispered them to me on those dark nights during the war. Tales of piskies and the hurlers, of giants and witches and merfolk. But they weren't *real*. They couldn't be.

I squeezed her hand again. A helpless gesture, but I did it nonetheless. "It's the grief speaking. No one will harm you or your son. I swear it."

She let out a brittle laugh, a sharp sound that froze me to my bone.

"You're in shock. You must eat. Drink something. It's all right to grieve your husband." *Even a dreadful one.*

She shot off the bed and began pacing the floor of her chambers. The wooden boards creaking beneath her. Back and forth. Faster and faster.

"Tam—"

"Grieve him?" she choked out, her voice ever higher. "Grieve a monster? I'd as soon pluck my own eyes out as give him a moment of pain. No. I won't give Edward that gift. But I will not allow the curse to take my son either. My misdeeds will not cost me my child! Edward was a snake, but my son is precious."

My breath caught in my chest. *Edward was a snake.* Images of Tamsyn, the life smothered out of her, flickered in my head.

Edward wasn't the only one in my dream last night. I stared at her unblinking. *A coincidence, Ruby. It was just a dream.* I opened my mouth to speak, to break the sickening silence between us, when she laid a finger on my lips, silencing me.

"If your promises mean anything, promise me this." She dropped to her knees before me, squeezing my hand painfully tight. "Promise me you'll protect him. No matter what happens. You'll take care of Jori. No matter what comes for him."

I nodded, unable to formulate the words, to shape them out and put them in the air between us.

"I need to hear it from you. Say it. Swear upon your sister's grave that you will not let the curse take my son."

"I swear . . ." Two words, and my die was cast.

I didn't believe in curses any more than I believed in the God who long ago abandoned me to my fate, but I was determined to get to the bottom of what happened here at Penryth Hall and to bring back the Tamsyn that I used to know. The one Sir Edward had destroyed stone by stone.

CHAPTER TEN

A Gin-Soaked Subterfuge

EDWARD Chenowyth died for a reason.

A human one.

He had to have.

And my dream was just that, a dream that shared an uncanny coincidence with real life. Edward was smothering Tamsyn. A reasonable interpretation. And I'd imagined carving him up at the dinner table. *That was all.*

I repeated those facts to myself over and over until I found myself slowly beginning to believe it. Once my thoughts had settled, I went off in search of Mrs. Penrose—after all, a good housekeeper knows every secret in the house and Mrs. Penrose struck me as the very best of her kind.

I found her in the kitchen, elbow-deep in flour with the front of her apron smattered with crusty bits of dough that she'd inadvertently wiped there. The room redolent with yeast and pleasantly spiced fruit tarts. Several empty bottles and jars sat on the windowsill, catching the light. I straightened my spine and summoned my most devil-may-care smile, one I wasn't at all feeling. "Care to join me for tea, Mrs. Penrose?"

The old woman looked up at me, flummoxed. Her brow

was creased with worry, a weariness she'd been carrying since leaving the orchard this morning. From the sheer number of pasties scattered across the worktable, it appeared that Mrs. Penrose had been trying to bake away her troubles.

I pulled the silver flask from the pocket of my neatly tailored twill skirt and offered it to her. "*Enhanced* tea. Lord knows after the morning we've had, I suspect we both need a moment to recover ourselves, hmmm?"

Her eyes widened in unspoken acknowledgment and she dusted her hands on her apron. Mrs. Penrose glanced to the doorway, but we both knew good and well Tamsyn wasn't coming back downstairs. If anything she was staring out the window again. The guilty part of me was glad to be away from her. Away from the sickening guilt that erupted whenever she was near.

Her shoulders relaxed. "I suspect I could use a cup myself. I'll be a moment. Are you hungry, maid?"

I shook my head. After seeing Sir Edward's stomach strewn across the lawn, the idea of putting anything else inside my own wretched organ remained highly unappealing, no matter how pleasant the kitchen smelled.

She didn't pay me a bit of attention. "You go on to the morning room and I'll bring a tray and some biscuits up, and you can tell me all about what the Pellar said after I left."

Of course she'd want to talk about *him*. I, on the other hand, wanted to talk about anything else but Ruan Kivell. Even his name irritated me after this morning. How he'd looked at me with such suspicion in his eyes. *Or a woman*, the irritating man had said. His name consisted of two syllables—*Rue Ahn* or an elongated *ruin*. Fitting as he'd utterly ruined my afternoon—oh, that wasn't true, Edward's killer did that all on their own. It was unfair to be cross with the man, but his gaze bothered me. A mixture of suspicion and apprehension. I blew out a breath. But as I was here, there was nothing for it—I'd have to talk about him, deal with him. Talk *to* him if I was to have any prayer of setting Tamsyn to rights and getting out of this godforsaken village. And in that case, it was best to know as much as I could to better prepare myself. *Prepare yourself for what, Ruby Vaughn?* This wasn't a war, but what it *was*, I didn't yet know.

TWENTY MINUTES LATER Mrs. Penrose joined me in the morning room with a full tray overladen with sandwiches, biscuits, and little teacakes iced in pink. Gauging from the spread, she'd been waiting her entire life for me to arrive at Penryth. My stomach let out a longing growl, reminding me I'd not eaten since breakfast the day before.

She gestured for me to sit and I did as she suggested, but not before snatching a ginger biscuit and plopping it into my mouth with an audible crunch.

"Has Ruan left?" she asked, picking up a pair of silver tongs. "Sugar?"

"Yes, please. I assume he's gone by now. I left him in the orchard." Then another thought struck me. "Oh, good God. What's he done with the body?" My imagination ignited with possibilities, some more macabre than others. None pleasant. The biscuit grew dry in my mouth.

"Nothing for you to worry over, my lover. Some of the lads from the village helped bring him up to the house while you were upstairs with the mistress."

"You don't mean he's here?"

She lifted her hands in exasperation. A serious slight for a housekeeper under ordinary circumstances, but we were beyond propriety now. "Where else would he be, maid? We've cleaned him up as best we can. The constable asked that we lock him in the cellar, to prepare him for burial and to keep the curious sorts from nosing about. Bothering the poor man's body."

"Do you mean to tell me he's in the storeroom?"

Mrs. Penrose looked wounded at the thought. "Well, it's not like we laid him alongside Sunday's joint, if that's what you're insinuating. No, he's cleaned up—the poor soul—and in the old wine cellar. He might have been a loathsome sinner, but that still don't justify not paying him the proper respects."

I tried to look suitably mournful for said sinner, but it was a difficult emotion to feign when I was growing increasingly puzzled over the whole situation. Pulling my silver flask from my pocket, I filled her cup first, then my own. "How are you?"

The edge of her mouth curved up slightly and she blinked at me. "Do you know, maid, you are the first person to have asked that this whole wretched day?"

Her words settled uncomfortably in my belly, as my motives for asking were far from innocent.

"I'm as right as I can be." She took a long drink of the gin-infused tea and sighed heavily.

"Mrs. Penrose . . ."

"What is it, maid?"

"It's only . . . I want to talk to you about what happened in the copse this morning."

She sucked in a sharp breath. "I suspected you might have some questions."

Some was an understatement. I had nothing but questions. "It's only . . . you seem convinced that it's the curse, as does Tamsyn."

"Because it is, maid. It is. I'd hoped Ruan would tell me different but it's just the same as it was before." The corners of her mouth tightened in strain and she blew out her breath. "I don't know why I'm telling you this, it certainly isn't proper but then again, nothing in your and my acquaintance has been, has it?"

I shook my head. From what I'd gathered, Mrs. Penrose had seen me at my absolute worst. And rather than taking my poor behavior as an indictment against me, she felt duty bound to take me under her wing. An oddly fortuitous turn of events.

"You may as well know the whole of it as you're in the thick of things." Seconds ticked by while Mrs. Penrose slowly drew courage from the contents of her cup, her lids heavy as she leaned back into the brocade chair. Black leather shoes, shined but worn, peeped out beneath her fresh gray skirt. "It's the same as it was afore. Even down to the way the body was laid. I'd hoped . . . I prayed that Ruan would have noticed something different. That the constable would agree and we'd be well shut of it." She crossed herself and then downed her cup before jutting it out for me to pour her another.

"Was the previous victim Sir Edward's uncle then?" I tugged a leg up underneath me in the chair, racking my brain trying to piece together the bits I'd learned from Tamsyn.

She ran her fingers over the rim of the cup hesitantly. "Sir Edward wasn't supposed to inherit the title. His uncle held it before him. An old bachelor." She frowned deeply. "They found him in the cowshed. Laid out like we saw this morning. His entrails ripped clean from him. At first they thought it was some sort of wild creature. But there's nothing in the countryside to kill a man in that fashion. Nothing natural at least. Oh, an adder might do a fellow in. Or he might get gored by a teasy bull. But this was different. This was—"

"Intentional."

She pressed her lips tight and gave me a firm nod. "That it was, maid. I've seen all sorts of things in my life, but I've never seen such evil done a soul in any other way."

The hairs rose up on the back of my neck at her words. "What killed the old baronet, then? Did they ever learn?"

"The curse, maid. The curse. But we didn't know it then. Not until his pretty young wife was found two weeks later."

I furrowed my brow. "But I thought you said he was a bachelor."

Mrs. Penrose set her cup down and leaned forward, the chair creaking softly. "He was, he married not long before his death. I had just been brought on to be her lady's maid, though I never set eyes on her alive."

"What happened?" I mumbled between bites of my tea sandwich.

"I don't know for certain. I was brought up to the house to work, but there was no lady here when I arrived. I toiled for weeks preparing the rooms for her, waiting for her to arrive. The master had said she would return once matters were settled, but Sir Joseph was a secretive sort—he wouldn't ever say what those matters were."

I frowned.

"After Sir Joseph was found dead, I'd gone to spend some time with my sister in Dorset. I returned three days later and found the mistress dead."

"Dead!" Well, that certainly explained why Tamsyn was so convinced of her own dire fate.

"That she was. Gutted and laid out in this room as her husband had been in the cowshed."

My teacup clattered on the saucer as I glanced down to the fine carpets beneath my feet. "Here?"

"Lady Chenowyth doesn't know. She thought it such a pretty room and I hadn't the heart to tell her what happened. It's been kept locked up for years because of . . . well, you see, don't you?"

"She was murdered . . . here?" I repeated, staring at the rug.

"It was thirty years ago, maid. I doubt there's a great house in this country without a death or twelve within its walls." She drained her teacup and refilled it, topping off my own in the process. "You see, we hadn't a Pellar then. They don't spring up like mushrooms after a rain."

I nearly snorted at the image her words conjured.

"Before young Mr. Kivell, we hadn't had one here in some three hundred years. So the townsfolk sent off for the White Witch of Launceton. She was one of the old ones. A seer and a powerful witch too." Her eyes took on a reverent expression and I found myself almost believing in her story. "Ruan was just a baby then."

Mrs. Penrose's once neatly kept graying hair had fallen slightly loose from the knot she wore it in, escaping her cap. Her face was flushed from having imbibed the better part of my flask on her own.

"Then did this woman get to the bottom of it?"

Mrs. Penrose made a sound of distress and shook her head. "We thought she had. She came and worked a charm that was to send the beast back from whence it'd come."

"Thought?" My brows rose.

"Well, it's back now, ain't it?" she grumbled, settling herself into her chair. Her body loose as she ran a hand over her face and blew out a breath.

"I don't see why everyone believes it's a curse. It's gruesome what happened to the previous baronet, yes, and there are similarities, but . . ."

Mrs. Penrose eyed my flask thoughtfully and then shook her head. "Because Sir Joseph wasn't the first. Nor was he the last. If I remember the story, it started over two hundred years ago—when another Chenowyth heir made off with a girl from the village. A bal maiden."

"Just like Sir Joseph and his wife, then."

Mrs. Penrose pressed her lips into a tight line and gave me

a curt nod. "The same. The young gentleman was intended to marry a wealthy wellborn maid from Devon. The young maid was furious for being cast off like rubbish, and for someone born so far beneath her? It was unthinkable. So she channeled her rage and went off to a local witch, begging the crone to bring her beloved's heart back to her. The witch, they said, was a cruel and evil creature that dabbled in black magic, having long harbored an ill wish toward the Chenowyths."

I furrowed my brow, enraptured by the story. It reminded me of the ones Tamsyn's cook would tell us when we'd steal away to the kitchen for late-night puddings. "And then what happened?"

"The witch set a curse upon the Chenowyth line vowing revenge. She killed the faithless heir and his young bride, removing his inconstant heart and delivering it to his betrothed in a silver box."

"I suppose that wasn't what the jilted girl had intended."

Mrs. Penrose let out a startled laugh and then straightened her features. "No, I imagine not, maid. Be it a lesson—always be careful in dealing with witches."

I refrained from commenting on the fact she sent for the same herself to help in this very matter. A witch, the constable had called him.

"But Sir Edward's heart wasn't removed, was it?"

Mrs. Penrose wrinkled her nose. "To tell you the truth I didn't have the stomach to look. Perhaps our Pellar knows." She sighed heavily, the morning's discovery weighing on her every movement. "I tell you true, my lover. If it weren't for our Pellar, I'd pack my bags and be off myself. I haven't the stomach to live through those dark days again, but I can't bring myself to leave the poor babe alone out here."

"Jori?"

She nodded. "He's an innocent in all this."

"As is Tamsyn," I protested.

Mrs. Penrose started to speak but then thought better of it. She frowned into her empty cup before setting it on the gilded tea tray.

"You don't think she had something to do with it, do you?"

Mrs. Penrose ran a hand over her hair, smoothing it nervously, and shook her head. "Of course not. But I wouldn't blame her if she had, the way he treated her. Poor lamb. It doesn't matter now, does it? Our Mr. Kivell will rid us of the curse for once and all."

I pinched the bridge of my nose trying—and failing—to look as if she hadn't told me that Ruan Kivell was more or less some type of arcane Cornish exorcist. "I suppose I don't understand precisely. What *is* a Pellar, Mrs. Penrose? The way you speak of him he sounds like a cross between a physician, a witch, and a priest."

She let out a startled laugh. "I suppose it'd seem that way to you, wouldn't it, maid? Though come to think of it, perhaps it isn't so different."

"You think he can do what that White Witch did before, then?"

"Oh, maid. You don't have any idea, do you?" She didn't wait for me to respond before continuing on. "He's the seventh son of a seventh son, from a family of charmers, he is. They say his mother's line is descended from the very first Pellar. I knew he had the gift. Knew it the moment the lad was born. The magic's in his very blood and bone."

"Is that so?"

She nodded, her eyes taking on a fanatical light. "Oh, yes. He never was sick. Never a day in his life. Nor any of his kin. Ask me, Miss Vaughn, how many we lost in Lothlel Green to the influenza?"

The word made my skin crawl. It was still too recent, I

didn't much want to think on it for fear the plague would consider it an invitation to return. "A handful?"

"Not. A. One." She flashed me the most beatific smile I'd ever seen. The woman was beyond foxed, but I daresay she'd earned it after this morning. "And it's all because of him. When he was still away in France, we lost dozens of young, strong lads to it. The mine even had to shut down because there was no one to work it. But he returned home from the war and instantly the illness fled. Tell me how else you can explain it."

I couldn't. But then again, the extent of my medical training covered battlefield triage, hasty tourniquets, and administering morphine to dying men. There was a plausible explanation for all of it. There had to be. "That's all fascinating, but Sir Edward was murdered, Mrs. Penrose. I don't see what a Pellar can do that a constable cannot."

The woman's eyes widened as if I'd struck her, and I immediately regretted my words. "Have you not listened to a word I said? It's no man that we're after. It's Old Nick. And Ruan Kivell is the only thing standing between the mistress and the grave. Mark my words." Her eyes drifted up to the ceiling, to the floor where Tamsyn was hopefully now resting peacefully. "And he's coming for her, make no mistake on that. Her and that poor lamb of hers, just as it happened before."

I cleared my throat and downed the rest of my cup. I'd encouraged her far too much on that score. Tamsyn was already convinced of this nonsense, and I needed to nip the conversation where it stood. "I've come to understand that Sir Edward wasn't a . . ." I bit my lip, weighing the words. "A saint."

The old woman snorted back a laugh. "Far from it. He was a menace."

"Well, it's on that point I want to know a bit more."

Mrs. Penrose's eyes narrowed in suspicion.

"You see, I want to help Tamsyn—" I caught myself. "But

there are some things women don't tell one another. Things that—" I glanced up through my lashes, as subtle as a bull dancing in the Trocadero.

"I shouldn'ta said what I did." Her brow furrowed. "It's not right to speak ill of the dead, but the things he did to the mistress weren't right."

I leaned forward, sensing my moment, and took her hands in mine. They were slightly damp. Cool. "Mrs. Penrose, was Edward unfaithful to her?"

She didn't answer, but the acknowledgment was written all over her face. Ah, so Tamsyn too had Mrs. Penrose's sympathies. I could work with this. "If there's anything at all that he might have been involved in. Perhaps it'd help Mr. Kivell in his investigations. Was there anyone who would want to harm him? Wish him ill?"

"Wish him harm? Why, Nellie Smythe wished him dead on the village green not three weeks past. But this is more than the evil eye."

The maids' Miss Smythe. I leaned closer to the housekeeper. "And no one thought to bring it up?" This was absurd. A completely reasonable, rational explanation was at hand and everyone was leaping to the most far-fetched conclusions. And a woman at that! Anyone who had spent even a modicum of time existing in humanity would know that one didn't need a dramatic conspiracy to explain away murder. The usual suspect was almost always the correct one. Jilted lovers. Money. Betrayal.

Mrs. Penrose shook her head and waved me off. "I see the look on your face, maid. But our Nellie is a good girl. She wouldn't have done something like that. Her tongue got ahead of her, that's all, and who would blame her? To be frank—"

As if she wasn't already.

Mrs. Penrose laughed again, the gin having done its job.

"Miss Vaughn, to be perfectly frank with you, there isn't a woman in Cornwall who wouldn't wish Edward Chenowyth to the devil. But I doubt a one would have bothered to lay a finger on him. Least of all our Nellie."

But a woman had. I'd seen her, dressed all in white going out into the orchard the very night he died. Though perhaps it hadn't been a woman at all. From the distance, it could have been anyone. Anything.

Even you. The thought sickened me. I'd been known to sleepwalk as a child, even to leave the house. Once when I was a girl, my mother found me at the edge of the pond, sitting there staring sightlessly into the water. But to kill a man in one's sleep? Was such a thing possible?

"Is everything all right, Miss Vaughn?"

"Yes. Yes. Quite," I lied, shaking the worries away. I would have to go make my own inquiries first, before I told anyone of what I'd seen that night. That was the best course. The only one as I was beginning to doubt my own eyes. Doubt what I might or might not have done. That thought sat heavier with me than it ought.

I managed to make it through the remainder of tea with Mrs. Penrose without learning anything else of measure. Unless you counted the seven minor miracles of Saint Ruan of Kivell. As I'd taken to thinking of him now. Three of said miracles were love charms that resulted in blissful marriages with passels of rosy-cheeked children each. The others more inexplicable, though each could easily be chalked up to chance. After all, there were plenty of reasons for the village to have been spared the influenza. And mine accidents happened all the time. You'd hear of them, with the workers somehow trapped in a bubble of air. A pocket in stone. It was luck. Nothing more.

Yet as I left Mrs. Penrose in the morning room, I began to

wonder if there might be more to Ruan Kivell than met the eye. But if I were to allow the existence of Pellars in this world, who was to say that curses were not also just as real—a thought I refused to countenance.

CHAPTER ELEVEN

Unlikely Bedfellows

HEAD swimming with thoughts of Pellars, curses, and a healthy amount of gin, I hurried up the stairs to my room in dire need of a nap. The door was wide open. I didn't recall leaving it in such a state, but the morning in the orchard had been so chaotic, I was lucky to have put my blouse on properly after my bath. Fiachna lay curled up asleep on the top of the muddied nightdress I'd shed this morning. I tossed my empty flask on the mattress with a thump. The cat lifted his head lazily in greeting, then set it back down again.

I sat at the dressing table and began unbuttoning my blouse so as not to wrinkle it, when a loud thunk came from behind me. Along with the sound of masculine swearing.

Glancing into the mirror, I spotted a pair of legs sticking out from the far side of the behemoth of a bed.

Ruan Kivell. Of course it was.

"Well, this wasn't exactly what I was expecting." I stood, leaning against the dressing table lazily. "I must confess, I've had quite a few young gentlemen try to finagle their way into my bed over the years, but this may be the first time one has actually worked his way beneath it—" I grew unable to contain my amusement at the situation. I ought to be angry for the intrusion, but all I could do was laugh. This day had truly done me in. "Though I suppose it has potential . . ."

His face turned a peculiar shade of red, his lips pressed into a thin line as he slithered out from underneath said bed.

He was unamused.

Pity, as I'd rather liked him when we first met. However, his ill mood today damped that sentiment quick enough. What was that word Mrs. Penrose had used downstairs? Teasy, that was it! A teasy bull . . . yes, that's precisely what he was.

If anything, he was glowering even more.

"Oh, good God, has anyone told you that you look rather like a cross frog when you do that? Besides, what *are* you doing lurking down there anyway?"

He grumbled something that was *not* suitable for delicate ears, before withdrawing what appeared to be a bottle from beneath the bed. In a quick and catlike movement he was on his feet prowling across the floor to me.

"What are you playing at?" He shook the bottle at me. The contents made a sickening sloshing sound as I struggled to focus on the object he waved in my face. It was ordinary—clear green glass—but inside was some sort of yellowish liquid with a desiccated *thing* floating in it.

"What *is* that?"

"I thought you might tell me what you are doing with it and why you're meddling in charmwork?"

I rolled my eyes. "That's not mine. I assure you of that. I would never dabble in . . . whatever that is."

"What it is, is an . . . an abomination."

"You'll get no argument from me there."

He sniffed angrily, raking his hair back from his brow with his left hand. "What I don't understand is why you are playing at black magic."

I let out a startled laugh. "Black magic? Indeed, Mr. Kivell, I'm beginning to wonder which one of us dipped into the gin today. I assure you, I know nothing about black magic, unless it's a cocktail and in that case . . ." I tapped my chin just to irritate him. "I think I've had it once or twice."

His nostrils flared. "This isn't amusing."

"Agreed. What are you doing in here anyway?" I folded my arms across my chest.

"Trying to understand what you are doing here."

I let out a sigh and rolled my eyes. "I brought you a box of books if you recall."

He shook his head angrily and took a step closer to me. "And yet you didn't just deliver them. You remained here, in a house no one visits, where a man has been murdered, and then I find this under your bed." He gave the bottle in his hand another shake. "Do you know what this looks like?"

"Like the great Pellar of Lothlel Green is skulking around grasping at straws? Come now, the only reason I'm in this wretched little town is because of you and your books. You can't truly believe that I somehow orchestrated the whole thing to kill Edward? Or that I'd be naive enough to keep the evidence of my crimes in my bedchamber?"

He folded his arms firmly across his chest in challenge. The two of us like a matched pair of bookends bullishly staring at each other.

Good God, why didn't he believe me? I hadn't even wanted to return to Lothlel Green in the first place—not truly. It was only my affection for dear old Mr. Owen that brought me here.

He blew out a breath, studying my face intently. Then his peculiar eyes widened for just an instant then shuttered again. The man was harder to read than my own penmanship.

"Hush," he growled.

"I'm not speaking."

"It's truly not yours, is it?" He sounded vaguely disappointed at the acknowledgment.

"Truly. Now will you tell me what that thing is, and what it's doing under my bed?"

He blew out a heavy breath and walked to the window, pulling the thick curtains back and gazing out onto the path into the orchard. "And you didn't see anything last night. Nothing at all unusual?"

I shook my head, grateful he couldn't read my thoughts. "No. Though I had a rather unsettling dream. I'm prone to them—bad dreams—but this one was strange, even for me."

He made a low sound of annoyance in his throat. "What sort of dream?"

I'd never told many people about them. Only my mother knew, and Tamsyn of course. Yet something about this irritating stranger made me want to tell him about them. In detail. Lay bare everything I'd never understood. Had to be the gin, that was all. "It was strange." My fingers rose to my throat, tracing over the spot where my skin still hurt. "I felt as if I were being strangled. Tamsyn was there, and a snake . . . so was Sir Edward. He was attacking me. And I was struggling with him. Then Fiachna had a fit—the cat, you see—" I left out the detail about the knife and gestured to the cat, who let out a timely wet feline snort.

"Your throat?" His variegated eyes remained fixed upon me.

I nodded, my fingers toying with the golden chain of my locket. He prowled closer, one hand shooting out, brushing my own hand away. His fingers rough and warm as he probed my skin.

I jerked away from his touch, stumbling slightly, causing me to whack the back of my thighs against the wooden dressing table. "Ow. What are you doing?"

"Turn around."

I jutted out my jaw, swatting his hand away. "That's enough of that. I don't understand what you are doing, what you're thinking storming in here with wild accusations. Putting your hands on my person and brandishing that . . . that . . ." I waved my hand airily at the jar he still held. "Whatever that is."

"A fetal pig."

I let out an involuntary shudder. "A fetal pig . . . lovely. Well, regardless. I do wish you would leave and take all that nonsense with you."

"Nonsense, is it?" He took hold of my shoulders and turned me bodily around to face the mirror, looming behind me—a bleak and angry expression on what I'd once mistaken as a rather kind face.

His warm hands tugged down the flimsy, white-lace collar of my blouse, revealing faint bruises on my skin. Purplish-green streaks spread across the tawny flesh. They were faint, but there all the same.

I sucked in a breath, my own fingers tracing the marks in the reflection. I hadn't been dreaming after all. And if that wasn't a dream . . . then what else might have occurred last night?

Mr. Kivell slipped the bottle into his coat pocket and started back across the room. "There's blood in your bed as well, Miss Vaughn. And if I don't miss my guess, I'd say that Sir Edward wasn't the only target last night. Someone here means you ill. Unless . . ." He trailed off, staring intently at me.

"Blood?" The color drained from my face, and I grew chilled. "Surely you don't think I . . ." But I couldn't finish the statement, as the farther he moved from me, the more the world began to shift beneath my feet. I sank back down onto the top of the dressing table, tilting my head toward his bulging pocket. "Is that what that is, then? An ill wish?" Tamsyn's old cook had mentioned such things, but I'd never paid much attention then.

He gave me a halfhearted shrug and sniffed in response. "I'm not sure what it is, truth be told. It's nothing I've ever seen before. It looks like black magic, but sometimes countercharms can be just as macabre to the untrained eye. I once saw a woman put nails into a bullock's heart and shove it up a chimney to break a curse. I can't be certain either way until I look a bit more closely."

"I feel rather sorry for the bull." I frowned. "How does one learn this sort of thing? I suppose they don't teach it at Oxford, do they?"

He let out a slight sound of amusement. "I'd say whoever put the charm there was either better versed in the craft than I am or wants it to look that way."

I wet my lips. "Which do you think it is, Mr. Kivell?" I sorely hoped his answer was the latter, but he turned on his heels and stalked out of the room, leaving me even more unsettled than before.

CHAPTER TWELVE

An Odious Visitor

"I came as soon as I heard." A cultured male voice came from the drawing room, bringing me to a dead halt where I stood. I hadn't known we were expecting guests. Though news of Edward's death must have traveled fast. It had been probably half an hour since Mr. Kivell left me in my bedchamber, as it had taken at least that long for me to regain both my wits and enough sobriety to make my way downstairs to speak with Tamsyn. I'd been in this house less than twenty-four hours and someone had not only murdered her ne'er-do-well husband but tried to kill me as well.

I paused outside the doorway for several seconds, my fingers toying with the golden chain of the locket at the base of my throat. My skin still burned from where Mr. Kivell had touched me moments before. Was it possible that Sir Edward had attacked me in my sleep? Could he have caused my bruises and I . . . My thumb ran over the back of the locket. *No.* No, it wasn't possible. There had been a knife in my dream, and I certainly didn't have one of those. Besides, how would I have gotten his body to the orchard if I'd somehow stabbed him?

And wouldn't there have been more blood than just the smattering on the sheets?

No. None of that made sense at all.

I took a fortifying breath and stepped into the morning room.

Tamsyn was seated in the very same chair I'd occupied during tea with Mrs. Penrose earlier this morning. My gaze flitted to her strained and vacant expression. Much the same as the one she wore at dinner with her husband. Her expressive hands were folded and still in her lap, bearing a distinct resemblance to a butterfly under glass.

Neither she nor her companion acknowledged my presence at all, so consumed by their conversation that I might have been a ghost myself, or some ephemeral thought not worthy of a second notice. I leaned against the doorframe, arms folded, and took in the tableau before me.

The man at her side looked to be a vicar, based solely upon the dog collar he wore. A rather rounded and jolly-looking man. Cheeks pink and flushed, possibly a score younger than Mr. Owen, but decidedly less clever looking than the old man. His skin, other than his face, possessed a rather mealy shade of pale. The sort of fellow who couldn't be in the sun more than a handful of minutes before taking on a decidedly porcine hue.

There was an almost tangible snap in the room when Tamsyn's eyes lit upon me and her expression brightened. "Ruby!"

My heart gave an irrational start at my name. She thrust her hand out for me to join her, and like a fool I went, settling my hip against the faded Chippendale chair she occupied.

She put my fingers in her own and clasped them tight to her shoulder. "Reverend Fortescue. This is the woman I was telling you about."

I could only imagine what she had said about me. Clearly not the truth of our connection or the good vicar would have run for the hills to save his own immortal soul, rather than sit across the drawing room with such unabashed admiration on his face. At the very least, the fellow would have begun rummaging the well-worn pages of his prayer book for a suitable bulwark against my corrupting nature. Amused by my own imaginings, I glanced down to his hands. Odd that he didn't have one. What sort of vicar came condoling without a prayer book?

"Ah, the estimable Miss Vaughn, is it?" He smiled at me with far too many teeth. Even and uncannily white. One should never trust a man with too-perfect teeth.

"I'm not certain on how estimable I am, but I'm Ruby Vaughn, yes."

He laughed at that, a bit too loudly. His smile indelibly printed upon his face as his blue eyes wetly took in every ounce of me. And while I wasn't up to snuff on religious affairs, I was quite certain that he was thinking things his maker would take issue with.

The room was close, stale, and thick. In stark contrast with how it had been a few hours before when I sat in here with Mrs. Penrose, polishing off the contents of my flask. I longed to yank back the thick damask curtains and unlatch the windows—let in the light of day. The birdsong. Something. Yet Tamsyn held my fingers in a vise, pealing out her fear clear as the Penryth Bells.

Her thin chest rose and fell rapidly. I squeezed her shoulder. Her bones far too frail as if she had been slowly wasting away over the last two years. A thought that I couldn't bear.

"It heartens me you're here with Lady Chenowyth in her time of need."

Another squeeze.

She was trying to tell me something. Her thumb drummed nervously on the side of my hand. I shifted my grasp enough to hold her still with my own. She was revealing too much to this man. Though I hadn't a clue what she was trying to tell me.

"As any good friend would."

His gaze shifted from Tamsyn to me.

"Yes, as I was telling Lady Chenowyth." He cleared his throat with a moist hack. "I've heard the most horrific whispers about her poor husband's demise. It's unfathomable what stories people will concoct to explain what's in truth naught but the devil's work."

Tamsyn's pulse galloped beneath my thumb. Her skin was growing damp. "The devil, Reverend? I cannot believe that an educated man of the cloth would believe in such things as curses."

"I don't, Miss Vaughn. I simply mean it's the sinful nature of man that's done the deed." His cerulean eyes sparkled with barely concealed glee. "All this talk of curses and beasts . . . It's heathen nonsense. Carryovers from the pagans. Popery even."

I schooled my expression into an imitation of well-heeled boredom and sniffed. "Indeed."

"You see, this is precisely what occurs when you allow the uneducated to self-govern. I was telling Lady Chenowyth the same just moments before you arrived. You see, the common folk need people like us—of good breeding—"

I nearly choked.

"To guide them with a firm hand. Shepherd them if you will. Otherwise, if left to their own devices, not only are they vulnerable to the most venal sins, but they also come to the most perplexing notions."

Like a man rising from the dead? But I didn't voice my annoyance. It was no good arguing with those whose minds were already iron-tight. The man perplexed me. Sir Edward was scarcely cold, and yet the vicar had already arrived. Hurrying to the house and secreting himself away with the grieving widow when it had only been perhaps a handful of hours since the body had been discovered. Perhaps he was only here out of Christian charity, but something in his demeanor told me there was another motive behind his swift appearance.

The vein at his temple bulged as he carried on the conversation entirely on his own. "I've heard that the mad housekeeper here has called for the *Pellar*." Reverend Fortescue's cheeks grew even more ruddy at the mention of Mr. Kivell.

"Mmm . . ." I'm not sure what devil had gotten into me. But I was beyond tired of listening to him go on. "Ah, yes, I left him not a few moments ago, your Pellar. Quite a charming fellow. Found him in my bed. Well. Under it, to be precise."

The vicar choked for a moment before recovering his composure. "Charmer's more like. Barely civilized, preying upon the poor, weak-minded members of my flock. You won't find him in a pew come Sunday. What may I ask was he doing under your bed?"

"Whatever he wanted, I presume, as I wasn't there to keep him company."

He sputtered again, and I could have sworn I heard Tamsyn hold back a laugh from behind me.

"I take it you don't believe in Pellars either, Reverend?"

He bristled, shaking his head once more. His color even higher now. For half a second, I worried all my goading might cause him an apoplexy. "Nonsense is what it is. If I were you, Miss Vaughn, I wouldn't spend more than five minutes with the gentleman—not that he warrants the term. He's as common as they come. Filthy, and there's something not right about him beyond those eyes of his."

Despite my general mistrust of Mr. Kivell, I felt a strange kinship with him. He was an outlier. Existing on the periphery of society as was I. And while I wasn't quite certain of his motives, I found I'd much rather take a chance and put my faith in him than the *man of God* sitting before me.

"Not a single redeemable quality to him, and while he did do his duty during the war—" Reverend Fortescue made a comically pious expression. "He's a dangerous sort. A rabble rouser. Likely a Bolshevik—"

I sighed with a bored examination of my free hand. "Pity . . . I'm fond of Bolsheviks."

Tamsyn squeezed the other in reproach, but I wasn't about to stop. Not now. I loathed this man even though I had no reason to do so. I'd met plenty others like him and been able to politely extricate myself from conversation with little effort. But Reverend Fortescue was a menace and he brought out the very worst in my nature.

He trembled again, his color brighter by the second. "But it's no matter. His kind will disappear before long. The modern world has no place in it for men like Ruan Kivell."

A growing pang of affection rose in my chest for the poor reviled Pellar, misplaced I was certain, but I swallowed it down and minded my tongue. Otherwise we'd never get rid of this odious man. Tamsyn sensed my retreat from the field of battle and steered the conversation back to safer waters.

It took another half hour of small talk before I could convince the vicar that Tamsyn was safe with me, and that there were no more witches hiding in the closets. We said our goodbyes and she walked him out.

Once the door closed firmly behind the pair, I collapsed whole-bodied on the settee and closed my eyes. The fabric even smelled of her. It was the most divinely terrible moment of my life. Her husband was dead, she was irrationally convinced she was going to die, and yet I longed for her—for the way things might have been—in a way I hadn't longed for anything in my life. She was free. Truly free and if I wanted, perhaps I could reach out and grasp our broken past and bring it into the present. And yet some piece of me remained wary. Afraid. And I didn't know why.

I heard the door snick shut. "That was poorly done of you, Ruby."

I rested my folded hands atop my forehead and didn't bother to open my eyes. "Wouldn't want him to get the misperception I'm redeemable."

Tamsyn sighed heavily and settled down beside me on the settee, lifting my head so it rested in her lap. "He's dreadful, I know. But you shouldn't goad him so. He's been the vicar in these parts for ages. He even christened me, if you'd believe it."

I breathed in, relishing the stolen moment. The faint lemony scent of her invaded every crevasse of my memory and I hated it. Her fingers grazed gently over my features in the sweetest agony I'd ever endured. She wasn't mine. Not any longer.

Her touch traveled slowly down my neck until it suddenly stopped at the collar of my blouse. "What happened to you . . . ?" Her cool fingers were again at my throat, shifting the collar of my blouse to reveal the bruises there, following the same path of Mr. Kivell's earlier, albeit with a bit more tenderness.

"I haven't a clue. I didn't even know they were there until Mr. Kivell so keenly noticed them."

Her breath hitched in her chest at the mention of his name. "Was he truly in your room or were you just goading the vicar?" She hesitated for a moment. "I know I have no right . . . no right to ask after how things ended between us."

"Honestly, Tamsyn, do you think me fast enough that I'd

have bedded your Pellar when I've been in town less than a day?"

She let out a little huff and shook her head. "No. Of course not, it's just . . . I'm sorry, I'm not thinking clearly."

I reached up, opening my eyes and touching her cheek softly. "It's fine, darling. He was looking for something. He thinks . . ." I rolled my eyes, wetted my lips, and pulled myself upright. It was easier to talk—to think—with some space between us. For someone who had spent the last several years running from the past, I seemed to be lingering a great deal in the place. "He thinks someone attacked me last night too."

"What?!"

"I thought it was a dream, you know how I used to have terrible nightmares after . . ." *After my parents died.* Before, even—but those I kept to myself. How I'd seen my younger sister disappear beneath the waves. Ribbons in her hair as she sank farther and farther away from my outstretched hand before at last she disappeared. It ached, even now some seven years after their deaths.

"Oh, Ruby, have they returned again? You should have written. You shouldn't have to be alone with that burden."

I walked to the window, hefting the heavy sash up. It groaned with the effort, but the sweet August breeze was worth it. Particularly vocal pigeons called to one another from a nearby tree. "I don't know if they have or not. It was strange. It wasn't like the ones I used to have. It seems I was saved by my stowaway cat. I woke up to Fiachna screaming bloody murder." Perhaps not the best choice of words considering the morning. "Mr. Kivell said there was blood on my sheets as well. All I can think is that he must have startled whoever meant to do me harm." *That or I murdered your husband and brought his blood back in with me.*

"Ruby, that's terrible! I don't know how to apologize to

you for . . . Oh, goodness. I'm ever so glad it wasn't you." She stood and ran to me, hugging me tight enough I couldn't draw breath.

"Yes, yes, I'm rather pleased it wasn't me either."

She laughed again, stepping away and wiping at the tears on her cheeks. "I'm glad you're here. I have no one to talk to but you."

"You mean the vicar isn't a good listener?"

She laughed at that, her smile not quite reaching her eyes.

"Were you the one who snuck into my bed and tried to do me in?" I teased, earning me a cross look.

"Do be serious."

"I'm nothing but."

She turned away, allowing me only the back of her head. The jeweled comb she wore in her hair winked in the afternoon sun. "I have something to tell you and I need you to listen."

"Very well then." I settled myself down on the settee, watching the curve of her neck apprehensively. "Tell me."

She didn't. Not at first. The silence stretched on. The ticking of the clock, the soft groan of the wooden floorboards as she paced back and forth. And then at last she spoke. "I didn't love him."

"Edward? I don't blame you. Who would? He was a dreadful man. I still don't quite understand why you married him in the first place."

"You shouldn't say such things. I told you why a dozen times, but you never listened."

I leaned forward, elbows on my tweed-clad thighs. "Tell me again."

She turned back for a moment, worrying her lower lip. "Do you recall when he was brought into the hospital? How things were then?"

"Of course, he was mad for you. They all were."

She shook her head. "Not that. How I was. . . . what it was like for me at Amiens?" She twisted her hands nervously.

I found myself watching them. The way her brilliant sapphire ring winked in the light. A pang of guilt struck me as I realized I didn't know. Tamsyn never spoke of herself, of her wants. Instead she'd let me go on about my bad dreams, the men I'd helped, the miles I'd driven under fire. I wanted to apologize, and yet I realized that perhaps my words weren't the ones she needed right now, so I kept my silence.

"Do you know what it's like to want something, Ruby? To want it so badly that you would do anything in the world to make it happen?"

"You loved him then? Desired him?" I couldn't conceive of it. But stranger things happened.

She shook her head. "No. Not like that. I think . . . I think I wanted things to go back to how they were. The war . . . the future." Her eyes squeezed shut as she struggled putting a voice to all the things we'd never said to each other. "Everything was coming so fast and Edward offered me something . . . Something I thought I wanted at the time. Do you understand what I'm saying?"

I didn't. Not at all.

"I suppose I cared for him a little then. And I regret he's dead, but I don't . . . I don't find myself sad that he's gone. I don't want to weep. And a part of me, the wickedest part, is glad that I'm free, that he cannot torment me any longer."

"Did he strike you? Is that where the bruises came from?" I asked sharply. "He's gone now. He can't hurt you."

She shook her head. "Sometimes I wonder if it'd have been easier had he done it. I'd have been able to lay a finger upon it and say ah-hah! *That* is why I should leave. But instead I stayed when I ought not. And now I've—" She caught herself from going further, and I was suddenly very curious about what she might have said. "—but I'm glad he's dead. What does that make me?"

"A merry widow?" I offered.

She laughed, throwing a frivolous little cushion at me. I caught it at once and placed it in my lap, toying with a bit of the emerald-green fringe.

"You shouldn't tease me so. I may not have loved him, but I didn't want him to die like that. But the women." She let out an exasperated laugh. "Oh, Ruby, you wouldn't believe the number of mistresses he had. Every week another would show up at the door. You'd think a man's cock would give up and walk away after that many. Surely it'd be exhausted!"

I snorted at the image of said beleaguered appendage. "I rather think the cock enjoys it. Otherwise what's the point?"

She stifled a laugh and then her expression grew grim again. "Oh, Ruby, it's just that I ought to feel something for him yet the only emotion in my whole wretched body is worry for my son. For myself. I couldn't care a bit about Edward. Isn't that horrible?"

I walked over to her, brushing her hair back from her brow and wrapping her into my arms. "Oh, my darling, you will soon. I knew men like this during the war. The initial shock numbs it, then the reality sets in. Enjoy the numbness while it lasts." I rested my chin on the top of her head.

She stilled in my arms, frowning against me. "Perhaps I didn't want you to be quite so serious."

"Beggars cannot be choosers, Tamsyn Chenowyth."

She frowned but remained in my embrace. Her head against my shoulder. "I suppose you're right. But I'm grateful you're here. I don't know that I could bear all this alone."

"You won't have to. I'll stay—as long as you need me."

She nodded with a weak smile, carrying all the millions of unspoken things between us. I should have probably asked her more. Seen who had access to the house, who could possibly have known I was here. But my own safety meant little when Tamsyn's happiness was on the line.

CHAPTER THIRTEEN

Another Sort of Garden Party

THAT evening passed at Penryth Hall without anything of note. I slept better than I had in months with a full stomach thanks to Mrs. Penrose's gustatory endeavors, and woke with a newfound determination to get to the bottom of this puzzle. And while Mr. Kivell might have found some sort of charm beneath my bed, I sensed whoever left that wasn't the same one who had attacked me. It seemed silly to ask for spiritual assistance to do something when one was more than willing to bloody one's own hands. No, whoever it was would go on as they'd begun that very first night, with far more direct methods.

Bright and early the next morning I began the three-mile trek from Penryth Hall down to the village of Lothlel Green, determined to speak with Nellie Smythe and find out her connection to Sir Edward. The rutted road wore a thick sheet of mud from the recent rains, making for a messy walk. I would have simply taken my own roadster down were it not quite such an oddity, and there was no need to make any greater of a spectacle of myself than I already had. I'd convinced Mrs. Penrose that I ought to do the market for her. Though it didn't take much convincing after our tea the day before. The older woman had taken a bit of a shine to me, and while I experienced an iota of guilt for playing upon her trusting nature, I couldn't be bothered with such tender feelings.

I was only a handful of yards from the gates of Penryth Hall when I saw a woman coming up the path to meet me, a matching basket upon her arm. She was pretty enough, probably in her mid- to late fifties if that, with a round cheerful face and dark hair all swept back beneath an oversized straw hat.

"Hello there," she said, lifting a hand into the sun. "Have you come from the house?"

I nodded. "I'm headed into the village."

The woman's brows knit together in concern. "You're not from here, maid. Do you know the way well enough?"

I nodded again, glancing down into her basket. It was full up on pasties and boules. Sausages and cheeses, jars of preserves and pickles, along with some fresh vegetables. My stomach growled just to look at it.

"Oh, forgive me. I'm Alice Martin. My husband has a small holding just over that rise. When I heard about Sir Edward I thought I'd bring Dorothea some things to ease her burden. I'm certain the poor dear has had her hands full with the comings and goings."

"Dorothea?"

"Dorothea Penrose, the housekeeper there. I've known her since I was a girl. We both grew up in this village."

Ah, so that made sense. "I think she's feeling poorly this morning. A headache. But I'm sure she'll be glad of the company."

Mrs. Martin nodded with a warm smile. "You be careful, dearie. There are all sorts of strange goings-on in the village lately. Odd visitors and now this business with Sir Edward . . ." She gave her head a long, slow shake. "Well, one can never be too careful."

No. No one couldn't.

I HADN'T SET foot in Lothlel Green since the wedding, but not much had changed in the eponymous village. The great center square was just as it had been, lushly planted with all sorts of flowering bushes and greenery. The dreary church where Tamsyn had married Sir Edward remained in its post of honor along High Street alongside the soulless-looking stone vicarage where the insipid vicar must live.

Fitting.

A tavern, a few shops—greengrocer, butcher. I could walk from one end to the other in a handful of minutes at most. I checked the list that Mrs. Penrose had given me and set to work. I stopped in at three different shops. At first the villagers greeted me with a bit of trepidation, but soon they warmed up. Picking up soap, a bit of thread—not that I knew one end of a needle from the other—and whatever information I could glean about the poor late Sir Edward Chenowyth and his goings-on. It seemed I wasn't the first outsider to be asking questions this morning. A man from the *London Daily News* had come in on the morning train and already been making the rounds. I bristled at the thought, knowing keenly how quickly things can go topsy-turvy when a good story was on the line. And what was more sensational than the idea of a curse? I'd been little more than a girl when my own scandal broke—but the gentle clack of a shutter, the gray typeface, those things left an indelible scar. I'd gone from the prized calf, fatted for the marriage market, to the great whore of Babylon overnight. And not even all my father's money could have saved me, so he did the only thing he knew to do—he sent me away. I swallowed the bitter memory down.

No. The press's appearance in town made it doubly important that I quash this curse talk, the sooner the better. I wasn't about to subject Tamsyn to that sort of scrutiny, have her chased away from the life she'd chosen, no matter how badly she'd hurt me.

I made short work of confirming Tamsyn's complaints of her perfidious husband. The first words on everyone's lips when the topic would arise: *That poor girl he'd married.* Followed by an account of Edward's libidinous indiscretions. By my loose reckoning he had five natural children—excluding little Jori—most of whom were conveniently sent off and their ill-fated mothers moved away from the village to stay with a distant infirm and fictitious aged aunt.

Honestly, the man was lucky no one had castrated him long before now. I made my final purchase, a pocketful of penny sweets for Jori, and set off to find Nellie Smythe.

She lived with her mother in a cramped cottage that looked no more than two rooms up and two down. Chickens pecked in the grass, and a meager garden plot sat on the sunny side of the lot. An undersized gilt pig snuffled and rooted around in an inadequate pen on the far side of the yard. Closer to me, I spotted a young woman digging into the dirt with a rusty trench knife, driving it into the loamy soil. A boy, perhaps five if that, sat at the edge of the garden picking peas and dropping them into a sack slung over his shoulder. His clothes were ragged and thin, and he could certainly do with a meal or two by the look of him. I glanced down into my basket full of meat, the contents of which were likely far more than the pair saw in a month.

"I'm looking for Miss Smythe, is this the right house?" I shielded my eyes and leaned over the wooden gate.

The woman looked up at me from beneath the wide straw brim of her sun hat. I probably had a handful of years on her. She had doe-like brown eyes and yellow hair plastered to her cheek with sweat. She was a handsome woman with a smattering of freckles across her nose and that lovely English Rose complexion that young girls bought creams and pastes to acquire.

"I don't know who you are or what you want, but I'll tell you like I told that newspaperman. I got nothing to say about Edward Chenowyth." She dug her knife hard into the soil with a grunt and pulled out a particularly large weed, throwing it into a bucket behind her.

"I—"

She looked up, her jaw firm, and pointed the muddied blade at me. "I had nothing to do with it. I wish to God I'd never had anything to do with *him*, but I can't change the past—" She rocked back onto her heels, brushing the sweat from her brow with the back of her hand, replacing it with a smudge of dirt. "That is why you've come, isn't it? To see if I've killed him. It's what everyone is thinking." Her anger was palpable. But there was something else behind it, a futility that sparked in the air between us.

"I don't think I'd blame you if you did. Seems he needed it, if what they say in town's the truth."

She let out a surprised laugh and resumed her assault on the unwanted vegetation in her paltry little vegetable patch. "You aren't from here." Another grunt.

I shook my head. The wooden gate creaked as I pushed it open and entered the garden. "What gave it away?"

She made a sound of amusement. "You're an odd one, Miss . . ."

"Vaughn. Ruby Vaughn." I jutted out my hand in offering. She examined it, then looked up to meet my gaze. She wiped her own hands on her apron before taking mine and giving it a shake. "Nellie Smythe. But I'm guessing you know that."

"I heard."

"I suspect you heard a lot if you've come from town." She turned back to her weeds.

I lifted a shoulder. "I heard enough. Mrs. Penrose said you used to work up at the house for Sir Edward before—"

"Before I lifted my skirts, eh? Is that what she said? She's always shown me a bit of kindness, but they all say it. At least when they think I can't hear."

"Not precisely, no. But I take it that's the gist of the story."

"It is, isn't it? Great men and their great cocks." A sentiment I shared. It was the plight of our sex, to bear the consequences of a man's lust. Nellie turned to her boy. "Go on into the house, Sam. Let us have a bit of peace."

The boy gave an uncertain nod, bounding off into the cramped little cottage.

I shifted the basket in my hands, setting it down by the stone fence.

"I'm sorry for my language, but it's not fair, is it? Men can do as they please, whatever they want. And we? What happens to us then?" She drove the knife hard into the ground. I flinched slightly, staring at her hands. She seemed more sad than angry. Tormented even. But pain didn't make one a killer. If it did, I'd have wiped out all of Britain in my grief ages ago.

"Were you here the night before last with your boy?"

Her eyes narrowed. "You don't believe me."

"Frankly, I don't know what I believe. But for whatever it's worth I do agree with you. It would have been difficult for a girl in your position to say no to an unwanted advance from the master of the house—a baronet at that. Unfortunately, I understand how these things work, far more keenly than I care to."

She looked at me thoughtfully, as if she saw the truth behind my words. "Isn't that the way?"

My fingers reached for my pocket where the flask usually rested and found only penny sweets. I popped one in my mouth instead, a sorry substitute.

She leaned back down, continuing to tug at the weeds in the rows of vegetables. Nellie didn't speak for a while before finally looking up. "I was up at the Hind and Hare that night." She tilted her chin toward the main road leading back to Lothlel Green.

"All night?" I sucked on the hard candy. Clacking it between my teeth.

She shook her head and cast her eyes down. "Until I left."

"And went where . . . ?" A few raindrops began to sputter from the sky.

She gave me a wry smile. "Where do women go when they need to pay the butcher and have nothing but parsnips to pay?"

A wave of understanding crossed me. "I see." No wonder the woman wished him to the devil in town. "Miss Smythe, I have to ask . . . I heard that you'd been engaged before . . ."

She sucked in her breath and nodded. "Aye, George Martin. God rest him. He was a good man."

I frowned. "Did Sir Edward have anything to do with your falling-out?"

She let out a bitter laugh and wiped the sweat from her brow. "No, Miss Vaughn. That fault lies squarely at Lord Kitchener's feet."

"The war?"

She looked wistfully up at the clouds stretching across the brilliant blue sky. "George wasn't quite right when he came home. But war does that to some folks, you know? Sir Edward? He was the same selfish bastard he'd always been, but George . . . I think it broke him, Miss Vaughn. And it wasn't me that could put him together again."

Wasn't me? That was a curious thing to say, but I let it go. There was no sense prying into her past. Not when she'd already been through enough. I took a step nearer to the garden patch. "Can I help you with anything?"

"Happen to have two tickets to America in that basket of yours?" she asked with a laugh then shook her head. "No, I don't want charity, miss . . . that's not why I told you what I did. I just wanted you to know I didn't kill Edward. Go down to town and ask, anyone there will know how I spent the evening, I'm not ashamed of it. They know well enough how I pay the bills." Her gaze drifted momentarily to the pigpen. "But all the same, I would rather be able to feed my son and be left in peace."

"I understand." I dropped down to my knees in the dirt beside her. "But I didn't offer you charity, I offered to help you weed this abysmal excuse of a garden. Are you growing barley or vegetables? I honestly can't tell at this point." I pressed my lips together in feigned amusement and she let out a laugh.

It seemed we understood each other, at least as much as an heiress and a former chambermaid could. But as we were both fallen women, there was a kinship there that could never be erased. We'd both been badly used by men we'd trusted, and it was only the fortuitous circumstance of my birth that kept me from the same straits she inhabited.

She pulled her knife from the soil and flicked it out to me handle-first. The old filthy blade against her pale wrist. "Start at the potatoes, we'll see if we can make it right again. Hmm?"

My eyes lingered on the knife for half a second before I took it from her outstretched hand, even though I knew good and well what ailed her could never be mended.

CHAPTER FOURTEEN

Sticks and Stones

I took my time on my way back to the village. Coward that I was, I couldn't bear to return to the house and face Tamsyn again. My conversation with Nellie had ripped open the memories of my exile from New York. The only thing that had made my fall from grace bearable had been Tamsyn. I'd briefly thought that she and I could forge a life in this new world together, but that too went up in glorious flames. And while I couldn't avoid her forever, it was a beautiful day and a few more minutes would cause no harm. The air was crisp with the first hints of fall.

By the time I reached the Hind and Hare, I'd resolved to myself that Nellie had nothing to do with the murder. Why, I didn't know. But I believed it all the same. It did her no good to kill the father of her child, and she didn't strike me as the sort of woman who would risk her son's security for her own petty vengeance.

As for the rest of the village? Good God, it could have been anyone. Most of the town had a reason or three to—

"It's her!"

I turned at the sound to see a young boy standing in the

doorway of the Hind and Hare. One I didn't recognize. His finger was jutted out at me in accusation. "It's the woman! The witch!"

Witch? "I beg your—"

Another man stepped out of a nearby shop door, malice on his mind. His face tight. Pinched and red as he snarled coming closer—a wild dog scenting prey. "She's a one who brought the demon with her, did she?"

"She's the one. The one from up at the Hall."

"I did no such—" But I couldn't finish the sentence as something thunked me hard in the back of the head. My vision swam, and I lifted my hand to the base of my skull.

I spun around toward the source of the projectile. In an instant, a crowd gathered surrounding me. I didn't know so many people even lived in this godforsaken village, yet here they were, all closing in and shouting.

This was bad. Before I could think on what to do, another rock struck me in the middle of my chest.

A third blow came hard and fast again to the back of my head. This one much larger than the first two, making the hollow sound of a melon cracking between my ears. The buzz of voices increased and I couldn't focus on them.

Could hardly keep my feet beneath me as I staggered toward the pub.

Crowds were dangerous things, able to turn on the head of a coin, depending on how the wind blew. Something hot and wet ran down the back of my neck, soaking through my dress.

I had to escape.

Run.

Taking a step back, I stumbled. Hands grabbed at me. Jostling. Tugging at my clothes. Something ripped.

The voices grew louder.

More shouting.

Piercing fingers dug deep in my flesh.

"Jago saw 'em, he did! All them devil books up at the Pellar's!" The mad dog shouted back, spittle flying from his lips. "You won't get our Ruan, you won't. Won't hurt another of our kind!"

The books, of course! But what on earth was *in* that trunk anyway? There was no time to think overmuch on that as another rock struck my shoulder, skittering to my feet. If I made it out of this alive, Mr. Owen was going to owe me a great deal indeed.

I tried to tug myself out of their grasp, to find an escape, but there was nothing. Nothing but the crowd and the ever-growing darkness in my eyes. I must be bleeding. That had to be it. Bile rose up in my throat as the jeers grew louder. They thought I'd killed Edward.

Another rock cracked me sharp and fast in my brow. The pain dropped me to my knees as the sticky wet substance filled my eyes.

Oh God.

I wrapped my arms around myself, curled up onto the ground in a futile effort to shield myself from the blows.

A hard kick came from behind. Then a second.

Spittle and dampness spinning farther and farther out of control.

I was going to die here.

The roar grew louder and louder around me, vibrating with their screams, growing into a crescendo until right before they reached a peak, when the voices all died away save one. One distant sound over all the rest, like a faraway mountain shrouded in fog.

"I said enough!"

Someone was angry. So was I. But my eyes wouldn't stay

open anymore. It was too late for that. I was too damnably tired.

"You should be ashamed of yourself, Freddy," the angry voice shouted again.

"But she summoned the demon. Jago saw the books at your cottage! Saw the devils on the page!"

I struggled to open my eyes to see what was going on. Jago must have been the boy. The other man shuffled on his feet, sweat beading up on his pink forehead, and then bowed his head. "Apologies, Ruan . . . Apologies . . ." he stammered out, but the Pellar gave him no quarter.

"It wasn't me that you attacked with your sodded fantasies."

"—B . . . b . . . but—" he stammered.

Ruan hushed him with a glance. "Do you really think this *girl* could harm me?"

Suddenly I was flying. No, that wasn't right. I was being carried. Scooped up and held against him like a small child. It had to be Ruan, but I no longer cared. The pain was ebbing away. I settled my head against his chest, listening to the eerily slow thrum of his heart, or perhaps it was mine. Either way, I fainted dead away.

WHY WERE THE wind chimes silent? I blinked up at the ceiling as my vision came into focus. They weren't wind chimes at all. They were herbs. Bound and hanging from the dark beam stretching across the ceiling above the settee in Mr. Kivell's cottage. They swayed gently in the breeze coming through the open windows. The birdsong chittered as the wind ruffled through the trees outside, like the sound of water. The air was sweet and herbaceous. Lavender. Lemon. Mint. Rosemary. Something else. Something I couldn't identify. Sage perhaps? But not quite.

"You're awake."

Fawnlike, I turned my head to the sound of the voice. Neck stiff, but not terribly sore. I startled to see the young constable sitting across from me, his elbows on his knees, with his jacket flung carelessly over the back of a worn armchair, leaving him in his rolled-up shirtsleeves. The skin on his forearm had its own mottled map of scars, much like his jaw.

"I told you she'd wake soon enough," Ruan grumbled. I tried to sit up, turning to the sound of his voice, but my head pounded with the movement. He loomed behind a large workbench, angrily mashing something with a pestle.

"Yes, but I've been waiting hours," the constable quipped.

"The human body does not run on your timetable, Enys." Ruan raked his unruly hair back with his hand, then gestured to me. "Well, you have her now. Ask her what you came for and be off with you before she falls back asleep."

The constable cleared his throat, a deep frown settling across his scarred jaw. "Miss Vaughn. Do you recall what happened?"

I started to shake my head, but thought better of it. "No. I'm afraid I don't recall much at all. I was attacked, and then I woke up here."

Ruan cleared his throat. "He's a boy, Enys."

"I've come to see precisely what started the attack, Miss Vaughn. I've heard three different stories this morning and your savior here has been less than forthcoming." He shot Ruan a cross look. "I've come to see what you have to say for yourself."

"Me? Say for myself?" A sharp pain kept me from raising a brow. I sucked in my breath, lifting my hand to the spot. Ah. Stitches. Lovely. "I didn't start it, if that's your insinuation. I was just outside the Hind and Hare and was—" Suddenly Ruan's words dawned on me. *He's a boy.* "Why did you come here, Constable?"

"There's talk of a strange woman in the village. She's been all about asking after Ruan, but no one can recall precisely what she looks like other than she has dark hair. Do you have any idea who they're talking about?"

"No. I hadn't even been into the village before today. Do you think they confused us?"

He gave me an uncomfortable nod. "I think partly. Strangers to town. The books. Sir Edward's death. It all spiraled out of control."

"Then why are you even here if it's just some badly timed misunderstanding?"

He shifted uncomfortably in his seat and folded his hands in his lap. His gaze went to Ruan briefly before settling back upon me. "A young socialite was almost murdered by an angry mob in broad daylight. I came to see her side of things before I went and collected the instigator."

Jago. The rational part of my brain told me that I should turn him over to the constable, let the law do what it was meant to. After all, he'd nearly gotten me killed. But the other part, the one I kept deeply locked inside, couldn't bear the thought of a boy's life being so upended for one mistake, not when I'd made so many of my own. "Let him be, Constable. No harm's been done."

He choked on air. "No harm, ma'am? Have you seen your face?"

"What would you have me do? Send you after a child because he's frightened? Someone has been murdered in his village and the rational adults who *should* be talking sense into the boy are blaming a curse and feeding him full of supernatural nonsense. I find I have a great deal of sympathy for him. Far more than I do for any of the lot of you."

The constable didn't even have the decency to look chastened.

"While I don't particularly relish being attacked, I can understand why he did it." I straightened my spine, feeling the swelling at the base. "So, no. I won't hold him accountable, and if you try to take matters further I'll simply tell everyone I fell over after too many pints."

"Madam, this is impolite to say, but you look like you did a bit more than fall down the steps of the Hind and Hare. Not to mention half the village saw what happened."

I shrugged. "I'm clumsy when I drink. Good day, Constable."

Across the room, Ruan's shoulders trembled with barely concealed amusement as he continued with his work. The scent of the crushed plants filled the room with reassuring sweetness.

Constable Enys stood tapping his hat upon his thigh before grabbing his jacket. "Very well. If you change your mind you know where to find me." He started for the door before pausing, turning to Ruan. "Have you discovered anything new about the Chenowyth matter?"

Ruan shook his head slowly.

The constable sighed and closed the door behind him.

I sank back onto the cushions, squeezing my eyes shut. That little encounter took far more energy than I'd realized, and the gravity of the situation settled upon me. All my life I'd been protected—in a fashion—by my money, my name, my status. But now all those things I'd come to rely upon were worthless. Useless.

"Thank you," Ruan said softly.

"Don't mention it. I'm not particularly fond of your young Jago after today, but at the same time I'd never forgive myself if his entire life was ruined because of this." A sharp pain settled in my temple and I whimpered. "What exactly happened by the way?"

"You mean you don't believe you stumbled?" The edge of his mouth curved up. "You fainted not long after I arrived.

Lost a fair bit of blood too, but head wounds can do that. You should be fit again in a few days so long as you rest."

I reached up to the back of my head where I'd been struck. It was tender and I could feel the stitches there as well. "Thank you, Mr. Kivell."

"Ruan. After all we've been through the last couple of days, the least you can do is call me by my name."

I smiled at that. "Ruby then. You should call me Ruby as you've saved me from an angry mob and sewn up the back of my head too. At least I assume this is your handiwork."

He snorted. "It wasn't many stitches considering the size of the rock that hit you. I also fished you from the sea before your husband got cross. Don't forget."

There he was again. The charming man from the shore. I vastly preferred him to the one hurling accusations of witchcraft and murder. "No. I won't forget that either. He does have a frightful temper."

Ruan chuckled as he reached over his head, grabbed a sachet of dried herbs, and plucked out a few pieces.

"I suppose it's a good thing I've a hard head."

"Indeed."

It hurt to laugh, another unwanted souvenir from my attack. "You shouldn't agree with that. It's not gentlemanly."

He sniffed and continued grinding herbs. "Then it's a good thing I'm not a gentleman."

"It's for the best, as I've never had much use of them myself. Thank you, though—I don't know what would have happened had you not shown up when you did."

"They'd have probably killed you."

"Lovely."

"They're rattled. Angry. Looking for explanations for what happened to Sir Edward. It's not entirely their fault, and yet squarely their doing. And as Enys said, there has been a stranger in town. Besides you of course."

"Besides me." I added wryly, "Do you have any idea who it is?"

He ran a hand through his hair, pulling it back and knotting it with a bit of leather. "No. She seems to be looking for me but I am not hard to find. I haven't seen her, that's for certain."

I stood slowly and walked over to the trunk of books I'd brought and lifted the lid, curious what it was inside that Jago had found that utterly convinced him of my wickedness.

"Careful."

"Of your books? I assure you I know what I'm doing. I am the one who brought them here." Good grief. Some were fifteenth-century demonologies. Recent reprints of the Big and Little Alberts. *Pseudomonarchia Daemonium.* A handful of grimoires. All five volumes of *The Lesser Key of Solomon* in pristine condition, which was a rather impressive find, even for Mr. Owen. No wonder the boy believed I was the spawn of Satan. Most were in Latin, though a handful were in ancient Greek. If he'd been able to read them, he'd likely be lighting the pyre for both me and his beloved Pellar.

Mr. Kivell laughed from behind me. "No, I mean mind your stitches. You are lucky to be alive."

I snorted, carefully setting the books one by one on the old wooden shelf. "Charming townsfolk you have here. Speaking of your murderous villagers, did you figure out what was in that bottle you found under my bed?"

"Not yet. I've been reading—" He gestured to an ancient tome on his worktable. I moved closer. "I've not quite figured out who made it, but as far as I can tell it doesn't do anything useful. The components counteract with one another. Some of them look like they might be for a protection charm, but others are less benign."

"You mean to tell me it's an ugly table decoration."

"More or less."

"A useless wish then." Didn't I have enough of those?

I pointed to another book on the table. One I'd never seen in Exeter. "Did I bring that one too?"

He nodded grimly.

I lifted the hidebound book and turned it over in my hands. It was ancient. Had to be fifteenth century as well. I opened the pages, but inside was a language I'd never seen before. Old English? No, it wasn't that.

"It's Cornish."

How did he do that? "And you speak it?" No one knew it, at least not anymore. The language had been nearly eradicated by the mid-part of the last century. Only a handful of native speakers remained, the bits and remnants being salvaged and preserved by traveling folklorists and linguists in a desperate hope to preserve it for future generations.

He nodded. "Enough of it at least to make out the important bits. With time, I'll probably figure out the rest."

This Pellar of theirs was full of surprises. "What does it tell you?"

He added something unctuous from a bottle into the herbs he was crushing and continued with the pestle. "It's the memoir of a sixteenth-century Pellar. Some of her charmwork. Countercurses. It's why I had Owen looking for it."

"Her? You mean there are female Pellars too?"

"Seventh of a seventh. From what I understand it doesn't matter which you are. You see, I'm the seventh son of a seventh son, but she was the seventh daughter of a seventh son." He shrugged.

"How very egalitarian. The constable called you a witch, you know."

"I am."

It hurt to laugh, but I did nonetheless. "You know I always imagined witchcraft was women's work, something the church used to control our sex."

Ruan sniffed, rubbing his nose with the back of his left forearm.

"But Pellars aren't those sorts of witches, are they?"

He shook his head.

Mr. Owen had spoken of older things when he lured me out here to Cornwall. Perhaps this was what he meant. A sort of earth magic that predated the church. An ancient thing not a weapon of control, but a means of liberation. Not that I believed in any sort of supernatural nonsense, but it certainly was a compelling image.

Good God, I'd lost a lot of blood if my thoughts had turned so radical. That or perhaps I was one of Reverend Fortescue's feared Bolsheviks seeking to unhinge the patriarchy one sleepy hamlet at a time. I ran my fingers over the ancient book cover. "*This* is why I'm here, isn't it? Why Mr. Owen refused to let me open the box."

"You see, to make the muddled mess even more complicated—" The grinding of the pestle echoed his words. He paused and pointed at me with the stone handle. "—the craft can only be passed from male to female or female to male. A male Pellar can't train another male. Nor can a female a female. So, I've spent the greater part of a decade looking for this one."

I cocked my head to one side. "How peculiar. Why is that?"

"Put the book down, Ruby."

I tugged it to my chest with a challenging look. "Why? Afraid you'll teach me something forbidden?"

He set the pestle down, reached across the table, and plucked the book from my hands. "Because you bled out like a slaughtered hog and I'd rather you not get any on the only link I have to what I am."

My cheeks flamed and I leaned on the bench beside him.

"You'll have to stay up at the house for a time."

I arched a brow. "I'll *have* to?"

"Yes. It's not safe for you to wander off the grounds. Especially not now."

"It evidently wasn't safe for me to be *on* the grounds either." I gestured toward the bruises on my throat, which were soon to be joined by many other purplish-green companions after today's adventure.

"I don't think it's real, for what it's worth," he said as he finished putting the herbal concoction he'd made into a little clay pot and stuffed a cork stopper into the top.

"My bruises? I assure you they are, and I ache like the devil. I can only imagine how rotten I'll feel come morning."

"The curse. I think someone wants us to believe that there's dark magic at play. But I'm not convinced."

"That's good news, right?"

"I'm not certain." He pressed the jar into my palm, closing my fingers around it with a frown. He frowned too much.

I glanced down at the object in my hand. "What is it?"

"Put it on your wounds three times a day. It should help with the healing and minimize the scarring. Though I'm afraid this"—he lifted a finger, touching my brow gently—"this will not fade. I'm sorry for it."

"Thank you. Truly."

He nodded and stood abruptly, walking across the room for his coat. "As I said, you'll be as safe at Penryth Hall as you would here. I made it clear in town that you were under my protection."

"Your pro—" Even in my battered state, I didn't care for the sound of that.

"It's the only way you can be safe. I am the Pellar here. There's a level of—" He paused, measuring his words, and then sighed. "You can't understand the weight of that to them. They'll mind me individually."

"They're afraid of you, you mean . . ."

"A bit."

"Why?"

He wet his lips and glanced back down at his hands. "Do I not frighten you, Miss Vaughn?"

"Should I be afraid?" I wasn't sure I wanted the answer.

Ruan's nostrils flared as he left his table, coming nearer to me. He had an uncanny way of taking up too much space in any given room. Partly because of his size—he was a great brute of a man—but there was something else too, an element that had nothing to do with his physical being that spoke to something long forgotten inside of me. A deep awareness, and *that* frightened me indeed.

I *knew* him. Except he was a stranger.

He folded his arms across his chest. "Do you recall what happened earlier today? One foolish boy and a drunk old man nearly caused a mob to kill you and you wonder why I'm concerned for your well-being?"

"But if you are fearsome—"

He snorted at that.

"—then surely they wouldn't—"

"Mobs are unruly things. If you're with me, not a soul will raise a hand against you—or if you're out of sight, they won't risk my wrath by seeking you out."

"Are you all that frightening?"

He gave me a slight smirk and continued glowering at me.

I settled back into the sofa. "Very well. I suppose I'm your captive then." I shot him a glance up through my lashes. "You don't happen to have a spare pair of clothes, do you? Something a little less . . ."

"Bloody?"

I pressed my lips together. "Yes. That."

"I'll walk with you back to Penryth Hall once you've eaten. Do not leave the estate grounds without me. No one will hunt you but I don't want to have to solve your murder too. I want your word on it, Ruby Vaughn." His expression was dark and foreboding. Brooking no argument.

I opened my mouth to argue anyway, but considering the way my day had gone, I tended to agree with him. I was rather fond of my neck. So Penryth Hall it would be.

CHAPTER FIFTEEN

And Promises Broken

IT took far longer than it ought for the pair of us to make it back to Penryth Hall. While my strength was returning quickly, my head felt precisely the same way it had the afternoon after the Armistice party I'd thrown in France. Now, *that* had been a spectacular debauch despite the scant rations.

Ruan let out a decidedly amused sound and I turned to him. "What?"

He started to answer and his affable expression faded away. "Oh, bloody hell . . ."

I followed his gaze to where I spotted the object of his ire. Reverend Fortescue was storming up the dirt path, his black coat flapping in the wind giving him the appearance of a great perturbed bat going up the gravel walk. Hands flailing as he muttered something beneath his breath.

"Morning, Reverend," I called out rather cheerfully considering I shared Ruan's sentiment with regard to the fellow.

Reverend Fortescue scowled as he crossed the distance between us. Likewise, over my shoulder, Ruan smoldered. Not in the attractive way that large dark-haired men had a knack for doing, but in the same fashion as a fuse on a munition, sizzling its way down to the shell before finally setting off a catastrophe.

"I thought I'd warned you, Miss Vaughn, about the sort of company you keep?" The vicar snarled in Ruan's direction.

I shrugged lightly, despite the deep ache in my muscles. I would pay dearly for this goading. "I've always been a terrible listener I'm afraid. Did you come from the house?"

If there were any truth to this Pellar business, the vicar would have incinerated on the very spot. Then again, the feeling was mutual. The awful man's upper lip curved into what could only be described as a sneer.

"I'm afraid I have things to do, Miss Vaughn," Ruan growled. "Can you make it the rest of the way on your own?" Wise man. Cut bait and run. I'd rather wished I could do the same, but as I was headed to Penryth there was no chance of avoiding continued conversations with the vicar.

I summoned a breezy smile and nodded. For a moment I saw the worry flash in his eyes. He couldn't possibly know how much it hurt to feign this ease. "I'm fine. Truly." My eyes met his and he gave me a curt nod, before abandoning the field.

Ruan wasn't even out of earshot before the vicar launched into a litany against the man, which I could not allow, even in my weakened state.

"—Reverend." I interrupted his tirade. "I am afraid I'm not feeling well. If you would excuse me."

He wagged a finger at me. "I warned you, Miss Vaughn. No good will come of carrying on with men of his sort. Just look at you. Your lovely face has been—"

I bristled. I didn't give a damn about my face, it was mine—for better or worse—and there wasn't a thing I could do to change what had happened to it. I turned without bothering saying goodbye and called back over my shoulder, "Say a prayer for it then, won't you?"

Mrs. Penrose met me at the door, having just seen the back of the *good* vicar. She glanced warily past me at the path from which I'd just come as if to reassure herself that he was not returning.

"I'm not overfond of him, maid. Always sniffing about the mistress like a dog in rut. Even before what happened to poor Sir Edward. Something isn't right about that one."

I wrinkled my nose at the thought. "What did he want today?"

"What does he ever want? No one can tell." She threw her hands up in defeat. "I'd think he was after marriage, but what could one like that offer Lady Chenowyth?" Mrs. Penrose sighed, shutting the door and sliding the bolt for good measure. Her expression fell as she got a good look at my face. "Oh, maid, you look a fright. Let's get you to the kitchen and see what we can do, hmm?" Tired from the walk, and half starved, I gave in to her maternal ministrations and followed her belowstairs.

Half an hour later, having downed two cups of warm honey milk and between bites of smoked turbot, I wheedled out of her that Tamsyn had spent the afternoon in the garden. She'd gone for a walk that morning and hadn't returned. My heart gave an irrational stutter at the thought. I had gone years without worrying for her safety, even thinking much of her, and yet now—it seemed to consume me the minute I was within reach of her. I dabbed my mouth and made my escape from Mrs. Penrose, not before snagging one of her ginger biscuits, then headed upstairs to change into some fresh clothes.

The darkened halls of Penryth were no cheerier this afternoon than they had been when I left this morning. Despite my head pounding terribly, I managed to turn myself out neatly enough in my riding breeches and a loose-fitted mint blouse and set off to find Tamsyn.

It didn't take long to spot her in the orchard, not far from where we'd discovered Sir Edward's body. She was seated on a bit of broken stone wall just to the left of the blackberry brambles, her legs swinging aimlessly, so preoccupied with her own thoughts she didn't hear me approach. The dappled light came down through the canopy, casting a kaleidoscope of shadows on the meadow floor. Brown shrikes hidden in the hedge beside her made my presence known.

"I saw you coming up the lane."

I settled myself alongside her on the broken stone wall. Little bits of lichen and moss grew in the cracks and nooks there. I plucked at a dried bit with my thumbnail rather than answer.

"Where were you all day?" She still hadn't bothered turning to face me. Instead keeping her gaze unfocused at some unknown spot in the distance. An odd space had sprung up between us, and I couldn't shake the sensation that I'd done something to offend her. Yet the fogginess in my brain kept me two steps behind.

"Sassing the vicar, it seems. Lucky you to avoid him." I tasted a bit of blood on my tongue from where my lip must have split back open.

She let out a slight laugh and shook her head, fiddling with a piece of long grass. "Mercifully so. I heard he had intentions to call upon me this afternoon to pray with me, so I decided to make myself scarce. For some reason I ended up here."

Tamsyn turned. Her eyes widened and she sucked in a breath as she saw the full measure of my injuries. I'd managed to avoid looking at myself thus far, but it must have been far worse than I imagined—as everyone else I'd come across felt compelled to comment upon it.

She ran her fingers gently over the cut along my eyebrow and the half-dozen stitches that Ruan Kivell had so smartly secured there.

"Did he do this? It looks like his handiwork."

There was no sense in using names. We both knew of whom we spoke. "He patched me up as best he could. It seems there was a bit of confusion in town."

"I'd say a bit more than confusion. Ruby, you could have been killed." She frowned deeper, lines forming at the edges of her mouth as she traced the bruise already forming on my cheekbone. "Does it hurt terribly?"

I swallowed hard and shook my head. Liar that I was. It hurt like the very devil, and I hoped that she couldn't see it in my expression. I didn't need to add to her troubles.

"I feel so guilty, Ruby. If I'd known I . . ."

"—I've had worse. Besides, Ruan was there to frighten them off. It was all a misunderstanding."

"Leave it to you to consider this a simple misunderstanding." Her expression fell. "Oh, Ruby, had I not invited you to come, then none of this would have happened. It seems I'm always causing you trouble."

I reached up, taking her hand from my cheek and placing it firmly in her lap. The very last thing I needed today was to have Tamsyn muddling my already cloudy emotions. My tether was frayed as it was.

"I had to deliver books for Mr. Owen. If anyone here deserves the blame for my face it's him for sending me. Or Mr. Kivell's unusual reading habits."

She set her jaw and slid closer. "But you could have died. I don't know how I would have borne losing you too."

You gave me up quick enough in France. The thought came so hard and unexpected it took me by surprise. Apparently, I wasn't quite as numb to her as I supposed. Bitterness snaked up inside me and it was on the tip of my tongue to ask the question. To rend open the old wound once and for all. As it was the one thing that never made sense, the part I never could puzzle out. Why she had left me a handful of miles west of the front lines with five meaningless words to ease my pain: *Forgive me, I love you.* She'd sworn to me the night before she left that she'd go anywhere with me. We'd open that bookshop with my inheritance and live with abandon. But those were the naive dreams of a girl. And I hadn't been that girl in a very long time. So I let the moment pass with Tamsyn none the wiser.

"It's strange to have you here again. There are times with you being back at Penryth I can almost forget the things that came before. And then others, like now, it's as if a great wall has appeared between us." She reached out, taking my hand in her own. "But I wanted to thank you regardless—for staying. You didn't have to. Not after what I did. How things ended. It was poorly done. I know that now."

The bushes rustled lightly, and from the corner of my eye I caught a brown hare darting from one to another. I wished desperately she'd change the subject.

"Where were you today anyway? I went to see if you wanted to have a picnic down by the water this morning with Jori, but Mrs. Penrose said you'd gone into town—and then I see you've . . ." Her voice sounded almost sharp at the question and I froze, uncertain how to answer as I wasn't ready to tell her about my fruitless inquiries. Though they'd undoubtedly make their way back to her in time.

"I needed a walk and thought to pick up a few bits and bobs for Mrs. Penrose in town. Her head was bothering her." *Because I gave her far too much gin.*

"That's what she said as well. It's not like her to be under the weather." Tamsyn traced the bone on the back of my hand with her thumb. "Who did you go see?"

Her voice took on a strangely jealous tone. One I hadn't

noticed before, but didn't much like. She'd lost her opportunity to claim that emotion long ago.

"I told you, I went to pick up some items. Who would you think I'd have gone to see?" A prickle of something ran up my neck. Warning? Probably. But I was so off kilter with Tamsyn, always had been.

Perhaps it was being out here in the copse, in the very spot where Edward was killed, but I was growing ever more sure that our killer was a woman. A certainty, deep in my subconscious, even though I had no evidence for it. The crime was exceptionally violent, gruesome enough that it would have taken a man—and not an inconsiderable one—to overpower Sir Edward. Someone like the Pellar. A deep vee formed between my brows, tugging the stitches painfully with the movement. I couldn't imagine him killing anyone, except the vicar perhaps. But the man was so odious, who could blame him?

"I don't know how you do it."

"Do what?"

She hesitated for a moment before replying. "You're not afraid of anything. Not the curse. Not—" She pointed at the bruises on my face with a brittle laugh. "Your poor face. You don't give a whit about your own safety. Even during the war, when all hope was lost you were never afraid. I envied you that then."

There was little to fear when one had nothing to lose. But I didn't feel like talking. My face hurt.

"I just sometimes . . . Oh, don't mind me. I'm emotional and lost and I . . . I've missed you." She glanced up at me through damp lashes, so brittle and perfect that I wondered if she might shatter if I reached out to touch her. I didn't have the heart for it. Or the stomach. I was so bone-achingly tired and sore and didn't want to talk of the war, the past, or any of it.

So I slid back a few inches in a desperate attempt to straighten out my thoughts. "Tamsyn—"

She reached up, touching my cheek, and smiled, bridging the span between us, and wrapped her arms around me. The ache in my head grew worse with each passing second. What ought to have felt normal, even pleasant, felt achingly wrong. It was this place. The sound of the cheerful birds singing out their songs. Even her lemony scent. Every ounce of it had my internal prey creature screaming for me to run.

But before I could gather my wits, reconcile what was going on to my wayward thoughts, she brushed her lips against my cheek in a tender mockery of the love we once shared.

And somewhere in my aching head I remembered why I'd stayed away all these years. Because when Tamsyn was near I couldn't think. The past, the present, it all came colliding together and I couldn't breathe. Couldn't tell up from down. I was a bottle tossed upon her waves and I hated it. I scrambled away from her and nearly fell off the stone fence for my effort.

Her eyes were dark. "What . . . what's wrong?"

I should never have come here. It was bad enough to have my head bashed in, entirely another to have somehow rebroken my own heart in the process.

It was only a kiss—the sort you would give your aged great-aunts should they exist. Lord knew I'd had far more exciting ones. Yet to me it was more. It was a reminder of all the reasons I should have never set foot in Lothlel Green. It would only cause me pain. I'd known it three years ago when I came for the wedding, and a wiser woman would have known it now.

I took a step back, raking my hand through my hair, wincing as I touched the raw stitches at the back of my scalp.

"Ruby . . ." She reached for me, concern etched in her face. "Ruby, talk to me. Tell me what's wrong."

I took another tremulous step back, shaking my head.

Flickers of France danced through my mind. Of how I'd once thought I'd known her so well, the secrets we'd shared. The promises she'd made. But if I was wrong about her then, couldn't I be wrong now? Another thought struck me, settling into my jaw with a coldness I'd never before known. My knees grew weak. Could she have killed Edward? And was that why she was sitting here all alone not twenty yards from where he'd been found?

Out of habit my hand rose to my throat for the locket chain. It wasn't there.

Tears pricked my eyes. I'd lost it. The only remaining link to my parents was gone.

I took a second step back and shook my head, unable to form the words. My vision grew dim. I needed to get out of here. Perhaps I'd lost too much blood as Ruan said. But I knew one thing for certain—I couldn't remain here at Penryth Hall. Not for one instant longer.

"I love you, Ruby!" she called after me, her hands limply at her side. "I always have. Let me help you. Please."

Love? She knew nothing about love.

Angry mob or not, I was leaving Penryth once and for all. She could protect herself, for I was beyond ready to wash my hands of this whole broken affair.

As I stormed out of the orchard, I thought perhaps I did have an ounce of self-preservation coursing through my veins after all.

CHAPTER SIXTEEN

A Growing Storm

I couldn't remain at Penryth Hall a moment longer. A fact I acknowledged long before storming away from Tamsyn in the orchard. It was all too much. Too much past. Too much present. And while I might have made promises to Tamsyn, surely those were negated by the fact that I'd nearly been killed. *Twice.* Not to mention she'd broken her share of promises to me. I was owed at least one of my own.

By the time I'd gathered my meager possessions—including one wayward feline—and settled into my roadster, the first crack of thunder echoed across the hills, followed quickly by a downpour of biblical proportions.

Lovely.

I splashed and bounced all the way to the Hind and Hare, feeling rather pleased with myself that I hadn't managed to get myself stuck in one of the deeper ruts. But I'd driven worse roads—albeit in an ambulance.

The innkeeper eyed me nervously as I stepped inside. If they'd thought me a witch before, I could only imagine what they thought now. Bloodied, bruised, and spitting mad, making puddles wherever I stepped.

The innkeeper stuttered a time or two while taking my information down, but accepted my money all the same. He placed a warm key in my palm. The taproom was crowded with men, all of whom kept their backs to me. Whether out of kindness or shame for what happened this morning, I neither knew nor cared. Instead, I turned on my heels and walked up the stairs head-high, as my mother had instilled all those years ago.

Let them see your spine, Ruby Vaughn. No one can take it from you. The last words I ever heard from her lips as I boarded the steamer for Southampton.

I sucked in a breath, wishing the memory of her voice hurt just a little less. One would think it would with the years, but it ached just the same.

"Be good for my head," I grumbled, shifting my burden in my arms to take the key in a steady hand. The hallway shifted beneath me, or perhaps it was just my own exhaustion. "Nearly broke the damned thing's what this trip did."

A brass number 7 hung crookedly from the door. I glanced down on the key to make sure it matched. Whoever had nailed it up evidently had had a pint or two downstairs before setting off to work. A rather appealing thought were the place not full up with superstitious countryfolk prone to stoning strangers.

I fumbled with the lock until it clicked then gave the door a shove. It wouldn't budge. Stuck on its heavy iron hinges. The whole inn must have been built three hundred years before considering the slant of the deep-black wood floors. I slammed my battered hip into it with a grunt, and the door swung open. A musty scent greeted me as I stepped inside, dropping my drenched traveling bag on the floor. Fiachna, tired of being damp, wriggled out of my arms and made himself a spot in the middle of the bed, pointedly licking his paws and commencing his evening routine.

Just as I turned to bolt the door, it flew back at me, revealing a very wet and angry Ruan Kivell on the other side.

"What are you doing?" he growled, his hand wrapped around the edge of the jamb. "Did you forget what I told you this afternoon?"

I waved him off, pushing futilely against the door. "That was this afternoon. Things changed."

"I forbade you from coming into the village alone. You gave your word you'd remain on the estate." With his free hand he slicked his hair back from his head and stalked into the room, letting the door slam behind him. He turned his back, and for half a second, I thought—no, hoped—that after asserting himself in a fit of masculine pique he would turn around and leave. But alas, he only bolted the latch with a sickening slide of metal to wood.

"As I said—" I straightened my spine, trying to look as prim as a soaked rat could be. "—that was before. Things changed. Now if you don't mind, I need to get out of these clothes before I catch my death." I tilted my head to the door hoping he could take the hint.

He did not.

"Very well. If you intend to stay, don't drip on my bed." Once behind the screen, I tugged off my soaked boots and began working to remove the rest of my woeful attire. A little puddle of water leaked out as I tossed the boots toward the unlit fireplace. "Be a dear, and do something about that, would you?"

"What are you thinking, trying to leave?"

My lace brassiere was wet enough it may as well have not been there at all, for all it hid. I unfastened it and tossed it over the screen along with everything else. "I didn't ask your permission, I'm a grown woman. Besides, who are you to forbid me anything? I appreciate you saving me earlier, and I admit that whatever you did to my head did ease the pain considerably—however, last I checked you were not my father, my lover, or my keeper."

He made a strangled sound in his throat as I heard a match strike and the sound of air as he worked to relight the fire.

"Oh, let me guess what comes next. You're going to say *you cannot leave* again as if my answer will be any different. I can. And I will. Now if you don't mind, please dig in that bag over there and see if there's something only moderately damp before I catch my death."

"People don't catch the ague from being wet." A deep roll of thunder shook the inn. He rustled around on the other side of the screen before tossing what looked to be a chemise over the top, followed by quite possibly the least attractive day dress I owned. A gray-and-cream affair I'd bought when I was feeling particularly glum. I snatched both up—blissfully dry—and commenced tugging, wriggling, and fastening buttons.

"It's not safe for you to leave here. Not yet."

Well, at least that was something different. I stepped out from behind the screen to glare at him. *And it's safe here?*

"Of course it's not safe."

I startled, staring at him. "How did you do that?"

"Do what?"

"You answered me." I narrowed my gaze, stepping closer to him.

"Of course I did."

"I hadn't *said* anything."

"Yes you did," he grumbled.

"And how did you find me so quickly? There was no reason for you to be out in the storm."

He folded his arms, shifting where he stood. His eyes downcast, not meeting mine. "I was in the village. We aren't discussing me. We are talking about you."

"And you just happened to see me. In the middle of a storm, with the street nearly flooded out?" I didn't believe him. But the alternative was impossible. A man could not simply read another's deepest innermost thoughts. No. He most certainly couldn't. I was going mad, that was the more plausible explanation. "I have no reason to stay. And your charming townsfolk have made it perfectly clear that I'm not welcome."

"No reason to stay . . ." he repeated gravely. His eyes bright. "You see no reason . . ."

"I can do whatever I wish," I grumbled, toweling off my hair. It was a mess of dark curls now. Ruan and I were a matched set. Both dark and unruly things. I'd never noticed that before.

He took me by my arms, pulling me close in a futile attempt to will me into compliance. "You cannot leave."

"And why, pray tell, can I not drive away from this godforsaken crossroads?"

"What do you think it would look like if you did?"

He hadn't shaved, I realized as I looked up into his face. Though he smelled clean, of rain and herbs and man. Pity he was such a brute.

His cheeks flushed for a moment, and his grip on me tightened, sensing my turn of thought.

"I think it'd appear that I am the only person in this town with a lick of sense."

"You'd look guilty of something, you little fool. Like you're running away."

"Well, they would be correct on that score."

"Miss Vaughn." Another crack of thunder shook the inn.

"Mr. Kivell." I snapped back, "Speaking of which, I'd like you to tell me how you knew where to find me."

He ignored my query. "Care to talk about what's really bothering you?" He let go of my arms, but he didn't step back. Neither did I. The fire was warming the room considerably, cutting the chill and damp from the air. It popped and cracked in the hearth.

"Not particularly."

"Oh, come on, I can tell you're in love with her. Why don't you tell me the rest of it? What happened? If you don't, certainly someone around here will if I wait long enough, but I'd rather hear it from your lips."

"How—" Feeling light-headed, I sank down onto the mattress, picking at the woolen blanket with my thumb and forefinger.

"You walk around looking as if she's ripped out your heart and is carrying it around in her pocket, and you can't decide whether to go fetch it back or leave it where it is. Anyone can see that."

I sucked in a sharp breath. How dare he? I reached into my bag and pulled out a cigarette case and lit one, moving to the window. I opened the ancient latch and shoved it open enough to let in the fresh air. "An apt metaphor. Are you going to judge me then? Assume that I killed her husband because my feminine passions have run rampant?"

"Of course not."

The embers nipped at the paper casing of the cigarette as I twisted it in my fingers.

"Unless you did kill him."

I jerked my head to face him. *I most certainly did not.*

"Didn't think so. But I had to ask."

He'd done it again. "That's unfair of you. Just because—"

"Because what? You were in love with a woman, return to town, and her husband shows up dead the very night you arrive. You don't think that sounds suspicious? It makes a great deal more sense to me than the idea that you summoned up a demon to strike him down, or some thirty-year-old curse has resurfaced. You *are* the rational explanation here."

My throat grew thick. "You don't believe me then?"

"I would be a fool not to consider it, especially after the ill wish under your bed. It's why I was in your room, but no, I don't think you killed him. I do think whoever did, placed that wish beneath your bed and meant to kill you as well."

I crossed my arms tightly beneath my chest and shot him a cross look. "Well, I suppose I should be relieved you don't think I'm dabbling in the occult in my spare time."

The edge of his mouth quirked up. "Even if you were, Old Nick has no power over me. Seventh of a seventh. Or so they say. Though I wouldn't know, as I don't recall ever meeting the fellow to have put the issue to the test."

I laughed, tugging my legs up beneath me on the windowsill. "Oh, come now, you can't tell me you've never been tempted by the devil. A big brute like you?" I studied him for a moment. His damp shirt clung to every ridge of his remarkably formed shape. The maids at Penryth had the right of it. He was rather pleasing to look at, if sad.

He kept his eyes dutifully averted from me. How very chivalric.

I could have sworn he grew pink.

He grumbled something beneath his breath and sat down heavily in a chair. "Not tempted by Ol' Nick, that's for certain."

"And you call yourself a witch."

He gave me a slight smile, eyes still downcast. "And me a witch."

The cigarette did wonders for my nerves. "Don't you suspect people will talk, what with you storming into my room? It's the stuff of gothic novels. They could think we're . . . that . . . hmmm." I wet my lips and snapped, "I have it! They'll think I've used my devilish wiles to lure the great Pellar into temptation."

He folded his arms, a mulish look on his face. "You mean, you're concerned that they think we're fucking?"

"Precisely. Oh, don't look that way, Mr. Kivell." I warmed to him a bit, the big hulk of a man, but he wasn't threatening in the least. Big men never frightened me much. It was always the ones you least expected that did the greatest harm. "And don't think you shock me either, Mr. Kivell, with your crass language. I'm an old hand at all that."

He raised an eyebrow.

"Besides, I plan to eventually leave this charming little murder-retreat and I don't give a jot what anyone thinks about me. But you might have a mind toward your reputation. It'd be a pity if they thought you were ravished by a witch up here."

"I'm the Pellar," he said grimly. "And this is not the conversation I should be having with a respectable young woman."

"Good thing I'm not respectable." I finished my cigarette, stubbing it out in the bottom of a glass, and frowned. "So how long am I your prisoner?"

"You're not."

"I'm not?" I repeated in shock. The blasted man had all but forbidden me to leave. Not that I wanted to anymore. I had to admit I was puzzled by the goings-on here. And truth be told, I *had* promised Tamsyn I'd protect her son and damn me for a fool, but I wasn't as good at breaking my word as she was.

He cleared his throat. "But if I'm to prevent you from getting yourself killed, I'm going to have to keep you with me until we've figured it out. Now come here."

"*We?*" I noticed the jar of salve in his hand. He gestured to the bed, and reluctantly I sat down on the mattress in front of him.

"Yes. I take it you're too stubborn to let things alone while I figure it out, and if I leave you to your own devices, I may not be able to stitch you up a second time." He unscrewed the lid and began applying a bit of the sweet-smelling salve to the stitches on my brow. Immediately the skin tingled beneath the liniment. A hint of mint, perhaps some honey?

His hands were uncommonly warm, but not in an unpleasant way. "You have a point."

He grinned at me. Bastard. "I know. But I need to get a better look at Edward's body first." He moved to the other bruises and scrapes along my face.

"Didn't you see it good and well in the orchard?" I mumbled as he rubbed the top of my lip with it. "Personally, I'd rather not go there again." *For a variety of reasons.*

"Tell me. Why were you talking to Nellie Smythe earlier?"

"Is there anything that happens in this town you don't know of?"

He let out a low laugh.

Apparently not. He was very near now. Our knees brushing. "The real question is how *you* knew about her . . ."

"Small town, Mr. Kivell. People talk."

The corner of his mouth twitched. He gestured for me to turn around. Reluctantly, I did, and he began to work on the wounds on the back of my neck and head. We went along that way for several minutes. In a strange silence with only the crackling fire and scent of his little jar of salve between us.

"You're clever," he said at last. "Nellie hasn't had an easy life. Not after getting thrown over by George, and then coming to Sir Edward's attention. I pity her position. Seems she was always second in everyone's list. Sweet enough girl, though. She deserves more than what life's handed her."

"But she didn't kill him," I said gravely.

"I never thought she did."

And yet he didn't suspect her, knowing that she had far more reason to kill Edward than anyone else in town. That boded well for me, I supposed. I blew out a breath of relief, still weighing whether to tell him the rest of it.

"You saw something that night, didn't you? That's what you're so afraid of."

I startled, turning around on the mattress to look into his unusual eyes. "How did you . . . Oh, never mind, I don't care how you do that—yes. I did. When I woke up from the dream, I went to the window to get some air, and I saw a figure in white headed into the orchard."

He paused, holding up a hand. "You saw a woman going into the orchard?"

"I didn't say it was a woman. It *looked* like a woman, but come to think of it I suppose it could have been a boy, or a slight man even."

He swore beneath his breath.

"What is it?"

But instead of answering, his shoulders began to shake and then he laughed. A deep, highly inappropriate laugh considering our present circumstances.

"Ruan . . . what is it? I don't . . . I don't see what's funny."

He took in a deep breath, his chest still trembling as he tried to control his very ill-timed amusement. "It's only that you seeing a woman in the copse narrows it down to precisely half the population of Cornwall as our potential killer."

CHAPTER SEVENTEEN

Awful Offal

AFTER having come to our uneasy truce, I followed Ruan down the stairs back to the tavern. With each step I took into the main room, every eye seemed to follow me. Hushed voices hunched over ancient wooden tables, casting not-at-all-subtle glances over the rims of their pints. Ruan sat me in a corner near the front window away from most of the patrons. It was dark and grim, though the hearty smells from the kitchen overpowered the room's lack of visual charms. I rested my elbows on the table in a decidedly un-lady-like manner, waiting until Ruan returned with what appeared to be calf's liver with a side of kidneys.

"Eat." He slid the plate before me and plunked down an overfull pint of beer.

I wrinkled my nose.

"You're ill. Eat."

"I heard you the first time." Taking up a fork, I reluctantly cut into the liver. Organ meat was disgusting, but if I was to get a moment's peace, it was best I heed him in this.

"It's good for your blood. I have all new mothers eat it for a month after they're safely delivered. Three times a week."

I took a bite. Grainy and wet, and I hated every earthy chew. "Three times a week?" I struggled to swallow then took a sip of the beer. That went down much better. "It's a wonder anyone has a second child."

He ran a hand through his mostly dry hair. The storm raged on outside the window, pelting the pane. "It helps replace the blood that's been lost. You should be fine within a week as long as you don't do anything reckless."

I scowled and took another bite. "I'll have you know I am never reckless."

His mouth curved up into an almost sinful smile as he watched me. I swallowed down a third bite. His expression shifted and he slapped his thigh. "I almost forgot!" He reached into his waistcoat pocket, pulled out a familiar gold chain, and laid it on the table between us.

I greedily snatched it up, rubbing my thumb over the tiny seed pearls set in the gold locket before flicking it open to make sure my eyes were not deceiving me. The warm smiles of my parents gazed back. My eyes grew damp as I snapped it shut and fixed it to my bruised throat. "How did you ever find it?"

"I didn't. One of the lads from town saw it in the street and gave it to me this afternoon thinking I could find its owner. I recognized you . . ." He gestured at the locket with his forefinger.

I shook my head, hand still to my throat. "It's my mother."

"I know, but you have the look of her."

My heart ached, and my fingers went to it again, holding the warm metal against my chest. For all he seemed to see through me, I was grateful he didn't ask more. I hadn't the strength to speak of them.

"Now eat."

"I don't see you eating. Besides, I don't care much for offal."

"I wasn't the one they tried to kill. You need the blood,

whether you want it or not." He leaned back in his chair, folding his arms across his chest. Behind him some of the other townsfolk had begun looking at us. Some more obvious than others. I caught the eye of a man—one I recognized from the mob—and stabbed another bite of liver, met his gaze, and plopped it in my mouth with a raised brow.

The man shifted uncomfortably and turned back around.

"You really shouldn't encourage them, you know." Ruan's voice was soft as he leaned close to me before shooting a warning glance of his own over his shoulder.

"But you can scold them with your glower, I suppose?"

"Pellar. I told you I'm given certain license." That worried crease between his brows had softened a bit.

Despite my argumentative nature, I was grateful for his presence. Pellar or no. Though I'd never admit it to the man's face. The liver wasn't quite as awful this time. Then again that probably had more to do with my lack of sustenance than anything else. "You mentioned before that you'd never met anyone else like you."

He nodded, his eyes fixed on something behind me. "The last known Pellar for miles around died long before I was born."

It shocked me how freely he spoke of such things, things that other people would only mention in hushed whispers. People here respected him. They came to him for broken hearts and sick children. Or if their crops wouldn't grow or if the well was dried. In that way, I supposed a Pellar was as much a part of the fabric as a butcher, a vicar, a teacher. Each with a role to play. Although his position was at odds with the modern world. There would always be a place for tradesmen and vicars. But what about witches?

He coughed loudly and shifted in his seat. The sound snapping me from my thoughts.

"Right. Sorry." I took another long sip of the pint, letting it warm me. I licked the yeasty foam from my lips. "What about the other witch? Mrs. Penrose said there was another one before with the previous curse killings."

"Mmm. The White Witch of Launceton."

"Yes!" I must have said it a bit loud because the old man I'd frightened earlier turned to me with a curious expression as another rattle of thunder shook the walls. Outside, the sky was streaked in the oddest shade of green. I always hated storms. The sentiment even greater now.

"Why do you ask about this?"

"It's odd to me is all."

"Which part?"

All of it.

He laughed at the look on my face. "Your point is taken."

"I didn't make a point!"

He raised an eyebrow to argue, giving me the sensation he'd heard loud and clear the words on the tip of my tongue. "How much did she tell you?"

I pulled my left leg up under my rump in the chair and downed the rest of my beer. "Not much, I'm afraid. I know you don't think the curse is behind it, but could they be related somehow? The killings then and the one now?"

He gave me a flash of a smile. His teeth bright and even. "Come now, do you believe in witches and ghosts after all, my dear Miss Vaughn?"

I grumbled beneath my breath and could have sworn I heard him laugh. The wretch.

"There could be a connection. But the problem is, no one really remembers precisely what happened before."

"What do you mean?"

"It was thirty years ago, the war . . . people have moved to town. Died. There aren't many of the old ones left who remember, and even if they do, memories fade. They get altered.

Shaped by the things that came before and after. That's all memories are, fading fragments of what came to pass."

"How very fanciful of a thought." That wasn't particularly helpful. I gnawed on my lower lip. "Is there anyone whose *fading fragment* you *would* trust?"

Ruan watched me for a moment, his eyes lingering on the cut on my brow. "There are a few of the old ones. Arthur Quick would be my first thought. Or Minerva Grose, though she's away for the summer. Both of them are well over eighty, though."

"And are they—"

"Sharp-witted as ever. If anyone would remember what happened then it'd be one of them. Dr. Quick was the physician here for decades, until his eyes gave out."

"Do you think he would have seen the bodies of the previous victims?" I nearly tipped over my pint glass with newfound enthusiasm.

"Possibly. No. I'm certain he would have. There were no other physicians in the village at that time. I'm sure he'd speak with us."

"What about the White Witch? Is she still alive to ask?"

His expression grew clouded. "I don't know."

"Don't know?"

"I was a babe in my mother's arms at the time of the last killings, and the White Witch vanished almost immediately after breaking the curse. For years folks would whisper of seeing her at the crossroads. Dark hair. Dark clothes. But she'd disappear just as soon as she'd come." His jaw tightened. Something was wrong.

"Dark hair . . . dark clothes . . . isn't that what the constable had mentioned earlier. The stranger in town."

Ruan pressed his lips together and shook his head. "It doesn't make sense. She hasn't been sighted in years. Not since before the war." He waved off that minor thought. "It doesn't matter, though—if she was still alive, I certainly would have known of her. They'd have sent me to her no doubt by my twelfth year. I assume she must have d—" His words were cut off by a thunderclap that shook the inn.

"Allo, Ruan!"

My dining companion turned to the voice. "Benedict!" He gestured to the empty seat. "Have a pint with us until the rain lets up?"

The other man nodded. He had a good-natured face. Older. Perhaps on the far side of fifty, but hale and straight. Slight with a gap between his front teeth—and unlike the two of us, he appeared to be dry as a bone.

"Miss Vaughn, this is Benedict Martin, he has a smallholding between my cottage and Penryth Hall. Some fifteen acres that he manages with his wife. Benedict, this is Ruby Vaughn. She's here from Exeter bringing me some books and got tied up in all this Chenowyth business."

That was one way to put things. "Martin? You don't happen to be related to Alice Martin, do you?"

He nodded with a warm smile. "My wife. Why do you ask?"

"I met her this morning." Had it only been this morning? "She was on her way to take a basket to Mrs. Penrose."

"Ah, yes, we heard about what happened to poor Sir Edward and thought Dorothea could use a hand. They're thick as thieves those two." His expression shifted and he sighed. "I heard about what happened this morning, maid. I'm that sorry about—" He drew his hand to his jaw, mirroring the spot where I sported a ferocious bruise. "Freddy gets into the drink and he . . . there's no excusing his actions. None. I'm glad you didn't come to no serious harm."

"Is that his name?" I asked with a graciousness I didn't feel. "The one who resembles a mad dog?"

Ruan snorted.

"That'd be the one," Benedict replied with a shake of his head. He clapped a hand on Ruan's shoulder. "I am sorry about it, but with our Pellar here it wasn't as if they could do any serious mischief to you."

The back of my head cared to disagree, but Mr. Martin was kind enough, which was something I had seen very little of from the denizens of this town.

"Speaking of mischief . . ." Benedict said, shifting to face Ruan. He leaned over the table. "There's a woman here looking for you."

My ears perked up at this. "A woman?"

Benedict nodded. "A strange one that. I met her at the crossroads on the way to the village this evening. Offered her a ride as it looked like it was about to storm."

I cast Ruan a curious look. A woman at the crossroads?

"What was her name?" Ruan asked.

"Wouldn't say. Nor would she say where she was from or why she wanted you. Only that she'd some business for the Pellar."

Ruan sucked in the air through his nose and exhaled slowly.

"Dark eyes. Sharp features. Truthfully I thought she was a ghost when I saw her at first, standing straight as a statue all in black. Odd. Terribly odd. But she was flesh and bone all right. Reminded me of the old stories. Remember 'em, Ruan? Like to scared me to death at first." Benedict glanced out the window into the storm. "I need to get back before Alice worries too much, but it looks like we're stuck here for a time." He sat down and turned to Ruan. "Is it really as horrible as they said? There's talk about the curse come back. And while I'm not sure as I believe that a demon got him . . . but the lads in town—the way they talk'd make even the vicar second-guess himself."

The muscles in Ruan's jaw clenched, and my own stomach knotted in response.

"What is it, lad . . . ?" Benedict's expression grew paler. "You don't mean to say it *is* the curse?"

He gave a noncommittal shrug and took a drink. "You know as well as I that Sir Edward wasn't a particularly well-liked fellow. During the war or after. You don't happen to know of anyone he'd crossed, do you?"

Benedict frowned deeply and settled himself in a chair beside me. "Not rightly. He wasn't liked, that's for certain—but I don't know of anyone who'd want to kill him." Ruan's question quashed any more mention of the curse. Benedict ran his fingers around the edge of his glass. A roar of laughter emanated from the table behind us, wedging itself into my still-sore head. I'd been forgotten. Or at least, wedged between these two men, I'd been deemed no longer a threat. A small silver lining to an altogether wretched day.

Benedict smelled of the fields. Not in an unpleasant way, but of nature and grass and livestock. "Curse or no, it's a terrible thing. And that poor wife of his," the older man said with a shake of his head and gestured for another round.

My head grew lighter, most certainly the result of imbibing after having my brains bashed in earlier. But I welcomed the warmth it brought, and the way it subtly dulled the ache inside my chest. The one that had begun the instant I saw Tamsyn again, and every rotten memory of my life came flooding back. I drank down the heavy beer and listened to the two men talk, slipping deeper into their West Country accents. Leaning against the window, I closed my eyes. The cadence of their voices, Ruan's slightly lower, lulled me to sleep. Odd, but after the day I'd had, I was grateful for the calm. For the oblivion. And I fell slowly into a dark and dreamless abyss.

The next thing I knew I was being shaken.

"Miss Vaughn."

My eyes jerked open, fixed upon Ruan's.

"The rain has stopped," he repeated and I had the sickening thought that he had perhaps said that same thing several times. My hand drew to my mouth. Thank goodness I hadn't been drooling. I glanced to the clock. It was late. Past ten, and the night was thick and clouded.

Almost everyone in the tavern was gone. Even Benedict, who had been here when I'd closed my eyes. I ran a hand roughly over my face, wiping away the last of the cobwebs.

"We should get to Penryth Hall before too much longer."

"Penryth . . . why?"

"I need to see the body."

Right. I'd nearly forgotten.

CHAPTER EIGHTEEN

Burglaress

THE rain made the roads impassable for my little car, forcing us to return to the estate on foot. My legs would regret all this scarpering about in a few days, but for now my thoughts remained foggy from the pub and the last couple of days' excitement.

In the moonlight, the house was even more foreboding. And devilishly dark. All the lights were out, aside from one on the uppermost floor. I thought of Tamsyn here, with only Mrs. Penrose and a handful of gossipy maids for company, and immediately felt guilty for the way I'd left things. She was emotional. Overwrought. That was all. And I'd once called myself her friend. I'd called myself more if I were honest with myself, which I didn't care to be at this moment.

"You don't have to come with me . . ." Ruan laid a warm hand on my shoulder. "I can find my way—"

His voice settled me, and I shrugged him off, heading on down the path to the house. "No, no. It's only I was thinking of the woman at the crossroads. Do you suppose she's our killer? I assume she's the one that Constable Enys was talking about."

Ruan didn't answer.

"That's not reassuring, you know. Mysterious woman comes to town. Dead bodies pop up."

He glowered.

"You don't think it is the White Witch, do you?" I asked suddenly.

He shook his head. "I told you. The White Witch is dead."

I was not convinced on that score, but wasn't about to argue with him. "Very well, what could this woman want with you?"

The moonlight had finally broken free of the thick clouds, illuminating the path. "People seek me out for all sorts of reasons. It could be anything."

"Or she could be our killer."

"Doubtful. Anyone who would *ask* for a Pellar isn't likely to be up to mischief. One of our many attributes, in addition to breaking curses, is finding thieves. Pellars redress wrongs, cure the sick. They don't abet murderers." He rummaged around in his pocket in the darkness.

Not even if the dead deserve it?

Ruan let out a strangled sound, and once again I had the uncanny sense that he knew my thoughts. "Ruby, these sorts show up from time to time. Curious folk. Or someone wanting a charm or poultice. I'm sure that's all it is. She'll find her way to me eventually and we'll sort it out then."

There was no sense arguing. Besides, there was nothing to link this strange woman to Edward at all. She *was* after the Pellar. Perhaps Ruan was right to not be concerned, but I remained uncertain.

The servants' entrance was locked when we arrived, as I'd expected. I dug around in my canvas haversack and pulled out my set of lockpicks. I held them up in the moonlight, looking for the one I needed, glinting steel in the night. The leather case was steadying. Normal.

As if any of this was normal.

"You . . ."

"I?" I arched a brow, glancing up from my palm. "I take it you had another idea for how to get inside the house without waking everyone?"

I dropped to my knees and set to work on the warded lock.

"I can't believe you're—"

I tried again, feeling for the obstructions, and bit my lower lip. Sweat beading up at my brow. "Picking a lock? Yes . . . yes I am. Now would you please be quiet so I can—" But I heard the telltale click anyway. "Ah-hah." I turned the knob and the door swung freely open. "After you." I gave him a jaunty little bow, tucked my pick back into the roll, and dropped the whole affair into my satchel. "What? Honestly, what did you think you would do? Walk in, *Please may I see the body?*"

"Yes. Yes I did. Pellar, remember?" He pointed to the center of his chest.

"Burglaress?" I pointed at my own. "Come on then. I know where he's at. Or where he was at least." The kitchens of Penryth Hall were uncharacteristically quiet without Mrs. Penrose bustling about. I stepped easily, careful not to make noise to alert her to our presence—though I doubted she'd say a word if she discovered her beloved Pellar scurrying through the house at all hours of the night. She'd probably fix him a pot of tea and some sandwiches.

The door to the wine cellar was locked as well. I dropped to my knees again. It was a simpler design, intended to keep hungry footmen at bay, not thieves—but for whatever reason it was giving me trouble.

"Where did you learn to do that?" he asked, more amused than horrified.

I shrugged. "Cabinets, closets. Cellar doors. You wouldn't believe how many times Mr. Owen has sent me on an errand only to find that the master of the house has lost the key to the trunk where he's kept his dusty twelfth-century volume of *Fancy Lords and Dubious Ladies*."

"You're having me on."

I fumbled, dropping the pick, and it skittered across the slate flags. "About the book only. I haven't found that particular title . . . But you would be shocked at the number of times I've had to unlock a desk drawer or seventeenth-century bookshelf to recover some inane tome. Bawdy books too. You would not believe how many copies are kept under lock and key as if the nude form is something to be ashamed of. Besides, it's been far easier to do it myself than to have to wait on a locksmith."

He let out a low laugh then bent over and picked up my tool, dropping it into my outstretched palm.

"Thank you." I brushed the hair back from my eyes and looked up at him. "Are you laughing at me?"

"Never."

I grumbled, jamming the pick back into the keyhole, and with one last click, the lock gave way. Ruby 2—Locks 0.

THE "OLD" WINE cellar was more modern than the one I had in Exeter, in stark contrast with the rest of the house. Tile, floor-to-ceiling in sterile white. Made to be easily cleaned out and washed down—but why one would want to wash out one's wine cellar baffled me. My breath came uneasily. I wasn't sure what to expect. I'd seen bloated bodies along the roadside back in France. Wounded men scarcely more than walking corpses, half starved. I'd inured myself to that sight during the war. Carnage no longer shocked me. Nor death. But somehow, seeing Edward in the orchard was beyond anything I'd experienced across the channel. It was real. In a way that little had been since long before the archduke had the audacity to get himself shot.

I took in a deep breath and stepped inside hoping I wouldn't be casting up the contents of my stomach. Yet what had been horrifying in the orchard was oddly less so here . . . in every conceivable way. Edward lay naked on the wooden worktable. A surface more suited to storing produce than cadavers. His hands were folded neatly over his chest, and his entrails tucked back inside, but he hadn't been sewn shut. Hadn't been touched at all besides the washing.

Ruan wasted no time in reaching the body. His hands running over Edward in the same reverential fashion as before. He stooped down, bringing himself eye level with Edward's bluish-green-tinged belly. The scent of death hung in the air, faintly. But ever present.

"The wounds are clean."

I snorted. "I'd assume so, Mrs. Penrose wouldn't allow anything else here. Have you seen the state of her cupboards?"

He glared up at me. "No. I mean they've been cut cleanly."

"Oh?" I moved closer to him, glancing down—against my better judgment—at Edward's lifeless form. I touched his chilled body with my bare hand.

"You aren't frightened."

"Not like this, no. I admit when I saw him at first it was a bit . . ." *horrifying.* "Off-putting . . . but now? He's not here anymore. It's a bit of flesh and blood and bone. And those things aren't troubling at all."

Ruan closed his eyes again, holding his hand over the body in the same fashion he had in the orchard. An eerie stillness filled the room, and something else. That sensation in the air, sharpness—like an electric storm.

"What are you doing?"

He opened his eyes then, and I could have sworn there was a bit of silver there. But it disappeared as quickly as it'd come. A trick of the light—nothing more.

"I was listening."

I turned to the door. "For what? Everyone's asleep, and I suspect most of the house would as soon someone make off with his body than to wake up with him still down here."

"Not for that."

"Ah . . ." I blew out a breath and began to pace the edges of the room. Each trip around, Ruan remained unmoved. By the time I made the third lap, I was downright frightened. He was *doing* something in his inaction.

"You did that in the copse too. When I saw you there. What are you . . . listening for?"

He bit his full lower lip, and my mouth may have dried in response. Oh, good God, I was lusting for a man over a dead body. Was that what that feeling was? The one I'd been too lackwitted to pinpoint. If so, this was . . . not good. It was this place—Cornwall—all it did was engender infidelity, lust, and murder. First Edward and his numerous inamoratas and now here I was having very *appealing* thoughts at a most *unappealing* time.

"I'm not sure. I don't understand it entirely but sometimes I can hear . . . oh, why am I even telling you this when you don't even believe in any of it?" He raked a hand through his dark curls, tugging slightly on them.

"Hear what, Ruan?"

"Things. I don't know how to describe it. Why it happens. But sometimes I get a sense of something."

"You mean like voices?"

He shook his head. "Not exactly."

"Do you hear anything from him?"

Another shake of his head.

A worrisome thought came to mind, one I dared not voice, but yet I knew the answer as well as my own name. All the signs had been there since the very first moment I met him, and I'd just been too stubborn to see. *Can you hear me too?*

His eyes met mine and he gave me the grimmest nod.

I should have been upset. Shocked. Angry, that the man had been mucking around in my thoughts for the better part of my time here, and yet a part of me always knew. It explained so much. The other thing I knew—straight to my bones—Ruan Kivell wasn't going to harm me. Strangely, I felt that the risk went the other way around. "It's why you knew where to find me tonight."

He nodded, eyes downcast. The poor man looked as if I'd accused him of the worst perfidy, when I'd simply put in the open what he'd known all along.

"Do you hear everything? Everyone?"

He shook his head, still not speaking. His left hand was jammed into his pocket. "I can't control it. I just . . . do." His shoulders slumped. "It's different with you. You're so loud and in the forefront. It startled me at first—how clearly I hear you—I don't know what it means. Or why."

I touched his arm. "It's all right. Truly." What a strange thing. Here I was consoling him when I was the one who should be upset. "Do you think that it actually means something?"

He blinked. "I don't know. I just don't know. It's never been like this." He straightened up, pulling away from me, and ran his hands through his hair again. We weren't to speak of it. I might not be able to hear his thoughts, but I could sense his mood well enough. "I don't think I'll learn anything else here. We should probably go before anyone realizes we've broken in."

"Oh, come now, Pellar, where's your sense of adventure?"

I turned toward Edward's body, walking around the table.

Nose wrinkled. I'd likely never forget the scent of this place. The way the air carried with it a bit of earth along with the stench of death and stillness you find inside a raised cemetery vault. I studied the body. He'd been a reasonably well-formed man in life. Handsome enough. I'd only seen him with his clothes on before, but here laid out to be prepared for burial his body was sunken. Veins visible against his discolored skin. Most of the cuts on his face and chest were superficial. I touched them gently. Some of my own were deeper. These were nothing but scratches.

I leaned closer, glancing over his body. The other wounds, those on his abdomen, were another story. Deep and grotesque, but still I saw no sign of puncture marks. Nothing ripping.

"What are you doing?" Ruan grumbled.

"Looking. I may not be a witch, or able to hear *your* thoughts. But I am rather observant. Even if it is crass to admit one's strengths."

He snorted and crossed his arms, retreating to the smooth tile wall. "See anything interesting?"

I bit my lower lip, much the way he had a few moments before, and ran a hand through my short hair. "I *see* that we need help."

"And you've only now come to this conclusion?"

"Well, no. But as you don't have any useful ideas—I think we need a physician. A real one. Someone who can help us narrow down what could have caused these wounds. It's nothing I've ever seen."

"Have you seen many dead men?"

"Enough."

Ruan nodded. Not pressing any further and I wondered how much of my thoughts he *had* overheard since we met. A rather unsettling thought.

"Do you suppose we could get someone to look him over? Get a professional opinion?"

He frowned for a moment. "Not before the funeral."

"Good God, why must everyone in this town be superstitious? I don't suppose—"

"And before you ask—no, you are not digging him up either."

"It was worth a try. Could you use your . . ." I gestured to him, unable to form the word. "Yourself to get them to delay the funeral. At least until we can get someone willing to look at him. I know a surgeon in Exeter, an excellent one—he's not the superstitious sort—perhaps I could have him come and see what he thinks."

"He's dead, Ruby. I think that's pretty evident."

"Of course he's dead, but perhaps there's some clue here as to how it happened."

"The giant glaring hole in his abdomen isn't clue enough?" he asked me, growing sharper than I'd ever heard him.

"Well, have you any better ideas?"

He didn't answer.

"Besides, we need someone from outside. Someone not bound to be swayed by all this curse business."

Ruan gave me a troubled look. "I'll see what I can do. I don't know that they can wait. The people here . . . they believe in this. And I know you don't and that's fine and well. You are entitled to your beliefs, but—" He took a step closer to me. "To some of them the old ways are as real as the air they breathe. I can try to see if they will wait, but I'm not about to discount their feelings on account of yours."

"This isn't about feelings, Ruan. There's a dead man on this table and you know as well as I do whatever killed him is of this world, not some other."

He didn't answer. His gaze cloudy.

"Ruan." I hesitated. "You do still believe that, don't you?"

But instead of assuaging that nibbling worry of mine, he turned for the door. "We should go." Which was infinitely worse.

CHAPTER NINETEEN

Doubts and More Doubts

IT was well past midnight when we finally escaped the grounds of Penryth Hall. The moon was full and bright overhead, and I remained shaken from our conversation. The shock of seeing Sir Edward, the victory of having convinced Ruan to allow a real physician to come to Lothlel Green, all now paled next to the slow realization that the very same man walking beside me was able to hear my thoughts. And it wasn't the intimacy that bothered me, but the dreadful knowledge that if such an impossible thing could be true—what else could be?

Somewhere in the distance a cock crowed and I shivered in the cool of the evening. "Do you think it could have been an animal after all?" I asked at last. That option was certainly better than the alternative. Any of them. "If you don't *hear* anything, or whatever it is you were trying to do—maybe that means it wasn't a murder after all? Maybe it was something . . ." *else?*

He didn't answer at first, his long strides making it hard for me to keep up.

My heart thundered in my ears as I hurried to match his pace. "Ruan, *could* it have been an animal?"

He stopped abruptly, spinning around to face me, the muscles in his jaw tight. "I don't know. Everybody expects me to know—" His fingers clenched into fists. "—every bloody thing. And I. Do. Not. Know." He turned back around with an annoyed grunt and continued walking across the dirt path that led to the cliffs and back to the crossroads leading into the village.

"Ruan, I need to know something."

"What?"

"Are you or aren't you a witch?"

He whipped around with the strangest expression in his eyes. "Must you always ask so many infernal questions?"

Yes. Yes, I must.

He must have heard that, as he let out a low growl and resumed walking. "You're the one who says I'm not. Always questioning. Always wondering what I am. Always doubting so loud it makes me question it myself."

His words gave me pause and settled uncomfortably in my chest, but it wasn't as if I intended him to hear my doubts. It wasn't my fault he was mucking around in there. Ever since coming here I'd been upended and lost. Not knowing which way to turn. I sighed and reached out for his elbow. "I don't know what you are, but I need to know if you're just the seventh son of a miner with a penchant for parlor tricks or if there really is something to this Pellar business."

That crease between his brows returned. "I don't know."

"You don't know?"

"I don't know!" he said in a harsh whisper. "Mind if you say it a bit louder. I suspect the folks in London haven't heard you yet. People ascribe miracles to me. They think I can *do* something but all I can manage is to mix up herbs and have a head that feels like Charing Cross station. So no, Ruby. I do not know what I am. And I don't know what killed Sir Edward."

I snapped my mouth shut. "How can you not know what you are? Besides the obvious fact that you are mucking around in my head—people come to you. They pay you to solve their problems."

"They come for poultices and medicines. Why do you think I have all those plants? I don't do charmwork—never have. Don't you think that if I could control any of this, I'd have done *something* worthwhile with it all?"

"What about those marriages? Mrs. Penrose was very eager to tell me about all the young couples you made love charms for."

He waved me off and continued on through the deep mud, which made an unpleasant sucking sound with his steps. "That wasn't magic."

The back of him was nearly as infuriating as the front. "You admit you swindled them, then?"

"Power of suggestion. Nothing more."

"Nothing more?"

He whipped around to face me, looming large, and I felt an unfamiliar stab somewhere deep in my belly as he looked down at me. "You see some lad mooning over the baker's daughter. Or a scullery maid making eyes at a stable hand who can't hardly string two words together whenever she's around. You just . . ."

I pressed my lips together to disguise both my amusement at his words and the unpleasant discomfort at his proximity. Not that I was afraid of him. It was frighteningly the opposite. "You're telling me you are a matchmaker."

He sighed heavily, rolling his eyes heavenward. "I don't matchmake. I just . . ." His voice was low in the darkness as we continued along the path to town. The wind had picked up not long ago and clouds had set back in. More blasted rain. "I see a pair who ought to be together if they could stop tripping over their own feet bungling the whole affair. One of them comes to me asking about their true love and I—"

"Give fate a nudge?"

"Exactly."

"Ruan Kivell, you are a hopeless romantic!" I traipsed along the moonlit path beside him as the first few drops of rain began to fall. I wiped them from my face. "But you are a miserable witch. I mean honestly, look at this weather!"

He snorted. I cast a glance over my shoulder, half expecting my needling to have upset him after his outburst earlier. But it seemed he didn't mind my teasing. It was the silent doubting that troubled him. Everyone in the county, save the vicar, worshipped the ground he walked upon. The chosen one. Hell, he'd likely give Christ a run for his money in their estimation, but to my sudden surprise—he didn't care for it. Not one bit.

By the time we made it to the crossroads, it was clear that I wasn't going back to town tonight. Water rushed over the bridge that led into Lothlel Green and my warm bed at the inn. And while I was an adventuresome lass—as Mr. Owen always chided—the idea of being swept down a flooded stream was not to my taste.

"My cottage is near, shall we wait it out?" Ruan shouted over the viciousness of the roaring water.

I nodded rather than wasting my voice. My feet stuck to the muddy road, making it a slippery and treacherous hike. But provided there were no flooded streams between here and there I was quite happy to shelter for a few hours.

But that was not to be.

Chapter Twenty

A Crisis of Bovine Proportions

ABOUT twelve minutes after walking in the door, a great commotion rose up outside. Banging and shouting flooded the small cottage.

"Ruan! Ruan Kivell!"

Marvelous. More excitement. I stifled a yawn beneath my fist. Ruan opened the door as another crack of lightning lit the night, revealing a very soggy Benedict something-or-the-other from the pub earlier.

"What's the matter? Get in here, man, before you drown," Ruan grumbled, stepping back into his rather cozy front room. It was small before with only the two of us; a third made the space positively cramped.

Benedict shook his head. "No time. It's my cow. Someone's put the eye on her. I'm certain of it."

"What's happened?" Ruan ushered him inside, despite Benedict's protests.

"She's laid out in the field, unable to get up. Frothing. Can you do something about her? She's my best breeder, she is. I can't afford to lose her."

Ruan sniffed and nodded. "I'll be along dreckly. Dry yourself by the fire while I gather my things." He turned and immediately began grabbing various concoctions from his shelves and placing them into his stained British Expeditionary Force haversack. Benedict remained by the door, arms folded across his chest. His worry palpable even to me. Ruan on the other hand remained steady, calmly lifting jar after label-less jar, sniffing, and closing them back before deciding which to secure into his pack.

I stepped closer to him and lowered my voice. "What are you thinking, going out again in this weather. You're liable to drown out there yourself. Can't it wait until morning?"

He shook his head and secured his satchel, slinging it over his shoulder. His voice was low. "It can wait if you want a dead cow. Are you coming along?"

I cast a longing glance at the fire crackling away in the hearth and then back to Ruan. *In for a penny* . . . "I suppose it isn't possible to get any wetter than I already am." I leaned forward and plucked the damp blue handkerchief from his coat pocket and tied my hair back. I half expected him to swat my hand away, but he just shook his head and turned and walked out the door. And I —fool that I was—followed the Pellar into the storm.

DURING THE WAR, I'd seen all sorts of creatures—man and beast—in various states of distress. Horses. Mules. Dogs. Stray cattle that had somehow survived crossing the lines only to be captured and turned into supper for the troops. But in all my life I'd never seen anything close to this. Well, I had once, but it hadn't ended well for the beast. The great brown cow was on the ground heaving, each breath a struggle. The contrast of the cool night air and the hot exhalations gave the impression that she breathed fire. She was in pain. Great amounts of it from my inexpert opinion.

I bit my lip, unable to take my eyes away from the scene before me. Ruan had been right. If he'd waited until morning the poor thing would be dead—granted, it didn't look long for the world as it was.

He leaned over the flailing creature, much as he had Edward's body earlier. A strange parallel. I shivered and hugged myself tighter against the unrelenting rain. His eyes remained closed—not that I could see them from this distance, but I knew it all the same—his hands on the creature's great flanks. Cold droplets beat down as the cow let out a great bellow that echoed in my ears. The ground beneath me shook with the violence of the animal's convulsions, and yet Ruan Kivell remained still.

He was liable to get crushed.

We all could be.

I took another step backward away from the cow. My own heart skittish in my chest. He needed to move. Get away from there. "Ruan, come back, you can't save her!" I called out to him through the rain, but my voice was lost to the night.

I started to call again, but it was useless between the cow's cries and the storm. I took a step forward.

Benedict reached out and tugged me to his side. His warm hand on my shoulder. "No, maid. Stay back. This is Pellar business."

I shook my head angrily. This was the second time someone had said that to me. "You won't *have* a Pellar if he goes and gets himself crushed to death. The cow is dying. Surely you can see that."

Benedict shushed me and pointed to the scene before us. "Watch," he whispered low in my ear.

I did. Unable to take my gaze away for fear that if I so much as blinked, Ruan would slip beneath the creature's flanks and be crushed in a slow agonizing death.

He leaned his head low, murmuring something in a language I didn't understand. His hands stroking the cow's neck and snout, causing her to still instantly. The black tongue reaching out and wrapping around his offering.

Whatever he'd done had silenced her. Eased her passing. Of course he would. Tears filled my eyes at the senselessness of the loss. It wouldn't be long now. She was dying. Any fool could see it, yet Benedict held me by my shoulders, forcing me to watch his favorite cow die. It was macabre. Cruel of him to make me witness such a thing.

Except she didn't die.

I watched through the rain and my own tears as Ruan stood up and stepped back. Seconds later the cow followed suit. Struggling unsteadily onto her feet like a just-born calf. He rubbed her great snout with a rough pat. Her mouth was still frothing, but she nuzzled at his chest before beginning to walk away in the rain, back to the shelter of the barn. One slow step at a time, tail flicking.

What . . . what had he done?

I stared openmouthed as he fumbled in his bag and began dumping something from a flask over his hands. "We need to get the rest of the herd into the south field. Are any of the others sick?" Ruan ignored me, looking directly at Benedict.

"Not as I could tell. I saw this one out here making a great fuss. The others are all bedded down for the storm. But not her."

Benedict set off across the waterlogged pasture, and Ruan followed suit. I stared after him for a moment, trying to reconcile what I'd seen with science—with reason—but coming up woefully short. So instead I turned and ran after

Ruan, slipping in the mud with each step. My feet ice-cold and wet.

He was halfway to the house when I caught up with him. "What . . ." I gasped, catching my breath. "What did you do?!"

He shook his head. "I gave her some charcoal. She was too far gone for much else."

"Charcoal?! Ruan Kivell, I'm no farm girl but even *I* know that you couldn't give a cow in that state charcoal. You'd have never gotten her to eat it. Maybe if you had ground it up with some liquid to funnel it down her throat. The thing was hardly conscious when we arrived. You mean to tell me you gave the old girl a pet and she licked it out of your palm?" *But she had.* He'd murmured something to her, and she'd obeyed him. My hand shot out, grabbing him hard about the forearm and pulling him back to me.

His skin was warm beneath my touch, his eyes eerily bright. "I told you what I did. You saw me. What more do you want me to say?"

I snapped my mouth shut. I didn't know. I was beginning to see why the villagers were afraid of him, of who he was—what he was. And if I allowed that Pellars could exist in this world, then maybe there was room for curses too.

Ruan and I followed Benedict in silence back to his farmstead. I traipsed along in my soaked-through boots. My toes now prunes in the woolen socks I'd thrown on earlier in the afternoon.

I'd offended him.

Again.

It was evident in the slant of his shoulders and the rather determined stride away from me. He didn't care if I fell in the mud or cow shit. A sentiment I returned. Perhaps it was cruel to be angry with him after he'd done—whatever it was—but it only made me angrier. I wanted him to reassure me that there wasn't a curse, that Sir Edward's killer was flesh and bone, that together we'd figure out who had done the deed—but his uncertainty earlier this evening was like contagion, festering beneath my skin, growing and spreading until I too began to doubt my convictions.

CHAPTER TWENTY-ONE

Hearth and Home

THE Martin homeplace was a small structure, rising up like the back of a tortoise from the surrounding land in stone and a slate roof. More squat than not. A warm light glowed from the window. And most important at the instant—it looked dry.

I shivered again, hugging myself in my flimsy gray-and-cream dress. I may as well have been in my underclothes, for the warmth it provided.

Ruan placed a hand on my shoulder. "Rest here. Warm up. Benedict and I will be back once we've moved the herd."

"I can help."

"You don't know this country. You're more likely to hurt yourself than be of any use. Stay with Alice. It shouldn't take long."

I started to protest, but the thought of frustrating him any further, combined with the warm glow of the fire, convinced me to surrender in this. The two of us walked in through the back kitchen door.

Alice Martin stood by the stove, her face grave. Her hair was pulled back with wisps coming loose at the edges, looking far wearier than she had when I first saw her outside the gates of Penryth.

"She's dead then?" Mrs. Martin looked to her husband, who was scraping his boots in the doorway behind me.

"No. Ruan said she should make it through the night. Thinks she poisoned herself. Got into some water hemlock that got washed out with the storms. He found some earlier on the edge of his property, where the cliff gave way this morning. We're lucky to not have lost the whole herd."

Mrs. Martin grew paler, if such a thing was possible. It was a sobering thought. One cow was a hardship, but to lose the lot of them was the sort of thing that meant complete ruin for a farmstead like this. "You're moving them tonight then?" She looked out into the growing storm. The wind picking up. Howling outside the little house. "In this?"

Ruan nodded. "There's no choice for it, Alice. We'll keep them safe. And you can have that lad of yours clear the root out of the pastures in the morning."

She let out a heavy sigh and hugged her husband tightly. Her eyes squeezed shut. "Be careful." She stepped back and Benedict wiped a tear from her cheek with his thumb. "I'll have a kettle ready for the pair of you when you return."

Ruan paused in the doorway and turned back. "Doesn't the Smythe girl forage here sometimes, over by the cliff's edge?"

Mrs. Martin nodded as she watched Ruan curiously. "She and half the village this time of year. There's some wild mushrooms growing up that way. The lass always brings me some back when she goes. My knee has trouble making it up there with the weather."

Ruan made a low sound in his throat. "Make sure to send a lad to tell her not to pick anything that looks like wild garlic or parsnips while she's there. Only mushrooms. Understand? Be sure word gets around to be on the lookout for it."

Mrs. Martin nodded grimly. "Aye. We will. Water hemlock you think it is? I'll send the boy around first thing in the morning."

Ruan gave her a grateful smile and dipped back out into the storm. The lightning flashed outside, illuminating the field like midday as the door shut behind them.

Alice cleared her throat and turned to me. "I've got some saffron cake left from Sunday. You hungry, child?" She didn't wait for a response, instead settled me near the fire. "Come, let's sit you down and dry off, mmm? You look a far sight worse than you did when I saw you this morning. More like one of the merfolk fished fresh from the sea. Pretty like one too, at least under all those bruises." She brushed a lock of damp hair from my brow and smiled at me.

She stooped down, knees creaking with the action, and tossed another log onto the fire.

"Thank you, Mrs. Martin."

"Call me Alice."

I untied Ruan's handkerchief from my brow, laying it before the crackling fire, and began roughly drying my hair with the linen cloth she'd handed me.

She poured tea from a deep cobalt pot into a delicate cup. "Sugar? Milk?"

I shook my head, taking it from her. The warmth ran straight through the thin china into my fingertips. I lifted it to my nose and took a deep breath. It wasn't tea. Or rather, it was but there was something else in the brew. I looked at her, puzzled.

"One of Ruan's concoctions."

I arched a brow.

"It's to help with settling my nerves. They've not been what they ought these last few years. The lad made this for me to help ease my mind. Except it's rather good and I've gotten into the habit of drinking it at night. Helps me to sleep and keep the dreams at bay."

I caught a strange array of herbs. Ones I'd not thought about drinking down.

"It's mostly chamomile I think," she said with a warm smile. "Some mint. Fennel too. But beyond that he won't tell me and I haven't been able to figure it out."

I took a slow sip of it. Hissing slightly as I burned my tongue. I blew on it before trying again. She was right. It was delicious, and definitely a hint of fennel.

"Benedict told me what happened in town today. I'm that sorry, maid. Some of the men get it in their head that they're going to protect us and . . ." She clucked her teeth. "Gracious, child, you look like you've been thrown from a horse."

I snorted. "It's been a while since I've ridden but if I recall, it hurt less last time I was thrown from one."

She laughed at that. "Ah, you'll be fit in no time, if our Ruan's put his hands on you."

My fingers rose unconsciously toward the stitches at the back of my head.

"Cold, love? Shall I fetch you a blanket?"

I shook my head and took another sip of the tea. The knots in my stomach slowly unwound. "Has he always been a healer?"

"Ruan? Heavens no. He grew up in the mines like most of the lads around here. Was down in them from the time he was six years old. He was a tiny little thing then—if you can imagine it now—able to get deep into places men full-grown couldn't reach."

"Six! Isn't that . . ." I recoiled at the thought. "Surely there were laws against such things, that's . . . barbaric!"

Alice drank her tea slowly with a distant frown. "I assume things are much the same way where you're from as they are here. The fancy folk will do whatever it is they can get by with, laws or no laws."

I swallowed hard thinking of my own fortune. I'd preferred to pretend that my father's money came from more noble gains. But was speculation and playing the markets any better than owning mines? As a girl I'd looked up to him, thought it dashing—like a glorified gambler—but in truth his money was as stained as anyone else's. A kingdom built upon another man's labor.

I wrung my hands together. Trying to block out the image of a little boy so deep belowground. But his face was clear as day, with those strange bright-greenish eyes looking back up at me beneath the dirt on his face. I shook my head to push it away.

"Ah, don't worry for him, the lad came to no harm. None of them did so long as he was underground with them. He's told you, hasn't he?"

I shook my head.

"About the accidents? Surely someone in town has?" She looked incredulous at the thought.

"No. Nothing. Mrs. Penrose mentioned something in passing but didn't say what had happened."

She gnawed briefly on the inside of her cheek, glancing toward the window to reassure herself that the men weren't returning before she started into her tale. "Well, the first time he did it, he was thirteen. The engine had failed and the mine flooded. All the lads were still underground. The captain was certain all souls were lost. Everyone came from the village up to the engine house. The bells—oh, maid—I will never forget the sound of the mine bells and the commotion. It was a terrible day. By the time they drained the shaft, we'd given them up for lost. But once the others got down there, they found a bit of the tunnel had collapsed saving them. He was still a slip of a lad then, he and the rest of the men all trapped in that cutoff shaft saved by a pocket of air. Dirty as could be, hungry to a man, but not a one was harmed. Not even a scratch."

I sucked in a breath. "But surely those things happen . . ."

"Once perhaps. But twice?"

"It happened again?" This time I glanced out the window knowing deep down I was an intruder here, stealing away with information I hadn't been given. But at the same time I needed to know. If I was to understand what Ruan *was*, I needed to know what he'd done. Where he came from.

"Aye, during the war. He did just the same. A collapsed tunnel, and not a single man was lost. But I get the feeling you're the sort of lass that needs to put her fingers in the Lord's side to believe. There's nothing wrong with that, my lover, it's just some folks need more than faith to believe."

I felt the heat rise to my cheeks as she took my hand in hers and gave it a squeeze.

"I don't mean anything by it. But our Ruan is a special one, he is."

Yes. Yes, I'd gathered that, but it still didn't ease my mind. In fact, with the recent trouble at Penryth, it did the opposite. I finished off my tea, its soporific effects slowly spreading throughout my body. Lulling me into a rather contented state of being. My limbs warm and peaceful.

"What brought you here anyway? I imagine you think us quite provincial. You came down on holiday and ended up in the middle of all this. I suspect you rue the day you set foot in Lothlel Green."

She filled up my cup again. "A bit yes. But it wasn't a holiday precisely. I work for a bookseller in Exeter and was bringing some things to your Pellar." I stifled a yawn behind my fist and shook my head. "Thought I'd stop by to have supper with an old friend." That ache that always rose in my chest when I mentioned Tamsyn was oddly absent, and I couldn't for the life of me figure out why. I blew softly over the warm tea before taking a second sip. "I have to admit, it's by far the most memorable of my deliveries."

She chuckled, casting a fond expression toward the door. "Ah, that explains it. Well, he's a good one. None of the lasses in town are half good enough for him." She gave me a knowing look.

"Oh, no. It's not like that. Not at all." I glanced down at myself. She was right in her initial assessment, I did look as if I'd been fished from the sea. Soaked to the bone, coming out in the middle of the night. The woman had every reason to wonder what I'd been doing with their Pellar. "You see, after the incident in town, Mr. Kivell though it safer for me if I stayed near him. He has this mad notion that I'm in danger here."

Something flickered in her expression, but it was gone as soon as it came. "I suspect if Ruan thinks something's after you, then you'd best heed him. He's seldom wrong about such things, that one."

"No. I suppose you're right."

"Shall we go to the parlor now that you're dry?"

I grinned and stood, following her deeper into the house. The next room had the same low ceiling as the kitchen. With great dark beams stretching across supporting the second floor. Wood and lime-washed walls. It was homey, though, warm. Happy. If a house could be such a way. Which was a silly thing to think—certainly chalked up to the day I'd had. Had it only been this morning I'd been in the garden with Nellie Smythe? Yesterday morning? The days blurred together—mostly as I hadn't yet slept.

I walked over to the large slate mantelpiece. A photograph

of a soldier sat in the center, surrounded with dried wildflowers tied with bits of faded pink ribbon. I lifted it up gently, studying the picture of the young man. "Is this your son?"

"Aye, that's my Georgie." A wistful look crossed her face.

He was remarkably handsome in his soldier's uniform. He had to be of an age with Ruan, but I didn't recall seeing him around the village. Then it struck me. George. George Martin. Her son must have been the one they were speaking of who died after the war. "George Martin? Was that his name?"

She nodded, taking the photograph and running her finger over the glass by habit. "I see they've been talking again in the village."

I shook my head. "I just heard his name mentioned in passing. That's all, and that he'd been engaged to Miss Smythe once."

"Nellie was a good girl. I sometimes wonder if a broken heart sent her to do what she did. I can't help but feel a little responsible. Had I not let George sign up, then maybe the demons wouldn't have come for him."

I stared at her for a moment. "I'm not following."

Her voice cracked as she reluctantly set the photograph back on the mantel. "They tell me he took his own life. He couldn't live with himself. It was eighteen months ago now." She paused for a heartbeat or two before continuing with the litany I suspected she repeated every day. "Three weeks. Four days."

I would wager she knew each hour, minute, second since her boy's death too, but I thought it was best to change the subject. I hadn't meant to bring up bad memories and that melancholy clouding her face was catching. It was a sentiment I knew all too well.

I yawned again into my fist, hardly able to keep my eyes open.

"Oh, child, you should go lie down. Stay here this evening.

You're as safe with us as you are with our Pellar. And I've got Georgie's room made up."

The thought of sleeping in a dead man's bed gave me pause, but after a moment's contemplation I agreed. Trudging all the way back to Ruan's cottage in my current condition was an unappealing notion. Not to mention I didn't particularly want to speak with him, not until I'd gotten my own thoughts in order.

"You don't think Mr. Kivell will be cross with me?" *Crosser than he already is.*

She laughed. "He'll have to answer to me if so."

"Are you not afraid of your Pellar?" I grinned back at her.

She made an amused sound and led me deeper into the house. "You leave him to me. All will be well, my lover. All will be well."

CHAPTER TWENTY-TWO

Things Both Lost and Found

I woke early the next morning, to the sound of Ruan's voice emanating from somewhere deeper in the house. As he hadn't thundered into the room yet and dragged me out of the bed linens, I took it to mean that he was no longer irritated with me. Not that I cared if he were.

I'd only managed to steal a few hours' sleep, but between the tea and Mrs. Martin's kindness, I felt more rested and at peace than I had since I set foot in this bloodthirsty little hamlet.

It was a dreamless and deep sleep. The sort of oblivion that normally only gin could provide, but without any of the residual fog that inevitably followed. Which was good, as I had a great deal to discuss with Ruan and no time to nurse my beleaguered head. We'd planned to meet with the elderly Dr. Quick in the village before I returned to Exeter to procure my own physician in hopes he would be able to shed some light on what had truly happened to Sir Edward, and if there were any links to the previous curse killings. It would be a long day. A terribly long one, but I'd had far worse. Yesterday, for example.

My tired day dress was dry and sat pressed at the foot of the bed. Mrs. Martin must have crept in sometime while I slept to return it to me. I slipped out of my borrowed nightdress and stepped into my own frock, fastening the smooth mother-of-pearl buttons up my throat. The stubborn bruises there were growing darker by the day. My fingers traced the prints of my would-be killer. My face hadn't fared any better. Green and purple blossomed above my lip, surrounding a dark scab. The stitched-together gash along my brow was a sight to behold, but it too would heal in time, leaving only a faint silver scar as a souvenir of my time here. I ran my fingers through my knotted hair, putting myself to rights. Visions of a nice long soak in my bathing tub flickered through my mind. By this evening, I'd be back in Exeter, miles away from here. It was a heady thought.

Mrs. Martin was in the kitchen already when I finally surfaced. "Did you sleep well, child?" She brushed a lock of hair from her brow, leaving a stray smear of flour in its wake. "Ruan's come early to fetch you. He said you were to call on Dr. Quick this morning."

"I did, thank you for everything. I can't recall the last time I slept so well."

"That'd be the air here. I'm convinced on this hill you get the best breeze in all of Cornwall."

I smiled faintly at her words. Out the window the golden morning light lit the field like a gilt engraving. Tall flowers danced in the meadow grass. Dots of white, yellow, delicate pinks. The occasional poppy just opening in the morning sun punctuated the scene.

"Where is he?" I glanced around the room, noting the very obvious absence of the Pellar.

"He's in the barn with the cow. He wanted to see to her again. I don't know what I'd have done if we'd lost her. And to water hemlock of all things. It's a mercy Benedict found him when he did. We could have lost the whole herd by morning."

I was struck by the tenuous line between life and death on a farm. Everything was more real. More vital here than back in the ballrooms and theaters of New York. Entertaining the Morgans and Vanderbilts or whoever else one chose to spend their days with as long as they were deemed *acceptable* to polite society. I'd bucked against that world long before I was cast out of it. There was also a bit of my mother in Alice. In her warmth and strength. The way only farm women are able to be. A combination of quicksilver and tenderness in the very same breath. Because one has to be changeable to survive. My mother had grown up on a farm before she married my father. Sometimes I wondered if her life might have been better had she stayed there. She certainly wouldn't be dead now if she had married someone with more humble aspirations. But no, my mother had been swayed by a silver-tongued charmer. Not that I faulted her, my father was an easy man to love.

"Ah, I see him now."

Heart heavy, I followed her gaze to where Ruan was speaking with Benedict beneath an old elm tree. His head bent low. Mrs. Martin must have sensed the encroaching dread in me, as it echoed in her own eyes. "Benedict is always after me to clear out George's room. Says he's not coming back and it's foolish to keep it ready for the lad. But it was a good thing I did, now wasn't it?" She flashed a half-hearted smile, and I felt a rare pang of unease at having slept so well in her dead son's bed.

"There's no reason to rush things. The healing will happen in its own time."

"You understand, don't you?" she said softly.

God, did I ever. My eyes pricked as the memories flooded over me, like that washed-out bridge to town. After my parents and sister were killed, I waited—weeks and weeks—despite the newspaper reports of the sinking of the *Lusitania*. Despite the casualty lists. Finagling leave from my duties at the front to comb through hospitals looking for survivors, grasping on to any hope that they hadn't drowned, and yet it was futile. I'd seen precisely how it had happened in my dreams. I knew. I just didn't want to believe it to be true.

She took my hand in her own roughened one and squeezed, a simple gesture reminding me that there was no need for words between us. No need to rehash the pain and in that very moment, I knew that we two were far more alike than I'd previously imagined.

RUAN AND I made it scarcely twenty yards from the Martins' farm when I grabbed him by the elbow. "Tell me about George Martin."

He sniffed, glancing back to the house. "What about him?"

Everything. "Who was he, what did he like? How did he die?" The words tripped off my tongue. All the thousands of things I refused to ask Mrs. Martin, and yet I had this unbearable need to know them all.

"Suicide."

The word hung heavily between us. "Did anyone know why? Did he leave a letter?"

Ruan shook his head. "No. Didn't leave anything at all. That was the peculiar part. But it wasn't long after we returned home from the war. He was having a time of it. Lots of us did back then."

"You were friends with him?"

Ruan shifted and folded his arms, his eyes focused past me on the distant treeline. "We served together. He, Enys, and me. George was a good man. Strong and clever. Half the girls in the village were in love with him before he signed up. The sort of bloke with more charm than the gods should allow."

"But he killed himself. And you're certain of it?"

"As certain as one can be. It was about a year and a half ago."

A year and a half.

Eighteen months. About the same time Tamsyn wrote me that letter. *I've made a mistake*, she'd written. But Tamsyn had nothing to do with George Martin. At least not that I knew of.

I gnawed on the inside of my cheek as we made our way through the west field on the way back to town. "Did you go to his body? *Listen* or whatever it is they had you do to Edward?"

Ruan's brows were knit up in confusion. "No, they didn't need me for that. Dr. Quick saw to him. Generally, I'm not brought in unless there is something suspicious."

"Ruan, if you are able to hear me . . ." I ran my tongue over the split in my lower lip. "Do you hear other people? For example, if we brought the killer before you—would you know what they were hiding?"

He placed his hands on his hips, thumbs resting just at the waistband of his trousers, and shook his head. "I wish it were that simple. I can't . . ." He looked up to the sky, where thick white clouds grew in the distance casting shadows across the field below, like in a Gainsborough landscape. "It's strange. I've never really spoken of this to anyone—but with everyone else— just for a moment imagine that you're in a crowded train station right as the train arrives. There's all this sound and commotion about you. A general feeling and buzz. An urgency even. You might pick up the errant word here or there, but there's a *sense* of something coming. Something important. Most of the time it's that way. It's not useful for much beyond giving me a great aching head."

I furrowed my brow and hesitated. "But with me you said it's different."

He nodded and blew out a breath. "With you, it's like

you're with me. In here." He tapped his brow with two fingers. "Not always—thank the gods—"

I wasn't sure whether to be grateful or offended by his deep relief.

"But when it happens it's as if you're speaking directly to me."

"Has it ever happened before, like that, I mean?"

"Once or twice. During the mine collapse when I was a boy. The first time I ever . . ." He raked his hand through his hair and glanced up at me sheepishly. "I assume Alice told you about that one."

I nodded with a frown. "So if I understand what you're telling me, it's that you have this ability, but you have absolutely no idea what to do with it or how to control it or even how to use it."

He let out a bitter laugh, shoulders trembling, and nodded. "Bloody useless, isn't it?"

Bloody useless indeed.

Ruan paused, turning his attention to the village. "Come along then, mmm? And we'll see if we can puzzle this out the ordinary way."

I followed after him knowing full well that there was absolutely nothing ordinary about the two of us, let alone the task at hand.

CHAPTER TWENTY-THREE

Old Doctor, New Clues

WITHOUT bothering to stop by the inn for a change of clothes, we hurried back into town. If I'd thought the whispers of *witch* and looks of suspicion would decrease after my attack, I was sorely mistaken. Only now the wary glances were more curious, less hostile. And the moniker had shifted to one of a cautious respect: *Ruan's witch*, the words lingering on the lips of every third person as we hurried through the bustling morning crowds picking up the day's meat from the butcher or carrying letters to post.

I blew out a breath, struggling to blot the voices from my head. Was this what it was like for Ruan? A constant drumbeat of chatter and information invading upon one's every waking moment? If so, it was a wonder he hadn't gone quite mad long before now.

Dr. Quick's home was situated a few doors down from the Hind and Hare. The middle of three stone rowhouses along the High Street. His door was painted a cheery shade of yellow, which I had to admire the fellow for. The old woman who greeted us appeared of an age with Mr. Owen, if not older.

Her eyes keen and cloudy as she peered at me through thick spectacles.

"Allo, Ruan."

He smiled at her. "Mrs. Tompkins."

She pulled the door farther open and gestured for us to enter. "I expect you're here to see the doctor again?"

Ruan nodded. "We have things to discuss."

She let out a coarse laugh. "I would imagine you do from what I've heard."

With that cryptic response she led us deeper into the small stone house, settling us into a snug drawing room—not much larger than the cramped chamber I had at the inn. A great window opened out onto the street, letting in the morning sun along with the sounds of village life. A rather quaint image, had I not nearly been killed some twenty feet outside it. In the corner of my eye I caught the shape of a figure in the crowd dressed in black head-to-toe. A woman. Dark hair. Dark dress. My heart stuttered and I turned my head quickly to focus on the image, but whatever it was vanished.

I shivered despite the warmth of the room and settled myself into a fine—if worn—armchair. I cast a nervous glance out the window, but whatever—whoever—I'd seen was gone. Not a reassuring sensation.

I heard the old doctor coming. The echo of his cane clicking on the herringbone wood floors. He made his way into the room, his left hand feeling his way around the back of a Victorian sofa, before settling down across from me.

"Morning, Dr. Quick."

The old man's head turned to the sound of Ruan's voice. "Ah, there you are, boy."

The small knot of tension in Ruan's brow eased, smoothing the omnipresent lines there. "I hope we aren't disturbing you."

"Ah, no, lad. Never you. I expect you've come about the killings, haven't you?"

"We have. Miss Vaughn and I were wondering if you recalled what happened to the previous baronet, the last curse killings?"

"Ah . . . I'd hoped it was a social call. But I suppose that was a foolish thought considering—" The old man's expression fell. "I remember. And that fraud they brought in from Launceton."

I arched an eyebrow. "Fraud? They say she broke the curse."

Dr. Quick let out a gruff harrumph. "There was no curse. Never has been. I am convinced she took the coin from the family and left town as quickly as she'd come. She was no more witch than I am. Sir Joseph was killed by someone in the village. Of that I'm certain."

Ruan gave me a hesitant glance before turning back to Dr. Quick. "Did you have any ideas of who it might have been?"

The old doctor shook his head long and slow. "If I had, I would have made my suppositions known long ago. I've seen all sorts of animal attacks in my years. The wounds on Sir Joseph would not have been that clean. They were cut with a blade. There was a nick in the breastbone too. No fragments of hair, tooth, or claw that I could find. What sort of creature would do such a thing?"

"Was his heart removed?" I asked, recalling Mrs. Penrose's story of the very first victim of the curse.

Dr. Quick nodded. "Aye. It was, but a hound dug the fetid thing up a few days later."

I wrinkled my nose. "Charming." And then a second thought struck me. One that hadn't dawned on me until this very moment. "Sir Edward's heart wasn't taken, was it?"

Ruan shook his head, tapping two fingers on the top of his thigh. "No. Which is another reason to think that this isn't the curse—regardless of what happened before. Just like that bottle under your bed, I think whoever is behind this means for us to believe in it."

"A misdirection, then." The doctor made a sound of agreement in his chest. "Not the work of a demon, I tell you that, Miss Vaughn. A man murdered Sir Joseph, and I'd bet my eternal soul that his nephew was killed by just the same." Dr. Quick was adamant in this. He smoothed his neatly pressed trousers.

Ruan raked a hand over his stubbled jaw. "Don't let the good vicar hear you betting away your soul like that."

Dr. Quick chuckled. "Ah, I take it he's still after your salvation, is he? You're wise to avoid him. The man might spin a pious tale from the pulpit, but he'd as quick see you in jail than he would in the pew."

Ruan grimaced, but didn't argue.

"You don't think they were killed by the same person, do you?" I asked.

"It'd be difficult for me to tell. A year ago, perhaps? My vision was still good enough then that I'd be able to look over Sir Edward and see if there were similarities. But now? I have lost almost all of my vision. Only shadows and light, I'm afraid, my dear."

I frowned and settled back into the chair, tugging my arms to my chest. We knew no more than we had before.

"Now, if you had a physician. One from afield perhaps. They might be able to look at Sir Edward and let you know what's what."

Hope bubbled up. Brief. But still there. "That was our plan. I was headed to Exeter this afternoon to see if I could bring a friend of mine back."

"Exeter, you say. He's not the superstitious sort, is he?" Dr. Quick looked rather affronted at the idea.

"Not a bit. I'm afraid he's German."

"Well, we can't all be Cornishmen, can we?" Dr. Quick flashed me a bright smile that faded away as he tilted his head to Ruan. "Boy . . . go over to that shelf, would you? There's a blue bound book on the second row." His gnarled forefinger pointed to the old rosewood bookshelf by the window. It was a piece from an earlier time, with diamond panels of glass criss-crossing the doors.

Ruan stood, made his way to the shelf, and pulled open the glass framing. His fingers traced over the spines before settling on the volume Dr. Quick described and retrieving it.

"It's my diary. I've kept one ever since I started practicing. Open the cover. Should be the period you want. I kept my reflections and notes on cases. Don't know much that would help you, but you might find something in there to help your doctor friend."

Ruan opened the cover, his dark brows drawn up as he read whatever was there before snapping it shut and dropping it into his jacket pocket. "Thank you. I'll give it to him."

Dr. Quick settled deeper into the floral cushioned sofa, crossing his legs. "I only wish I could help you more, lad. There's nothing worse for a man who spent his whole life being useful than to have nothing to do but sit around and wait to die."

"Come now," Ruan said with a start. "You've earned your rest."

Dr. Quick snorted. "I'd rather be tending the ill. Don't let time catch you, lad. For she's a terrible thief."

The edge of Ruan's mouth quirked up. "I'll try to avoid it." The two men were alike. Similar in so many ways that it heartened me to see it. There was at least one person in this village who wasn't afraid of Ruan Kivell. Granted he was near-ing ninety.

That same parallel symmetry between two people put me in mind of Mrs. Martin and our conversation this morning. "George Martin," I said softly. "Do you remember him? Did you see his body as well?"

Ruan sighed. "I told you, Ruby. He killed himself. I cannot fathom why you are so interested in the poor fellow."

I shook my head, not quite certain either. But there was something there. I was convinced of it. Though I doubted it had anything to do with Sir Edward.

The old doctor's expression shifted to one of suspicion, his fingers lightly on the tops of his trousers. "What makes you ask me such things, child?"

"I don't rightly know. I spent the evening with Mrs. Martin and I cannot get George from my thoughts."

He let out a wry chuckle, shifting his weight as his sightless eyes moved toward the light of the window just past my shoulder. "You and half the maids in the village. But I will tell you, something about his death didn't sit right with me."

I furrowed my brow, glancing to Ruan, who shifted in his seat.

"Do you mean to say you don't believe he killed himself?"

"Ruby!" Ruan shot me a quelling look. As if he had the right.

Dr. Quick shook his head. "No. I am convinced of it. That boy didn't kill himself any more than I have."

I sat with the revelation for a few seconds. If George didn't kill himself, someone else must have. I wet my lips, repeating the words again in my head. I'd never believed in coincidences, and for two murders to occur within eighteen months in a town as small as Lothlel Green—it was inconceivable that there wasn't something connecting them. Before I realized it, the words tumbled out on their own. "Do you think it could be somehow connected? Sir Edward, George Martin, the previous baronet?"

Dr. Quick sucked in a breath and shook his head. His spotted hand drew up to rub his smooth jaw. There was something about his face that reminded me of an old pocket map. Folded and unfolded time and again. "No. I don't see how they could be. And rightly I don't know what to think of the whole affair, only that Reverend Fortescue didn't want me to ask questions—which is what first raised my suspicion. At first, I assumed he wanted to keep everything quiet—being a suicide and all. But Fortescue has never been one to avoid a chance to prove his virtue over that of his flock."

"Quite," Ruan growled.

"Well, why should the vicar care one way or the other? If he was already known as a suicide, what harm could come from you inspecting the body?"

"See, that was my thinking as well. I had mostly settled into my retirement, as my eyes had begun to fail me, but I could still see enough in bright light to know what was what."

I leaned forward, resting my elbows on my knees.

"I paid a call on the curate at the time. Lad's been long since cast out—sent to the Outer Hebrides likely for having let me in that night, I'd imagine—you see, young George's body was being held in the chapel the night before the ceremony. Ordinarily it would have been at the family home, but the reverend was worried for Mrs. Martin's mental state. Rightly so, if you ask me. Said it was too terrible a thing for a woman of her delicate constitution to bear and insisted he keep the body at the church overnight."

Alice Martin delicate? Brokenhearted, yes, but she didn't seem to me the sort of woman to crumple in time of crisis. "Is that unusual?"

"Very. Alice Martin was a sad and broken woman, but she deserved to have her son with her the night before he was interred. So I decided I'd go see for myself what the vicar didn't want me to know."

I pressed my lips into a barely disguised smile. I found I rather liked Dr. Quick. "You mean to say you let yourself in and looked at him?"

"More or less." The old doctor braced his elbows onto his knees and dropped his voice low. "There was clear evidence of a struggle. Bruising on the back of the lad's neck. Someone had hidden it with powder but it was clear as day. His face didn't look quite right either."

"Could he have been in a fight before he killed himself?"

Dr. Quick sighed and shrugged. "It's hard to say with any certainty, but there were other signs. Scratches and scrapes. All hidden beneath his clothing. And why put powder on a part of the body beneath his clothes unless there was something to hide? Someone didn't want us to see those wounds."

I frowned. It did sound that way. The back of his neck would be covered with the collar of his coat, laid out in a casket; no one would ever be the wiser. Unless whoever killed him was eliminating any chance that someone would learn the true cause of death.

Dr. Quick clenched his fists on his knees. "I would stake my career that someone killed him on the moor that night. That they struggled and drowned him in the mud themselves."

Ruan raked a hand through his hair, his expression pained. "Who would have had reason to kill George? He was better liked in these parts than I am, and I've never once thought I had to look over my shoulder should someone want to drown me."

"Perhaps you should start."

He shot me a dark look, but I could see the flicker of humor in his eyes.

Dr. Quick continued. "I haven't an idea who. But if anyone knew, it'd be the vicar. He was awfully eager to keep it all quiet and to put the lad in the ground before anyone asked questions."

"Can you think of anyone else who might know something? Who George might have confided in?"

Dr. Quick hesitated, as if he couldn't decide whether to say his piece or let it die. Though he'd said quite a fair bit up to this point. The old doctor sighed, folding his hands in his lap. "If it were me I'd ask your friend."

"Tamsyn?"

He hesitated again, gauging his words. "There were rumors. Whisperings. The two had been close once. Some say . . . well . . . it's not my place to repeat what some say. But I would start there. If it were me."

His words struck me like a slap. Surely Tamsyn hadn't been carrying on an affair beneath her husband's nose. Then again, she'd betrayed me once. Who was to say she wouldn't break her vows before God just as easily as promises made in the dark? Ruan gave me a curious look before turning back to the doctor and thanking him for his time.

As Ruan said our goodbyes, I remained stuck in my own head. Tamsyn? Surely she'd have said something to me about an affair. *Ruby, I've made a mistake.* That's what she had written at about the same time as George Martin was found dead. Could she have harmed him? Or had Edward discovered her affair? I swallowed back the bile that rose in my throat. Two things were painfully clear. One, while I needed to get to Exeter, I needed to speak to Tamsyn more. And second, there was most certainly no curse. Oh, I'd barely scratched the surface of all the murders and secrets and lies in this confounded place, all bound up so tight, I'd be damned if I could unravel the knot. But I had to try, and unfortunately my warm and inviting bathing tub in Exeter was going to have to wait a few more hours.

Chapter Twenty-four

A Wayward Feline

MRS. Penrose greeted me at the door with an unusual bout of cheeriness considering the fact I'd fled here without even saying goodbye the day before. She bussed me on the cheek and ushered me inside, chattering on about how quiet the house had been lately. The hall itself was darker today. Or perhaps it was just my fevered imaginings after speaking with Dr. Quick. Why had he pointed me back to Penryth instead of telling me what he knew? It would have saved me a great deal of trouble.

"I've been that worried about you after you ran out last night, maid. Have you come to fetch your cat then?"

I blinked, turning to her. "My . . ." But before I could finish a familiar black puff of a tail hopped down the center stairs, flicking endearingly in greeting. "You little devil . . . how did you . . . ?"

"The poor creature showed up in the kitchen this morning, soaked to the bone. I assumed you'd left him here and he'd gotten out somehow and couldn't figure out how to get back inside before the storm came."

A reasonable assumption, except I had left the little nuisance safe, warm, and dry back at the Hind and Hare. How on earth had an Exeter house cat managed to find his way across a storm-flooded stream and back to a house he'd been in for barely two days? It was beyond comprehension. I narrowed my gaze at him, but he remained unfazed, blinking up at me with his golden eyes. Then—damn him to perdition—he walked over and nuzzled himself against my ankles.

"Thank you for taking him in." He rumbled loudly, sounding like a motorbike engine.

"Oh, it's nothing at all, I have a soft spot for the Lord's creatures. He had quite the appetite too. I fixed him some salted pilchards and dried him off and he's been happy as a lark following me around this morning."

No wonder he forded raging streams to come back, the cat had found a mark. "I'm certain he has . . ."

She bustled me down the hallway into the library to wait on Tamsyn, continuing to fuss over my poor battered face with promises of biscuits and tea. I hadn't the heart to tell her I wouldn't be here long enough to enjoy them.

She shut the door behind her, and I set Fiachna down on the carpet. Immediately he began patrolling the corners of the room, sniffing at the wall. Likely seeking out a mouse or a stray crumb that someone had long forgotten. The library was by far the most impressive room I'd found at Penryth. A great leaded-glass window rose up floor-to-ceiling overlooking the front lawn. From here you could see the comings and goings of the house. The bookcases reached the ceiling full to bursting with tomes collected over the centuries. A week ago I would have been running my fingers over the spines, examining each one with breathless curiosity. But now with three dead men on my mind, I could scarcely summon the energy to care.

I ran my hand through my tangled hair, catching in a knot at the back near the stitches. I was beginning to agree with Ruan that a curse might be simpler after all. It didn't completely beggar belief—after all Ruan could apparently hear my thoughts and just last night I watched the irritating man bring a cow back from the dead—but before I could finish the thought, Fiachna let out a bloodcurdling yowl. The sort of screech you heard in an alleyway right before you ended up on the wrong side of a pair of claws. I turned. Fiachna was fluffed out fuller than I'd ever seen him. Nearly twice his ordinary size and staring at the wall with murderous intent. A low guttural growl coming from his not-insubstantial feline chest.

Fabulous. Even the cat had gone mad. "Fiachna, what's gotten into you?"

He screamed again, stubbornly positioning himself between me and the wall.

My heart leapt to my throat. "Good God, cat." I stepped closer to the area he was inspecting. It was a wall. Nothing else. I crept carefully around him, running my hand over the mahogany panel, tapping lightly with my fingers. It was solid. Wood. I breathed out a sigh of relief, not certain what I'd been expecting. "See? Just a wall."

Fiachna flicked his tail, which I assumed was a sign he was satisfied. Caught up in my conversation with my meddlesome house cat, I didn't hear the door open or Tamsyn quietly creep into the library.

"I wanted to apologize for yesterday. For the things I said."

I whipped around to face her. She was pale with dark circles beneath her eyes, as if she hadn't slept in days. Her lovely strawberry-hued hair was tied back into a stern knot at the nape of her neck. "Apologize?"

She nodded and gestured to the settee. "Would you sit?"

I shook my head, lips pressed tight. "I'd rather stand."

The words hurt her, but I wasn't certain how to go about asking what I needed to know. I wasn't even certain what I needed to ask. *Dr. Quick insinuated you had been involved in extramarital fornication.* Right. That would go over like one of the kaiser's zeppelins full of holes.

"As you wish." She toyed with her fingers before continuing. "I . . . I didn't think you'd come back after the things I said. I know you are never one to look back. It's only . . . it seems to be all I can do now. And I apologize if it caused offense."

"Tamsyn, it isn't you who needs to beg forgiveness. I'd just nearly been stoned to death. I was not at my best. Besides, I'm afraid after I say what I've come to say, you might wish they'd succeeded in the task."

A faint flicker of amusement flashed in her green eyes. "It can't be that bad."

I drew my brows up regardless of the pinch of my stitches. I would beg to differ. "It's only . . . Tamsyn . . . it seems I'm going to go digging into the past after all."

"Well, as the past is my forte, have at me." Tamsyn mustered the smallest smile, and it made what I was going to say hurt all the worse.

Well . . . there was nothing for it. I sank down into an armchair, back decidedly to the door. "Tell me about you and George Martin."

Her breath caught in her chest with his name. The denial was formed on her lips and then she snapped her mouth shut. "How did you know?"

The desolation on her face told me everything I needed to know. She was guilty. Of what, I didn't quite know. Bitterness clawed its way up my throat, taking hold. "I stopped by to speak to Dr. Quick this morning. He seemed to think that George had some help in departing this mortal plane, and said that I ought to speak to you."

Tamsyn studied the carpet, not speaking.

"Now, I can imagine all sorts of things, Tamsyn Turner—"
I hadn't used her maiden name in years and it felt good on my

tongue. Erasing Edward Chenowyth bit by bit, though in truth it was far too late for that. "And I need to know everything. No lies. No omissions. There are now two dead men." I held my fingers up in the air. "Both of them clearly had something to do with you. And considering someone tried to strangle me in my sleep here, I don't relish the idea of being number three on the list of bodies at your feet. So if you would please start at the beginning and I'll do my best to keep up."

She jerked her head away, lit by the window. "I'd never hurt you. I thought you'd at least believe that."

I didn't know what to believe. In truth, I'd never given much thought to what she was capable of. To my mind Tamsyn had always been gentle and kind, but as the death toll linked to her rose, I began to ask that precise question of myself. Could she have killed them? I didn't know. And that uncertainty frightened me more than it ought to. I cleared my throat, shaking that thought away, struggling to maintain the higher ground. "You did that job years ago. We're both well past that now. I need the truth." I folded my arms across my chest. "Now."

"You were never cruel before, Ruby."

Her eyes were damp and I couldn't summon remorse for causing those tears. Not with the fresh ache of betrayal mingled with suspicion in my heart. No one would have blamed her for killing Edward. The man was a menace. "Before, I didn't question whether my best friend, the woman I used to love more than anyone else, was capable of murder."

She straightened, nostrils flaring. "I didn't love Edward, but I didn't kill him either. I want you to know that. And I *thought* you knew me well enough to believe that but evidently I was mistaken."

"I still cannot understand it. Not a bit. Why would you marry someone you didn't love when you had other options? I gave you a way out. A third choice. We could have run away and lived in London as we'd planned. I had enough money for the both of us, with or without your father—"

She stood up, walking to the window and resting her forehead against the cool glass before answering. "Because you are you, Ruby. So brave and fearless. I've never had the luxury of courage, even before the war. I was born to marry well. To run a household. To bear children. That was my duty. And you—you made it all sound so easy. But some of us weren't made to break the rules. Some of us must follow them." She struggled for the words, folding her fists tight. Her even nails boring dents into the soft flesh of her palms. "During the war you hared off without a fear for your life. Do you know who feared? I did." She pointed angrily at her chest then turned to face me. "I feared for you every single day and I couldn't live that way any longer. That's why. I don't know how you bore it."

I let out a bitter laugh. "Because when your entire family has been wiped off the earth, there's very little left to fear."

"You might have claimed to love me once, Ruby, but you never allowed anyone to love you. How could you expect me to spend my entire life waiting for the day you didn't come back? Because I knew that day would come. And I wanted a life, a life that Edward could give me. It might have been a mistake to marry him but it was my mistake to make." She let out a strangled sound that echoed the emotion that was just beginning to rise in my chest.

Had I truly pushed her away? I tried to think back on those days. On the grief and anger that I carried with me in those years after my family died.

"You wear your pain like armor. Daring anyone to challenge you, and yet you never let anyone beneath it." She paused and shook her head. "It was a lovely dream, Ruby, of being with you. But that's all it was. We never suited each other, one day you'll wake up and realize it too."

I stared at her thunderstruck, her words breaking beneath that very same armor she spoke of and digging into my flesh. I had to change the subject, to move away from the thousands of ways I was wrong in my feelings for her. I folded my arms. "I ask again, tell me about George."

Tamsyn lowered her eyes and sighed. "You would never understand."

"I'll simply have to try then, won't I?" I grumbled, hugging my arms against my stomach.

She turned away, silhouetted in the window. "We grew up together, George and I, playing the games children do, and . . . well . . . I don't know. I always assumed I'd marry him. But Father would never allow such a thing." She let out a heavy sigh, tugging at her bare fingers. "The summer before you came to stay with us, Georgie went and asked for my father's permission. Of course we were barely more than children, but Father refused to entertain the notion and promptly carted me off to London so I couldn't shame myself with him—that's what he'd said. Then you arrived in my life and I tried to forget what I couldn't have."

"Why didn't you simply run away with him? Your father would have come around in time, I'm certain of it."

"Not all fathers were willing to forgive every transgression like yours, Ruby." Tamsyn shot me a cross look. "Besides, my wants meant very little to him and I trusted my parents knew what was best for me, for my future. I tried to put him out of my mind, and George was going to marry Nellie anyway. Everything was as it was supposed to be. The proper order, Father called it. So when Edward offered for me during the war . . . he was precisely the sort of man Father wanted for me. And at the time . . . he gave me an alternative. A way out of all that."

"So you wouldn't have to settle for me," I grumbled, trying—and failing—to not sound aggrieved.

"You still aren't listening to me. How many times must I tell you this?" Tamsyn snapped. "My choices were never about you, they were about me. I was tired of the war. Tired of waiting for you to get yourself killed—or worse, tired of waiting to die. I wanted to go home, and back to the way things were before the war changed everything. I wanted peace, Ruby. You would never give me a peaceful life. You couldn't. And it would have all been fine had George stayed away like he'd promised."

"What do you mean like he'd promised?" Fiachna hopped up in my lap, settling himself there, and I ran my fingers over his silky fur.

"Georgie came back and . . ."

Georgie? The way she flipped between his given name and the nickname made me dizzy, then I realized what she was saying. Perhaps she was right that I didn't listen. A thought I wasn't about to dwell upon at present. "He's Jori's father, isn't he?"

Tamsyn nodded as she toyed with the edge of her skirt, her eyes fixed on the floor. "Edward knew right away. He was gone when . . . when it happened. He'd been in the city for business for months and while we might have fooled the village, Edward knew he wasn't the father."

Having the truth between us at last was a relief. No more swords drawn, no more fighting. It was one thing to quarrel with a stranger, another to do the same with someone who knew the very contours of your heart, as those battle wounds were far graver.

"Did Edward . . ."

She blinked the wetness back from her eyes. "I don't know. He was angry at first. George came here as soon as he found out, telling me we should run away and I wish . . . I wish I had but I was frightened. He was talking nonsense. Saying Edward wasn't the heir, that he had a plan. That everything would be right again if I'd just trust him."

"Edward wasn't the heir? Is that . . . is it true?"

Tamsyn shook her head. "I don't know who else would be if it wasn't Edward. His uncle died childless. Killed by the curse as was his wife." Tamsyn took on a shade of green. "According to the legend, any Chenowyth heir who marries beneath his station would die at the hands of the beast the old witch summoned."

"I told you, it's not a curse."

Tamsyn clenched her fist tight enough her skin grew white across the knuckles. "But it happened to Edward's uncle. He'd married beneath him as well. And me . . . I'm not gently born. Not like Edward was. His family is ancient. I'm the granddaughter of a butcher. What if *I'm* the reason that Edward is dead?"

I placed a hand on her shoulder. "You're not—and there's no such thing as curses. They're all about control. That's all any of those old stories are. Ways to keep girls like us from reaching too high. You can't possibly believe that the curse killed your husband, not when there are any number of angry husbands and brothers who would have done it themselves."

Mention of Edward's infidelity calmed her, though more likely it was the logic in my words. The only real question was who *didn't* want Edward Chenowyth dead? "Then you don't think that I'm in danger?"

I wanted to say no. Promise her that nothing was going to happen and that the worst was over, but I couldn't bring myself to lie. Because while I didn't truly believe in curses or demons, I'd nearly been stoned to death in the town, all because of a misunderstanding. "Do you think Edward could have had something to do with George's death?"

She shook her head. "No. That I'm sure of. We were . . .

well . . . George and I understood each other. After the war . . ." She held her hands up to silence me. "I know you don't like to go back there, but it changed me, Ruby. And it changed him too. He had returned home with every intention of picking back up with Nellie, despite the fact Edward had saddled her with his bastard. But when she looked at him . . ." Tamsyn bit her lip with a frown, grasping for the words that didn't want to come. "He told me when he looked at her, he saw all the things that the war stole from him. When he tried to talk to her, to speak of it, the words became like ash on his tongue."

"But he could talk to you?" I said softly.

"Broken people make the best companions. That's what he told me," she said with a frown. "And George, well, he had a bad war. Had a harder time adjusting to life at home than you or I. It changed us all—even Edward. I don't know how it couldn't affect one a little."

"Did he . . . tell you what he was going to do?"

She pulled a handkerchief from her pocket and twisted it in her hands, then shook her head. "No. But I wasn't surprised either. His mother. She didn't want to believe he'd done it. Neither did Nellie. But you should have seen him, Ruby. The man was eaten up with what he'd done in France. No one could reach him. Not in those last few days."

A lump formed in my throat as I remembered the way Mrs. Martin spoke of her grief. "Who found him?"

"Mr. Martin. He had half the village out looking for him when George didn't return from . . ." Her hand rose to her throat. "Oh God . . ."

"Had you seen him? What is it? What did you remember?"

Her eyes grew wide. "Honestly, Ruby, you can't think I'd hurt him. He's the father of my child. And . . . and if he were still alive I—"

"You'd be with him now," I finished. The words stung a little less than I'd expected.

"I love him. Even still. I know you can't understand, considering what I've done, and you think me fickle and foolish, but I . . . I wouldn't have harmed him for the world. We understood each other, George and I."

"Where was he before he disappeared? Tell me, Tamsyn."

"I sent him away and told him there was no future for us." She choked down a sob. "He'd been drinking and was going on about how he had found it. The answer to our problem. He wasn't making any sense at all."

A trickle of tension rose at the back of my throat. "Was Edward home when this happened?"

She shook her head. "He came home the next day, he'd been called away to London for business."

But I couldn't help but wonder if that was truly the case. There was a connection between the two deaths, I was convinced of it. I just hadn't pieced it together. Tamsyn was at the center of it all. But how? And why?

RUAN WAS AT the gate where I'd left him when we arrived an hour before. Lost in thought—or whatever it was that went on inside that frightening mind of his. His head was bowed down as he fumbled with something held between his hands. It was a vulnerable position, that of a man at prayer. He didn't see me nearing him, or if he did, he didn't respond. His head tilted low as he leaned against the old bronzework. Its ornate metal scrolls reaching high, catching in the sunlight that was finally peeking through the clouds.

"You knew George was Jori's father." It was an accusation and statement of fact rolled into one.

He didn't lift his head. "They'd been sweethearts off and on. I'd assumed so but it wasn't any of my affair."

"None of your affair? You, who make love charms, say this is none of your affair?"

He glanced up briefly with a slight tug at the side of his mouth. He lifted a finger. "Ah, but I don't make un-love charms. I couldn't mend Sir Edward's marriage any more than I can change the tides. It's none of my concern who is tupping who. I can neither control nor contain a soul's passions. What's the point in interfering?"

I arched a brow, the stitches there stinging with the movement. Blast it. "I could argue it's hypocritical of you to aid in one and not intervene in the other when one is having an *affair*."

"As you say."

"As I say?"

"Why do you care who the lad's father is?"

Good God, save me from hapless men. I took in a long breath. "Because her son isn't Edward's and Edward knew it. This could have some bearing on why there are two dead men in this charming little murder hamlet of yours."

That caught his attention. Ruan shifted slightly from where he leaned and glanced up. "Does anyone else know?"

I shook my head. "Besides Dr. Quick? I have no idea. I seriously doubt Tamsyn would bandy the fact about."

He wet his lips. "No. No. You're right. Edward doted on the boy as well. If he knew it wasn't his, he at least wasn't holding it against the child."

"There was no talk of the baby? Honestly I don't know how I didn't see it before. He looks nothing like Tamsyn or Sir Edward."

He shook his head slowly. "None that I'd heard. Just my

guessing from the way George spoke of her when we came back from France. I truly think he loved her."

Infuriating man. I frowned, half afraid to put the thoughts I had to voice. "What if the first victim of this murder isn't Edward at all? What if it's George? Or . . ." I trailed off before saying the part that I didn't want to admit. Not even to myself.

"What if it's the curse?"

I narrowed my gaze at him. It was unfair that he could do that.

"Try to not think so loudly, mmm?" Ruan frowned. The humor disappeared as he considered the idea. A faint dusting of silver stubble had sprung up on his cheek sometime between yesterday and today, giving him a wilder look than before—Ruan Kivell, when I first met him, looked only partly civilized. But now, disheveled as he was, his dark hair tangled and loose about his shoulders and whiskers forming on his jaw, he was a feral creature from my darkest imaginings. An image of him striding through the ancient Briton woods flickered to mind. More pagan priest than anything else.

He groaned as if in pain—interrupting my overly distracted imaginings. Good. He'd heard that too. That's what he got for eavesdropping. "Well, we'd best be off then."

I looked at him again in the clear light of day. No. He wasn't some sort of mythical thing. No matter what folks around here said. No matter what I saw, or thought I saw in the Martins' field that night. He was a man. No more and no less.

Chapter Twenty-five

Visitors in the Night

THE road back to Exeter was treacherous thanks to the recent flooding, causing the journey to take twice as long as it normally would. But I had my thoughts to keep me company, especially as Fiachna was sleeping off his adventures on the seat beside me. My body ached, my heart was sore, and my mind confused. I didn't begrudge Tamsyn her choices, at least not rationally. I suppose they made sense in a way. She longed for a past that was dead, and I longed for a future that had not yet been born. We were hopeless then, more so now.

I arrived home as the sky began to cloud up again, rising above the tall brick town houses from the latter part of the last century that flanked the narrow cobblestone street. Mr. Owen's residence took up the better part of the block, with a high iron fence blocking it from the street. I'd never in my life been happier to return here. Not since I first stood in this very spot on the sidewalk answering a newspaper advertisement. House for let, it said. Oh, I'd listened to the obsequious man who arrived before me, as he lectured Mr. Owen on how badly he'd kept up the old place. How the whole thing should be

202 · JESS ARMSTRONG

demolished and built again. It was obscene the things he'd said to Mr. Owen.

I tucked a sleeping Fiachna back into the luncheon basket and lifted it out of the car before walking up the granite steps. A large bronze knocker in the shape of the Green Man sat in the center of the black enameled door. I'd scarcely gotten my key in the lock when it flew open.

Mr. Owen stood there in his dressing gown, barefooted and looking as if he'd not slept in days. "I read all about it in the papers, my girl." His weathered old hand moved up to cup my cheek. His eyes were glassy as if he'd been weeping. "My poor lamb. What have they done to you?" In an uncharacteristic show of affection, he wrapped his arms around me, squeezing the breath right out of my lungs. In the last three years I'd shared his home, he'd never given me more than a tap on the shoulder or chuck on the chin as a reflection of his sentiment.

He held me there for several seconds, smelling of pipe smoke and old leather, before stepping back and shaking his head, but I couldn't mistake the wetness he wiped from his eyes. "I shall have a word with Mr. Kivell about this."

"It's thanks to him I'm not any worse."

"Oh, lass . . ." His voice cracked as he held my face in both his hands.

I shifted my basket-of-cat, eager to rid myself of my uninvited traveling companion. "Do you mind if I come in? We're making a scene here." It was then that he noticed the curious gaze of Mrs. Grimshaw, the greatest gossip in all of Exeter, craning her neck from across the street to watch our little tableau.

He grumbled beneath his breath about nosy bits of baggage and opened the door wider, ushering me in.

"You said something about the papers . . . ?" I'd not seen a newspaperman, only heard of one being in town. But I had been rather preoccupied in my short stay in Lothlel Green between the murder and my brush with death.

"Have you not heard? It's all over the country about the Pellar and the Heiress."

A ball of bile rose in my throat. I'd spent over a decade of my life blissfully out of the headlines only to be suddenly thrown back in the fray, and for reasons not of my own doing. "What are they saying?"

Mr. Owen took me by the arm, leading me down the hall. "The usual. Mostly it's Kivell they're interested in—poor lad— but it has the press in an uproar. You know how it is. Ever since the war ended, the occult has been all the rage. I'd be shocked if the lad won't be fighting off the charlatans before long."

"By the way, I am very cross with you on that score, you could have at least warned me what I was headed into."

The old man had the temerity to look offended. "Me? You know good and well if I'd told you about Ruan you'd have never set foot into Lothlel Green. Besides, I *did* say he was a folk healer."

He had me there. I wasn't about to tell him about the strange connection between Ruan and me; he'd get ideas. And it was never a good thing when Mr. Owen had *ideas*.

"I do regret it, though. I had no idea I was sending you into danger. Had I known, I'd never have let you go. I've lost too many children to risk you as well."

"I'm not your child."

He didn't respond, only tucked my hand into the crook of his arm and continued down the black-and-white-marble-tiled foyer hall. A fine sheen of dust had taken up residence in my absence. Mr. Owen must not have procured a replacement for our housekeeper yet. I rested my head on his shoulder as we followed the faint glow of light to his study, feeling wearier by the instant.

"What are your thoughts on what happened to Sir Edward?"

He nodded grimly as he settled himself into his chair and picked up his pipe, taking a puff from it. "Terrible business, curses."

"It's a disaster. What are they saying about him? I haven't the energy to read."

"Then sleep, lass. There's nothing in the papers that won't keep till morning." He waved a hand dismissively. "All they're saying is that it's stumped the local constabulary. 'Man or Mythical Beast' I believe is how they've been referring to it when they aren't commenting on the war-hero-turned-warlock." Smoke curled languidly up from his pipe. My eyes drifted upward with it to the dark wood-paneled ceiling, not so different from those at Penryth, and yet the two buildings were worlds apart. The townhome was comfortable, a grand lady in dishabille after a night of debauchery. Whereas Penryth was an older relation swathed in mourning crepe and drowning in her own grief.

"I don't believe a word of it. What really happened out there, Ruby? Tell me."

I shook my head. Unable to speak of it. Tomorrow. Tomorrow I'd tell him everything. I curled up in a large leather chair in front of the fireplace and rested my head on the high back. "Have you had any luck replacing Mrs. Adams?"

"As if you don't have more important things to concern yourself with."

"I concern myself with your comfort. And my own prospects for a proper breakfast. I have grown very spoiled by Tamsyn's housekeeper. I should have nicked some ginger biscuits before I left."

He laughed and shook his head. "Not as of yet, girl. Not as of yet. I'm glad you're home again. I don't care for the idea of you all alone out there with murderers afoot."

I yawned sleepily, pulling a soft knit blanket over my lap. "I'm not alone. I have Ruan. Besides, you'll have to get used to it as I'm back to Lothlel Green in the morning. I'm only here for the night. Is Dr. Heinrich in town? I've come to beg a favor of him."

"Are you feeling poorly? I would have thought Ruan would have mended you if something was amiss."

"No, no. We want him to look at Sir Edward's body. Get his opinion on things."

Mr. Owen made a sound of agreement and resumed reading his latest serial novel. I could have gone to my room. Probably ought to have, as I'd been fantasizing about being able to take a good soak in my bathing tub for at least twenty-four hours. The thought of rinsing away my troubles, then drifting off to sleep watching the night sky behind the spires of the cathedral appealed. But instead I was unwilling to leave the comfort of the old man. I hadn't had a glimpse of paternal affection in years—not since I left my father in America more than a decade ago now. He'd always been an indulgent patriarch. Too much so, Tamsyn's own father complained. Perhaps she was right, not all men were like my Papa. Though I imagined Mr. Owen and he would have gotten on rather well. My hand rose to my throat, toying with the gold chain there.

I fell asleep in the study to the low snore of Fiachna on the back of the chair, punctuated by the subtle sound of Mr. Owen's turning of pages. I was safe now. Far away from the horrors I'd seen in Lothlel Green. Far away from Ruan Kivell and whatever ancient and invisible cord bound us together.

I WAS BACK at Penryth Hall. Or someplace very like it. The flower-papered walls on either side of me quivered like the surface of a summer wheat field in the breeze. Rippling. Dancing.

There was a light in the distance. Faint and glowing. Flickering.

I followed after it.

With each step the walls swayed and trembled.

On and on I went, making my way through the maze-like corridors and up the undulating stairs.

Continuing, as a somnambulist would, until I at last reached the third floor.

And that was when I saw her.

The woman from the orchard. Standing at the end of the hall. More wraith than human. White robes billowing in the still air. I reached out to touch her, but she shook her faceless head and turned away from me.

Again, I followed. An automaton now—not a woman—wound and obeying the mechanics I'd been designed to perform. Emotionless walking. Watching.

The wraith paused outside a door, her bony hand outstretched, and turned the knob. The door swung wide as the walls around me began to melt. The flowers now weeping red wax as a great golden serpent slithered between my legs and after the wraith.

It turned.

I should have run. I should have screamed.

I did neither. I simply stared back into its hollow visage. The cold boring into my soul, robbing me of breath.

Then it turned away and entered the nursery, pausing over the cradle to gather up Jori where he lay sleeping.

I opened my mouth to cry out. To stop it. Anything.

But no sound came.

And then the air around me was rent with a scream.

* * *

BANING. SO MUCH banging. It took several seconds after I woke before I remembered where I was. Exeter. Yes. And someone was at the door. I jumped to my unsteady feet. The fire had died in the hearth.

It was just a dream.

A loud crack of thunder shook the house. A thick blanket lay pooled at my feet.

The pounding on the door continued. I reached down, grabbing the blanket and wrapping it around my shoulders as a bulwark against the cool night air. Pausing in the hall, I looked up at the great wooden grandfather clock. Half past two was rarely a propitious time for guests.

The hall table drawer scraped on its track as I reached in and withdrew Mr. Owen's ancient Webley revolver and confirmed it was loaded.

My breath grew surer as I finally shook the last remnants of my nightmare from my thoughts.

I pulled the bolt on the front door and slowly opened it, the gun in my left hand. Too damnably tired to be afraid of whatever might be on the other side.

"Ruby . . ."

It was Ruan. What was he doing here? He stood there huddled in the narrow portico, soaked to the bone, his hair plastered around his shoulders as he had been the evening he found me in the inn. His face as ominous as the flashing sky behind him.

Oh God, the dream. What if it hadn't just been a dream? My stomach clenched and I stumbled backward, squeezing my eyes shut, willing him to be just another aftereffect of exhaustion. It couldn't be happening again.

I opened my eyes. Throat tight.

He was still there. *Oh, no. Not again. Please not again.*

"Not again what?" He stepped inside, taking me by the shoulders.

I shook my head, unable to speak.

Get out of my head, Ruan Kivell.

Get out.

I blinked back tears until finally the words escaped. "Tell me. Tell me Jori's not dead. Please tell me he's not dead." I should have stayed at Penryth. Tamsyn was right to worry. She was right and I quarreled with her and didn't believe. I left her and now her son was dead.

My knees gave way and I slid down to the marble floor, tugging my legs to my chest.

"Ruby Vaughn, you're going to shoot me, put that thing down," Ruan grumbled as he stepped inside the doorway, pulling the revolver from my hands and setting it on the side table. "Jori is fine," he added curtly as water from his clothes dripped on the floor beside me. The door slammed shut behind him.

"Fine . . . ?" *Fine? Fine . . .* It took a few moments for those four sweet letters to settle into my mind, but once they did another thought struck me. One that hurt nearly as much as the first. "Tamsyn?"

"Also fine."

I nodded again, my breath coming a little steadier now. I hazarded a glance up at his face. His eyes were dark. Dangerous. "What's happened? You wouldn't have come if something wasn't wrong."

"We need you back." He took a step forward, placing his hand on my shoulder. Warm and damp from rain, but the strangest sensation crossed my body. A wave of calm washed over me from where his skin met mine. Shoulder to throat to mind, then down my spine, surging through my veins in a way not even the finest imported opium could provide. My breath eased. Heart slowed.

"There's been an attack," he said softly.

"Who?"

He shook his head. "There's plenty of time for that later. Go pack your things. We need to return."

My hand rose to my throat. "I should wake Mr. Owen . . . I . . . I shouldn't have left . . . Perhaps we'd have found the killer before . . ."

Ruan placed his forefinger beneath my chin, tilting me up to look him in the eye. "There's nothing you could have done. I don't think the boys were the intended target anyway. They're alive at least and Benedict and I thought it was quicker if I came to get you and bring you back with your doctor."

"Boys? Ruan, sit, you must tell me—"

"No . . ." He glanced warily down the darkened corridor. "I don't belong here. I wouldn't have come if it wasn't dire."

"Give me a few moments to get dressed and speak with Mr. Owen."

There was plenty of time to learn what had come to pass on the long drive to Lothlel Green. I would simply have to wait.

As I HADN'T unpacked my belongings, it was a simple matter readying myself to leave again. I latched my trunk, threw on a fresh ocher blouse and riding breeches—tied my woefully tangled hair back from my brow with a dotted scarf—then crept down to Mr. Owen's bedroom. His snore was loud even through the door. I rarely intruded on his privacy, except when he was ill of course. I knocked once. Another snortle.

Quietly I pushed the door open and came to his side, sitting down on his mattress and giving him a slight shake.

He startled awake. "What is it, girl? Is someone dead?"

"Ruan's come."

"Kivell's here?" The old man shifted himself to sitting. His white chest hairs poking out from atop his nightshirt. "Ruan Kivell's come *here*?" he repeated numbly. "To Exeter?"

I nodded.

Mr. Owen rubbed his face and groped along the nightstand for his spectacles. "Then it must be grave indeed to summon him this far from home."

"There's been another attack, I don't know the details but I need to get back. Can you be sure to bring Dr. Heinrich to Lothlel Green first thing in the morning?" I glanced out the window as another crack of lightning rent the sky.

"You know I cannot drive, lass."

I bit my lip, watching the stormy darkness out his window. "I have to go. Tonight. Let Heinrich take my automobile."

Mr. Owen let out a cynical laugh. "You're letting that Hun drive your Crow Elkhart?"

I pressed a kiss to his brow. "You had said you were growing bored of Exeter. Perhaps this is what you need. A vacation to clear your head." My voice lighter than my heart as his hand covered mine. "Come with him." *I need you there.* I didn't want to voice the fact. But I did. There are times a girl wants her father. And despite my protestations to the contrary earlier, Mr. Owen was the closest thing I had to one.

"Be safe, lass. Promise me that."

"I'll see you in a few hours. All right?" I didn't wait for his response, just turned and hurried back to Ruan and the long road to Lothlel Green.

The way was treacherous and slick as Benedict navigated the darkened path in his farm truck, a carryover from army days redone to serve less violent purposes. If I'd thought the roads bad earlier, they were doubly so now in the height of the storm. Visions of the three of us drowning in an overswollen stream flicked through my mind as I sat in the darkness.

I closed my eyes. "Tell me."

Ruan nodded as we hit a large rut, throwing us both against the edge of the truck, the back of my head narrowly missing the side paneling. A small mercy. "Jago and another lad were attacked in the woods behind the churchyard."

"Jago . . . wasn't he the one—" *who'd tried to get me killed?*

"Mmm. The same. No one knows what they were doing out there, but lads do what they do. Charles has been very tight-lipped about it. He ran into the village to get help. By the time the others came, they found Jago lying in his own blood."

I sucked in a sharp breath. "Is he . . ."

Ruan shook his head, laying a hand over my own, warm and reassuring. "He's alive. He hasn't woken yet. It'll be good to have a real physician in the morning to tend to him. Make sure I haven't missed anything."

"Ruan, you know you're as good as many a properly trained doctor. I've seen plenty of them during the war, and what you did for me . . . it was remarkable."

He might have flushed under my praise, but it was too dark to tell in the back of the truck. He cleared his throat. "Yes, but this is the bit that worries me."

"Worrying a Pellar? That doesn't sound good."

"A wraith attacked them. That's what Charles said. That a wraith did it. He's nonsensical. It's all he would say. *The wraith, the wraith.* And then he wouldn't speak another word. I thought that maybe—maybe he'd talk to you."

"Me?" The faceless being from my dream flickered to my mind. I swallowed hard, hands shaking in the darkness. What if the killer was a *thing* after all? I wet my lips, not quite ready to voice the concern. "What do you think I can do?"

"I mended them up as best I could, but I . . ." He paused and I heard him shift in the darkness. There was something he wasn't telling me. "I have a feeling about you. And I can't say whether I hope or fear that I'm right."

"About me?"

Ruan sighed and leaned his head against the side of the truck. His body visibly exhausted. "Ignore me. I'm nattering on. See if you can get him to speak, Ruby. I don't know what else I can do."

I gave him an unsteady nod as his large hand covered my own and the trembling ceased at once. Wraith or man or curse come to life, we had to find this killer and stop it once and for all.

Chapter Twenty-Six

A Professional Perspective

DR. Heinrich was an eccentric older gentleman. German, as his name betrayed, but his family had been in Britain for at least a century. He had no hair remaining atop his head, and silver eyebrows, but his beard was black as jet. He wore a stern dark suit, with the only flash on him being a silver pocket-watch chain that dangled, catching my eye where it swung jauntily before him. He and Mr. Owen arrived at Ruan's cottage approximately three hours after we did, and we immediately brought him to the injured boy's bedside.

Dr. Heinrich leaned over young Jago, who slept steadily. He looked nothing like the angry boy from the Hind and Hare; he was smaller now and appeared a handful of years younger than his age. Despite the harm he'd caused me, a deep anger rose in my chest that someone—something—would harm him, a child. Perhaps there was a mote of Christian charity left in my blackened heart after all.

A deep cut sliced through the side of his face but had been stitched up neatly. Ruan's hand, I suspected. Jago's stricken mother watched from the corner, her fists knotted in her skirt, frustrated agitation visible. She couldn't be much older than I was, if that, but she looked a dozen years more.

"This is deft work, whoever did it," Dr. Heinrich mumbled to himself as he held the boy's wrist in his hand. His lips moved as he counted to himself. "I don't think I've seen such clean stitching in years. I certainly couldn't have done a finer job."

I glanced over my shoulder at Ruan, who shifted uncomfortably at the doctor's words.

"Ah, that'd be our Pellar," Jago's mother said with a note of pride in her voice.

Dr. Heinrich began to question, his brows drawn up and mouth opened, but I caught his eye and shook my head.

He nodded in understanding. We'd discuss this later. He placed a hand on the boy's shoulder. "He's well enough. I suspect he'll wake no worse for wear. I see no reason for him not to."

"And the scar?" his mother asked, twisting her stained apron in her hands.

"Should heal well enough. But this . . ." He picked up a jar of salve on the bedside table and unscrewed it, sniffing it for a moment. His eyes then went to Ruan with a strange expression. "You made this for him, did you?"

Ruan nodded gruffly.

"Mind if I buy some off you? I'd like to try it in my practice."

Ruan made a stern sound of assent, uncertain what to do with the olive branch that Dr. Heinrich offered.

I excused myself into the front drawing room where the other boy sat anxiously on a wooden chair, his hair long and face dirty. Charles, I think, was the name Ruan gave me. I had no idea what he thought I could do, how I could make a boy speak to me when any number of people who had known him his whole life had failed to do the same.

"You're Ruan's witch!" he said, eyeing my breeches curiously.

"I suppose I am." I still didn't care for the moniker, but as long as it wasn't being hurled alongside stones, I could learn to live with it.

"How is Jago?" he asked softly. "My mam almost wouldn't let me come."

I sank down on the sofa beside him. "He's fine. I brought a physician friend from Exeter back with me. Dr. Heinrich says your friend should wake up soon. And you? How are you faring?"

He shook his head tight-lipped.

"I don't blame you. I don't like to talk about things like that either."

Charles bore a few scratches on his face, but nothing else of note. "They wouldn't understand."

"That's my experience as well. But these people care for you, they want you to be well. So sometimes you do have to . . ." I paused and cocked my head to one side, touching his hand softly. "Sometimes you have to trust that they'll try to understand. Even if they might not be able to." I thought back to what Tamsyn had said when we quarreled last. How adamant she'd been that I kept everyone outside my armor. Was Charles trying to do the same?

Something in my words must have rung true, as instantly his body relaxed, his shoulders sagged, and he shook his head. "It was frightful, miss . . ."

"I can imagine so. It did a number on young Jago's face."

He closed his eyes and drew in a shaky breath. He couldn't be more than fifteen, if that. Not so much younger than I was when I left New York on that steamship.

"I don't know rightly what it was."

"Can you try to describe it . . . what you saw? It might help Mr. Kivell if you can tell me precisely how it happened. Do you think you can do that, Charles?"

His hand remained beneath mine. Still and warm. From beyond the tightly drawn curtains, I began to hear voices. People were gathering, but Charles didn't hear them. Instead he was staring at the back of my hand. "I'll never forget it, miss. Never."

I squeezed his hand again.

"It was in white, all white like a ghost from the Christmas pageant. Except instead of holly, it had a claw. I'd never seen such a thing. Sharp and glistening in the morning light." He gestured with his free hand, drawing a bit of a hook in the air with his two fingers.

"Glistening? Was it a knife?"

"I only saw it for a moment. I was so afraid, miss. But I don't . . ." He stumbled over his words, swallowing hard. "I know it sounds odd to say, considering how bad Jago is, but I don't think it was after us. Not truly."

"Not after you? What makes you say that?"

He wet his lips, dropping his voice to a whisper. "It told us to run."

"It *spoke* to you?"

He nodded, eyes wide. "It did. Hissing out some infernal thing. Said to leave. Run away. I ain't no fool, miss, I ran. But Jago, he . . ."

"He what . . ."

"He fought back."

"Did he do any damage?" It was a hopeful question. After all, if the boy had harmed his attacker, it should be as simple as looking for someone with a corresponding wound.

"I don't know." His voice cracked with the admission. "I . . . I didn't think meself a coward but I ran . . . Jago." He shook his head and brushed away tears with his other hand. "When I realized he wasn't following me I went back. That's when I found him. But the ghost was gone."

I let go of his hand and took him squarely by the shoulders, forcing him to look at me, much as Ruan had done the night before. "You're not a coward. You did right, Charles. It was the sensible thing to do, to run. And you brought help. If you hadn't gone back with the others, he might have died like Sir Edward."

I still had a difficult time believing it was some sort of creature after them, despite the very otherworldly description Charles provided. Ghost. Wraith. Curse. Whatever it was supposed to be. Though after this sighting, it was clear the village would never let that pass. Someone around here meant to do harm, but who was it after? And why? It was one thing when it was a single man killed in an unusual way, but a sighting of a murderous ghost attacking mere boys? That was another thing entirely.

The commotion outside grew louder. At least a dozen voices clamoring for attention.

I moved to the window, pulling the curtain back to reveal a crowd outside. Folks not from here by the cut of their clothes, men and women alike dressed more suited to London than Lothlel Green.

"Were they here when you arrived, Charles?" I asked him with a deep frown.

"Three newspapermen and a photographer. They wanted to take my picture but I wouldn't let them. So was she."

I growled low in my chest. These must be the ones Mr. Owen warned me of. The press and charlatans both. And then my eyes lit on *her*. It was the woman I'd spotted outside Dr. Quick's. She must be the one who had been asking for Ruan. The one spotted at the crossroads. She stood apart from the rest. Youngish, middle-aged at most. With a Roman nose and keen golden eyes keeping a watchful presence over the crowd. She was dressed in an old-fashioned black gown, a decade or more out of fashion, but it was clean and pressed. Her hair was dark like a raven's wing and falling loosely around her shoulders. There was an odd stillness about her, a sense that if I didn't know better, I'd have imagined her a statue, frozen in place. In time.

"What about the woman? Is she the one the townsfolk have been talking about?"

He nodded grimly. "Yes, ma'am. Something's not right about her. I saw her a time or two at the crossroads asking after Mr. Kivell."

"Did you tell her anything about him?"

He shook his head. "I don't like the looks of her, miss. I know it's not right to say, but anyone who has business with the Pellar knows where to find him. So why didn't she just go on to his cottage like everyone else does?"

My sentiment exactly. Curiosity and caution warred within me. I could go speak with her, find out once and for all what she wanted with Ruan and no one would be any the wiser. But something told me not to. She was after Ruan. And that was a thought I didn't like one bit. No. We'd take the back door. There was something wrong about her, terribly wrong.

HOURS LATER, AFTER having narrowly avoided the crowd outside of Jago's house and somehow placing the woman in black squarely from my mind, Ruan and I were strolling through the gardens at Penryth. Dr. Heinrich remained sequestered with Sir Edward's body. He'd shooed us both away over an hour ago in order to focus upon his *work*, though I was beginning to think that Ruan's proximity unnerved him much as he did everyone else in this village.

Everyone except me. "What do you make of what Charles

said?" I walked slightly ahead of him, along the path between yew hedges. The air sweet and green.

"It doesn't fit with the previous killings, nor Sir Edward's either. And if we *were* to entertain the possibility of the curse—"

I sucked in my breath. I did *not* want to entertain that possibility.

"*If . . .*" Clearly he didn't either. "Then it wouldn't have gone after the boys. They have nothing to do with the Chenowyths."

"Then do you think they are involved somehow? That they saw something? Did something to offend the killer?" I shot Ruan a glance over my shoulder.

Ruan pressed his lips together in thought. "They're troublesome lads I grant you, but I cannot fathom what mischief they could have gotten into that would lead them to this. Neither ever worked on the estate, or had any dealings with the baronet."

"Which only means they had to see something."

Ruan nodded thoughtfully, pushing a low-hanging branch out of our way. "Or got in the way. But of what . . . I don't think they even know what they saw out there."

The edge of my mouth curved up, despite the twinge of my cut. "Then you still agree with me the killer is human?"

"Of course I do."

Which was a relief, as I was beginning to doubt everything. "I'm still not convinced they didn't make it up."

"No. They saw something. Charles for certain. I'll have to wait until Jago's awake to speak with him. Perhaps he got a better look at it."

"Did you . . ." I didn't want to put it into words but Ruan gave me a grim nod.

"What's it like . . . eavesdropping on people's thoughts? I still have a hard time wrapping my mind around it."

He chuckled beneath his breath and shoved a hand into his coat pocket. "Bloody inconvenient."

I could imagine. I rather enjoyed not knowing what people thought of me. To be subjected to their most unfettered thoughts and feelings with no control must be hell.

Something shifted in his expression, and he turned me to face him, gently holding me by the shoulders. "It is, you cannot—" But whatever he was about to say was interrupted as we heard the telltale sound of footsteps on the gravel. I spun out of his grip to see Dr. Heinrich coming up the path, wild with excitement.

"You found something?" I called out, hurrying down the path to meet him.

Dr. Heinrich twirled his silver pocket watch by its chain. "Indeed. The marks on the body match those on the lad. Whatever weapon sliced up Edward Chenowyth is most certainly the same one used for the boy. A blade of some sort. Curved. Very sharp."

Ruan shot me a victorious look. Bastard.

"But I found something very intriguing that I think might interest you both." He glanced between the two of us, pausing for dramatic emphasis. Dr. Heinrich, while overly erudite, had a penchant for theatrics. It was why he came to my salons in the first place. After all, a man can only be so staid and proper before becoming an absolute bore.

"Well, get on with it."

"Ever the impatient one, Miss Vaughn." The doctor laughed. He tucked his pocket watch away and folded his arms across his chest, puffing it out proud as a prized peacock. "Edward Chenowyth was poisoned."

"He was what?"

"I'm certain of it. He was dead several hours before he was carved up like a Christmas goose."

My stomach heaved slightly at the memory. Good God, I might never eat meat again after this venture.

"Mr. Owen said you had some notes about the previous set of killings. Do you still have them? I'd fancy taking a look at them if you don't mind."

Oh! I'd almost forgotten all about Dr. Quick's diary. "They're back at the cottage. If you come with us, I can let you have them. Perhaps they'll help us determine if there's a connection between them?"

He nodded slightly, his forehead screwed up in thought.

"Do you know what the poison was?"

He shook his head. "I can't be certain, his stomach contents are in a state of decomposition. I'd need my laboratory back in Exeter to do much more with this. Or a fresh body."

"Well, hopefully we won't have any more of those," I said with the nagging sensation that we would indeed have another; the only question was whose and how soon.

CHAPTER TWENTY-SEVEN

The White Witch Returns

THE birds sang out along the hedge by the dirt path as we made our way back to the cottage from Penryth Hall. Ruan was quiet in thought, a strange and new undercurrent of tension flickering between us. One that hadn't been there when I left Lothlel Green yesterday. I'd only caught glimpses of it here and there since returning, but with Dr. Heinrich's proclamation of poison it became crystal-clear—Ruan was afraid. But of what? We walked together toward the cottage, a deep divot between Ruan's brows, as he mumbled to himself beneath his breath. Something quiet enough I didn't have a prayer of understanding.

And that was when I saw her. Again. The solitary figure at the junction where the rutted road curved upward to Ruan's cottage just as Benedict had described the night of the storm, when he offered her a ride. Unease ran up into my throat at the sight of her. The woman's uncannily bright eyes were fixed upon us. She'd been waiting. She knew where we'd been and where we were going.

I grabbed Ruan by the arm, halting him. "We should go back. I . . . I don't think we should speak to her."

The muscles in his arm tensed as he glanced up. He must have not seen her before. Ruan furrowed his brow before brushing my temple with this thumb. The tightness in my chest began to dissolve. Slowly at first, but with growing intensity.

"You're terrified," he whispered.

"I'm not afraid. I simply don't like the look of her. She was back in town as well, watching Jago's house. Charles told me she's been asking about you. This is the woman. The one everyone has spoken of. I'm certain of it."

"All the more reason to see what she wants. Don't tell me you're afraid of witches, Ruby Vaughn." His unusual eyes sparkled with the barest hint of teasing. The wind was picking up again as we drew nearer to her. Cool and angry, with the first few spitting drops of rain. I hastily wiped them from my cheek.

She possessed the same strange agelessness Ruan did. Or perhaps it was just my imagination. The only signs that she wasn't carved in stone were the way her eyes would follow Ruan along with the faint rise of her chest beneath the dark fabric. She didn't pay me any mind at all.

Only him.

Always him.

And I loathed her. For no reason at all, other than I knew she was a threat to us. *Us?* The word came to my mind on its own. But it was true all the same.

"I've been looking for you, Pellar." She lifted a finger pointing at his chest, revealing a pair of brightly pigmented enamel bracelets—the only hint of color on her.

Ruan's nostrils flared in annoyance and the muscle in his jaw tightened. He wasn't as unfazed by her as he pretended. I wasn't certain if that knowledge made it better or worse. "And what need have you of me?" he called out.

"Need?" Her voice rose shrilly "Need you, Pellar? What need I of a whelp?"

The air grew still around us, as if even the wind was afraid to intercede between the two of them. Perhaps nature was wiser than I. "Well, if you haven't need of him, I do. Come along, Ruan." I grabbed his wrist to tug him away from the crossroads and back to his cottage, but he remained steadfast. Not giving an inch.

"I have no need of a Seventh. It's you who needs me, boy. I bring a warning to you."

"Well, you could have left a note like ordinary folk," I grumbled, my fingers remained loosely around Ruan's forearm.

The woman gave me a sharp look. "You do not understand our ways. You understand *nothing*, morvoren-born. Your kind never do."

My kind? I bristled. How dare she speak to me in such a way.

Ruan jerked to attention at her words, whether in defense of me or something else, I didn't know. "Who are you, witch?"

"It's none of your concern who I am and who I'm not."

Something in her voice gave me pause. In the chilly cadence, or perhaps Ruan's response to it, giving me the distinct feeling that I was interrupting something. Something ancient that I had fallen into entirely by accident.

"I was once as you are. Overproud and certain in my powers. Failing to read the signs just as you fail to heed them." Her frenzied words grew more rapid as she fixed all her intensity upon the man at my side.

Ruan's breath caught in his chest as he glanced to me, then back to the woman. Yet his pulse remained steady and slow as always beneath my fingers. "Who are you? How do you—?" He took a step toward her, but he was bound by my grip. I was afraid. For the first time in my life, I was afraid of what might happen if I let him free. My fingers tightened.

She laughed, her voice rich and deep. "Because I see things. Things that have come to pass, things that are not yet written. Just as you hear the truth, boy—I see it. Whilst I may not be the Seventh, I have seen your path. The curse will not take you as it once tried to take me, but she—" The woman pointed a finger at me. "She will destroy you. Take everything from you until you have returned to the earth from which you were born. Leave the morvoren-born behind, Pellar. She can bring you nothing but death." Her gaze softened as she looked at him, pleading now. "They are not for our like. Heed me, boy, and look to the heir. Look to the heir, Pellar, before it's too late."

A cold wind rose up, from the lowlands below, howling through the trees and setting the chill deep into my bones as the raindrops fell from the gray skies.

I tugged again on Ruan's arm. *We should go.*

He heard me. He must have, as he swallowed audibly, shaken by what she had told him. For a moment I thought he might resist; then whatever war was raging within his mind concluded, and I felt the moment of surrender in my fingertips. I let him go, and he turned and followed me away, back toward his cottage as the bitter rain fell in earnest. I thrust a hand into my hair to push it back from my brow, trying to put my mind around what had happened. The woman had to be mad. She had to be, and yet I knew to the very marrow of my being that there was truth in her words.

She knew of the bond between Ruan and I. An impossible bit of knowledge, yet she had sensed it.

Ruan muttered something beneath his breath in a language I didn't know. Cornish, most like, which was just as well as I didn't have the heart to hear his thoughts. We had made it perhaps a dozen steps away with her hot gaze boring into us when her voice rang out again. "I have seen it written. Forsake her, Pellar, or you will die before the year is out."

Ruan's nostrils flared and eyes flashed with a dark fire, and he spun on his heels away from the woman and stormed back to his cottage as the fickle Cornish weather turned again.

He didn't slow down until he'd nearly reached the crest of the hill. The roof of his cottage peeked up through the mist and fog just ahead.

"Ruan . . . what was that word she said? *Morvoren?*"

He shook his head angrily, every muscle in his body wound bow-tight. "It's nothing. Just the ravings of a madwoman . . . Pay it no mind."

I didn't think so. Not the way he responded to it.

I'd just slipped a bit in the mud when something else struck me.

The dark hair.

The clothes.

The crossroads.

It all suddenly came into perfect focus. A sense of fatal dread settled into my belly. "Ruan . . ."

He continued storming back toward his cottage, boots sticking in the mud with each step. I hurried after him, reaching for his elbow to tug him back.

"Ruan . . . stop and look at me."

He paused and spun around, slicking his rain-wet hair back from his brow, both hands resting futilely atop his head. There was a pain in his expression. A forlorn exhaustion that was unmistakable. The woman's words had broken something in him. And I hated her doubly so. "What is it, Ruby?"

I hesitated for a moment. "Could . . . could she be the White Witch of Launceton?"

He started to deny it out of hand, but then his eyes met

mine and I saw it on his face. The emotions rifled through him like the pages of a book. The denial. The possibility. Then the panicked acknowledgment of truth. "*Look to the heir,*" he whispered with a shake of his head. "Gods, I've been a fool." He swore loudly before taking me firmly by the shoulders. "Get to Penryth, quick as you can. I'll go for Enys and then find the witch."

"Jori. It's after Jori," I breathed out, understanding the warning. The dream had told me, if only I'd believed in it. Believed in the unbelievable.

Look to the heir, Pellar.

"Go, Ruby. Run!" he shouted, and we both darted off in the rain in opposite directions. He to the village, and I to Penryth Hall. Where I prayed the bells did not toll.

CHAPTER TWENTY-EIGHT

As It Might Have Been

I was soaked to the bone by the time I reached the estate grounds, huffing and puffing, my side aching. I no longer felt the cold, the wet—any of it. My sole focus, sole thought was to reach Jori. To not be too late.

I was always too late.

But it was quiet when I burst through the front doors of the house. "Tamsyn!" I shouted, racing through the halls. "Tamsyn!" I called out again, until I finally came upon her in the morning room with Dr. Heinrich. She set her teacup down on the saucer.

Alive. Safe. The information barely registered into my mind.

"Ruby, you look like you've seen a ghost!"

I wasn't quite sure I hadn't.

She shot up from her seat, coming to me. Taking my face in her hands. The ridges between her brows grew deeper. "What's happened? Dr. Heinrich . . ." She turned to him.

The doctor hurried over, cosseting me as I tried to spit out what had occurred at the crossroads, but all I could get out was a feeble, "Where's Jori?"

Tamsyn placed her palm on my clammy brow. "You need a

bath, and a hot bottle. Jori's fine. He's with Mrs. Penrose, what has happened?"

"Let me see him. The boy. Let me see him."

Tamsyn nodded uncertainly, taking me by the hand and leading me to the kitchens, where Jori was standing on a bench, drawing shapes with his finger in flour. He looked up at his mother and beamed. "Mama!"

"Satisfied?" Tamsyn asked me.

I gave an unsteady nod, and let her lead me up to my room to change. They were safe. For now. But I could only guess how long that would remain true.

RUAN MUST HAVE located Enys quickly, because not long after I'd taken a cursory cloth to the mud that splattered my body and put on a dry frock, the men arrived from the village— only a handful, but heavily armed. As the hours passed and I received no further word from Ruan, I began to try to reason away my worries. It was absurd to think I would harm him, and that woman—whoever she was—was a liar. A charlatan as Mr. Owen warned. He said they would come, and come they did—never mind the fact she'd been in town before the news-papermen. Likely before Sir Edward was even killed.

Two cups of tea—and a considerable amount of brooding— later, I had managed to convince myself that it was simply my exhaustion causing me to leap to conclusions. It was far more likely that the woman at the crossroads was somehow involved in the killings and just trying to frighten us off, and not actu-ally the White Witch. Though that hypothesis didn't bode well for Ruan hunting her down, but he was a grown man who'd been to war and back—and was beyond able to take care of himself. My focus needed to remain at Penryth. It was a better use of my time to be hunting through Sir Edward's things for clues, than it was fretting that somehow I was going to kill Ruan Kivell. The idea was preposterous.

Constable Enys had performed a cursory sweep of the estate in the hours after Edward's death, but no one had looked terribly closely into his personal affairs—believing in the killer's tricks. A faint glimmer of hope dwelled in my chest, the idea that somewhere among Sir Edward's nightshirts and handkerchiefs would be some tiny bit of ephemera linking him to his dead uncle, or even to George Martin. The missing piece of one of those jigsaw picture puzzles that would make everything clear to me. Then again, it was always more than one lost piece needed to figure out a puzzle. And so far, I was short an entire box.

After supper I passed the guards that Enys had stationed by the doors. They were hearty-enough-looking fellows, and I couldn't help but feel a bit safer with their presence here. I started down the darkened hallway for my room.

"Ruby!" Tamsyn cried out from behind me. I spun on my heels. She was standing in the doorway by the library, a flood of warm light washing out onto the dark wood halls casting deep shadows across the floor.

"Is everything well?" My eyes searched her face, looking for some clue. But she simply smiled and shook her head. Her hand rose up to her cheek and then she dropped it again. She'd changed her clothes after supper, now dressed in a fine green silk robe over a white nightdress.

"Where's Jori?"

She tilted her chin to the floor above. "With his nurse. Enys put a pair of guards outside his room and another inside. I suspect he's better tended than the Prince of Wales."

Despite my conviction that the killer was mortal, I couldn't shake my dream. I'd seen someone—something—try to take him. Tamsyn retreated deeper into the library and I followed along, linked by our shared past and our present troubles.

She refilled her sherry from the sideboard, and then poured a second for me, pressing it into my palm. A jolt of awareness shot through my fingers as hers brushed my own. I swallowed down the confused emotion and took a drink from my glass. But instead of assuaging the sensation, it only made it worse. I'd had lovers since and I most certainly would have lovers after, but what I shared with Tamsyn was legions beyond all of that. There was a closeness between us, an intimacy that surpassed the physical. But seeing the changes in her since the war, the secrets she'd carried alone, and the newfound shadows in her eyes muddled my thoughts—as if I could only make her out through frosted glass. I thought I'd understood her once, known her as well as I'd known myself. But the way she spoke to me now, the things she said, I realized that perhaps I never had understood her. She was a stranger, perhaps she'd always been and I was too foolish to notice.

Tamsyn pressed her lips to the glass and frowned. "Is it better or worse that it's not the curse? I admit I cannot decide."

My fingers rose again involuntarily to the bruises at my throat. We had not spoken of the curse since my return, and it shocked me that Tamsyn had reached the same conclusion I had. "What makes you change your mind now? Especially with that odd woman threatening Jori?"

She ran a hand over her lap, smoothing her already smooth skirts. "Dr. Heinrich is such an interesting man. I think he finally talked me 'round this morning. What with how Edward was killed, not to mention the attack on the boys. There is no reason for the curse to strike outside the Chenowyth line. I suppose it should be a relief, and yet it's a bit more troubling in some aspects."

I chewed my thumb, sinking down onto a low sofa. "Do you know if Edward had any dealings with them. Jago or Charles? Did he know either of them?"

Her dressing gown shimmered nearly black in the dim lighting as she sat beside me. Outside I could hear the low voices of Enys's men, too quiet to make out what they said, but they provided an odd bit of reassurance.

"Not as far as I know. I'd only seen them at church and Edward never set foot inside the place. Have you any ideas?"

Not a one. "We drink? It's typically what I do when out of decent alternatives."

She giggled, tinking her glass gently into my own. "An excellent notion." She hesitated for a moment before looking at me with a sober expression. "I feel wretched that I'm so relieved. There is a murderer out there." She swung her glass to the open window. "And those poor boys could have been killed, and yet I can't help but be happy that it's not the curse."

I rested my head on her shoulder and closed my eyes. "No, darling. It's only human. Besides, I think we should celebrate that you are no longer to be in fear of your life. Though you might need to be concerned about the state of your storerooms."

She wrinkled her nose. "I know . . . don't remind me that Edward is down there still. He's to be buried in two days, and not a moment too soon."

"I meant because of your housekeeper. Did you know she's been cooking for my cat?"

Tamsyn snorted and took another sip, licking the drink from her lips. "Oh, yes, there isn't a creature Mrs. Penrose wouldn't take under her wing. Did I ever tell you about the pig?"

"Pig?" Something nibbled at the edge of my thoughts and I batted it away.

Tamsyn's face grew animated as she smiled, leaned back into the settee, and crossed her legs. "Last summer, she found an enormous sow running loose in woods, sorely neglected. It'd been there for weeks and she'd failed to be able to corral it. Then one day she stumbled across it caught with a leg in a trap. The thing was nearly dead. So Mrs. Penrose stormed back to the house, got a rope, and led the wretched beast back into the paddock and spent the next week finding its owner."

"And did she?"

Tamsyn nodded, her hair slipping from the comb holding it back. "Mmm. She did and gave him a right tongue-lashing too. Refused to give the pig back. It was breeding too. Can you imagine someone being so careless with their livestock as to let a breeding pig run loose?"

Another prick at the back of my neck as I recalled the bottle Ruan had found beneath my bed on the very first night at Penryth Hall. A fetal pig he'd said it was. I wasn't quite sure I wanted to know more and yet I had to ask. "And what happened to it?"

"Oh, Edward planned to shoot it and have it cured for the winter larder once it'd had its litter, but Mrs. Penrose wouldn't hear of it." Tamsyn laughed. "Of course, the creature eats better than the rest of the household. Honestly, I think if the world wouldn't think her mad, she'd let it live in the house with us, put it up on the third floor with satin bedclothes. But it is rather nice for a pig. Jori likes to take it sweets."

"And the piglets? You said it was breeding."

"Lost most of them. But I allowed her to give the survivors to the poor in the village."

I laughed at that, the unease loosening a bit. A woman who gave away piglets to the poor was not about to put an ill wish beneath my bed.

The idea was absurd. I drank down some more of the expensive sherry and rested my head along the back of the sofa. "I must admit I'm rather fond of your eccentric housekeeper."

"She's a lot like you. One wouldn't know it to meet her, but she has the kindest heart of anyone I've ever met. Once she takes a soul into her affection, there's nothing she wouldn't do to keep them safe. Another way she reminds me of you. You were always so fierce, Ruby. With far too much heart—I suppose that's why you've always locked it away from everyone."

That selfsame organ seized up at her words. I kept my eyes closed, massaging the back of my neck with the edge of the sofa. Rocking back and forth. It was seductive to be with her like this. Easy and unafraid in our conversation. Almost as it used to be, and for a moment I understood why Tamsyn dwelled in the past. And while I wanted to give in, to surrender to this moment, there was something about this new Tamsyn I could not trust, and it burned that I couldn't puzzle out the reason.

"What's wrong?"

My body must have told the truth that my words would not. I shifted away from her and took a sip of the wine. "I've not slept properly in over two days."

"Well, I'm glad you're here. Regardless the reason."

"Have you any new thoughts as to who might want to kill Edward?"

She fetched the bottle of sherry and brought it back to the sofa, refilling both our glasses for yet another time and settling it in the cushions between the two of us to save a return trip. "Anyone. Honestly, he was abominable. You should have seen the way he treated the staff here."

"I still cannot fathom why you stayed, even if I grant you your reasons to have married him in the first place."

She took in a deep breath through her nose. "Please don't

quarrel with me. Not today, Ruby." She reached out, taking my hand and twining her fingers in mine.

I closed my own around hers. No, not today, then.

I'm not certain if it was the wine or simply her presence pulling me back to our girlhood days—the time before my parents died, long before the war, when we were into mischief. Much like Jago and Charles. Somehow, we found ourselves with a second bottle of wine in Edward's room. Clumsily rummaging through his drawers, a pair of drunken thieves searching for treasure.

"Property disputes?" I suggested, dumping out his hand-kerchiefs onto the bed and shuffling through them.

"No. Nothing recently." She popped her head out from his wardrobe, hand still in a dinner jacket pocket.

I giggled to myself, taking another sip of wine and wobbling a bit on my feet. "Not recently? Murder is murder. Come now, Tams, think!"

She laughed. It was wrong to be cavalier with her when her husband had been killed. Edward. A darkness crept over my thoughts. "He didn't strike you, did he? That bruise . . . I know you said before that—"

"And it's the truth. Edward never raised a hand to me. I'm certain you won't believe me—I wouldn't if it were me—but it's the God's honest truth." Suddenly the color drained from her face as her eyes fixed upon the bruises at my throat. "You don't think that whoever harmed you could have tried the same to me?"

I hadn't thought of that. Not truly. My throat grew thick at the idea, but Mrs. Penrose did say that the room I'd slept in was Tamsyn's favorite. I swallowed down the fear and lied. "No. No, I don't think so. I'm sure it was just an accident as you said."

She sighed, and I couldn't be certain if she believed me or

just went along with the farce. "I know I should have left him. I thought about doing it dozens of times. It's only that I couldn't ever come up with a good enough reason. He was respectable and I had a comfortable life here. It made it simpler to excuse his bad behavior when he wasn't quite as horrible as he could have been. Besides, by the time I made up my mind to leave, I already had Jori. He'd have never let me take his heir away."

The conversation sat uneasily with me, so I returned to safer waters. "No property disputes then? What about business deals? Did he cheat anyone out of money?"

She thought on that for a moment, tilting her head before deciding against it. "No. But the man had rutted with almost every single woman between here and Exeter. Does that count?"

"For what it's worth, I don't think it could be related to his sexual adventures."

She shook her head. "Me either, if it were, surely someone would have done the job ages ago."

I snorted, returning to the dresser. "Ah, well, onward I dig." I stooped down to the ground and ran my hand under the empty spot where the drawer I'd removed had been. Nothing. "What's in here, you suppose?" My fingers traveled along the base of a particularly deep drawer. "You know in stories there's always a secret compartment. Something very clever. Hiding important things. But I tell you something—"

"Ruby—"

I glanced over my shoulder and she smiled. The sensation shot straight to my core, settling there. Or rather, *unsettling* there.

The floor shifted slightly beneath me. The wine was stronger than I recalled. Or maybe it was the fact I hadn't eaten much in days. If it weren't for that combined with my brush with death, I'd have assumed that there was something else in the wine muddling my thoughts. I braced myself on the dresser with my free hand to keep from falling over.

"I'm glad you came back."

"You said that already." Dozens of times.

"I know. But I am."

I turned my attention to the drawer, pulling it fully from the tracks. *Me too.* But I could never put voice to things like that or it would open up a Pandora's box of emotions. And I detested the things. I set the newly freed drawer on the floor and started to reach into the gap, feeling around the top for something. Anything. Even a jammed-up piece of paper stuck in the bracing, but there was nothing. Nothing at all.

I rocked back onto my heels and then plopped down onto the carpet, reaching backward for the glass of wine that I'd set down. It was half empty.

Tamsyn came over and sat down beside me with the glass decanter. "More?"

I lifted my glass. "Always."

"Ruby, I . . . I want to tell you something." She fiddled with the diamond bracelet at her wrist nervously.

I struggled to focus my gaze, my vision growing fuzzy and dim. "What is it?"

Something flickered in her expression I couldn't make out. Her light eyes guarded. "It's nothing. Nothing at all."

If my head weren't such a jumble I might have pressed her, but instead I let it go and took another drink.

CHAPTER TWENTY-NINE

Finally a Clue

I woke the next morning on the carpeted floor of Edward's room, struggling to piece together snippets from the night before. Songbirds aggressively chirped out the window, and the sun—drat it—had risen far too early for my tastes, considering the aching in my head. The last thing I recalled was sorting through the dresser and then everything faded to black. I had no recollection. None at all, which in all my many years of overindulgence had rarely happened. And certainly not with this intensity. I struggled to my feet, smoothing my wrinkled clothes, and glanced in the mirror. Over my shoulder I spotted Tamsyn, fast asleep on the narrow bed. She looked younger, the years fading away leaving only possibility with a dash of regret. I turned away and finished putting myself in order.

I raked my hand through my hair, combing the messy curls with my fingers, and glanced around Edward's room, eager to resume my search through his belongings. There was no sense being quiet about it. Tamsyn had always been a heavy sleeper, able to sleep through a bombing raid if she was tired enough, but there was a strange stillness to her slumber.

I needed to find something. Anything at all to guide us toward the killer. I went on for half an hour rummaging through the papers in a wooden cigar box. Receipts, lists. Nothing particularly useful. Until I finally lit upon a small scrap of paper sandwiched between a pawn broker's ticket and a jeweler's receipt.

My blood froze in my veins as I read the words there, scarcely believing my good fortune.

My silence comes with a price and you are testing my patience. If you renege upon our agreement I will consider my silence no longer necessary. And you know what that will cost you. Thursday. No more games, Chenowyth.

Well, that couldn't have been clearer if it'd been spelled out in newsprint. Not that I knew what Edward's secret was, nor what his blackmailer wanted, nor even who wrote the dratted thing, or when it had been sent. But I at least had something, which was a far sight more than I had when I woke up with a splitting head. I squinted at the script. It looked masculine, if script could look so. And the letters were well formed. Whoever the writer was, he or she was educated.

I held the paper to my nose and sniffed it. Nothing. It smelled like clean linens and the vaguely stale insides of a drawer. Not that I particularly expected anything grand to jump out at me. The paper wasn't particularly expensive or thick. Nothing special there.

I blew out a breath and heard a rustling behind me.

Tamsyn had stirred. She sat up in the bed, her hair a tangle around her shoulders, and stifled a yawn in her fist. "Dear God, I don't know how you endure waking up this way." She blinked, rubbing her temples and squeezing her eyes shut.

I snorted. "I take it you're worse for drink too."

She nodded and hugged her knees to her chest. "You found something?"

I had, rather. I sucked at my teeth and climbed up beside her on the mattress and showed her the note.

She gasped, tugging her long hair off her neck, and glanced up at me uncertainly. "Well, that certainly *is* something."

"Do you have any clue who wrote it?"

She shook her head. "And before you ask, I have no idea what his secrets were either. I mean, beyond Jori not being his, but I cannot imagine he'd care enough to pay to hide that. Why would he? He could have divorced me, set me aside, and disowned the child. No one would blame him a bit, then he could remarry and have a legitimate heir. In many ways, he might have even preferred it."

"Yet Jori would still be his heir by law, wouldn't he?"

She pressed her lips together in thought. "I believe so, but I'm not certain. I never really thought much of it since Edward was always keen on having a son. I suppose we'd have to consult a solicitor to determine how the inheritance travels in cases of divorce and illegitimacy." Her shoulders slumped. "Oh, gracious. I hadn't even thought of the title." Her expression became hopeless. "You must think me simpleminded."

"Darling, this isn't precisely the normal course of things. One doesn't plan for this sort of thing at their come-out." I stared at the letter again before getting another idea. "Do you happen to have your condolence letters?"

She blinked at me, eyes wide, unable to follow along. Then again, sometimes I had trouble keeping up with my own wayward thoughts.

"The letters that you've been getting. About Edward."

"Of course, they're downstairs in the study. I haven't had the heart to read them yet."

"Go back to sleep. I'll be back if I find anything." I grinned at her, bolting off the bed and racing down the stairs.

I pressed the study door open to find Mrs. Penrose inside, straightening the desk, Fiachna at her heels. "What is he doing here?"

Mrs. Penrose looked from the cat to me and sighed. "That Scottish fellow who came with the doctor. Owen, I think he said his name was."

"He's here? Mr. Owen?"

She shook her head. "No, he and the doctor are with Ruan this morning. I offered to watch the little fellow as you seemed to have your hands full."

Quite the understatement. I glanced down at the cat who was now rubbing himself against the hem of her skirt. The traitor. I supposed I'd worry about my faithless cat at another time. I had more important matters at hand.

"The letters. Where are they?"

She dusted her hands on her white apron and tilted her head to one side. "Which letters do you mean, maid?"

"The condolence letters. Tamsyn said they were in here."

Mrs. Penrose gestured to a stack on a small silver tray on the left edge of the table. "Right there. I brought in a few more that came this morning. I don't believe the mistress has read a one yet."

I walked around the desk and sat down in the chair beneath the inscrutable gaze of Mrs. Penrose.

"Would you care for some . . . tea?"

"Coffee if you have it. And some sandwiches if there are any. I know it's early but I'm half starved and I fear we have a great deal of work to do."

The older woman turned to go then paused at the door as my words struck her. "*We*, maid?"

"Unless you've something more important than finding Sir Edward's killer?"

She sucked in a breath and shook her head. "I'll be back in a trice."

I grinned at her, and I could have sworn I saw a hint of excitement in her eyes. I had a plan. A mad one, but was hoping that it would work.

CHAPTER THIRTY

An Unlikely Accomplice

TWO hours and two strong pots of coffee later, Mrs. Penrose and I had gone through all the condolence notes, comparing the handwriting from the blackmail letter to those delivered since Sir Edward's passing. I reckoned that whoever killed Edward knew him, and anyone who *knew* him would feel compelled to send a condolence note to his poor grieving widow. After all, society had its rules, and while murder might be outré, it was even more reprehensible to shirk one's social responsibilities. A reasonable enough assumption to my mind, though Mrs. Penrose remained skeptical of the notion. However, midway through the first pot, she came around to my way of thinking.

I bit into a cucumber-and-cress sandwich, staring at one of the more recent letters before handing it over to my semi-unwilling accomplice. "Thoughts on that one?"

"The vicar? Have you lost your wits, maid?"

"Probably." I laughed, licking the remnants of the sandwich from my finger. "Most likely actually. But you can't tell me that doesn't match. Look at the *t*'s." I laid the page down in front of her on the table, tapping the suspect letter.

Mrs. Penrose leaned forward, adjusting her spectacles as

she studied the script. She smelled of bread and jam. A rather pleasant thought. A far cry from the last few housekeepers we'd employed who carried a whiff of brimstone about them and looked at me like I was the very devil herself. It was a wonder we kept any staff at all, but from all indications Mrs. Penrose knew precisely what sort of troublesome woman I was and cared not one jot. She'd seen me at my worst at Tamsyn's wedding, the details of which remained mercifully foggy, and still found an ounce of sympathy for me. She sighed with a shake of her head. "He's pompous, that's for certain. And conniving. But I still find it hard to believe he's a murderer. Murder is work, and that man never cared for the condition."

I snorted back a laugh, biting into a second cucumber sandwich, grateful that Mrs. Penrose had avoided any animal flesh. If anyone around this village was a witch, it was her, as she somehow possessed the power to know precisely what I needed—wanted—without a single word. "Mrs. Penrose . . . ?" I asked suddenly. Tamsyn's words about the pig came to mind again. "Mrs. Penrose, would you know anything about a bottle underneath my bed?"

She looked affronted at the accusation, except for the slightest bit of pink flushing up by her ears. "Why on earth would there be a bottle beneath your bed?"

I frowned and shook my head. Perhaps I didn't want to know after all. I cleared my throat. "Never mind me. What about the others?" She leaned across, quickly dismissing my questioning, and shuffled through the piles of letters. We'd divided them into three categories: Definitely nots, Probably nots, and Maybes. She placed the vicar's card reluctantly in the latter pile.

And now there were three: the vicar, an earl who lived in Cheshire, and Sir Edward's solicitor. While the writing wasn't an exact match to *any* of them, there were marked similarities in the script, as if they'd all attended the same school.

I blew out a breath, staring at the letters laid out together, wishing that I were as clever as all those bright young things back in Exeter believed. In this instance, I felt a giant fraud. All of the condolence stationery was far finer than that used for the blackmail note, but that was to be expected. Who would use their best paper to threaten someone? I chewed slowly on an anise biscuit. Not my favorite—but it fit my mood.

"Do you have any idea who might have had something over him? You've worked here for years, haven't you?"

"Thirty. I worked for the old master as well, remember."

"At least now you believe me it's no curse that did the killings."

She gave me a mutinous look, but her eyes told the story, and I admired her all the more for it. It was the mark of a strong mind to be willing to change it when given incontrovertible evidence. And frankly, a threatening blackmail note was as good a proof as any of human intervention.

"This one, I'll grant you. But I still don't think it's the vicar who done it," she added gruffly before taking a sip of her coffee. She wrinkled her nose in distaste. Perhaps even Mrs. Penrose had limits to her open-mindedness.

"No, no, I actually agree with you for once. I don't think he's the killer either. But I do think he's the blackmailer. He has to be. Why else would he have been sniffing around the estate so soon after Edward's death? You cannot think the man actually meant to console Tamsyn. He didn't even bring his prayer book." A detail I had almost forgotten until this very moment.

Mrs. Penrose let out a surprised laugh. "You know, now that you mention it, that did strike me odd as well."

"Will you tell Tamsyn when she comes down that I've gone to call on the Pellar?" I gathered up the blackmail note and the letter from the vicar, tucking them into the pocket of my smart riding jacket.

Mrs. Penrose nodded. I bussed a kiss to her cheek and breezed out of the room wondering briefly if Tamsyn would hate me terribly if I poached her housekeeper. Then again, I supposed she owed me after all we'd been through.

CHAPTER THIRTY-ONE

Missing Vicars

IT was nearly midday before I tracked down Ruan, unable to wait for him to come to me. He'd likely be cross to discover I'd left Penryth unaccompanied, but I wasn't about to delay any longer to satisfy his transient moods. Besides, I now had two reasons for my haste to find him. First, I was inordinately curious about whether he'd found the woman from the crossroads. Second, I'd grown giddy with my own discovery. I'd done it. I'd found something to lead us on a new angle, and I'd done it all on my own. Oh, fine. I had some much-needed assistance from Tamsyn and Mrs. Penrose—but nevertheless I had done *something* useful in the handful of hours we'd been apart.

He was deep in the woods behind his cottage gathering bits of bark with a wickedly dark blade in his hand. The sun barely broke through the thick canopy overhead, and all manner of birds and small animals seemed to have made a home here in this heavily shadowed sanctuary.

"You're not going to use that on me, are you?" I said lightly as I reached his side, glancing at the knife in his hand. The blade itself was nearly eight inches long and slightly curved, more suited to gutting an animal than gathering herbs—yet that appeared to be precisely what he was doing with it. The edge was honed shaving-razor-sharp.

He startled at the sound of my voice, knife skittering across the bark of the tree. "Woman, are you trying to get me to cut my finger off?" He turned around, his expression hovering between frustration and exasperation. The dappled sunlight came through the canopy overhead, catching on the hints of silver in his hair.

"I'm sorry. I thought you could hear me."

He grunted, pulling a bit of the bark off and dropping it into a cloth in the basket beside him. "It doesn't work that way . . . I apologize, I'm a bit distracted. Murderers in the village and all."

And a woman claiming I would destroy him.

He shot me a dangerous look. It seemed he heard *that* at least. "No one is going to harm me. Least of all you." He sounded oddly disappointed in the notion.

I cleared my throat, changing the subject. "Did you find her then? The woman?"

Another grunt as he struggled with a particularly stubborn bit of bark. He drove the knife a bit harder beneath the trunk. "Gone without a trace. I was up half the night trying to track her down. No one saw hide nor hair of her. You'd think she was a ghost."

I furrowed my brow. "Could she have been?"

"At the crossroads?" He shrugged as if this were an ordinary conversation. "I don't think so. She was flesh and bone. But as for what her motives are, and where she's from . . ." His voice trailed off.

"What do you make of her?"

He let out an exasperated sigh and gestured at me with the knife. "The inn is full up on the curious sort. Take your pick of what she could be. With the papers and the stories . . . she could be any sort of fraud, coming to stir up trouble. A charlatan." That was the same word Mr. Owen had used, and yet I could tell that Ruan didn't believe his own words. He was lying. And I needed to know why.

"Ruan—"

"Say your piece and leave me be."

Shifting on my feet, I took another step closer to him. Who was this uncertain creature I'd become? He was to blame for all of it—him with his unusual eyes and mercurial temper and ability to see straight through me. I was adrift at sea, with no mooring. No anchor. "I—"

He whipped around to face me. "You what?" A bloom of red dropped from his finger.

"You're bleeding . . ."

He glanced down at his hand, then shoved his finger into his mouth, sucking on it. "So I am," he mumbled, the edge falling from his voice. "What did you come for, Ruby?"

"A clue." I beamed, reaching into my pocket and withdrawing the blackmail note. I shook it at him. Paper rustling. "Someone was blackmailing Edward before he died."

Ruan steadied my hand, his eyes quickly darting across the letters there. The witch temporarily forgotten. "It's not signed."

"Of course it's not signed. But I also have this!" I whipped out the vicar's letter from my pocket and put it on top. I tapped the paper, unable to contain my excitement. "Look at it, Ruan! Look at it! It's the vicar! It has to be!"

He glanced from the pages in his hands to me, back and forth until he finally stopped altogether and settled upon my face.

My breath caught in my chest, hanging there desperate for his approval. A *Good work, Ruby*, would have satisfied me for days. Anything at all. The perils of being a fatherless child, I'm sure Mr. Freud would have claimed. At least that's what I blamed this tightness in my chest on. It had absolutely nothing to do with the fact that I was utterly fascinated by the man before me. The same one who was staring at me as if he'd discovered fire. A look somewhere between admiration and something else I couldn't countenance. My mouth was dry. "Say something."

He swallowed hard, finally looking away and shoving the letters back to me, his fingers brushing my own. "You did well." He turned back around and moved on to another tree deeper into the shadows.

That was it? I huffed out a breath.

You did well?

I traipsed off after him deeper into the wood as he continued whatever it was he was doing with that plant.

"Yes, that's it."

Infuriating man. "Well, we need to go call on the vicar. See what he has to say for himself."

"You suggest knocking on his door." Ruan grunted as his blade slipped on the tree and he nicked his thumb again. At this rate he'd soon be out of fingers.

Tree 2—Ruan 0. Today was not his day.

He shot me a cross look.

"Yes, yes, I do suggest doing something of the sort."

"Won't work," he mumbled over his second wounded appendage.

"Why won't it?"

"He's gone."

"Gone?" The birds chittered cheerfully in the brush nearby while I waited for him to elaborate.

"Until morning. Was called away to London, I'm to understand he's fetching the new curate."

I opened my mouth and shut it again. "Did you suspect the vicar and not even bother telling me?"

"No. I told you I was in town all night trying to find that bloody woman." He paused, weighing his words cautiously. "I overheard."

Ah. Well, that would make sense. "What are you doing out here anyway?"

"What do I *appear* to be doing?"

"How would I know? I never know what you're doing, what you're thinking . . ." I blew out an irritated breath. He turned his back again and headed deeper into the woods with me storming after him. "Well, what do you suggest we do until the vicar returns?"

He went back to his terse tree-mutilation, or whatever it was he was doing in this dark and lonely wood.

Very well, I clearly was getting nowhere with him in this foul mood. Instead of banging my head against the proverbial tree trunk of a man, I turned on my heels and walked back to the cottage. Surely Mr. Owen would prove better company.

WHATEVER ILL SPIRIT possessed Ruan earlier this morning had abated by the evening. He remained sullen, but at least we were comrades again, of a fashion. The low sound of Mr. Owen's snore emanated from an oversized armchair. Fiachna, the fink, was curled up on the old man's lap. Occasionally lifting his oversized head to look at me, blinking slowly, as if to say, *You really thought he'd leave me in Exeter?*

The only creatures in my whole dismal life who never once failed me were an overly fluffy black house cat and an eccentric Scottish bookseller. I peered into the empty tin cup in my hand, willing it to be full again.

Ruan was stooped over that ancient Cornish grimoire. One hand along his brow, tangled in his hair, the other making careful notes in pencil in a hidebound journal. Notes he refused to share. Something was bothering him, and whatever it was had everything to do with that woman's warning. He hadn't been the same around me since. He glanced up at me curiously as if trying to convince himself of something, but then turned back to his books—knowing good and well I was watching him. I'd had far too much whiskey by now to bother disguising it. I picked up the rather uninspiring demonology in my lap and snapped it shut, walked over to the half-empty bottle of whiskey, pulled the cork, and refilled the cup before returning to where Ruan was working. While he was not an overly educated man—at least not formally—he was by far one of the cleverer specimens of his sex that I'd ever encountered.

I threw my head back, letting the amber liquid burn its way down my throat. Not my preferred drink, but it did the trick.

"You drink too much."

I narrowed my gaze at him. "You don't drink enough."

He let out an irritated grunt in response. Infuriating man.

"Honestly it's the only thing helping me endure your charming little village."

"You don't like the country?"

"I don't like being accused of things. I don't like people being murdered and attacked every time I turn around. I don't like some woman coming and claiming that I'm going to somehow kill you. And I especially don't like that you know what it means and are hiding it from me." I poked him hard in the chest. Wobbling a bit on my feet.

He let out a low rumble of laughter, steadying me with a hand to my elbow. "Ah, Miss Vaughn, you don't particularly enjoy being a spectacle?"

There was a double-edged meaning in his words, which stung more than they ought. I'd thought him my friend, and now he was . . . distant. Worried. "I won't harm you, you know . . . that woman . . . she . . ."

Ruan sighed, running a hand over his stubbled jaw, clearly not wanting to discuss the witch's warning further. "You should go to bed, Ruby."

I stifled a yawn with my fist and eyed the impossibly tall ladder leading to the loft.

"You'll never make it up there in your sodded state. Take mine."

"I am not—"

"You're drunk. My bed, Miss Vaughn. No arguments."

The rickety ladder leading up to the loft looked even more treacherous than it had two hours ago when I started into this bottle. My lids grew heavier. Mounds and mounds of books were piled upon the table. Half of them I'd gone through myself. And while I had long ago accepted there *was* something unusual about Ruan Kivell, I was ever more convinced there were no such things as demons. No monsters. No dragons. Just evil men. And hopefully the vicar would be the one to tell us the truth. Except he wasn't even in town, not returning until the morning train.

"Do you think he did it?"

"Do I think that Reverend Fortescue killed Sir Edward?"

"Edward, George. Maybe even the uncle . . ." I paused, still unable to remember the blasted man's name then shrugged it off. "You know who I mean."

He nodded, wetting his lips and not responding.

"Do you think he's capable of murder?"

"He's capable of blackmail, that's for certain—" Ruan rubbed the back of his neck and stretched. "And while he wishes me to the devil, I don't believe he's the sort to do the job himself."

I frowned. "Would he hire someone, though?"

Ruan shrugged.

That wasn't helpful.

"Once someone starts down that path, I suppose it's an easy enough one to follow. Killing a man isn't particularly hard. Not when it's in your head that you must do it. Perhaps Fortescue has more mettle than I've given him credit for these past years."

Outside a cock crowed. I checked my timepiece. Four in the morning. If we were to see the vicar after he arrived home, we'd have to get some sleep soon. I stared at the scattered papers in front of me. I didn't want to close my eyes, though. Because the moment I did, the memories would return. I could handle them in Exeter, but here the wounds were all too fresh. Too entwined. My parents. Tamsyn. Everything I ever loved—ever touched—turned to dust. She'd been the only one with me when they died, and being with her again—it brought their loss back in force.

I bit my lower lip, examining the now-empty glass in front of me. "It was a mistake, Ruan . . ." *Coming here. Seeing her again.* I couldn't say the words, and yet I needed him to know I wasn't as brave as I pretended. That I drank to forget the things that would never go away. The ones I could no longer run or hide from. But that armor Tamsyn spoke of, it had failed me at last.

His hand came down warm and gentle on my shoulder. I could feel his thumb against the curve of my jaw when I finally looked up at him, his eyes fixed upon mine. Something passed there. Something I'd never felt before. Comprehension.

"I know."

Some consolation that was. And then he stood, turned on his heels, and started climbing up that ladder, taking it two rungs at a time, leaving me with a maelstrom of thoughts. None of them pleasant. And a pile of old books.

Chapter Thirty-Two

Piskie-Led

I woke early the next morning, my head full of wool and rocks. The only benefit of said state was that I was too exhausted to care about how badly the rest of me ached. Perhaps Ruan was right about my drinking, as it no longer helped me keep the memories at bay; lately it had the opposite effect. But as I lay there snug in his bed, which smelled disturbingly like the man himself, I realized one pertinent fact.

Ruan Kivell was missing.

Not that he wasn't in his bed—that part was no shock as I'd watched him climb the ladder to the loft long before I laid my own head down. Rather he wasn't in the house at all. I scrubbed my hands roughly over my face before pulling on a sensible brown walking skirt and white blouse. I fastened the mother-of-pearl buttons at my wrist, then reached into my satchel and pulled out the little jar of salve Ruan had made, applying it gently to the cuts on my face. They were healing nicely beneath the garish bruising. Perhaps in another week or two I might look more like myself. Though I sensed I'd never feel the same again. Lothlel Green had changed me and only time would tell for better or worse.

"Morning, lass," Mr. Owen said from the doorway. He wore a paisley dressing gown and looked altogether too pleased with the world for such an unchristian hour.

"How long have you been standing there?" I watched him through the mirror.

The old man shrugged. "Waiting on you to wake up."

"Where's Ruan?"

He lifted a chipped teacup to his lips. "Fancy a cup before breakfast?"

"Where's Ruan?" I repeated.

"Don't worry yourself, he's due back anytime now. But there was a note for you." He held his hand out. "Thought you might want it as it's from the house."

Penryth.

I turned and went to him, taking the envelope from his outstretched hand. I slid my thumb beneath the seal, breaking the wax, and skimmed over the words hastily.

My lady has need of you. Come at once. There is danger.

The letter was unsigned. The hand unfamiliar. "You said it's from the house?"

He nodded. "A maid brought it just after dawn. Said to give it to you straightaway."

"And you waited?"

"You haven't been sleeping, lass."

A frisson of fear crawled up my spine. "The guards?"

"At the house? Aye, they've orders to remain until the killer is found. Why are you so shaken? What's in there?" He leaned forward and I crumpled the note into my palm, sliding it into my pocket.

I shook my head, unable to voice my worries. "And Ruan . . ."

"Called away before dawn. You must speak to me, child. What's happened?"

"Nothing." I hoped. "If he returns, tell him I've gone to Penryth to check on some things." *To check on Jori.*

"Shall I join you?"

My heart jumped at the thought. If there were danger to be found, I wanted Mr. Owen as far from it as possible. I pressed a kiss to his furrowed brow and shook my head. "No. You wait here on Ruan. Send him to the house when he is finished."

And with that I jumped into my automobile and headed off down the rutted road to Penryth Hall, terrified of what would be there when I arrived.

"RUBY!" TAMSYN'S WIDE eyes lit up as I raced into the drawing room. Immediately upon seeing her, all my worries, fears, and concerns dissolved in an instant. "What are you doing here?"

"I was summoned. The note said there was danger. Did you not send for me?"

"No. And I can't think who would have," she said, settling down at the tea table, a tray set out before her full of pasties and a pot of hot tea. "Perhaps Mrs. Penrose sent a note. There's been some business in town and she was called away early."

She and Ruan both. I gnawed on my lower lip, my tongue running over the metallic-tasting cut. I glanced around the empty room. "What do you mean business? And are you alone? Mr. Owen said the guards were to stay until the killer was found."

Tamsyn sniffed and gave me a nod. "Don't worry. It won't be for long. Mrs. Penrose sent Mrs. Martin over to sit with me this morning. I finally managed to convince the woman to go back to her farm—that no monsters were about to leap from the cupboards to kill me. She didn't want to go, but I finally prevailed upon her."

"But why are there no guards?"

"Didn't you hear?" Tamsyn's eyes widened in surprise.

I shook my head.

Tamsyn gestured for me to sit and I did, reluctantly. None of this made sense. Not one bit.

"How could you have not known? Everyone is talking about what happened. Nellie Smythe was poisoned. Enys called his men back to help investigate."

Edward's former mistress?

"She almost died last night. Poor pitiable thing." Tamsyn picked up a decanter of brandy from a side table and poured two glasses. It was a bit early for a drink, even by my generous standards.

She pressed it into my hand regardless.

"What do you mean *almost died?*"

Her throat worked as she swallowed down her glass in a long slow sip. "I'm not certain. Mr. Kivell seems convinced that it's poison, though I'm not convinced she didn't have a hand in it herself."

"Ruan?"

A pang of annoyance crossed her features that a wiser person might have construed as jealousy. Scrawled out in capital letters across her face. "Yes, your *Pellar*. Once he let Enys know that he suspected poison, the constable brought half his men back into town. There are three or four still wandering about the house somewhere. At least I think they are. I haven't seen a one in ages."

I stepped back toward the settee, wrapping my fingers around the crystal glass. "Is she going to be all right?"

Tamsyn shrugged and flicked open a cigarette case, toying with the paper. "Depends on what you mean by *all right*. She's with child again. I didn't know that until Mrs. Penrose told me this morning. Apparently she was several months along. Could scarcely feed Edward's bastard, and then to have a second . . ." Tamsyn shuddered visibly, snapping the enameled case shut and tossing it carelessly onto the table beside the decanter.

I winced at the clatter.

She poured herself another glass of brandy, hands shaking. This wasn't like her. Not at all.

Tamsyn lit a cigarette, taking a drag and slowly blowing out the smoke. "I hear she'd gone to your Mr. Kivell a few weeks ago asking for some herbs to rid herself of it. But he wouldn't help her, the fiend. Mrs. Penrose said he'd told her that she was too far along for him to help safely, and she'd have to see a real doctor for that sort of intervention, and you know how unlikely that would be—even for someone with our means. He'd been mixing up some sort of tea for her to prevent the condition in the first place . . . But either she wasn't drinking it, or it didn't work."

"How do you even know all this?"

She shrugged, tapping the ashes off her cigarette into the bottom of an empty rocks glass. "Mrs. Penrose. The woman knows everything. But she spends a lot of time down at the Smythe place. I think she feels guilty for what Edward did and it's her way of making amends."

Nellie's hollowed cheeks appeared in my mind. Her hungry child. The anger flashing in her eyes when she spoke of Edward. I didn't want to hear anymore. I set my crystal glass, brandy undrunk, on the table between us. "I'm glad he went to her, then."

Tamsyn shot to her feet, pacing around the room. Her pale-pink dress swished as she walked. Something was wrong. And I sensed it was more than Nellie Smythe's fate that bothered her.

"Why didn't they send for Dr. Heinrich?" After all, he had been staying at the Hind and Hare, which was only a handful of minutes away. It would have been far faster to fetch him than to send all the way up the cliffs for Ruan in the middle of the night.

"Doctors cost money, goose. But it doesn't matter. Your Mr. Kivell seems to have saved the day."

That was the second time she'd said that and it grated. "He's not my anything."

She waved a hand dismissively. "Whatever he is, he managed to pull both Nellie and the babe back from the grave." Tamsyn picked up my untouched glass of brandy and began drinking it too. Her eyes cloudy.

"Was it Edward's?"

"How would I know?" Tamsyn snapped. "Does it even matter who it belongs to if it's another mouth to feed? Regardless, I've decided to offer her a position here at the house once she's recovered enough. It's a strange arrangement, I give you that, but the guilt is intolerable. She wouldn't be in this predicament were it not for that monster I'd married. Besides, her son has every right to be here. More than mine, truthfully. The thought she might have died and I've spent the last few years trying to pretend her situation was none of my affair when I had the power to do something." She frowned deeply at the thought.

"And what of Mrs. Penrose . . . ?"

"She's staying with her for now, but will be back and forth until Nellie's in the pink of health. And Mrs. Martin is to keep watch over me to make sure I haven't been piskie-led." Tamsyn laughed at her own little joke, then grew grave again. "I'll have the whole Smythe family under my roof before long. But I've been thinking on it all morning and as it's my money anyway, perhaps I could do some good with what's left of my wretched life after all."

The last part was said with a bitterness I didn't recognize.

A hardness just below the surface of her skin that appeared every now and then. Edward did that to her, and I'd never forgive him for it. It turned the girl I knew into a woman I could scarcely comprehend. One capable of . . . anything. That nagging voice whispered again in my ear. *Do you truly know her?* This new creature was one of Edward's making. My hands grew damp at the thought.

"What is it, darling?"

I picked up my still-untouched glass of brandy, hand shaking a bit as I took a sip, and sat down beside her, letting the heady liquid fill my senses.

I shook my head. "Nothing . . ."

"You're troubled. Come eat something." She nudged the plate of pasties toward me. I glanced at them for a moment, taking one in hand. I didn't want it. But she was right, I probably ought to eat something.

"I'm not. At least not particularly. I've just been trying to decide what the vicar could be blackmailing Edward over. Ruan and I were going to question him yesterday afternoon but he was in London. Now with Nellie taking ill, it'll likely be days before we get the chance to corner him."

She sucked her teeth, evidently placated by my answer. "Jori. It's the only thing I can think of. He must have discovered that the boy isn't Edward's." Her answer was simple, and yet I'd already ruled it out. It was *too* simple. And not a good enough reason for murder. *Unless she was the one to do the killing.* My mouth grew dry. What if Edward hadn't been so accepting of the child as everyone was to believe? Appearances were often deceiving, and Edward was a master at deception.

I bit my lower lip, toying with the flaky crust of the pasty, letting a crumb fall to my skirt.

"It doesn't make sense."

"No, it doesn't." She nudged me with her elbow. "Eat, Ruby.

You're making a mess of your food. Mrs. Penrose had them sent up from the village a little while ago. She'd be very put out with you if she knew you picked it apart instead of eating it."

I laughed at that, struggling to shake off the growing sense of dread. Mrs. Penrose *would* probably be very cross. An outcome I would not abide, so I lifted it and took a bite. Bits of heavily spiced lamb, potatoes, and parsnips on the inside, all in a hot-water crust. I wiped my lips with the back of my hand and swallowed. "I thought you hated parsnips."

She wrinkled her nose. "I do. Edward adored them, she must have forgotten—though I can't think why she would. I suppose it's a good thing my stomach is in knots. Do you want to take them with you?"

The flaky crust was perfection. I peered at the tray, debating the merits of taking her up on the offer when she stood and turned. The pale underskirt flashed slightly beneath the light-pink netting. Catching in the wind. And the image of that first night returned to my mind in force. The figure all in white.

Doubt washed over me like high tide. I'd been watching from such a distance that I couldn't be sure—not entirely—of what I'd seen that night. *Who.* And were I not blindfolded by my feelings for her, perhaps I'd have given it a bit more thought before this very moment. My breath grew short.

Largesse to a woman in dire straits did not negate the possibility she killed her husband.

My hand hesitated over the tray. "Tamsyn, I would understand if you'd done it, you know."

"Done what?" she asked, blinking.

"If you hurt Edward. No one would blame you. I don't know how . . . but I won't let anything happen to you. I'll find a way to get you out of—"

"Why would you say that?" Her face grew stricken. "Why would you think I'd harmed my husband?"

One would have thought I'd run her through with the elaborate fire poker sitting on the hearth. Or worse, perhaps she was able to hear my thoughts the way Ruan could.

Her face screwed up in an expression somewhere between surprise and pain. Then suddenly her green eyes flashed in anger. "After all these years, you are unable to see what is right before you. You say you hate the past, but in truth you refuse to let it go, Ruby. You cling to your grief and I won't play this game anymore."

"Game? A man is dead, Tamsyn. It's not a game."

"You think I don't know that?" Tears welled up in her eyes. "I don't know why I even try to explain myself to you. It's senseless. You can't even stop doubting me long enough to listen to the truth. But it doesn't matter. None of it does. You'll be gone soon and I'll be left here and I intend to be perfectly, blissfully happy for whatever time I have left at Penryth. Without you."

Yes. Yes, I would be gone without question. Coming here had been a mistake, just as I'd told Ruan last night. Spending time with her doubly so. My stomach ached. "It's a simple question, Tamsyn. And not an unreasonable one. You are the one person he's harmed the most. You and poor Nellie—" My stomach knotted tighter. "All I'm saying is, I wouldn't blame you, and I would help you. I promise that."

She whipped around, eyes flashing with a fervency that I hadn't seen before. "And how can I trust you?"

Her words cut through my gut. Sharp and hot through the heart of me. This was how it was to end—she and I—with angry words and misunderstandings destroying everything that had come before. "You doubt me?"

Tamsyn turned back to me, her eyes glistening. "I don't even know who you are anymore, Ruby. Go. Just leave."

"Tam—" I began to sweat. I hated arguing with her. Hated

this feeling that had come over me. A physical pain. No wonder people claimed to die of broken hearts. I might do the same right here on the parlor floor.

"Get out!"

Without another word I turned and walked out the door, knowing I would never ever set foot into Penryth Hall again.

I'd made it almost as far as the gate when my stomach began to roil. I was going to be sick. I'd never been one to cast up my accounts over nerves but it seemed there was nothing for it. The pain came again, sharper this time, making me double over. I heaved again. And again, stumbling a little farther down the path. The ground beneath me trembled unsteadily—or perhaps it was me that shook.

One step. Two. The road began to quiver as I carried on, counting to keep myself upright. A small child appeared in the distance, dressed all in rags. Its feet bare.

It beckoned and I followed.

Like in one of my dreams, except this was all too real. Stumbling through the undergrowth and brush. Intermittently the ragged little one would pause long enough for me to catch up—then turn and gambol on ahead, leading me on a not-at-all-merry chase. Miles and miles I must have walked over increasingly rough terrain. The path grew more treacherous and yet I kept on, unable to turn back. Unable to do anything else. I stumbled again, falling to my knees in the mud, and that's when I saw it—a great dark stallion beneath a stunted tree. And in an instant the ragged child was gone.

My strength had fled. I tried to pull myself to my knees to crawl, but fell back to the boggy earth, and the last thing to flicker through my addled mind was a single name. A plea. *Ruan.* But it was hopeless. He'd never hear me now.

And then there were no more thoughts. All that remained was white, furious pain. And death.

CHAPTER THIRTY-THREE

Long-Forgotten Secrets

I was swimming. Deep in a fathomless lagoon, with ice-cold water rushing over my limbs surrounding me. Somewhere neither here nor there. Cold water touched my brow. A dribble ran down over my eye, then slipped like tears to settle in the hollow of my throat.

It took every ounce of energy I possessed to crack one eye open. Then the other.

Ruan. An echo of my futile prayer on the moor.

The edge of his mouth curved up slightly as relief washed over him. "Good morning, Miss Vaughn."

I blinked again, trying to focus on his dear face, on the very shape of him. He sat beside me in a chair, a great hulk of a man with a porcelain washbasin in his lap and a soft damp cloth in his hand. *Morning?* My unfocused eyes drifted to the window, but the curtains were closed tight, hiding the sun.

"You've been sleeping for two days."

"Two . . ." My voice croaked, rusty from disuse. It scratched to swallow. "Two days?"

He nodded, running a gentle hand over my forehead, his thumb caressing my scarred brow. Instinctively I closed my eyes, turning into his palm. He traced the line across my forehead with his thumb, back and forth in a slow rhythm.

"What are you doing?" I murmured beneath my closed lids.

"Something my mother used to do." He continued with the gentle caress, chasing the pain away with each touch.

I opened my left eye, shooting him a look that might have been skeptical had I the energy for the notion. At the moment I was grateful not to be dead.

"What did you eat last? Can you recall?"

I shook my head slowly and struggled to sit up in the bed. My body weighed a thousand pounds. Limbs leaden. He leaned over to help lift me up but I shooed him away. I needed to do it myself. Gingerly, I straightened myself in the large brass bed. "Where's Mr. Owen?"

"Safe. Here. He went for a walk a few minutes ago, he's been worrying himself sick over you. Fairly raving until I assured him that you were not the sort to die so easily."

I breathed out a sigh of relief.

"Do you remember where you had gone when you left Penryth?"

My head ached to shake it.

He took in a slow breath and let it out again. "Ruby . . . I don't want you to be alarmed . . ."

I frowned. Anyone who began a sentence with that was about to say something quite alarming indeed.

"You'd wandered all the way to Bodmin Moor."

"Bodmin Moor?!" my voice squeaked. "That's ridiculous. That has to be . . ."

"Five miles, yes. Do you have any idea how you got there?"

It was impossible. Completely impossible.

"Do you remember anything? Anything at all? Did you eat something, talk to someone? See anyone?" His voice took on an almost frantic tone with his questions.

I closed my eyes, trying to remember exactly what had happened. But there was nothing there, only a giant void in my memory. "Just a child. There was a child. And a stallion. That's all. I'm sorry, Ruan, I just don't recall anything."

His eyes widened for a moment in surprise. "A child?"

"Dressed in rags. I think I dreamed it, it doesn't seem probable, does it? Following a child for miles into the moors?"

He ran a thumb over my brow tenderly and shook his head. "It sounds as if you've been piskie-led."

I rolled my eyes and closed them shut. "Doubtful."

"From what I can tell you walked all the way there, or certainly wandered through the moors. You're quite lucky you didn't drown yourself with all the rain we've had."

"Who found me? And why would they have even thought to look for me there?"

He shifted uncomfortably, unable to meet my gaze.

"It was you, wasn't it?"

He nodded.

I furrowed my brow. "How?"

Ruan looked as wretched as I felt. Unchained, lost, and scared to death. "You were calling for me."

I tugged the wool blanket up over my chest and took another sip of the water, letting it run pleasingly down my raw throat. "The way you can hear what I'm thinking?"

"It was worse. I've never had anything like it happen before. I don't know how or why you of all people. You . . ." His rough fingers grazed their way along my forehead. "What was it you called me? The seventh son of a miner with a pocket full of parlor tricks."

I leaned my head against the brass bed frame, stretching my neck slightly. "Penchant for them, I believe." The faintest hint of a smile crossed my face. "I do have a rather elegant turn of phrase, don't I?"

He snorted. "I'm glad you're alive, Ruby Vaughn. So very glad."

I am too. Inordinately so.

Another snort. This one of the cynical variety. The man could likely carry on a conversation with the sounds he made.

"I do appreciate you saving my life."

"Again."

His strange eyes burned brighter than normal as he watched me. As if they had their own ability to shine.

"I may not put any stock in curses, but I'm beginning to believe in you, Pellar."

He shifted in the chair. "Then you'd be the only one of us."

"I'm sorry for the things I've said to you."

"No need."

There was need. I'd have to prove my sincerity to him eventually. "Yes, well. Whatever you've done, I am starting to feel rather fine now." It was strange, but the longer he touched my brow and I sat here talking to him, the more I began to feel myself again— and I desperately needed to feel alive. To be alive. To remember how I wound up wandering Bodmin Moor. "But as much as I appreciate your skill at poking around in my brain, couldn't you read the thoughts of people who might actually have killed someone? That'd be a far sight more useful at this moment."

His laugh came again, slow and low. "You are the most confounding woman I've ever met."

"Most troublesome, probably."

"Without a doubt." The flicker of amusement returned to his face. Perhaps things would be right now and we'd solve this puzzle. Just as soon as I remembered where I'd been and why I'd been there.

THE NEXT TIME I woke, Dr. Heinrich was at my bedside wearing the very same expression he'd had that time I'd thrown that

Antigone-themed costume party and he'd missed that minor detail in his invitation and showed up in the parlor halfway through the party dressed as Napoleon. He was not amused then, nor now it seemed.

Evidently, Ruan had gone into town earlier, leaving me alone with Mr. Owen, who had in turn summoned Dr. Heinrich to fuss and worry over me lest I expire on the spot. Why he trusted my initial care to Ruan rather than a very fine surgeon, I still couldn't comprehend. "You're lucky to be alive, you know that, don't you, Miss Vaughn? Do you recall anything at all from before you woke?"

I shook my head, taking a cool sip of water, struggling to wash away memories of the ragged child, lest I start prattling on about him to the doctor. Or was the child a girl? Already I could scarcely recall its features. It was bad enough I'd admitted my hallucinations to Ruan, but a girl did possess a bit of pride. "I was going somewhere. To Penryth Hall perhaps? Though I don't know if I ever made it? Surely not if I was all the way to Bodmin, don't you think, since it's in the other direction."

Dr. Heinrich sniffed. "Perhaps you were pixie-led?"

"That's what Ruan said as well." Odd that both men would come to the same conclusion. "I don't believe in curses. Or pixies, thank you. Though I believe they call them piskies in this part of the world."

The doctor gave me an exasperated look and leaned back in the chair.

I tugged the woolen blanket higher up my legs, settling myself deeper into Ruan's mattress. "Where is Ruan anyway?"

"Seeing after Miss Smythe. Did you hear about that?"

I shook my head. There was something faintly familiar, as if I *ought* to know but had forgotten. "What happened?"

"You must be feeling a great deal better if you're looking

to catch up on village gossip." He touched my brow with the back of his hand. Whatever he found seemed to reassure him.

I flashed him a brief smile. "I'm really fine. I don't know what Ruan did, but I applaud his efforts because I feel at this moment like I had a bit of hashish and half a bottle of cognac."

"Then a typical Thursday morning for you?" Heinrich had evidently been invited to far too many of my parties. He stroked his beard. "It's my understanding that he gave you an emetic, followed by charcoal. But it does not explain your swift recovery. I've spoken with him at length, and there's no medical reason for it. At least none I can fathom. The man truly is an extraordinarily gifted healer."

"Yes, I've firsthand experience it seems."

He laughed again. "I can tell. Unfortunately, I believe you and Miss Smythe were destined to be the killer's next victims."

I shifted on the mattress, body stiff from being in one spot too long. "Why is that?"

"You both seemed to have ingested water dropwort."

I blinked and shook my head. "I don't understand."

He paused and clarified. "Water hemlock. In quantity enough, it ought to have killed the both of you straight off. There is no reason on this earth either of you ladies should be alive today. The fact Mr. Kivell found you on the moor is a miracle. That he managed to save you out there, now that is . . . quite remarkable."

I stared at him dumbfounded. Water hemlock . . . "You mean like Mr. Martin's cow?"

"So Mr. Kivell tells me. It appears you and Miss Smythe are two extraordinarily lucky young women. I did some reading on it as well. I also have reason to believe that it's the same poison as killed your baronet."

"How can you tell?"

"You see, one of the side effects of the poison is that it

contorts the face into a sardonic smile. I asked Mr. Kivell after he mentioned the dropwort and he described a very similar expression on the baronet."

I nodded numbly. "It doesn't make sense. None. The two failed attempts, and one . . . whatever it was that happened with the boys . . . they don't match any of the others. What I don't understand is why would someone want to kill me? And what does Miss Smythe have to do with this?"

His mustache twitched in amusement. "My dear Miss Vaughn, I think the real question is who *here* would want to kill you?"

I shot him a cross look, but he wasn't incorrect in his assessment. I'd lived rather freely after the war, of that I'd admit, and while I had my share of detractors, I hadn't quite made any enemies. Oh, fine. A few. But none who would bother killing me. "Parsnips . . ." I murmured. "Doesn't the root look like parsnips?"

"Of water hemlock? Yes, why do you ask?"

"Sir Edward had parsnips for supper the night I arrived. I only recall because Tamsyn cannot abide them. And the way he bit into it." I shuddered at the memory, which came back in a flash. "And then he felt ill . . . it all fits perfectly. I think you must be correct. But how would it get into his food? You can't think Mrs. Penrose did it. The poor woman was white as a ghost the morning she found him."

"It's an easy enough mistake to be made, someone slips the root in with the other vegetables. The person who prepared the dish might not be any the wiser."

"But then that would mean the killer didn't care who they killed . . ." I sank heavily back into the pillows and inhaled. The room smelled sweetly of sage and mint. I closed my eyes as my head was beginning to ache again. "When is Ruan returning?"

"I'm not his keeper. But speaking of the fellow, I did learn something curious about him while you were asleep. Did you know that you and he are exactly the same age?"

"Is that so? Did you sit down and spend your afternoons chitchatting over tea while waiting on me to die?"

He chuckled low and reached into his pocket, pulling out Dr. Quick's old notebook. "You were born November fourth, were you not? I seem to recall you telling me that."

I wasn't certain how I felt about Dr. Heinrich recalling such minutiae of my life.

"I was bored while you were asleep, thought I'd read the rest of the journal. It seemed there were several births around the same time in the village. It appears, if Quick's records are correct, that you and Mr. Kivell were born on a full moon. Granted on opposite sides of the world."

"I had no idea. Mother never kept up with astronomy. Though she did say I was born in the cowl, whatever that is supposed to mean."

Heinrich made a startled sound, then schooled his expression, setting the journal down on the bedside. "Now, that is curious. It's rather unusual for a baby to be born that way."

"I wouldn't know." I picked up the book, flipping to November. "You said several births . . ."

"Four. Which for a village of this size seems a remarkable number. Dr. Quick had quite the busy week."

And that's when I found it, barely six hours from my would-be deathbed, with the brilliant August light streaming in the window and birdsong filtering through my still-clouded thoughts. I couldn't believe my good fortune. The connection I'd been seeking had been there all along, I just hadn't read far enough in the journal to know. Because two pages after the doctor noted the healthy birth of one Ruan Kivell, seventh son of Arthur and Elizabeth Kivell, was a very curious note.

Went to Penryth Hall. Pt. delivered of a boy. No complications. Ordinary presentation.

A simple line of text. I had likely skimmed over it in the past, not paying any note at all, aside from the fact that a nameless child was delivered to a nameless woman at Penryth Hall some eight days after Ruan was born.

Joseph Chenowyth had no heirs. None that were acknowledged. None known.

It could have been a servant's child. What had Tamsyn said? That George told her that Edward wasn't the heir. What if George was right and *that* was what the vicar knew and was blackmailing Edward over? A baronetcy—even an impoverished one—might be worth killing someone for. My breath trembled in my chest. Surely an aftereffect of my illness.

Look to the heir, Pellar. Look to the heir. The woman at the crossroads had given us the answer and it had nothing to do with Jori. There was something else—someone else—at play here.

Slowly I stood, testing my unsteady legs on the cool wooden floor. I stretched for a moment, bracing a hand on the bedpost to keep myself from toppling over.

He glanced at me over the rims of his spectacles. "Dare I risk telling you that you should stay abed for at least a fortnight until we are certain you've recovered?"

"You might. But you know good and well I never listen."

He gave me a slightly worried smile. "Don't overtax yourself or else I will never hear the end of it. And drink water. No alcohol for a month."

I wasn't about to argue on that score. My stomach, while steady at the moment, felt a bit like someone had run it through a wringer and stuffed it back inside my belly. "I wouldn't dream of it."

"Where are you headed, then?"

"To the vicarage."

"Are you mad, Ruby?"

Most certainly. "I have to go through the parish register. The births, deaths, marriages. The answer is there. I'm convinced of it." I bit my lower lip for a moment, weighing the thought.

His eyes widened and he reached out to steady me, but I waved him off. "I'm fine."

"Well, as I don't have any prayer of making you remain here, absent tying you to the bed, I suppose I'll tell you to go with God then."

I grinned at him. If my supposition was correct, God had nothing to do with any of this.

Chapter Thirty-four

Godless Men

ISAIAH Bishop was an appropriate name for a curate. I studied the reason for the vicar's most recent trip to London, and couldn't say I was terribly impressed with the man before me, though a holier, more brimstone-looking fellow, I'd never met in all my years. We sat in the cramped snug of the vicarage, he, Mr. Owen, and myself. While I hadn't intended to rope the old man into my visit this morning, I was rather glad he'd insisted on coming along.

Mr. Bishop wore a pinched expression as he looked down his aquiline nose at Mr. Owen. "Why, no, Reverend Fortescue is out for the day. I'm afraid I don't know when he'll be returning."

The vicar's absence might provide just the chance we needed to look through the register as I doubted he'd allow me within a mile of the thing if he were here.

"A shame. A terrible shame as I've come all this way to speak with him," Mr. Owen said with a sad, low shake of his head. He paused before looking up at the curate. "But perhaps you could help me in his place."

Sometimes the ease with which Mr. Owen obfuscated the truth frightened me. But today was not one of those times.

I kept my face as emotionless as possible, a shockingly easy feat as I was bone-tired. Perhaps Dr. Heinrich was right and I should have tied myself to the bed and slept for a month, but then how were we to find Sir Edward's killer, especially as Ruan was now distracted with Nellie's recovery?

"Oh, how unfortunate. Are you in town long? I am certain he'll be available tomorrow. Perhaps even later this evening."

Mr. Owen frowned deeply. "No, you see, I've been ill since I've arrived and I must be back to Exeter in the morning. But as you are the new curate, perhaps you can aid me with this?"

Mr. Bishop leaned forward, arms resting on his bony knees. "Of course, my dear sir. Though I don't know how much assistance I can provide as I just arrived two days ago."

"So soon? And with all the dark business going on in Lothlel Green. Oh, good heavens, lad." Mr. Owen summoned an overwrought expression and sighed. "This is a great deal of pressure on your young shoulders then. But you look like the sort of fellow to rise to the occasion. Why, this tragedy might be the making of you, Mr. Bishop!"

The young curate preened at the compliment, and I found myself remembering why I adored Mr. Owen as much as I did. Wily old thing.

"I was hoping to see the parish registry, if it's not too much trouble."

Suspicion instantly clouded Mr. Bishop's features as he leaned ever more forward, precarious on the edge of his chair. "What could you possibly need with the registry? Vicar is very particular about who can see it."

Interesting.

Mr. Owen's eyes dropped to the floor between them, giving him the distinct appearance of a forlorn hound. "You see, it's my poor daughter. She married in this village some years ago, before the war, you see." Mr. Owen took this moment to sniffle loudly. The cad. He dabbed at his eye, and for half a second I wondered if he was unwell, except I knew good and well he wasn't. "You see, her husband was killed in Gallipoli . . ." *Yes, yes of course he was . . . Just as the old man was in possession of about seven great-aunts.* He never even had a daughter, only sons, all of whom were killed during the war—though not a one at Gallipoli. The Marne, Jutland, and his youngest on a hospital ship on the way back home. Yet the old man took in a haggard breath and continued his sorry tale. "And the War Office. Bloody fools—pardon me, my lad—but they won't give her his pension without proof that they were legally wed. Doubting my girl's honor." His voice grew louder and more rattled with every word. "Can you believe the audacity of those popinjays? Questioning my sweet darling in her moment of need and grief? What good does poor Gilbert's pension do them, I ask you!"

Gilbert? Of all the names for a false husband. I wouldn't marry a Gilbert any more than a Humbert. Or Humphry or Jeremiah. Not that I was inclined to wed at all, nor was I certain whether the curate believed me to be this wretchedly unlucky widow, but in the event he did, I dabbed at my eyes dutifully for poor dead Gilbert. God rest his soul.

I cast a surreptitious glance to the curate beneath my lace-edged handkerchief. The young man was clearly affected by the tale. Cheeks pink with rage on my . . . her . . . someone's behalf. "Oh, that is abominable of them." The curate's frown deepened. He offered an arm to Mr. Owen, who stood slowly with a stooped stance. "Come. Let me take you to his study, perhaps you can find what you need there and compose yourself. It is a terrible burden for a father to bear. I'm sure Vicar would agree were he here."

Mr. Owen's damp eyes blinked away his crocodile tears, and he allowed the young man to lead him through the house. His step enfeebled and unsteady as they went into a dark paneled room. Books stacked high on the walls. Spines in exacting lines, not a one taller or shorter. With gradual gradations in shade. The man who organized these was clearly a monster. Who else would be as exacting? My own shelves were stacked whimsically based upon whatever mood struck. Horizontal, vertical. Sorted by interest rather than topic. Truth be told it was a wonder I found anything at all back home. And me a bookseller! A grave failing, indeed.

It wasn't until the door closed and the curate's footsteps retreated down the hall that I finally spoke. "All right . . . where to first?"

Mr. Owen went to the desk, trying the drawer. Locked. "You're pale, Ruby. Sit, use your picks, and I'll check the shelves."

I made my way across the room, pulled the rolled parcel from my crimson handbag, and selected my tool of choice.

"We're looking for December 1892, possibly January 1893," I said softly. "For the baptism of a Chenowyth child. November possibly if he died. But my guess is he lived. Is still alive, perhaps even somewhere in the village." My voice was scarcely over a whisper as I stooped down in front of the drawer and set to work on the lock. There were only a handful of men the right age, not a one of them was likely to be the long-lost heir.

Mr. Owen went to the bookshelf, his hand running skillfully over the titles, as he skimmed them, lips moving as he read each one. Within seconds I managed to unlock the drawer and began carefully perusing its contents. Paper. Pen. Some coins. Nothing terribly incriminating. I turned over a small enameled snuffbox in my hand and popped it open. Empty. My head swam and I paused, closing my eyes for a moment to right myself.

Mr. Owen on the other hand appeared to have had success. He lumbered over to me, setting a large book down on the desk. It landed with a thump, rustling the papers, and I cast a worried glance to the door before his dark eyes met mine. He appeared years younger now, with a vitality he hadn't possessed back in Exeter, and I had a suspicion it was the adventure that had brought on this effervescence.

"I found the baby."

Greedily I grabbed the book from him, skimming down the baptismal record.

Blackwells, Burns, Carson, Cartwright . . . my finger ran down the page until I landed on it.

George Chenowyth b. Nov. 12, 1892. To Sir Joseph Chenowyth Bt and Lady Elizabeth Chenowyth.

I looked up at Mr. Owen.

"You don't suppose. This George is . . ." *George Martin.*

"There are no coincidences, my girl, I taught you that. Right age. Right village."

I ran my tongue over my teeth going back over what I knew thus far. Both Joseph Chenowyth and his wife were killed by the curse. But no one. *No one*—had mentioned the existence of a child. Surely Mrs. Penrose would have known if there were a baby.

Well, that certainly complicated matters. Sir Edward had every reason to kill George. Not only had he stolen his wife and placed a cuckoo in his nest, he was the legitimate heir to the baronetcy. It also made it quite clear, at least to me, that the vicar was the blackmailer. But that still didn't explain who killed Edward, or why? It would suit the vicar to leave Edward alive and continue his tidy little income stream. There had to be something I was missing, another piece that hadn't quite fallen into place. I pinched the bridge of my nose, thinking, when I heard voices from the hall.

Both Mr. Owen and I froze in place.

"I've only come to pick up a few items. I have an appointment in town, which should take some time." The vicar had returned. This was bad. Very bad. I looked to Mr. Owen and scrambled to my feet. We had to get out of here, and it certainly wasn't going to be by the same means we entered.

The vicar wasn't going to look too kindly on us snooping around his office. I should have thought this out more carefully. What a muddle. I hurried to the door and slid the lock into the latch.

Mr. Owen raised his white eyebrows in confusion before quickly understanding my plan—bad as it was. He hurried to the window and threw open the sash, climbing out first and offering me a hand.

I scrambled out the window after him, sliding the sash back closed. The vicar would piece together what we'd done, but hopefully by then we would be better prepared to deal with him. Mr. Owen and I hurried through the shadowed churchyard, past the tilting gravestones, into the woods. The same wood where the boys had met the wraith earlier in the week. It seemed so long ago. A lifetime even.

Out of breath from the excitement I paused, leaning against a tree, and shut my eyes tight, trying to catch my breath despite the stitch in my side.

"I told you, you should have stayed in bed," he chided. With his forefinger he slid his wire-rimmed spectacles up his nose. The man baffled me. Of all the things, *that* was the first thing he had to say to me.

I opened my eyes long enough to glare at him.

"You aren't well, Ruby. You should rest."

There was no time to rest. We were close to the killer. I felt it. But I needed help. "We need to find Ruan, see what he makes of all this." And I hoped . . . hoped between the two of us we could make it clear, because at this point, hope was all I had left and I was running short on the stuff.

CHAPTER THIRTY-FIVE

The Final Piece

WALKING far slower than I would like, Mr. Owen and I left the village and headed for Nellie Smythe's cottage in hopes that Ruan was still there. Perhaps it was the aftereffects of my near-death experience slowing my thoughts, but I could not figure out what the two dead baronets, George Martin, Nellie Smythe, and I had in common.

I pushed the wooden gate open, much as I had when I first came to speak with Nellie. Except this time there was a pall over the house. The only sound was the large sow rooting around in the pen at the corner of the yard. The garden was overgrown again, weeds taking over, and a bucket of slop sat just on the outside of the pen as if whoever had been bringing it was called away in a hurry. Something about the scene gave me pause, but my mind was clouded with memories that refused to be placed in order.

I left Mr. Owen by the garden gate and went to the house. The wooden door was ajar and I could hear voices from inside. All female, though. I nudged it open with my foot and called out, "Hello?"

Another hushed conversation ensued before an unfamiliar

voice called. "Miss Vaughn, come on in. You've just missed our Pellar."

I let out a silent groan and stepped into the main sitting room of the house. Nellie was curled up on a worn sofa beside the fireplace, a woolen blanket over her lap and a fresh basket of wood on the hearth. She looked a hairbreadth from death, if even that far. Her skin held a faint bluish tint, her bones sharp and visible beneath her too-thin flesh.

"I heard that you were taken ill too." Nellie's voice cracked as she squinted across the sparsely decorated room to where I stood. "Come. Sit with me for a spell."

"Now, Nellie," an older woman protested, likely her mother by the look of her. She wore a simple woolen dress and resembled a wearier version of Nellie. "You need your sleep."

"I can come back another time. I actually came to find Rua . . . Mr. Kivell." I caught myself.

Nellie shook her head, wincing with the effort. Her mother grabbed an earthenware pitcher and refilled the glass before pressing it into her daughter's outstretched hand. The fire cracked and popped in the hearth. "Sit. Please. I'm tired of being fussed over, it'd be nice to have a bit of conversation for a minute."

Something inside me told me not to stay. That tarrying would be a mistake, and yet I pitied her. The two of us had survived what should have rightly killed us both. I could spare her a few moments. "What all did they tell you about what happened?"

She shifted and readjusted her blanket. "Only that I was poisoned. They said you were too, but you seem quite hale to me."

"I certainly don't feel hale."

Nellie smiled faintly at that. "Nor do I. Be grateful you are walking. I still don't have the strength to make it to the chamber pot."

"Do you remember anything from before?"

She shook her head, tucking a loose strand behind her ear. "You?"

"Nothing. It's strange. It's as if part of my life has been scissored entirely out. I can recall the day before, and I recall waking up." I carefully omitted the fact that I also had *hallucinated*. People already thought I was eccentric.

"Can you think of who'd want to do it?" I frowned. "I've been racking my brain and I cannot seem to find the connection here between the two of us."

Nellie whimpered as she pulled herself upright, tucking the blanket tighter around her legs. "If it were just you, I'd say it was Sir Edward's killer. That—pardon my saying—you'd been nosing a bit too close for comfort."

A reasonable thought. One that hadn't struck me, though it ought to have.

"But what do you think now?"

She glanced at me hesitantly, fiddling with the edge of her blanket. She was afraid. Visibly so. Her skin so thin, I could see her pulse fluttering away at her throat, blue veins visible.

"Nellie. It's all right. If you think you know something. Saw something, suspect something. Please tell me. It's important. I won't tell a soul where I heard it. I promise you that."

She wet her lips and drank a sip of water. "I'd better not. I don't know for certain and I know how quickly rumors can spread."

The hair on the back of my neck pricked to attention as I took another step to Nellie and settled myself on the floor by her. I covered her hands with my own, holding them gently against the cup. Her skin was damp and cool. "Tell me."

Nellie took in a haggard breath. "All I mean to say is I think you should talk to *her*."

"Her?"

Nellie nodded, her eyes downcast. "Your friend."

"Tamsyn? You think Tamsyn would . . ."

She sighed heavily as the fire cracked again, causing me to jump.

"It's just that she's the only one who has a reason to kill me. I'm talking out of place, I know it. And I don't know anything for certain, but . . . well, you already know about George and me."

I nodded slowly, mind racing to keep up with what she was saying.

"Nellie, hush. You can't speak of these things," her mother said. "Miss, my daughter is barely lucid. She's . . . she's been having dreams, she doesn't know what she says."

I glanced over my shoulder to where Mrs. Smythe watched her daughter helplessly.

"It's okay, Mother. She should know. She should know it all."

Mrs. Smythe threw her hands up and sank down into a chair on the other side of the room, defeated.

Nellie looked once more at her mother before she turned her full attention back to me. "George came to me the day before he died. Said he was going to talk to her, that he had a plan and that he was sorry that things didn't work out between us. He'd given me some money. Said it wasn't much but it would make him feel better to know I wasn't completely destitute. He also said that if things went to plan there would be more."

"That was kind of him . . ."

"Yes, well, that was George. He was a good one, and I knew he'd never marry me. I knew as soon as Sir Edward's child grew in me that no man would take me to wife. At least not easily."

I wanted to protest on that score, but it wasn't important right now. "You don't think he killed himself . . ."

"I didn't know what to think. His words didn't make any

sense." She shook her head. "At least not until recently, you see . . ." She tenderly ran her fingers over her rounded belly. "I'd gone up to the house to plead my case to Sir Edward again, see if he'd do the decent thing for his son. He was a miserly sort, wouldn't give without getting . . . if you catch my meaning. So we took back up again."

"Took back up . . ." I repeated, staring at her uncertainly.

She nodded. "He had food sent over and paid the rent. I'd pop around every few days and keep him company. Lady Chenowyth quit his bed over a year ago and he was a man of . . . considerable appetites." Nellie took another sip of water. "He was a talker, Sir Edward was—Anyway, one day he was saying how he was tired of his wife. How he'd divorce her if he knew that the brat—that's what he called the boy—wouldn't inherit."

My skin crawled.

"When was this . . . ?"

She rubbed her hands together as if to warm them. "I can't recall. Perhaps a month ago, maybe less? He threw me over not long after. I think he may have grown bored with me too. He was like that, you know."

But I'd already stopped listening. I'd pieced it together, the last little bit tying all of us together. Sir Edward, George, Nellie, and I.

It was Tamsyn.

She was what we all had in common and I had to go.

WITH A VIGOR I hadn't known I possessed, I bolted out of Nellie's cottage, past Mr. Owen, and straight through the village. I had to get to Penryth. I had to get Ruan. As much as I didn't want to believe she was capable of murder—that she could do such a thing—there was no other answer. Not now. She could easily put parsnips on her table as she never ate the things to begin with. I'd been dancing around the most obvious answer since the beginning and felt like an utter fool for missing the truth.

My breath scarcely would fill my lungs by the time I reached Ruan's cottage. My sides split and my body ached as I crested the top of the hill. Storm clouds loomed overhead, dark and foreboding. The wind had begun to pick up, sticking my blouse to my body.

"Ruan!" I shouted as I burst inside the small dwelling.

It was quiet.

Still.

Not even Dr. Heinrich remained inside. Where could he be? I hurried into the room where my trunk sat and dug around until I found Mr. Owen's Webley revolver and stuffed it into the waist of my crimson-striped walking skirt. I had to get to Penryth Hall and prayed it wasn't too late.

"Ruan!" The wind stole my voice as I called out behind the house. Useless. Utterly useless. He'd vanished, without a trace. I ran back around to the front garden, my skirt brushing along the herbs filling the air with their scent, when I saw the very last person I ever intended to see again.

The vicar. The man must have been looking for me ever since I escaped out the window of his office earlier in the day.

His face was redder than I'd ever seen it, his lips pressed into a tight line, and in his right hand he held a riding crop, smacking it against his left with a sickening slap. "How did I know I'd find you here, Miss Vaughn?" He took another step closer, blocking the gate and, along with it, my means of escape.

"I really must ask that you let me leave. I have somewhere I urgently need to be." I looked past him to the lane, gauging whether or not I could manage to jump the drystone fence without him catching me. Doubtful in my pitiable condition.

"I don't know why you couldn't leave well enough alone, Miss Vaughn. A pretty thing like you." Another meaty smack against his palm. "Should know better than nosing around in things that don't concern you."

"I haven't a clue what you mean . . ."

"Stop playing coy, Miss Vaughn. We both know what you discovered in the vicarage. You cannot imagine that my curate would fail to identify you? You are a most distinctive woman, even without the bruises."

Well. I'd known he'd identify us, I just hadn't cared overmuch at the time. "If you'd please just let me pass." My heart raced in my chest. Why would the foolish man not *move* out of the way?

"Well, it's no matter, Miss Vaughn, as I propose we trade, you and I." His eyes wetly raked their way over my body and I took a step back out of instinct. "You see, I have heard some delicious things about you and Lady Chenowyth. Things I'm most certain you would not want spoken of. That *she* would not want spoken of and I'd be more than happy to keep to myself. For a price of course . . ." Good God, did the man have no moral center? Evidently not. He rapped the crop again on his hand with a slap and at long last I lost my temper. The one my mother had always cautioned me to guard. I jerked the crop from his hands and threw it behind me into the garden where it disappeared beneath some leggy chamomile.

"I have asked you enough. If you do not move, I will have no other choice but to make you move. Now, please, let me pass," I gritted out, my fingers moving to the revolver tucked in my waistband.

The vicar let out a laugh, deep and sickening. "As if you'd have the stomach to strike down a man of God." He reached down, lifting the latch, and took a step inside the gate, closer to me, his pink tongue running roughly over his lips. The man's breath reeked of liquor, which explained his sudden loquaciousness. He eyed the stand of chamomile where the crop had fallen. "Spare the rod, Miss Vaughn . . . I'm sure you've heard that adage. And I have a mind to—"

But before he finished another word, I'd balled my fist, pulled back, and punched him with a decade's worth of unspent anger. The man dropped like a sack of Irish potatoes. I'd knocked him clean out, likely doing irreparable damage to my immortal soul in the process. Then again, I doubted God—if he even existed—cared much for blackmailers.

I hurried down the lane, and for the first time in my life I wished that I believed in something beyond reason. The figure from my dream danced through my thoughts. How she'd leaned over the child. Could it have been a warning? Would Tamsyn harm her own son? I couldn't believe it—wouldn't—but I'd been wrong before. So many times that I could not take the chance. Not again.

The sky was dark as a sound of low thunder rumbled over the distance.

There was nothing for it.

I ran.

CHAPTER THIRTY-SIX

A Waking Dream

THE halls of Penryth were eerily quiet in the dwindling daylight. My lungs didn't want to take in air and my body ached from lack of food and my recent exertions. But I had to get to the nursery. Had to know that my dream was just that—a dream and nothing more.

I skidded to a stop, slipping on the kitchen floor. Blood pooled beneath my feet in the doorway to the servants' stair. I took in a bracing breath and procceded slowly, afraid of what or who I'd find on the other side of the wooden frame.

The broken and beleaguered object within my chest stuttered as I followed the oozing dark substance into the kitchen to find Mrs. Penrose sprawled out on the floor. In the same room she'd been drawing shapes with Jori days before. I dropped to the ground beside her, laying a hand on her chest. She was breathing but her eyes remained closed. Her graying hair was matted to her head with blood. She must have surprised her attacker. A basket lay on the floor with the contents upturned, teacakes and biscuits mingling promiscuously with her life-blood on the dark flagstones. I gently probed the wound on her head. It was hot. Sticky.

She jerked upright, eyes flying open.

"Oh, maid, it's you." Her body relaxed slightly and she drew in a shaky breath, her eyes dazed and unfixed. "She's gone mad I tell you. Completely mad. I couldn't stop her."

I nodded, reaching up for a cleaning cloth to wrap around her head to slow the flow of blood. It wasn't serious, at least I didn't think so. Her eyes weren't dilated, they were clear and bright. "Go. Go, maid. Get the boy. I'll be fit in a moment." She rolled over onto her hands and knees before pulling herself to stand. "Go!"

"I'll come back. I promise." I pressed a kiss to her bloody temple.

Fingers wrapped around the revolver, I bolted from the kitchen and ran up the back servants' stair to the nursery, taking the steps two at a time. My thighs strained from the effort, but I couldn't feel them now. I would tomorrow.

If I see tomorrow.

I started down the third-floor hallway, floral wallpaper precisely as I'd seen in my dream. The only difference was that the ground beneath me was firm as stone. Though my weary legs begged to differ. Wobbling slightly, I stumbled against the wall like a sailor just returned from a year at sea.

Dammit, Ruby, there's no time for weakness. I braced myself for a moment and paused, sucking in a breath. Then a second. Hoping that whatever moments I stole wouldn't make the difference in life or death.

Footsteps creaked ahead on the old wooden floors, and I took in a final breath. It was time. The nursery door was only a few feet away and I had to believe—trust—in my dreams, as I'd not allowed myself to since I'd watched my entire family drown. I summoned the memory again, of the figure leaning over the cradle. There was no time to tarry.

I rounded the corner and turned the knob to the nursery.

CHAPTER THIRTY-SEVEN

The Wraith Revealed

MY eyes adjusted to the dimness of the nursery, the scene before me playing out exactly as it had in my dream. Light barely came in through the pulled dark curtains. And in the center was the woman from the orchard. Shrouded in white, leaning over the cradle and humming something low and soft. With her back to me, the creature was unaware of my presence.

A muted shuffling came from the corner, and I turned to the sound. *Tamsyn.* She was strung up precariously balanced on the tips of her bare toes. She wore only her chemise. Nothing else. The thin muslin damp with sweat. Wrists bound behind her back. My gaze slowly traveled upward, to the cloth shoved into her mouth. Her eyes wide. Frantic as she gave her head an imperceptible shake. I followed the sinister, yellowed rope wrapped around her delicate neck all the way to the rafters. She begged me silently, darting her gaze from me to the cradle.

I gave her a slight nod. She'd asked me from the beginning to protect Jori. She'd been right to be worried, in ways she was incapable of knowing then.

The shrouded figure remained still, softly singing an old

Cornish folk song. One I'd heard sung before late at night. I could only make out a fraction of the words but I recognized the cadence all the same. And the voice.

Alice. Alice Martin. My heart and head and eyes were at war with one another. Alice Martin? I didn't want to believe it, she'd seemed so kind and gentle.

"Oh, Georgie. That wicked woman stole you from me," she cooed against the boy's struggling form.

"Ma . . . ma . . . mama!" Jori's cries cut through the room.

"Your mama's dead, my little love. That evil man killed her. But I won't let you come to harm. No, I won't."

I was helpless exactly as I'd been in the dream. Watching. Powerless to do anything. Any hint of struggle risked knocking Tamsyn from the chair, likely to her death. And I couldn't shoot Alice for risk of hitting the child. She didn't seem to be a threat to him at the moment, but goodness only knew what she was thinking. *If she's thinking at all.* There was something dreamlike about her movements. Her actions. Even her voice sounded strange and lilting. No wonder she was mistaken for a ghost.

I was out of options. I'd have to roll the dice and hope my father's gambler luck ran through my veins as well.

I took a step closer, tucking the revolver back into the waistband of my skirt.

Alice hummed again before continuing on her song in that odd and otherworldly tone.

My blood chilled. I had to get her attention, to get her to put the boy down. "Alice? Alice, is that you?"

She turned at the sound of my voice, Jori in her arms struggling against her. His face red and angry. Wet with tears. We were all connected on a tenuous thread. One bound to break at any second as his cries grew louder and louder.

"Miss Vaughn." She cocked her head to one side in confusion. That was something. She recognized me at least.

"He seems terribly upset, would you like me to hold him for you?" I reached out my arms.

She smiled faintly and brushed a kiss to the squalling child's temple. "Oh, no, I lost him once. I won't lose my little lad again. Will I, Georgie?" She nuzzled his cheek as Jori strained against her.

She's gone mad.

Mrs. Penrose was right. Only the madwoman was not Tamsyn as I'd supposed. It was Alice. How could I have missed the clues? George was dead, likely murdered by Sir Edward, leaving his grieving mother to take justice into her own hands.

"He is a handsome lad." I took a step closer. Sweat pricked up beneath my arms and my breasts.

"Looks like his mother. She loved him so. But that monster killed her. Like a beast he did. But I taught him." She nuzzled the baby, who only screamed louder. "I taught him, didn't I, Georgie?"

Somewhere deep down I knew that Alice wouldn't harm Jori—or so I hoped. I swallowed hard, taking a step nearer.

"Don't you think he has the look of Elizabeth?" She held the squirming boy down for my approval.

Biting my lower lip, I nodded. My mouth dry. "Yes. Yes, he does rather."

"Have you met my sister?" Alice's expression shifted and she tugged Jori back against her chest hard. "You've never met my sister, have you?"

"I—"

She turned slowly, placed the boy into the cradle, and tucked a blanket tightly around his arms. Jori's wails grew loud enough to wake the dead.

"That's a lad," she murmured before turning to me, her eyes cold. Emotionless.

Perfect, now if only I could get her a little farther away from the cradle.

She stalked across the room, the white robe billowing around her with each achingly slow step. She shifted slightly, and a sharp curved knife appeared in her hand. "He has her eyes, doesn't he? Her beautiful brown eyes. Look. Look at my Georgie. Doesn't he have the loveliest brown eyes?"

I hadn't a clue what color the child's eyes were as I'd only seen him a time or two and never paid it much mind. I wet my lips, stepped closer to the cradle, and made one strategic error that any heroine in one of Mr. Owen's prized collection of gothic novels would never ever do—I turned my back on a madwoman. Within an instant she had that same curved blade at my throat.

"Elizabeth, you see, had blue eyes." Her voice was hot and damp as she hissed into my ear.

"I knew that. I was only—"

The blade pressed tight against my skin. A trickle of blood ran down my clavicle. If I were the praying sort, I might have said one—but instead I held my breath.

"And here you've come to take him too. Everyone trying to take my Georgie from me." Alice pulled me toward the window, ripping back the curtains, flooding the room with midday sun while Tamsyn stood helplessly on the chair.

This was how we'd die. The two of us stared at each other in disbelief that somehow this was how our story would end. And I couldn't help but regret all the thousands of things that went unsaid between us, and the thousand more terrible ones said.

I'd been wrong. Judged her. Blamed her. Thought her the villain in my play due to my own stubborn inability to let go of the past. And my failing would doom us both. One heartbeat. Then another. My chest barely moved at all as I counted the seconds waiting for the moment when Mrs. Martin's tenuous grasp on reality finally snapped.

CHAPTER THIRTY-EIGHT

Fly Away, Fly Away Home

"ALICE Martin!" Ruan's voice roared from behind me, bringing with it a peculiar blend of relief and terror. "What in God's name do you think you're doing?!"

With the knife pricking at my throat I was hoping he wouldn't startle her and cause the blade to slip. I was rather fond of my neck, even if I was contemplating my own mortality just seconds before.

"They've tried to take my Georgie!" Her voice cracked as her muscles tightened around me. I leaned deeper into her body. To think, I'd found her a charming woman. This did not bode well for my judgment.

"That's not your George and you well know it. Look at him, Alice. Let go of the girl and look at the child." Ruan's voice took on a slightly softer edge. Alice moved me toward the cradle with a jerk.

He stood there motionless, hands open, arms outstretched. "Let her go, and look at the baby."

Alice's grip on my belly tightened.

"George is dead, Alice. He's dead. You're mistaken. Your mind is clouded. Listen to me."

Don't remind her, Ruan. He shot a glance at me. His peculiar eyes showed something in their depths. Acknowledgment. He heard me. I knew it then. He gave me a slow steady nod, the riot of my pulse drowning out all other sound.

"He's not dead, he's . . ." She turned her head to look at the cradle when the air in the room took on that same electric scent. Sharp and crisp. The one I'd first noticed in the copse with Ruan. Then I'd felt it again when we were examining Sir Edward's body in the cellar.

I *felt* him. It.

Whatever *it* was. *It* began with the gradual softening of her grasp on my belly, the knife falling limply to her side. Followed by the tremulous breath she drew in that lifted the hairs on my neck with her exhalation. In an instant her grief washed over her, flooding through me like a dam break by extension. And at last the knife clattered to the floor at her feet.

"He's Georgie's boy . . ." Alice turned to Tamsyn, her face stricken, before looking back to me. "Oh God, what have I done?" Mrs. Martin touched the scabbed-over cut on my brow uncertainly. "I almost killed you, maid." Her unblinking eyes searched my face as if she'd woken from a dream and could not quite understand what had come to pass.

Ruan had done something. He remained there immobile, hands outstretched, eyes unnaturally bright with that same intense expression he'd worn in the copse. She began to repeat herself. Nonsensical words I couldn't make out, nor did I care.

I dropped down, scooping up the blade, and hurried to Tamsyn's side, cutting at her bindings. Nothing else mattered but freeing her. The knife, sharp as it had been against my flesh, took ages to make its way through the worn hemp. As the last bit broke free, Tamsyn scrambled down from the chair, sending it tumbling in her haste to reach Jori. She scooped him against her chest, pressing frenzied kisses to his mop of dark curls. He wrapped his chubby arms around her neck, and the two of them slid to the floor.

It was done.

Done. Yet I couldn't quite believe it.

Alice stood frozen in the middle of the room, her hands limp at her sides. She didn't move. Didn't utter a word. She simply looked at Ruan with that familiar thousand-yard stare that I'd seen during the war.

"We should tie her up, I suppose?" I asked tentatively.

He nodded warily as he watched Alice. It seemed neither of us quite knew what to do next. "And then we'll wait on Enys."

"No." Tamsyn's chin rested atop her son's dark curls. Even Alice turned at the sound of her voice. "There will be no more bloodshed. I've had my fill." The red marks at her neck where the rope had chafed were already visible against her skin. "You will not have my child. You will not have my life. Do you understand me, Alice Martin? But neither will I have your blood on my hands."

The older woman sucked in a sharp breath. "I'll hang either way. I've killed a baronet. But after what he did to my sister. To his own uncle!" The silence in the room crackled as we all watched Alice, Ruan's arms now folded across his chest. The familiar divot formed deep between his brows. "Someone had to do it. He couldn't get away with it."

Tamsyn looked up suddenly in surprise. "Get away with what?"

I tried to remember what Mrs. Penrose had said about the previous killings, and then it struck me—the meaning behind Alice's words. "Alice, do you mean to say that Edward had a hand in what happened here thirty years ago?"

Her face was wet as she gazed upon Tamsyn, almost as if she sought forgiveness for her actions. "I was only a girl then, mind. Promised to my Benedict. We was to wait to wed until he'd managed to purchase a bit of land of his own. To set us up proper." Alice took in a shaky breath. She turned toward the open window. The sweet late-summer breeze causing the heavy curtains to sway ever so gently. "Joseph Chenowyth was a handsome man and he turned our Lizzie's head. It wasn't like it was with Sir Edward, his uncle was a decent man. A good one. He'd been widowed for years, and I like to think my sister made him happy. She was beautiful, Lizzie was, with hair just like that." She pointed to the back of Jori's head. "All roan curls and bright eyes, eyes that could put the sun to shame."

Tamsyn ran her hand over the back of her son's head, her own eyes glistening.

This was all fine and well and touching, but it didn't take away the fact she'd killed a man. I folded my arms across my chest and wet my lips, waiting for her to continue.

"Their love was a scandal before the marriage to say the least." She let out a cold laugh that settled in my veins. "But they loved each other, and she found herself with child. Sir Joseph couldn't deny the lure of having himself an heir at last. It was his greatest dream." She pressed her eyes shut hard against the memories.

"But dreams never last, do they, Mrs. Martin?" I took a step nearer to her. Ruan shot me a warning glance, halting me in my tracks.

"No. That they don't." When she opened her eyes again, they were clear. A far cry from the woman who'd tried to cut my throat seconds before. Whatever madness had possessed her had flown away, out the window, and had been borne to sea upon the Cornish winds. "Edward found out about the marriage and was furious. And my Lizzie was worried, so Sir Joseph sent her away. I went with her of course, because she was near her time. I'd lived at the hall with them for months. Lizzie showed me the passages in the walls, all the secrets of the house. She was proud to be its mistress. But even the house and all her secrets couldn't keep us safe. Not once Edward realized the child would be legitimate."

"So it was you that Fiachna noticed in the walls."

She nodded grimly.

"And you that attacked me in my bed."

She nodded again. "I didn't know it was you. I didn't, maid. Not that it makes it right what I did."

"You thought it was her." I tilted my head to Tamsyn, thinking back on the bruises I'd first spotted on her cheek. Mrs. Martin squeezed her eyes shut.

"I did, maid. I thought you were her. With Sir Edward out of the way, if she were gone then . . ." Tears fell down her cheeks and she hastily wiped them away. "I don't know why. I don't understand what happened, what came over me."

"It's all right," Tamsyn said softly, her chin resting on her son's head. "What's done is done and we can't change it. Now tell us the rest."

It most certainly *wasn't* all right. But I held my tongue all the same.

Alice frowned, her hands trembling as she fiddled with the sleeves of her robe. "We stayed in Falmouth with my mother's cousin. He'd have never found us there—Edward, that is." Her voice hitched with barely tethered emotion. "Sometimes I wish I hadn't let her return. I argued with her. I did!" Her hands formed into fists. "I wanted her to stay in Falmouth with little George. Sir Joseph told her that he'd come for us once he'd settled things with his nephew, and it was all fine and well until his letters stopped. Lizzie grew frantic. We all knew of the curse, everyone in these parts does. And she was convinced some evil befell him."

"Some evil did," I grumbled.

Ruan shot me a quelling look, his back straight and expression grave as he focused every ounce of himself on the task at hand. "Go on, Alice." His voice was so even and cool I scarcely recognized it. He was their Pellar now.

"We left Georgie in Falmouth and traveled back to Lothlel Green. She had to know why he'd stopped writing. When we returned, the village was in a panic. The curse had returned and taken him."

"But it wasn't the curse, was it, Mrs. Martin?"

"No. It was Edward. He'd killed his uncle. Just as he killed my sister. I saw him do it. I'd gone for a walk while she was at her prayers. Thought to give her a little peace with her grief. If I'd known . . . if I'd even thought that he was coming for her as well, I'd have never left her side. I was coming back through the hidden passageway to the morning room and I saw him. I should have done something. Anything. But I was so young and afraid that I ran."

Like Charles had in the churchyard.

"And you'd have been killed too if you'd tried," Ruan said gently. "You can't blame yourself for that."

She took in a shaky breath. "I suppose not."

"Did you tell anyone what you saw?" Tamsyn asked, looking among the three of us.

"And who would believe me? My word against the Chenowyth heir?"

"But why now? Why hurt the boys? Why me? Why Nellie? Why . . . Alice? After all this time, tell me why." I threw my hands up in frustration, the knife still in my palm.

"Enough, Ruby." Ruan's voice was low. But he was correct. This moment wasn't about me. Not now. I blew out a breath and took another step backward, the three of us in some sort of unholy triangle around Alice. The witch. The heiress. And the mother. We could have been etched on a page from one of

Ruan's grimoires, set in gilt. There was something ancient in what was happening in this room. Something I couldn't quite understand. Not yet. Perhaps not ever.

"It doesn't matter, Pellar. There's nothing she could say to me that I wouldn't deserve. I . . . I don't know what came over me. I'd been coming here for years, visiting with Dorothea, and then a few months ago I saw the baby. Saw him in the house and I knew he was George's boy. So I'd come more often, bringing treats and sweets. I thought I could live that way, that it would be enough to share in that tiny piece of him. Then something changed. A few weeks ago I . . ." Her gaze was fixed on the back of Jori's head. "I grew convinced . . . I *was* convinced—certain he was my boy . . . I—"

"You let your grief take hold?" Ruan's voice was tender when he spoke. It was a wonder he could summon the emotion considering Alice was quite literally a step away from slitting my throat when he walked in the nursery.

"For weeks now I've tried to get him. Waiting until he was alone, or someone was asleep, but there were always people about." Her eyes remained downcast, unable to witness what her pain had caused. "I couldn't help myself, couldn't stop it. The voices were too strong, telling me to take him. That Sir Edward would kill him as he did my Georgie. That this was the only way to keep him safe . . ." Her voice broke.

Weeks . . . she'd been trying for weeks. I swallowed down the lump in my throat. What if I hadn't come to Lothlel Green when I did? "But why kill the boy's mother?"

Alice had no answer. She opened her mouth then shut it again tight. "There's no excuse for what I've done. Nothing I can say for myself."

Tamsyn darted her gaze between Ruan and me. She paused, wetting her lips. "There is another choice."

"The woman tried to kill you. There is no other choice."

Tamsyn ignored me, her expression unreadable. "She could leave here. Leave Cornwall and never return."

"What?!" I'm not sure whether Ruan or I said the word first. The pair of us equally incredulous at the suggestion.

"She's nearly killed half the village in some sort of misguided sense of vengeance!"

Tamsyn shifted Jori in her lap. "You can't say Edward didn't deserve it for what he did. He was a murderer. Can you truly bear to see a woman hanged for meting out the justice that was denied her?"

I huffed out my breath. "Yes, well, that would have all been fine and well had she not nearly killed me and poor Miss Smythe in the process with her damned poisons! Why did you poison us, anyway?"

"It was an accident, both of you. Neither you nor Nellie were meant to eat the pasties."

"No, because I was," Tamsyn whispered. Her eyes fixed on the floor. "Wasn't I, Mrs. Martin?"

Mrs. Martin nodded.

"Dorothea was supposed to take some to the vicarage at first. But when that failed, I had her bring some here."

The vicar? At last the final piece snapped into place. "So the boys weren't supposed to be harmed either."

Alice shook her head. "No. That terrible man. He's the reason my son is dead. Had he not told George the truth of his birth and used it against Sir Edward . . . then none of this would have occurred. But when Jago and Charles stumbled upon me in the woods . . . I . . . I thought I could frighten them away but—Oh God, what have I done?"

I had no sympathy left for her, at least not anymore. "You could have killed them. All of them. And had Mrs. Penrose eaten one of the pasties, you'd have killed your oldest friend too. As it is, you've nearly made a murderer of her."

"Ruby . . . let her finish her tale," Tamsyn warned.

Alice blanched, her hands going to her throat. "I hadn't thought of that. But Dorothea never cared for parsnips. That's what gave me the idea in the first place. It's why I gave her the water hemlock. I knew she'd mistake the two and put it out for supper for Sir Edward. It would have been so neat and tidy."

"Except I was there . . ."

She nodded. "Sir Edward left the house and went for air. He often took a turn in the gardens in the evening. But for some reason he went out into the orchard. I'd only meant to watch him die. To make sure he knew I was the one who'd done it. But I couldn't help myself . . . I . . . cut him, and then I came back for his wife . . ."

"I've heard enough." These were not the doings of a sad woman. These were the actions of a monster. Surely Tamsyn had to see this. I cast a glance to her, but her expression remained as unreadable as before.

"You cannot take vengeance in your own hands, Alice. No matter how richly deserved," Ruan said softly. At least someone in this room saw reason.

"Where were you going to take Jori?" Tamsyn asked, ignoring both Ruan and me.

"America."

She was thinking, twisting one of Jori's curls around her forefinger, before she turned to Alice. "Then go. Take your husband and start over. Away from this place and all of us."

"Tamsyn, you can't possibly think to let her go."

"Her guilt will eat away at her more than any prison cell could manage."

As the sense of panic fled my body, it was replaced by

another headier emotion—exhaustion. Every second of the last twenty-four hours had etched itself deep into my bones, and I had no will to argue with her. Not anymore.

"If we go along with this mad scheme—and I am not saying we are—" I held up a hand. Ruan furrowed his brow. "How on earth are we going to explain this?"

Tamsyn stood, shifting the weight of her now-sleeping child in her arms. Clueless to the devastation that almost occurred in his name. Or rather, his true father's name. "It's the curse, of course. The Curse of Penryth Hall. No one will question it. Will they, Pellar?"

Ruan shook his head, raking his dark curls back with his left hand.

No. No, I supposed they wouldn't.

"It's settled then. You'll go to America and we will find a way to begin again."

Tamsyn had changed this week into someone else entirely. Soft on the outside, but with an inner core sterner than I'd ever realized her capable of being. Or perhaps—she hadn't changed at all, it was I who had changed, finally seeing her for who she was, who she'd always been.

"I can see why he loved you, my lady. And I wish . . ." Alice blinked back her tears. Eyes glassy. "I wish things could have been different for all of us."

Tamsyn swallowed hard. "As do I."

Silent tears streamed down Alice's face. She turned to Ruan, laying a palm on his chest, reaching up to cup his cheek with the other in a display of maternal tenderness.

He sucked in a sharp breath, his eyes widened. "No, Alice. Don't."

She straightened her spine and stepped backward. First one foot, then its mate. "Set me free, Ruan Kivell. Set me free."

He didn't blink. His gaze never wavering from hers. Ruan's

lips were a thin line as he shook his head. His voice cracked with quickly unraveling emotion. "I won't. I can't, Alice. Don't. Please."

What was happening?

She took another step backward in this strange dance between the two of them.

"This is the only way forward for us. We all know it. Even if you won't accept it."

Alice took a determined step backward into the large open window, and suddenly I knew how the tale unfolded. She was going to jump.

Her hands gripped the sill, knuckles white. Her body silhouetted by the sun making a shadowy cross on the nursery floor. The white robes flapped in the wind.

My heart lodged in my throat. *Do something. Stop her . . .* Yet I couldn't move, couldn't even draw breath for fear it would make her slip and fall to her death. Ruan watched her, his steady unblinking gaze fixed.

"Let me go, Pellar. Please let me go. I want to fly free with my George. I don't deserve it, God knows I don't after all I've done, but grant me that."

Several seconds passed before Ruan took in a haggard breath and gave in, closing his eyes.

Silence.

A flutter.

Then a sickening smack.

I scrambled to the window and leaned over the ledge, knowing good and well what I'd find. Alice Martin's broken body lay on the cobbles below. Her head at an unnatural angle from her shoulders as a pool of dark blood ran out beneath.

Alice Martin was free.

CHAPTER THIRTY-NINE

A Separate Sort of Love

RUAN didn't speak after Mrs. Martin jumped from the window. But she didn't jump. Not really. She stepped. Falling backward waiting on some unseen hands to reach out and ease her fall. The eerie fan of the white gown sprawled around her brought to mind the snow angels that my sister and I would make as children in New York.

My eyes burned.

I looked up at Ruan, his jaw set firm.

"She . . ."

"Dead."

I glanced back down at her broken form. "How . . . how do you know?"

"How is she not?" Ruan walked out of the nursery, the door closing behind him, leaving me alone with Tamsyn and her boy. She hadn't moved. Not an inch since she'd grabbed ahold of her son. The two of them cradled together on the clean dark oak floors. Brilliantly polished in the midmorning sun.

Alice was dead.

It was over. Truly over. Tamsyn and her child were safe at last and yet I didn't know whether to be grateful or horrified at how it all unfolded. Tamsyn had been willing to let the woman go. To allow her to walk free from all the terrible things she'd done, and yet Alice didn't take the chance. She chose a third option. To die in her own way.

I couldn't make sense of it.

I didn't know what to do, whether I should speak to her, to go nearer, or just leave this godforsaken place and never return. The final one being the simplest and wisest choice.

Tamsyn reached out for me with her hand. "I know you don't understand why."

Her sentence answered my question. Instead of fleeing I walked over, took her hand, and fell to the floor beside her. Her eyes were dry and clear with a resolve and certainty I did not share. My fingers closed around hers, rubbing the bones along the back of her hand with my thumb.

"You'll be returning to Exeter, I expect."

I swallowed hard and nodded.

"I think that's for the best. I . . ." Her voice caught in her throat, the slightest tremor there revealing her distress.

"Tamsyn, you've been through a great deal. There's no need for you to spea—"

"Hush. You always talk and talk and talk and I need to say my piece for now. I need for you to understand me. Truly understand me for once. You and I have been at sixes and sevens ever since you arrived here. I've tried a dozen ways to explain to you, but I think . . . I think perhaps now you can understand."

I snapped my mouth shut.

"I gave Alice Martin freedom. Something I never had. I wish to God that someone would have given me that same gift. Though I don't know I'd have been brave enough to grab on to it. Not then at least."

I frowned, not understanding.

"You see, my entire life, ever since I was a little girl, has been mapped out for me. First, my father. Then my dreams with George. Then you. You remember our plans, don't you? Where we'd go. What we'd do? Flittering around like larks. Never staying in one place too long. Seeking warmth and excitement, but never anything deeper. Never anything with roots. Permanence."

I did. I'd built my hopes upon those dreams. Dreams that she'd dashed upon the rocks. But to hear them spoken back to me, they sounded hollow. Shallow. Not that I longed for permanence—never that—but I longed for . . . something, something intangible that I couldn't articulate if I tried.

"I realized along the way that those things were never my dreams at all. They were yours, Ruby. Your dreams. Your plans. Your passion. It's why I left. I loved you too much and I knew if I had stayed, you'd have either broken my heart or clipped your own wings for me. I saw it then and made the decision for the both of us."

"But—"

She held up a hand to silence me. "No. You see, I have never begrudged you your dreams. Not a one. I thought—believed—that loving you enough would make your dreams my own. That I could be happy to live in your shade. That my loving you would make you stop taking those risks and stop being so . . . *you* . . . but we shouldn't ever try to change those we love, should we?"

I swallowed hard, still adjusting to her words. But she'd asked for my silence, so I was giving it to her. Letting her speak until no words remained. I could do that.

"But I've come to realize only recently that I subsumed myself to you then. To everyone who ever mattered." She turned to me with a sad small smile.

This might be the most honest we'd been with each other, and I didn't know what to do with her truth.

"One can't live like that forever." Tamsyn pulled her hand from mine and shifted the sleeping child on her lap. He let out a little moan and curled back against her. "Existing as nothing more than an appendage. An afterthought. Daughter. Wife. Lover. Friend. I suppose I followed along in that way because it was easier. Simpler not to fight the tide. It's my nature, you see—I'm not brave like you. I'm not particularly ambitious either. It would have been enough for me to marry George and live here in this village. Raise our children. I could have been happy like that. Picking flowers in the meadow, being a mother. A wife. Perhaps having a dog or three. I've never even had a dog, come to think of it. I might have even been able to make a good life with Edward, were he faithful. You see, I'm not a dreamer, Ruby. I never was."

Tears welled up in my eyes, not for myself, but for her. Had this woman truly been standing there before me all these years and I never saw, never listened to what she had to say—just ran roughshod over her like all the men in her life had done since the day she came into the world? But the truth was evident, starkly written across her lovely face. I'd just ignored all the signs.

"But the truth is, I was afraid. Terrified to stand on my own feet. To claim something for my own. You see, it was easier to stay with Edward, vile as he was, because I had a place in this world. I was so afraid of what it would make me if I broke away. If I left him, who was I?"

Her words struck like little shards of broken glass, embedding themselves into my chest. "I never meant to make you feel that way."

"Of course you didn't." She tucked a lock of hair behind my ear and kissed me softly. "I made that choice for myself. To put myself second to everyone. But I think . . . I think . . . that for once I'd like to live a little more like you do." She flushed at the implication of her words. "Not perhaps in the particulars. I've never been quite that daring, but I think I would like to discover who I am and see if there's anything of substance left beneath my skin."

"You know there is."

"I suspect there might be, but I need time to find her, I think. To be alone for a while."

I furrowed my brow. "But you aren't alone. You have your son and your writing."

"And that's why it's become important. I hadn't really thought . . . hadn't imagined that I could lose Jori before to-day. And in an instant with that woman holding my son in her arms, I almost lost everything that truly mattered. But I know now who I need to be. For myself and for him. It's a separate sort of love—the kind one has for one's child. The sort that makes you want to be better, try harder. To be worthy of this little creature entrusted to you even though you know you're destined to fail." Tamsyn took my hands in her own. "You see, Ruby, I think I need to grow up. Be someone my son can be proud to call his mother—because right now I don't think I'm that person at all."

I swallowed hard.

"Please say you understand. Of all people in this world, I thought you might."

She looked up at me through damp lashes and in that mo-ment I supposed I did. I'd found her again during this blood-filled week—my dearest friend—hidden beneath all the pain and lies and secrets, and I couldn't help but be glad of it.

SITTING ON A bench in the formal gardens outside the house after leaving Tamsyn, I rolled an unlit cigarette between my fingers. I was worn to the bone, if not to my very soul—if such a thing was possible. The image of Alice's broken body was not one I would easily forget. Constable Enys had come and gone, and her lifeless form had been loaded up on a cart and taken back to the Martin farm for a quiet burial.

I could only imagine how hard the news would be for Benedict. Did he even know the depths of her crimes? Surely not. And yet, I didn't know how he could have missed his wife's descent into madness. Though I hadn't seen it myself until it was nearly too late. But it all made perfect sense. Alice had always been *here*. Always around, waiting for her opportunity to strike. I swallowed hard.

The spot where she'd fallen, visible from where I sat, was now empty aside from the dark stain upon the cobbles. I closed my eyes and blew out a breath. Could a broken heart drive a person to such lengths? *A separate sort of love,* that's what Tamsyn had said. Perhaps it was that after all.

The birds quieted, and I opened my eyes to discover the Pellar there in front of me. Ruan. I wasn't certain which he was now. It had all blurred together in the last couple of days and I no longer knew what was real and what was false when it came to him. The only thing I did know, was he wore his troubles upon his face as I did. Alice's death weighed upon him and I didn't need to read his thoughts to see it.

The edge of his mouth turned up. He must have heard that. He remained motionless, silent and unmoving, like one of Tamsyn's Cornish giants of yore.

I reached up, smoothing the divot between his brows with my thumb. "You know you do need to speak at some point. While you might be privy to my thoughts—I lack that same ability."

"Don't blame Alice for what she's done."

I glowered up from beneath my lashes. "Maybe don't say that."

He smiled at me then in earnest and shook his head. Creases had formed at the corners of his eyes. "I don't have to listen to them to know. I know you, Ruby Vaughn. I think I've known you my whole life—whether you care to admit it or not."

Oddly, I'd had the same sentiment as well. As if Ruan and I were opposite sides of a coin. Bound by something I didn't care to ponder. "What do you suppose will become of Benedict? How will he take the news?"

Ruan flexed his broad hand before answering. "Not well, I'm afraid. Alice was his whole world. But he'll survive. It's part of life—the going on—oh, he knew she was unwell, but none of us knew how deep the sickness went. She was far more ill than any of us realized."

"Do you think he knew she killed Edward?"

Ruan shrugged.

"But if he did . . . how could he?"

"He loved his wife. Men have done far worse things, for less foolish reasons. I worry for him, though; his life has revolved around Alice and that smallholding. They never had children of their own, and they raised George from a babe. I cannot imagine he'll want to stay long with all those memories without her."

I nodded grimly. "Why didn't you stop her? I saw her. She wouldn't have jumped if you'd told her no."

He took a deep breath and let it out again. The air whipped up around us, snapping at my striped skirt, causing it to billow up beneath me.

"I let Alice choose her fate. She chose death."

Freedom. Ruan too had given her freedom.

He wet his lips for a moment. "I'm their Pellar. Not an angel of mercy."

Nor I. Ruan reached in his pocket and struck a match, offering it to me. I lit my cigarette, sucking in the smoke and exhaling. "So you let her choose her death."

Another grim nod. "What's done is done, Ruby. I can't bring her back, she paid for her crimes." He glanced down at my bruised knuckles and took them in his hand, running his fingers over the raw skin there. "And it seems you're no angel of mercy either."

I followed his gaze to my wounded hand. It seemed so long ago that I'd laid out the vicar with a decent left hook. Even now that the danger had passed, I still couldn't bring myself to regret the decision. "He deserved it."

Ruan let out a soft laugh, my hand still in his. "Would it please you to know that I was speaking of the man with Enys just a few moments ago?"

That piqued my interest. "Were you? Did you tell him about the blackmail?"

"I didn't need to. Turns out that Sir Edward wasn't the only one helping to line the vicar's pockets. Enys has been quietly gathering information for months now. Had Sir Edward not been killed, likely charges would have been brought already."

"That's something at least," I grumbled and pulled my hand back, running my own fingers over the roughed-up flesh.

"It doesn't please you?" Ruan furrowed his brow in concern. "I thought you'd be glad that he was finally going to face some retribution for what he's done. He might not be charged in connection with Sir Edward, but at least he'll not be able to do it again."

I sighed. I should be happy, and yet I wasn't. Not at all. "It's not that . . . I'm glad of it, I am, but I cannot stop thinking about the poison. In her madness how many people would Alice have killed? If you hadn't found me . . . or if you hadn't gone to Nellie that night, then we'd both be dead. Who knows how many others?"

He reached out, touching my cheek softly with the back of his hand. "But I did go to you."

I'll always go to you. He didn't say it, but I knew it all the same. Something lived between Ruan and me, it wasn't love— nor even lust. It was something else entirely—something far more powerful and far more frightening than either of those. He brushed his roughened thumb over my brow. "You're a tempest, Ruby Vaughn. Never let that change." His palm cupped my cheek as he looked down at me.

I struggled to swallow. My throat was thick as I warred with the urge to lean closer. Perhaps there might have been an ounce of lust in there as well. Only a bit. I sniffed and looked away from his face. "In a teapot perhaps." My words came out weak, feeble as my heart thundered in my chest, like the fool girl I'd been back in New York before my downfall. Bookish and awkward. Unsure. Unsteady.

He drew nearer. Pulled on some sort of invisible tether between us and, God help me, I wanted him closer yet. It had to be the day we'd endured, or the fact I'd nearly died more times than I cared to count. Or that I'd watched a woman throw herself from a window. Because there was no way he should affect me so. It was . . . improbable. Impossible. I'd been around the world, to war and back, and done things that would make the most wicked of men blush. And yet here I was, utterly undone by the most impossible of men. *This* man.

"You haven't even discovered a portion of who you are yet to be. It takes time and courage to do that." He leaned nearer, absorbing every bit of my focus, making it difficult to breathe. "And we know you've both of those in spades."

"Who is talking now, the witch or the man?" My voice

cracked as I stared up into his unsettling eyes, only inches from me.

There was nothing left in this world but him. His green scent. The warmth. This moment. This . . . this was terrible. This was . . . and before I finished my thought, he kissed me. At least I think he did. Everything flew out of my head but the sheer sensation of him washing over me. *Ruan Kivell.* The softness of his lips brushing mine and then it was gone as quickly as it had come, taking along any good sense I might have had. His voice came out just over a whisper, and yet it echoed in my jaded little heart. "Both."

He sat down on the bench beside me with a heavy sigh. I leaned my head on his shoulder and closed my eyes. "You should give Benedict the tickets."

"Tickets?" His voice was raspy. Good. At least I wasn't the only one who'd lost their head. Served him right to kiss a girl like that.

"To America. Give him a new start away from all this." He straightened and ran a hand over his jaw. "For what it's worth, I truly don't think she meant to hurt you. Nellie either."

I let out a strangled laugh. "Now, that's a fine thought. I am grateful that you saved me. However it was done." The word struck me hard the moment I said it. I was done here. Going home. I couldn't bear to leave him. Not like this, but at the same time I had no reason to remain. I'd done what I meant to—more than I'd meant to. "So . . . I suppose this is goodbye then? By the afternoon I'll be back to Exeter with Mr. Owen and my demon-cat."

"Mmm. Oh. I meant to tell you, I thought you'd find this amusing."

The stitches tugged as I arched a brow. *Damn.* I'd never heal at this rate.

"It was Mrs. Penrose who placed the bottle beneath your bed."

My jaw fell. "She what?"

He smiled faintly and shook his head. "She thought it would protect you. She'd asked dozens of times before if I'd make charms and I refused. I guess she took matters into her own hands."

"You're having me on . . ."

He shook his head. "No. The poor woman. I was stitching her up in the kitchen and I think her conscience overtook her. Once she admitted to what she'd done, I think she expected me to give her a proper scold."

I smiled at that. At least it wasn't an ill wish after all, simply a misapplied one. "How long had it been there?"

"She claims she'd placed it there the morning that Sir Edward was found. She'd seen the bruises on your throat in the woods and thought to protect you from the curse."

I sighed and shook my head in disbelief. "You mean to tell me that after finding a disemboweled man in the apple orchard, she went and took matters into her own hands?"

Ruan nodded gravely. "So it seems."

"Remind me not to cross Tamsyn's housekeeper."

Ruan stretched his neck to one side, putting me in mind of Fiachna. "I don't know how much longer she'll be that either. I think three murders during her time here was one too many."

"I can't say I blame her." I hesitated for a moment before looking up at him again. "Write me when you get back. Let me know what Benedict decides to do."

"I'd best go see to him. He'll need a friend tonight." Ruan stood and started to go, his footsteps quiet on the gravel path.

"Ruan!" I called as he got about ten paces away. He paused and turned back with his dark brows raised in silent question.

"Ruan, what *are* you going to tell everyone? You can't truly think they'll all believe this was a curse!"

He shot me a wicked smile. One I didn't think a man as provincial as he could possibly possess. "That's the thing about curses, Ruby Vaughn. Sometimes you have the devil of a time figuring them out."

EPILOGUE

A week later, I was settled comfortably back into the town house in Exeter, feeling a hundred years wiser and twice as restless. Perhaps that's the problem with solving murders: the return of ennui. More likely, I needed to get back to work—to do something to keep my darker thoughts at bay. I still wished Mr. Owen would let me join Howard Carter on his expedition to Egypt, but he'd made his stance on the matter perfectly clear. I was—under no circumstances—to cavort with archaeologists, professionally or otherwise.

Alas.

I dove into the still, warm waters of the jade-tiled bathing pool. Water slicking over my body as I swam the length before flipping, kicking off the wall, and going for another lap without surfacing. My lungs were fit to burst but I felt gloriously alive for the first time since leaving Lothlel Green. I surfaced and gasped for air, slicking my short hair back from my brow.

"Morning, lass."

Mr. Owen wore a garish lilac dressing gown and sat at the

water's edge beneath a large parasol, balancing a yellow china cup on his knee. He was looking well. Better than well. Perhaps having a small adventure did him good too.

I swam over to where he sat, rested my chin on the smooth decking, and blinked up at him. It was dreadfully sunny. But then again, give it fifteen minutes and it'd probably be raining again. That was the way of it this week. "How long have you been watching me?"

He lifted a shoulder. "Just wanted to make sure you didn't drown yourself. Heinrich said I was to keep an eye on you for at least a month. Make sure you weren't up to any of your usual antics."

I snorted. I doubted I'd be up to my *usual* tricks anytime in the near future. My body hadn't quite forgiven me for our most recent adventure.

The edge of his mouth twitched. "Though he said you should exercise. So I shall allow your daily exertions in the death pit. If I must."

I kicked my legs, treading water ever so slowly. "I'd never be foolish enough to drown. I'll have you know, I am an excellent swimmer."

A flicker of something crossed his expression, and I had the rapidly growing sense that Mr. Owen was afraid of water. Curious. He cleared his throat and reached over, grabbing a towel. "Come dry yourself off. Mrs. Penrose said she would bring coffee, we could break our fast out here before the clouds come in. I've received a letter from your Mr. Kivell."

"He's not *my* Mr. Kivell," I grumbled as I pulled myself out with a heave and wrapped the thick cloth around myself before taking the wicker chair beside him. But I couldn't say I wasn't curious about the contents. "What did he say?"

Mr. Owen held an unopened envelope, which I took from his outstretched hand. The writing was sparse. Simple. Like the man who'd penned it. I flicked my thumb beneath the seal and ripped it open.

Ruby, I've just returned from Portsmouth. Benedict finally took the ship. He debated for a couple of days but in the end realized there was nothing left for him here. I admit I shall miss his company. But considering all, it's for the best. Ever yours, R.

Ever yours. A normal closing, and yet there was something in those words that bothered me. What did he mean? Probably nothing. But with Ruan, one could never tell. I folded it back up and set it on the table.

"Anything interesting?"

I shook my head. "No. Nothing at all." I closed my eyes and settled back into the sun. I'd worry about Ruan Kivell another day.

It was good to be home, though I'd never say such a thing to him. Sentiment had no place between us—despite his uncharacteristic display of paternal affection when I first returned from Lothlel Green.

Mrs. Penrose appeared, silent as a cat, setting a loaded tray down on the round table between us.

"You are far too thin, maid." She straightened herself and placed a hand on my brow. "And your color is terrible. Just terrible. But we'll fix that, won't we, sir?" She cast a conspiratorial grin to Mr. Owen.

Blast and hell, what had I gotten myself into?

It was bad enough to have Mr. Owen worrying I might drown in my own backyard, but now I had added an overprotective housekeeper to the mix? I hadn't fully expected Mrs. Penrose to jump at my offer of employment when I casually extended it before leaving the estate—but I suspected that discovering that one's lifelong friend was a murderess tended to make one rethink one's outlook on life. I couldn't blame her for that. Nor could Tamsyn, as it were. She too had decided to take a holiday, just she and Jori, to the Continent. Perhaps my running from the past was contagious. Or maybe she just needed a change.

Mrs. Penrose's bags were packed and she was on the train to Exeter within two days of my departure. Fiachna had never been happier than when he saw her arrive at the back entrance with her trunks. My sole condition for her employment here was that there were to be no more attempts at charmwork. While Ruan might have been amused by her misguided attempt to protect me, I found myself far warier and unwilling to dabble in the inexplicable.

"I've been thinking . . ." Mr. Owen flicked the newspaper, making it stand fully upright in his hands.

"I do always despise when you start sentences that way." I picked up a ginger biscuit from the breakfast tray and plopped it into my mouth. One thing was certain, with Mrs. Penrose here I would not go hungry.

Mr. Owen had the temerity to look affronted. "I'll have you know, there are very few pleasures available to a man of my years, and thinking is one of my favorites."

"Last time you started a sentence that way you assured me I would not get arrested."

"And you weren't."

"No, instead you nearly got me killed," I laughed, finishing off the cookie. God bless Mrs. Penrose. No wonder Fiachna scarcely left the kitchen. "You cannot try to tell me that's better."

"Nearly isn't completely. If they'd killed you, then you could kick up a fuss. Besides, did it do you any good?"

"Three times, Mr. Owen! I nearly died three times."

He cleared his throat and turned a page in the paper. Both

of us fully aware he wasn't reading a word. "My great-aunt Persimmon always said facing one's mortality improves a girl's vigor."

"Well then, in that case how do you gauge my vigor?" I smiled at him. Truly smiled. This was where I was supposed to be. I knew it now. Somehow I'd made a home for myself in Exeter. Accidentally, to be sure, but I belonged with the secretive old Scot, my high-handed housekeeper, and a fickle house cat.

"I think it's past time you and I took a holiday."

Crumbs from the biscuit lodged in my throat and I coughed, but it didn't stop me from grabbing another and putting it into my mouth, chewing more slowly this time. "A holiday?"

He laid the paper down, and looked at me squarely. "Scotland, to be exact."

I narrowed my gaze at him, "We, or me? You hate Scotland."

His white mustache twitched in amusement. "I know a chap with a lovely castle there. He's turned the thing into a bit of a resort, but he's asked if I'd come sort out some medieval illustrated manuscripts for him."

"What are you plotting?"

"Plotting? Dear girl, who do you take me for?"

I refused to take my eyes off him, the fiend. I knew him too well for that—he had a plan. Though what sort, I couldn't begin to fathom. "At least promise me no more curses."

But the old man didn't say a word, he just laughed.

ACKNOWLEDGMENTS

The author is only one part of what it takes to deliver a novel to readers. There have been so many people involved in bringing Ruby to life. The team at Minotaur has been incredible from the very first step to publication—and none of this would have been possible without their hard work and dedication.

My incredible editor, Madeline Houpt, who from the very first moment we spoke understood both Ruby and the story I was trying to tell. This novel is so much stronger for her insightful comments and feedback. Also, my amazing agent, Jill Marr, I could not imagine having a better advocate in my corner on this wild journey.

To the production team at Minotaur who have worked so hard to put a Times New Roman Word doc into the gorgeous format that it is here. Ruby would not be here without all your hard work.

My non-publishing friends, Ashley, Corey, and Laura—y'all know far more about this industry than folks outside publishing would ever want to know. And you've put up with my out-of-the-blue writing texts with far more grace than I probably deserve. I'm sure I've scared you away from ever wanting to write a book yourselves, but your support and friendship have been so important to me.

My writer friends, Reine Dugas and Lyn Liao Butler. A

writer doesn't live in isolation, and you two have been bedrock for me through the ups and downs of the process. You were always there for DMs, late-night emails, texts, and random snippets of out-of-context plot. For commiseration and celebration. I couldn't ask for better folks to bounce ideas off of and to hold my hand (if virtually) through the good times and the bad.

My poor mother who endured daily angst calls of HAVE YOU READ IT YET?! And my sister, who would get roped into ongoing family group chats about characters she didn't know. Thank you both for putting up with me and loving me all these years.

My dad, who never got the chance to read this book. You always believed in me, probably more than I ever believed in myself. I think you knew this day would come, long before I ever did. Your love and support have been everything, even if you're no longer here with us.

And last (but most certainly not least), J and the boys, who gave me up on weekends, late nights, and holidays while I frenetically chased after my own dreams. You three have been rooting for me since day one, and I hope to make you proud. I'm not sure I would have had the inspiration or drive to write this book without you.

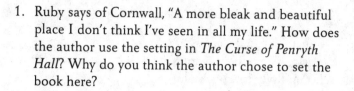

1. Ruby says of Cornwall, "A more bleak and beautiful place I don't think I've seen in all my life." How does the author use the setting in *The Curse of Penryth Hall*? Why do you think the author chose to set the book here?

2. The period during and after the First World War was a time of incredible technological and social change. The novel's heroine, Ruby Vaughn, stands out among the crowd throughout *The Curse of Penryth Hall*. How does Ruby interact with the technological, gender, and social conventions of the time period? Is she constrained by them? Does she challenge them?

Discussion Questions

3. Which characters are foils of each other? Why do you think the author chose to do this?

4. At several points in the novel, Ruan comments about people being afraid of him, or indicates he is alone—despite being a respected member of his community. Yet he is less of an outsider than Ruby. How—if at all—does Ruan serve as a bridge between the villagers of Lothlel Green and Ruby?

5. Ruby is skeptical about curses and the supernatural world at the beginning of *The Curse of Penryth Hall*. How—if at all—does her view change by the end of the novel?

6. In Chapter 24, Tamsyn tells Ruby, "You wear your pain like armor. Daring anyone to challenge you, and yet you never let anyone beneath it." But Ruby is not the only character with traumas—many others carry theirs with them as well. How do trauma and grief intertwine in *The Curse of Penryth Hall*, and how does it affect the characters' decisions and interactions with one another?

MINOTAUR BOOKS

7. What do you make of the connection between Ruan and Ruby? Does anything surprise you?

8. What do you believe were Mr. Owen's intentions for sending Ruby to Cornwall?

9. Which character do you relate to the most? Is this also your favorite character?

10. Were you familiar with Pellars prior to reading *The Curse of Penryth Hall*? If so, where have you seen them? If not, what do you think of Pellars, and did your view change at all as you read?

Turn the page for a sneak peek at
Jess Armstrong's new novel

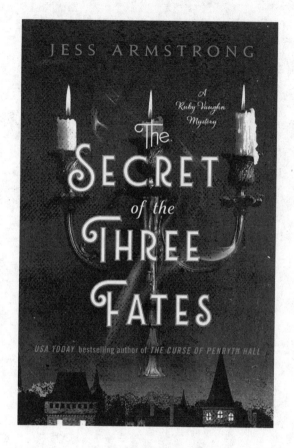

Available Winter 2024

Chapter One

Sic Semper Tyrannis

MANHURST CASTLE, SCOTLAND
OCTOBER 1922

I was going to murder Mr. Owen, there was simply nothing for it. Blood thrummed through my veins as I looked up at the librarian of Manhurst Castle, struggling not to lose my temper. It certainly wasn't *this man's* fault that I'd been brought here under false pretenses. No, that blame lay squarely at the feet of my octogenarian employer who was currently enjoying his midmorning nap.

"What do you *mean* there are no illuminated manuscripts?" I asked for the second time, my voice far more strained than I intended.

Mercifully, the young man remained unaware of my rising ire as he turned back to the dark mahogany bookcase behind him, pulling the newest copy of Debrett's guide to the peerage from an overburdened shelf containing every edition published from the company's eighteenth-century inception to now. He set it on the long low study table beside me. In a desperate hope that the young man had forgotten a cache of illuminated manuscripts secreted away with the most recent month's serial novel, I scanned the spines of the next nearest shelf. Mostly modern fiction alongside some late-nineteenth-century poetry. Nothing awe-inspiring. In fact, there wasn't a single interesting book in this library—it was a rather insipid collection all told. As if someone hastily purchased everything from a rummage sale in an attempt to fill the empty shelves.

"I told you earlier, Miss Vaughn, there are no illuminated manuscripts left in the collection. The lot of them were sold off two years ago, not long after Mr. Sharpe took over the estate. I understand they paid for the renovations here."

My attention snapped back to the young librarian and I blew out a breath, my eyes lingering on the most recent copy of the who's who of the peerage on the tabletop. A more generous soul might assume that Mr. Owen had simply gotten his estates mixed up. After all, he was in his eighties and I'd known plenty of other folk his age—younger even—who had begun to forget harmless little details like that. Though Mr. Owen never forgot *anything*—an annoying habit of his.

Besides, even if he *had* gotten his estates confused, it didn't explain the telegram in my pocket offering said missing manuscripts for sale. No. I was certain that Mr. Owen was up to his old tricks again.

"Is there anything else here Mr. Sharpe is thinking of selling? Perhaps there was some mistake . . ."

The librarian shook his head, glancing to the open door leading into the main hall of the hotel. "Nothing, miss. I was surprised as you were when you came in asking for them this morning. Mr. Sharpe sold everything of value from here not long after acquiring the estate. From what I understand, Manhurst Castle was falling apart when he bought it—and it took everything he had and more to fix this old place into a resort suitable for the sort of guests we entertain."

"You've not been here long then?" I raised a brow.

He shook his head. "I come from Edinburgh, miss. I was hired on earlier this year when the resort had its grand opening. Mr. Sharpe believed that any proper estate ought to have a librarian."

I couldn't argue with the elusive Mr. Sharpe on that score. A nagging worry lingered as I unfolded the telegram that Mr. Owen had handed me the morning we left Exeter and offered it to the librarian. He took it from me, reading it with a frown.

Have a dozen twelfth-century manuscripts for sale. Please come at once. M. Sharpe.

The young man reached up, rubbing at his smooth-shaven jaw. "That is peculiar, miss. Very peculiar. I shall ask Mr. Sharpe about it, but feel free to take your time to look around. I warn you not to get your hopes up; if there was anything of value here—I'd know it." He looked again at the door behind me, scooping up the newest copy of Debrett's and holding it under his arm. "I'd best be off. The dowager countess has requested this delivered to her rooms."

I groaned at the mention of the horrid woman. Every time I'd come across Lady Morton and her young daughter the elder avoided me as if I carried some twelfth-century pestilence. It was a wonder the woman needed the book at all. I'd assumed a soul as pompous as she would have the whole of Debrett's memorized already. I fiddled with the telegram before folding it back up and thrusting it into my pocket. There was only one person who could *illuminate* our reason for being here, and he was currently upstairs taking a nap.

I RUSHED THROUGH the fashionably decorated hallways of Manhurst, recently redone in *le style moderne*. A stark contrast to the sparse Georgian exterior of the building. The lush green, black, and gold paper on the walls must have cost a fortune. There was no wonder this Mr. Sharpe, whoever he was, sold off everything of value to fund the renovation.

Pillaging a library for wallpapering. The very idea made my skin crawl. I blew out a breath, brushing past a cadre of well-heeled gentlemen coming in from a game of golf smelling irritatingly of sunshine and the Scottish hills.

The only positive of my morning's discovery was that now we could board the first train back to Exeter and return to our bookshop there. Perhaps Mr. Owen would feel more like himself once we returned home. As it was, he'd spent most of the forty-eight hours since our arrival shut into his room, not even taking his meals with me, leaving me to wander the castle alone. Decidedly *not* my idea of a restful vacation.

The real puzzle was *why* Mr. Owen had brought me here in the first place. It was unlike him to hare off after mysterious manuscripts without knowing absolutely everything he could about the seller. The old man was a born meddler, and possessed investigative skills that would put the Home Office to shame. He could sniff a fake from miles away—so why would he have come all the way to Scotland for manuscripts that had been sold off years before? Mr. Owen ought to have known they were not here the moment he received the telegram.

No. Something was amiss, and I was about to find out what.

My throat grew dry as I turned the knob on the door connecting our rooms.

Locked.

I rattled the handle as a frisson of tension inched its way from my palm up my spine and settled itself in my jaw.

"Mr. Owen . . ." I rapped on the wooden panel.

Still nothing.

I waited on the plush crimson carpet for any sign of life from the other side but was met with silence. "Mr. Owen, you're beginning to worry me. Please open the damned door."

Still no response.

He never locked the door in Exeter, not even when he was sick. Of all the times for him to get missish about privacy . . . My satchel sat on the dressing table and I took two steps in that direction with the intention of digging out my lockpicks, when I heard the hinges creak behind me.

Mr. Owen appeared in the threshold, wearing his bright blue silk pajamas with a garish pomegranate-and-black dressing gown tied at his waist. His fluffy white hair looked as if he'd just awoken and my stomach unknotted in response.

"Good grief, Mr. Owen I thought you were dead. Or worse!"

He let out a bitter laugh and shook his head. "It'd take more than this old place to do me in. You should know that, lass. Now come sit and tell me why you look like you've drunk curdled milk."

I huffed out a breath. All my worry from a few seconds before evaporated. He was fine. *Fine.* Mr. Owen was the closest thing I had to family, as my own father had died upon the *Lusitania* seven years ago now, along with my mother and younger sister, Opal. At times it seemed a lifetime ago that I received word that their bodies had not been recovered, and yet at others it was as if I'd just received the telegram.

The telegram. Suddenly I recalled my reason for seeking him out in the first place. *The missing manuscripts.* I dug into my pocket and waved the folded-up paper at him. "Do you know anything about this?"

He wrinkled his nose and took it from me, holding it at arm's length as he tried to read it without his spectacles. "Ah yes . . . that."

"Ah . . . that . . ." I repeated dryly. "I take it there are no illuminated manuscripts here?"

He shook his head, then crumped the telegram and stuffed it into his dressing gown pocket before turning and gesturing for me to follow into his room. As I entered, I caught a whiff of whisky—likely expensive stuff if his normal taste held true. His room was far darker than my own with the curtains pulled tight against the sun and the fireplace providing the only light.

I sank down into an old armchair with an irritated grunt. "I sense there *is* a reason we're here, and that you didn't just change your opinion on Scotland after all these years?"

He settled himself slowly into the chair across from me. His left hand trembled as he ran it over his white beard before picking up a half-full glass of whisky. Its twin sat there on the table, equally full.

"Was someone here with you?" I glanced from the pair of whisky glasses to his face. The man had scarcely left his room since we'd arrived; I couldn't imagine who he'd be entertaining in here. While I knew he'd grown up in Scotland, he had no family to speak of—at least none I knew of besides his litany of fictitious great-aunts he'd pull out of his pocket whenever he needed to make a point.

"Leave off, Ruby. It isn't important."

Of course it was important. Mr. Owen never did anything without a reason, and I knew he had no desire to be here. His temper had grown shorter with every moment we remained at Manhurst Castle. Something about this place bothered him and if he wasn't going to tell me, I'd have to figure it out myself. There was a faint scent of flowers in the air. Lavender perhaps. No, that wasn't it. But I couldn't quite place it.

I leaned forward, placing my palm on his forehead. It was cool and clammy. "Mr. Owen, you are clearly unwell. It's time we go home."

"Not yet, Ruby. Another night. We must spend another night here."

"Not yet?" I almost squeaked, my hand flying into the air. "There is no reason on earth good enough for us to stay. There are no manuscripts, the entire library is devoid of anything even remotely interesting. I cannot fathom why you want to remain here when you are clearly miserable!"

He turned back to face me, brushing away at the moisture gathered in his eyes with his palm. "I take it you haven't seen the papers yet."

The skin at my neck prickled. Newspapers were the bane of my existence. I still recalled the glee with which the New York newspapermen had picked apart my every flaw after my disgrace. I'd been scarcely sixteen at the time—manipulated and misused by a grown man I'd believed to be honorable—but it made no difference to society that I'd been the victim. *A proper girl would never . . .* that's how every backhanded comment would begin. For the truth didn't matter to society, nor did it matter to the men who profited from my pain.

My expression must have betrayed me, as Mr. Owen reached out, touching my hand tenderly. "No, lass, not those sorts of stories. This has nothing to do with you. Nothing at all. You are safe with me. I promise you that."

I let out an amused sound—*safe* was a matter of perspective considering he'd nearly gotten me killed six weeks before on an errand to Lothlel Green. My relief was short lived, as the meaning behind his words became clear. If it didn't have to do with *me*, it had to do with *him.* "Oh no, Mr. Owen . . . what have you done this time?"

He eyed his glass of whisky, tilting it in the firelight. "I did not think you would come with me if I told you the truth straightaway."

Not again. "Told me what . . . Mr. Owen, *why* are we here?"

He grimaced, picking up a folded copy of *The Scotsman,* turned it over, and laid it flat on the table between us, allowing me to read the advertisement beneath the fold.

The Three Fates, at Manhurst Castle for one night only.
Join them to commune with the dead.
War widows. Grieving mothers. Brokenhearted sweethearts.
Take heart and find your consolation and peace for ten pounds.
TONIGHT!

I stared at it in disbelief. *Mediums?* Mr. Owen had brought me all the way to Scotland for us to commune with the dead? Anger. Annoyance. Dread. I wasn't quite certain which emotion would win out. "You have to be joking. You've brought me here for a séance?"

He rubbed at his thick white beard, and tapped the paper. "This is why I did not tell you earlier. You would have gotten all into a tizzy over it."

I shot to my feet, hands on my hips. "I do not get into tizzies. It is perfectly reasonable to be annoyed when your employer *lies* to you and brings you to the middle of nowhere under false pretenses."

He shrugged, his eyes not meeting mine. "I did not lie, Ruby. I obfuscated. There *is* a difference."

"I'm not in the mood for semantics this morning. Aren't there plenty of fraudulent mediums closer to home willing to take *my* money from *you*?"

He harrumphed, not rising to the barb, as both of us knew that Mr. Owen lived off my fortune. It was part of our agreement. I had free rein over the bookshop and permission to run his household however I saw fit and his name was on the bookshop door in large painted letters. My money bought me anonymity and freedom—two things I treasured above all else.

But arguing with the man was not going to bring Mr. Owen

around. I leaned against the arm of his chair, softening my words. "You know as well as I do that they're all frauds. I saw my share of their kind in France after my parents died. They'll say anything to get your money. I thought we were in agreement on that . . ."

His jaw grew slack as he stared at me. "After all you saw—after all that happened in Lothlel Green—you still mock the other world? You doubt its existence?"

He had me there. A great many things happened in Cornwall a mere six weeks ago, things I didn't dare think on at present. "I am not mocking it. I am simply pointing out that the dead are dead—they aren't coming back. And whether I believe in ghosts is immaterial. What *is* material is that you lied to me to bring me out here."

Mr. Owen did not believe me. His bushy white eyebrows rose in unison.

I crossed my ankles, looking away. "Nothing happened in Cornwall out of the ordinary."

"Curses and witches aren't out of the ordinary?"

Well . . . *almost* nothing. Mr. Owen didn't know half of what I'd found there when he sent me to deliver a box of books to his Pellar friend, Ruan Kivell. Nor did I even know what a Pellar *was*. I still wasn't entirely certain, only that Ruan was a type of folk healer—a witch of sorts.

Mercifully, Mr. Owen also remained unaware of the fact that Ruan could somehow hear my thoughts without me speaking, or the uncanny way I could sense his . . . well . . . whatever *it* was he did. I still was not certain how much I believed in the supernatural, but I did know that Ruan possessed . . . something. Something I feared to put to voice. He could *do things*. Things he didn't understand nor could he control. Things unbound by the laws of science, at least any science I knew. And the less anyone knew of what he was—the better.

A loud thunk came from the floor overhead, startling me out of my wayward thoughts, and causing me to bite my tongue. The metallic tang of blood filled my mouth. "Damn."

He arched an eyebrow in challenge. "No such thing as ghosts, lass?"

"Very amusing. All I mean to say is that it's well known about these types of women. They go to the most absurd lengths to wheedle well-meaning people out of their money. Goodness knows, I've seen plenty of them in my life, all of them telling me . . ." *That my mother lived.* No, I couldn't bring myself to speak it—not even to Mr. Owen. Those horrible frauds had given me false hope for far too long.

"It's only . . ." He paused, twisting a simple gold band on his finger. "Ruby, I need you tonight. Please don't make me ask you twice. I do not think I'm brave enough to face the dead on my own and I need you by my side."

My eyes widened at the rawness in his voice. "But Mr. Owen, it's not *real*. You can't possibly be planning on—"

He held up a hand, silencing me. The golden ring winked in the electric lights, catching my eye. "I must speak with my son." He pulled out a letter from his pocket and handed it to me. The paper trembled in his outstretched hand.

Owen, I know it has been years since we've spoken but I have a message from Ben. He has come to me in my dreams. He is angry and will speak to no one but you. If you have any love for your departed wife, you will come. You will come and hear what your son wants to say.

—L.C.

"Who . . . who sent you this?"

"Lucy Campbell," he said with a vague wave of his hand, as if that name meant anything to me. "In another life, I knew her well. She is a true spiritualist. The only one I've ever known to possess the gift of speaking with the dead."

"—and she's here . . . one of these *Fates*."

He nodded. "She has a message from Ben. From my darling boy. How could I do anything but come to hear what he has to say?"

Mr. Owen rarely spoke of his life before I came into it. I only knew the barest of sketches. Ben was the youngest of his children, and I got the sense his favorite. He'd been an aviator during the war and would have been about my age, had he survived. But he was shot down somewhere over the lines and wounded near the end of the war. By some minor miracle he managed to live through all that, only to die on a troop transport on his way back home.

"I understand how you feel, Mr. Owen, but how do we know that letter is any more real than the telegram we received about the manuscripts? Ten pounds for a public séance is an obscene amount of money. If this Lucy Campbell woman truly wanted to help you, wouldn't she just meet you in private to deliver Ben's message?"

Mr. Owen's eyes were glassy and bloodshot in the dim firelight. "I lost him once. I cannot bear to lose him again. I will not take that chance. I would offer up all the illuminated manuscripts in the world, burn each and every one until not a single page remained if it brought him back once more." A tear slipped down his face, running along the well-worn ridge by his nose, sealing my fate. "You of all people must understand that. If Ben has a message, I must hear him out, no matter the cost to me."

He'd won this battle before it even began, touching that fathomless wound in me that refused to heal. I reached across the table, taking his wizened hand in my own, and squeezed. "Very well. I'll go. But I won't like it."

"And no scenes, Ruby. I mean it. I need you to be by my side for this. I depend on you lass, more than you could ever know."

"Me? Cause a scene? I'd never dream of it." I struggled to keep my tone light, to bring him away from that dark place that he'd entered. Mr. Owen needed closure—and that was the one thing I could not give, but perhaps these Three Fates could.

ABOUT THE AUTHOR

Christy Lorio

Jess Armstrong is the *USA Today* bestselling author of the Ruby Vaughn Mysteries. Her debut novel, *The Curse of Penryth Hall,* won the Minotaur Books/Mystery Writers of America First Crime Novel Award. She has a master's degree in American history but prefers writing about imaginary people to the real thing. Jess lives in New Orleans with her historian husband, two sons, yellow cat, speckled dog, and the world's most pampered school-fair goldfish. And when she's not working on her next project, she's probably thinking about cheese, baking, on social media, or some combination of the above.